Julian Symons is a novelist, critic, biographer and poet. His novels have brought him wide critical acclaim and his biographies cover such diverse characters as Dickens, Carlyle and Poe. In 1990 he was awarded the Cartier Diamond Dagger for services to crime literature.

He lives in Kent near the sea. His most recent novel is *Something Like a Love Affair*.

JULIAN SYMONS

# THE
# ADVERTISING
# MURDERS

AN OMNIBUS EDITION COMPRISING

*The Thirtyfirst of February*

AND

*A Man Called Jones*

CRIME

**PAN BOOKS**

LONDON, SYDNEY AND AUCKLAND

*A Man called Jones* first published 1947 by Victor Gollancz Ltd
*The Thirtyfirst of February* first published 1950 by Victor Gollancz Ltd
Both titles first published in this edition 1992 by Pan Books Ltd
Cavaye Place. London SW10 9PG

1 3 5 7 9 8 6 4 2

ISBN 0 330 32266 4

© Julian Symons 1947. 1950
Phototypeset by Intype. London
Printed in England by Clays Ltd. St Ives plc

*For my mother*

# A MAN
# CALLED JONES

# CHARACTERS IN THE STORY

### In the Hargreaves Advertising Agency

| | |
|---|---|
| EDWARD HARGREAVES | *Founder of the Agency* |
| LIONEL HARGREAVES | *His elder son* |
| RICHARD HARGREAVES | *His younger son* |
| GEORGE TRACY | *Creative Director* |
| JACK BOND | *Production Manager* |
| CHARLES SINCLAIR | *Copy Chief* |
| JEAN ROGERS | *Copywriter* |
| ONSLOW | *Another copywriter* |
| MUDGE | *Studio artist* |
| MISS PEACHEY | *Receptionist* |
| MISS BERRY | *Her friend* |

### Outside the Agency

| | |
|---|---|
| MR JONES | *A mystery* |
| MRS LACEY | *A landlady* |
| EVE MARCHANT | *An actress* |
| MYRTLE MONTAGUE | *Another actress* |
| JOSEPH VAN DIEREN | *An art agent* |
| POLLY LINES | *His secretary* |
| ARNOLD CARRUTHERS | *A freelance artist, Cousin of Lionel and Richard Hargreaves* |
| WILLIAM WESTON | *Lawyer to the Hargreaves family* |
| EDWARD SINCLAIR | *Brother of Charles* |
| JULIA BOND | *Wife of Jack Bond* |
| JACKSON } WILLIAMS } | *Servants in the Hargreaves family* |
| DETECTIVE INSPECTOR BLAND | *Of Scotland Yard* |
| DETECTIVE SERGEANT FILBY | |
| DETECTIVES { BURK HEMMING | |

# I

## 6.15 to 6.45 p.m.

Charles Sinclair paused for a moment on the steps of the house in Redfern Square, and looked at his watch. A fine mist of rain blurred the dial, and he had to hold it close to his face before he saw that the time was 6.15. He shivered involuntarily as he hesitated, for some reason that he could not have named, before the open door of the house; as he turned, with a second decisive shiver, to go in he heard his name called and the figure of Jack Bond, jaunty and over-dressed, appeared through the drizzling rain. Bond's dark face was rich with malice, and he tapped the steps with the silver-headed cane which he used, a little unnecessarily Sinclair thought, to conceal a slight limp. His voice, like his manner, was unsympathetic, harsh and grating and curiously unfriendly.

'I hope you feel it an honour to enter these portals, Sinclair? To step upon rich carpets that have been trod by all the advertising talents of Great Britain?' Sinclair grunted. 'As our American friends say, a pretty nifty joint.' Bond bent down to examine with comical carefulness the plain red hair carpet. 'But the old man's been practising economy in the hall. The pile carpets are kept for the places where they matter.'

Sinclair found himself annoyed, as he frequently found himself annoyed, by Bond's facetiousness. 'What sort of carpet do you expect to find in a hall?'

'My dear chap,' Bond protested, 'here I expect flunkeys on every side, bearing salvers of beaten gold on which we shall drop the cards we haven't got, so that we may be announced suitably. And here comes the flunkey. But no salver. Very disappointing. My hat, certainly,' he said, giving to the man a hat with a small red feather in it, 'and my stick and case.' He passed over a small brown leather attaché-case. 'And here we are,' he said, as another servant opened a large white panelled door, 'entering the scene of revelry. How delightful – by which I mean, of course, how dull – to see the old familiar faces we saw an hour ago.'

The scene was hardly one of revelry. The room they entered was fully forty feet long, and some sixty people were standing in it, looking rather depressed than gay. In front of a pair of folding doors there was an improvised bar, with two bartenders. An enormous iced birthday cake with twenty-five candles stood on a buhl table: this cake commemorated the twenty-fifth birthday of the nationally famous Hargreaves Advertising Agency. And when people thought of this Agency with admiration, distaste or envy, they did not think of it as Hargreaves & Hargreaves, which was its established name now that Edward Hargreaves had taken his eldest son into partnership; they thought of the Agency in terms of the initials E. H., which stood for Edward Hargreaves.

Among these thousands E. H. was in a small way a legend. He never spoke of his past life, but it was known, or at least said with all the familiarity of truth, that he had been a newspaper-boy, an invoice clerk, a gravedigger's mate and a maker of model aeroplanes, before he was twenty-one: and he had not merely held those jobs, but had been dismissed from all of them. The steps by which he had started his climb to wealth and success were hidden: but when at the age of forty he came from America to his native country he brought a few thousand pounds and some unexpected ideas with him. It was said that these ideas were not always what the conventional might call respectable; that Edward Hargreaves, in those early days, was not only a little smarter than any of his competitors, but that his smartness might, in any more tediously ethical occupation, have put him in some very awkward situations. But those stories were all of the past and lent, in a way, a flavour of romance to the name of Edward Hargreaves. Nobody could deny that now, at sixty-five, E. H. had become conservative, traditional, a Grand Old Man of advertising. His knighthood was expected yearly by his staff. He had married twice; the first a thin, faded woman who had borne him two sons, and whose presence in the household had become less and less noticeable until at last she seemed less to have died than simply to have vanished from a scene where her presence was no longer required. A year after her death, when he was sixty-two years of age, E. H. had married a girl of twenty-two, who met her death in a yachting accident within six months of their marriage. Such was Edward Hargreaves, the owner of the Hargreaves Agency. On the Agency's twenty-fifth birthday a party was being given, a cake was being cut, and a speech was being made; dancing was to follow the speech.

All the members of the staff had been invited, from the other directors down to the girls in the Accounts Department, who giggled whenever anyone over the age of thirty spoke to them; only the messenger-boys had been given a pound note each, and told to go out and enjoy themselves. The invitation was an order: but there would in any event have been little inclination to refuse, since all the women on the staff were anxious to show how delightful they looked away from the office and in evening dress, and almost all the men thought it might improve their standing if it were known that they had been to a party at the old man's house in Redfern Square. 'Evening Dress – Optional' had been marked clearly on the cards which, in order to give the occasion importance, had been sent by post to each member of the staff: but very few, Sinclair saw, had decided to avail themselves of the option. He got a glass of sherry and a biscuit, and sipped the sherry reflectively, while he looked round.

The party, he thought, could hardly be called a success at the moment. Little departmental groups had gathered together, and were talking almost in whispers. The four Accounts girls, quite overcome by the occasion, were giggling together over their gin and grapefruit. Onslow and Mudge, two young copy-writers, were standing firmly together in front of the buffet, and drinking hard and fast. Mrs Rogers, who looked after copy from what everyone except Sinclair, who had charge of the Copy Department, called the woman's angle, was talking to Tracy, the Creative Director, and Bond. Lionel, the other Hargreaves in the name, was standing at the side of the room, near the windows, fiddling with a small box on a table. There was no sign of E. H. or his youngest son, Richard. Sinclair was debating which of the several little groups he should join, when Lionel Hargreaves beckoned to him. Lionel was a well-built, fair man of thirty-five, with a weakly handsome, sensual face, an amiably supercilious manner, and, Sinclair had always thought, very little aptitude for advertising. He greeted Sinclair with the friendly condescension of a duke who is being pleasant to a baronet.

'Looking lost over there, Sinclair. Devilish bore these things, aren't they?' The question was almost rhetorical, and Sinclair did not answer it. 'You know what the old man's like, though – loves that touch of ceremonial.'

'Oh, yes,' Sinclair said. 'E. H. couldn't do without the cere-monial.'

Lionel ran a finger round his collar. He was wearing a dinner-jacket. 'I could do without it myself, and without these damned monkey jackets, too.' There was a particularly loud giggle from one of the Accounts girls, and Lionel's eye strayed towards them. 'That girl – what's her name – Miss Gardner. Got a fine figure, hasn't she? Pity she giggles so much.'

Sinclair was rather short. 'She's engaged to be married.'

'Is she, now. Hell of a thing, marriage – can land you in a devil of a mess. Certainly has me.' Lionel suddenly looked alarmed, as if he had said something he had not intended. 'This buhl furniture and these Aubusson carpets now – I don't like that kind of thing, do you? Ornate.'

'It helps with the ceremonial – and it must have cost a mint of money.'

'Money, oh ah, yes.' Lionel's attention had wandered. With an almost visible effort he pulled it back to Sinclair and laid his hand on the box which stood on the table by his side. 'Never been here before, have you?' he asked, and although it could not be said that his tone was offensive, it was too noticeably that of the lord of the manor congratulating one of his retainers on a step up in the world to be agreeable to Sinclair, whose 'No' was rather stiff. 'You won't have seen any of the old man's musical-boxes, then.' He lifted the rosewood lid of the box on the table, and Sinclair saw a long brass cylinder with small spikes sticking out of it, which impinged on a steel comb. At the back of the box sat three little figures with drumsticks in their hands and drums in front of them. Sinclair, although he was annoyed by Lionel's manner, was too interested to be sulky. He bent close to look at the box and said, 'Charming.' Lionel moved a switch at one side of the box, and stood back with a slightly self-satisfied smile. The cylinder revolved, the figures beat on their drums, and the box gave a pleasant, tinkling rendering of 'The Blue Bells of Scotland.' Heads in the room turned towards them, talking stopped for the necessary and polite few seconds and then recommenced. Bond left Tracy and Mrs Rogers, and joined them in looking at the musical-box. 'My word,' he said. 'That's a fine box – one of the best forte-pianos I've seen. I did't know the old man went in for such things.'

Lionel affected a faint surprise. 'You know about these things, do you, Bond? Shouldn't have thought they were your line of country.'

Bond's laugh was loud. 'Precious few things that *aren't* my line of country. Always been interested in mechanical devices, and these musical-boxes are damned ingenious things. Does the old man collect them?' Lionel did not answer, and it was plain that his abstraction was such that he really had not heard what was said. 'Where *is* the old man, by the way?'

'He'll be along,' Lionel said vaguely. 'Had to go to some meeting or other. But he wouldn't miss this for worlds – gives him a chance to perform you know.'

'My word,' Bond said, 'look at Tracy and Mrs Rogers over there – they are going it, aren't they? I let them because I thought they'd like to be al-o-o-ne.' He exaggerated the last word comically. Sinclair looked across the room and saw that Tracy and Mrs Rogers were certainly engaged in what seemed to be earnest conversation.

'Don't know what you're damned well talking about,' Lionel said.

'Well, I do think it's a bit scandalous. Jean Rogers is all very well, but, after all, Tracy is supposed to hold a certain position in the firm. I don't know what E. H. would say if he knew about it.'

Sinclair did not much like Lionel, but he liked Bond less, and he could not help feeling pleased when Lionel said shortly, 'Should keep that sort of gossip to yourself if I were you, Bond. Ah – there's Dick. You're a bit late, Dick, old man. Haven't seen you since lunch.'

Richard Hargreaves was two years younger than his brother, but he looked less than his age. His face was smooth and unlined; it showed, like Lionel's, marks of weakness round the mouth and chin, but he had a willowy handsomeness emphasized by his choice of clothes. He was one of the few men not in evening dress. He was wearing a dark double-breasted lounge suit slightly tapered at the waist, with a red carnation in his buttonhole, and dark brogue shoes. He said in a gentle, rather high-pitched voice, 'I'm sorry. I got held up. Haven't even had time to change yet. I'll slip upstairs in a minute or two.'

'Been hitting the highspots?'

Richard Hargreaves said in the friendliest possible tone, 'I think you can give me lessons on that, Lionel. I've been out with Eve Marchant – we went back and had coffee in her flat.'

'Eve Marchant!' A flush mounted slowly from Lionel's neck to his face. 'You're a bloody fool if you mix yourself up with Eve – she's poison.'

Richard took a cigarette from a thin silver case, and tapped it deliberately, and a little theatrically, before he said with a faint smile, 'Didn't I hear something once about one man's meat . . . ?'

Lionel's face was alarmingly red as he said, 'My God, Dick, you're a bloody fool. I must talk to you about this.' It was at this point that Sinclair pressed Bond's arm gently, and led him away. Bond went unwillingly, and with a slight leer on his face. 'What do you know about that?' he said.

'I know it's time I had another sherry, and I know if some of us don't fraternize a bit with the juniors this party's going to be a flop.'

'Damn the party. They shouldn't wash their dirty linen in public if they don't want anyone to watch them doing it.'

Sinclair had had enough of Bond. 'I should put on a false beard and do some eavesdropping, since you're so interested. I'm going to liven up the lads from the Studio.' He made his way over to where half a dozen young men and women were talking in whispers, and looking rather gloomily at the floor.

'Look, George,' Jean Rogers said, 'there's Sinclair gone over to talk to the Studio boys. You should go and cheer them up – they do look pathetic. After all, they are your department, aren't they?'

'Hell with the Studio,' George Tracy said, 'and to hell with it all, and to hell with this party. I've had enough. I've a good mind to throw in my hand altogether.' He made an eloquent gesture, a throwing out of his hand as it were, in the air. He was full of eloquent gestures.

Jean Rogers sighed. 'Yes, George.'

'God preserve me from advertising men,' Tracy said, by no means in an undertone, 'but God preserve me most from top-class advertising men. If there's a lower species of life, I don't know it.' He made another eloquent gesture in the direction of Lionel and Richard Hargreaves. 'One of them without the faint-est knowledge of advertising or, indeed, of any other subject that requires the application of intelligence, the other a stuffed, tailor-made dummy who should be in the window of a multiple clothes store as a example of natty dressing.'

'George, I think we've been standing and talking long enough. We agreed it wasn't a good thing. I think I should – '

'A good advertising man, Jean, is nothing less than a creative artist. He has a soul. You and I have souls – and souls are delicate things. The treatment they get from these insensitive idiots is enough to drive any creative man mad.' He ran his hand through the black hair that stood up like pins on his head. Jean Rogers, looking at him, thought again that he was one of the most handsome men she had ever seen. She said placatingly, 'Richard's not bad. He's rather sweet in a way. I think I – '

'Rather sweet?' Tracy snorted, and made no further comment on Richard. 'And as for E. H. – you know what I think of E. H.'

She sighed again. 'Yes, darling.' Then: 'Here he is.'

Onslow and Mudge from the Copy Department had arrived early. They had each drunk six cocktails and eaten three biscuits, and they were feeling cheerful. Onslow was in his late twenties, and Mudge was a year or two younger. Both of them had taken advantage of the option on dress; they were wearing corduroy trousers and sports jackets and knitted woollen ties. Their opinions of their seniors were not more favourable than the views Tracy had expressed on the Hargreaves family.

'Do you know what I think of advertising agencies, old boy?' Onslow said. 'I think they stink.'

'Right you are,' said Mudge.

'But what stinks worst in them is the executive class – the managerial class.' Onslow tapped Mudge's chest with one finger and enunciated clearly. 'An advertising agency can only exist in full perfection in a capitalist system which is showing the – the iridescence of decay. It thrives in an atmosphere of commercial competition – '

'Right you are,' said Mudge.

' – and exists to sell people goods they don't want at prices higher than they can afford to pay. Its owners are sharks and its personnel are rats.'

'I say, old boy.'

'Yes?'

'What about us? After all, we're personnel of an advertising agency, aren't we?'

'Until the overthrow of the capitalist system,' said Onslow, scoring points rapidly on Mudge's chest. 'After that we shan't be. In the meantime what do you want us to do, starve? But if you ask me what I think of E. H. and his bloody birthday cake, I think he's a – '

'He's here,' said Mudge.

Edward Hargreaves was standing in the doorway.

## II

### *4.0 to 4.15 p.m.*

The person who used the name of Jones put down a book called *The Abbotsford Murders* and crossed to the window. The clock outside the optician's shop opposite said two minutes past four. There was plenty of time. Mr Jones (that was the name given when the room was booked) thought back again over the things already done, and the things that were still to do. Up to the present, at any rate, there had been no mistakes. 'And there won't be any mistakes,' Mr Jones said to himself. 'There won't be any mistakes.' From a battered suitcase Mr Jones took out a Smith and Wesson revolver, rather clumsily because he was wearing a pair of lemon-yellow gloves. Mr Jones put the revolver in his overcoat pocket, relocked the suitcase, and opened the door of the first-floor room. On the ground floor, down a flight of narrow dark stairs, was a telephone. Mr Jones called down the stairs in a curiously deep and harsh voice, 'Mrs Lacey.' The landlady's head, in a mob cap, appeared at the foot of the stairs, peering up into the shadows where her lodger was standing.

'What is it you're wanting?'

Mr Jones said in the same harsh voice, 'I have to go out in a few minutes, Mrs Lacy, and I am not sure when I shall return. May I make a telephone call before I go?'

'Sure you can, Mr Jones. Just so long as you put in your twopence, otherwise you won't get your number.' She laughed at her joke, but there was no answering laugh from the lodger. 'Thank you,' Mr Jones said – and then, instead of coming down to telephone, returned to the room and closed the door.

# III

*6.45 to 7.30 p.m.*

Edward Hargreaves was rather above medium height; he had a florid complexion and a fine head of white hair, and although he was now in his middle sixties, his walk was as brisk and his back as upright as it had been twenty years ago. There was a weight and portentousness about his words and gestures which fitted well with the part of Grand Old Man of advertising which he constantly played ('E. H. passes you the salt,' a friend had said, 'as if he were giving you a five-pound note.') Sometimes the pomp spilled over into geniality: but the heavy brows, the flaring nostrils and the downward curve of the thin mouth, told a story easily read. One did not have to know Edward Hargreaves well to know that beneath the surface of pomp and geniality lay a ruthlessness which was not the more pleasant because it was concealed. His first sight of that mouth convinced Sinclair that most of the stories he had heard about Edward Hargreaves' early life had not been exaggerated. At the present time, however, the corners of the mouth were curved upwards into a smile of palpable falsity. There was hardly a person in the room at that moment, including his sons, who liked E. H. or would have felt any sorrow if they had been told of his death; and yet such is the power of money and convention that when he smiled and said, 'Good evening. I am very sorry to be late,' every one of the faces that greeted him smiled in return.

With the smile fixed firmly in place E. H. walked round among his staff, giving them words of welcome. A dispassionate observer, if one had been present, would have noticed that although all the words he spoke to his staff were in appearance friendly, most of them looked more relieved than happy when he had passed on: and the conversation, which had been flowing a little more easily, was checked again to whispers. He stopped before Tracy and Mrs Rogers, and said amiably to Tracy, 'I'm so glad you're looking after Mrs Rogers, George. But we can't have any conspiracies between copywriters and artists tonight. Time off from business this evening, you know, time off from business.' If Bond had been within earshot he might not have said so confidently that E. H. knew nothing of an affair between Tracy and Mrs Rogers.

Tracy was foolish to rise to this palpable bait. 'We weren't talking business.'

E. H. was almost arch in reply. 'I thought you looked so much as if you were – I *do* apologise.'

By the time E. H. had sympathised with Onslow and Mudge on their lack of dinner-jackets, congratulated Bond on his wit in making the Accounts girls giggle, asked Sinclair anxiously whether he thought the boys in his department could stand so much strong drink, and made similar observations to the heads of the Research and Space Departments, he was looking almost benign in his cheerfulness. But as he walked across the room to where his two sons were standing the smile was cut quite suddenly and sharply off his face. The mouth turned down and the heavy brows contracted: the effect was not pleasant. Lionel and Richard awaited him with the air of two soldiers who are about to be inspected by their Commanding Officer, and are guiltily aware of spots on their tunics. They said in unison, 'Good evening, E. H.' E. H. looked at a point somewhere between them and said, 'Good evening. Lionel, I shall want to talk to you for a few minutes after the dancing has begun. I hope you can find it convenient to make yourself available. Richard, I shall be glad if you can make arrangements to change into appropriate clothing as soon as possible.' He turned, a Commanding Officer who had found the inspection even less satisfactory than he had expected, and marched away leaving Richard looking dejected and Lionel looking alarmed.

# IV

## *4.15 to 4.25 p.m.*

Mr Jones opened the door of his room. Feet clattered uneasily
on the uncarpeted stairs. At the bottom of the stairs stood the
telephone; the door of the room down the passage that Mrs
Lacey called her parlour was slightly open, and a thin gleam of
electric light shone through to the hall. Mr Jones carefully placed
his old suitcase on the floor, and took out from his pocket two
pennies which he regarded for a moment with a purposeful look.
He picked up the telephone receiver, inserted the two pennies,
and dialled a number. The shaft of light coming through into
the hall grew almost imperceptibly wider as the two pennies
dropped to the bottom of the box. Mr Jones had pressed Button
A.

He spoke for a couple of minutes and then hung up the
receiver with an inaudible exclamation of annoyance. He called
out suddenly, 'Goodbye, Mrs Lacey,' picked up his suitcase,
turned the round knob of the Yale lock and was out in the
street. He was still wearing the lemon-yellow gloves.

Outside in the street Mr Jones's shoulders were raised and
lowered almost imperceptibly in a sigh. Well, thank God *that's*
over, he thought, and began to walk briskly towards the main
road, which led to the Elephant and Castle. Just once he patted
the left pocket of the big raglan overcoat he was wearing, and
the corners of his mouth moved in the ghost of a smile.

## V

### *8.10 to 8.30 p.m.*

E. H. had been speaking for twenty minutes, and had the appearance of a batsman who after a shaky start is settling down to a good solid knock, when his serene expression changed suddenly to a look of lowering concentration. His eyes searched among the audience as though he were looking for someone, and he noticeably quickened the pace of his speech. He slowed down, however, as he came to the crucial point:

'I hope,' he said, 'that this brief history of the Agency's past activities and successes will have been of some interest to you. H'rm. All of you have shared in these successes, I do not hesitate to say that you have been in large part responsible for them. On this silver anniversary of the Agency's birth I propose to show some concrete appreciation of the long service rendered by you all. This appreciation will take the practical form of a 10 per cent rise in salary for the whole of the staff present here tonight, from our valued directors, to the stenographers, receptionist and switchboard operator whose work is equally valuable in its own sphere' (here there was a slight rustle among the audience). 'I hope that this step will meet with your approval. And now, without making any further call on your interest or time, I propose to cut this cake.' And E. H. was as good as his word: but he cut the cake with a look which showed that his mind was on other things. Suddenly he called on his son Richard, who, now wearing full evening dress, was standing looking rather moodily at his feet.

'Where is Lionel?'

'Eh? Isn't he here? I suppose he must have slipped out.'

E. H.'s look of concentration became converted to a frown. It was obvious that he did not approve of people slipping out while he was talking. He cut several slices of cake in a perfunctory manner, and then said, 'Look after things for me, my boy. I'm going to find Lionel.' Richard Hargreaves shrugged his shoulders as his father strode out of the door from the dining-room to the hall. Then he made a faintly comic deprecatory gesture to the assembled members of the staff, and they all crowded round the cake. There were mixed feelings about the 10 per cent rise. What would happen, Bond asked Sinclair, when next they asked for a rise in the usual way? They would be told they had had one recently. '*And*, my lad,' Bond finished up with the dogmatic tone which many people found offensive, 'it so happens that a rise is just about due to me. Now – I've had it.'

'There may be something in what you say. I wonder where Lionel's got to. I haven't seen him for some time.'

'Here he is. No he isn't – it's E. H. alone. I say, he looks as if he'd picked up sixpence and lost a ten-bob note, doesn't he?'

E. H.'s face was mottled, and his cheeks were puffed out with anger. 'Richard,' he said, 'I insist on knowing where Lionel is. Jackson, who is on the door, says he went outside at about half-past seven. If that's so, he wasn't in here while I was talking.'

Richard Hargreaves shrugged his shoulders again. 'It's no use asking *me*. Maybe he's gone out.'

'Nonsense. He knew that I wished to speak to him.'

'Maybe he's in the – ' Richard made a gesture, and E. H. seemed momentarily disconcerted. 'Oh.' His cheeks puffed out again. 'Well, let's see.' He slammed the door as he went out. Richard went on cutting slices of cake.

'When the old man gets on the warpath, the sparks certainly fly,' Bond said with a grin. He seemed to be enjoying himself. Sinclair was about to take another piece of cake when the door to the hall opened again. E. H. was standing there, an expression on his face was one of such shocked ferocity as no one in that room had ever seen. He looked from face to face and then, without speaking to anyone, crossed the room to the telephone, and dialled a number. They were all staring at him openly now.

'Scotland Yard,' E. H. said. His voice had a thick, choked

quality. 'My name is Edward Hargreaves. I wish to report a murder.'

# VI

## 8.50 to 10.0 p.m.

The cake lay untouched on the plates, the drinks stood half-empty on the tables. Nobody spoke. One of the girls from Accounts had hysterics and was taken outside by the bartenders. No one else left the room. Richard Hargreaves sat well away from his father, turning over idly in his hands the knife with which he had been cutting the cake. Tracy leaned against the wall and stared at the door: he did not look at Mrs Rogers. Other people sat uncomfortably on the edge of their chairs. Occasionally somebody coughed. E. H. himself sat on a stiff chair near the single door in the room, that led out into the hall, rather as if he were on guard. He had not spoken to anyone since making the telephone call. It was a relief to all of them when the police arrived.

They came in the person of a man of middle height, about thirty-five years old, wearing a light fawn raincoat spotted with rain, and a snap-brimmed trilby hat which he held in his hand. He had a fresh complexion, well-brushed fair hair and a round, smooth face; the curious innocence of his expression was contradicted by the watchful look in a pair of blue eyes which were not unfriendly but impersonal. He paused in the doorway and looked at them, and probably there was nobody in the room who did not feel a little disturbed by that look. It was not unsympathetic, but it was detached: it seemed to say, 'I can well understand that you are all upset, and that you may behave oddly. At the same time I am bearing in mind the fact that you may be behaving oddly because you have recently committed a murder. I am here to understand everything, but what I am most concerned to understand is a murderer's mind.'

As he stepped into the room the man said in a voice which was pleasant enough, but was curiously flat and expressionless, 'Mr Hargreaves, Mr Edward Hargreaves? I am Detective Inspector Bland from Scotland Yard.'

E. H. said, 'Yes,' in a hoarse voice. 'My son Lionel has been killed. This is my house. His body is in the library.'

Bland looked at his watch. 'Were these ladies and gentlemen present when he was killed?'

'They were all here. It – happened some time between half-past seven and half-past eight.'

'Oh.' Bland looked again at the rest of the people in the room. 'I shall be glad if you will remain here. I may have some questions to ask you.' As E. H. and Bland moved towards the door Richard Hargreaves said to his father, 'May I come too, sir? I may be able to help.' E. H. merely inclined his head.

They walked out of the large drawing-room into the hall, where the two footmen who had received the guests were standing together. 'These men say my son left the drawing-room – God know why – about half-past seven. They also say nobody came out after ten to eight.'

'That was about the time when you started speaking,' Richard said. In answer to Bland's unasked question he said, 'It was a special occasion, and my father made a short speech.'

Bland looked at the elder of the two servants. His voice was hard as he said, 'What's your name?'

'Jackson, sir,' the man said. He was a man of about fifty, with grey hair and a hooked nose. He looked rather like the popular conception of an Ambassador, but his voice was soft with years of deference. 'And this is Williams.' He indicated a young and perky man with bright black eyes who stood beside him.

'Were both of you on duty here in the hall?'

'That's right sir. We were on duty all evening. We haven't had very much to do so far, but we were to be on hand all the evening to give any assistance required.'

'Have you been here long?'

There was a touch of reproachful dignity in Jackson's voice. 'Ten years, sir. And Williams has been with us for five.'

'And you were on duty here in the hall, both of you, after Mr Lionel Hargreaves left the drawing-room? Neither of you left the hall for any reason?'

'That is correct, sir. As a matter of fact, neither of us left the hall during the whole evening, from six o'clock onwards, for more than two or three minutes.' There was almost a touch of acidity in Jackson's gentle voice as he said, 'This is our place of duty, sir.'

'And you are absolutely sure of the time when Mr Lionel Hargreaves came out of the drawing-room?'

'Within a minute or two, sir,' Jackson said, and Williams nodded agreement.

'What makes you so sure?'

Jackson coughed. 'A moment or two before, sir, Williams had looked at the clock and remarked that it was nearly half-past seven, and we should be late for our supper. It had been tentatively arranged that the dancing should start at eight and that we should go off for supper in turn after that time. Very soon after that, Mr Lionel came out of the drawing-room and walked down that passage.' He indicated a passage that ran along the side of the drawing-room.

'Do you confirm all this, Williams?'

'All absolutely right, sir,' Williams said emphatically. Both of them, Bland thought, looked more curious than distressed. 'The passage leads to the lavatories and through the library out into the garden. And it leads to the dining-room, too.'

'Did you see which way Mr Hargreaves went? Which door he entered?'

'Oh, no sir. You can't see that from the hall. Of course, we thought he'd gone to the lavatory.'

'And did you notice that he had not returned?'

Jackson spoke again. 'We noticed it, sir, but we did not remark it specially. We thought that perhaps Mr Lionel had gone to smoke a cigar in the library. And of course, sir, it was not for us to enquire into Mr Lionel's actions.'

'I realize that. Now, think carefully, before you answer this. Are you able to remember who came out *after* Mr Lionel Hargreaves – that is between the time Mr Lionel Hargreaves came out and his father went to look for him?'

Jackson bowed his head slightly. The gesture was impressive. 'Williams and I have discussed that point already, sir. We realised that it might be important. And the most we can say' – Jackson included Williams with a wave of the hand – 'is that we think we could pick them out. We knew Mr Lionel. We don't know most of the other gentlemen here, and so we couldn't be absolutely sure of identifying them.' He hesitated, and Richards said quickly, 'I came out for a couple of minutes. Don't be afraid to mention that Jackson.' Jackson did not reply, but merely bowed his head again.

Bland's face showed neither pleasure nor annoyance. 'You mentioned gentlemen. What about the ladies?'

'On that point, sir, Williams and I are positive. No lady came out of the drawing-room between the time Mr Lionel went down the passage and Mr Hargreaves came out to look for him.'

E. H. had listened to this dialogue with growing impatience. 'I can't see the point of all this.'

'It has a point,' Bland assured him. 'One of my men will come along and ask you both some questions about the people who came out of the drawing-room. Answer them as fully as you can. You've been very clear so far. Thank you.' They walked down the corridor, and came to two doors on the left-hand side, and two on the right. Richard acted as guide. He pointed to the two doors on the left. 'Men's washroom and lavatory, ladies' washroom and lavatory. On the right, dining-room and then library, with an interconnecting door between them.'

Bland nodded. They were standing outside the library door. He said to E. H., 'You turned the handle of this door, I suppose?'

'Why, yes, man. It was closed.'

'Did you enter the dining-room?'

E. H. seemed a little taken aback. 'No, I didn't. I didn't

suppose Lionel would be in the dining-room. As Jackson said, he might have gone into the library to smoke a cigar.' Bland said nothing, but turned the handle of the door.

The library was a large square room. A glass-fronted book-case over eight feet tall ran along the wall to the left of the three men; in the wall in which the door was placed stood another bookcase, and a bureau with a writing desk; in the wall opposite to the door curtains were flapping in front of a pair of French windows. Almost in the centre of the room the body of Lionel Hargreaves lay on the floor. The dead man was lying on his face with one arm flung out above his head. Bland knelt beside him. 'Shot through the back,' he said, and sniffed. 'From close range. Powder-burns on the jacket.' He made a gesture towards the curtains. 'Was the window open when you came in?'

'Yes. I've touched nothing. The window leads out into the garden.'

Bland walked across the room and looked out into the dark-ness. Three steps led down from the French windows into a garden. He spoke from the window. 'I'm right in thinking, am I not, that there's no possible exit from that drawing-room where your party took place?'

'Yes. Normally the folding-doors provide another exit which leads into the dining-room, but we had the buffet arranged in front of them, and they were locked.'

'And your guests are – ?'

E. H. said harshly. 'I am an advertising agent. You may have heard of me. The people here are members of my staff.'

Richard Hargreaves had been staring at the body on the floor with no particular expression. Now he looked up and said, 'Perhaps we'd better explain some details to the Inspector. This was a little party to celebrate the silver jubilee of the Hargreaves Advertising Agency, Inspector, and all the members of the staff are in the drawing-room.'

'Where does this garden lead to? Is it easily reached from the drawing-room?'

Again it was Richard who spoke. 'Anyone coming out of

the drawing-room could reach the garden by coming down the passage and into the library as we have done. Otherwise he would have to go out of the front door, walk round the back of the house, and come in through a door in the wall, which leads into the garden.'

'And if Jackson and Williams are telling the truth, nobody came that way. Do you think they are telling the truth? Are they absolutely reliable?'

E. H. exploded wrathfully. 'Good God, yes. There can't be any doubt about that. They'd have no reason to lie.'

'This door in the garden wall. Is it kept locked?'

'As a matter of fact,' Richard said apologetically, 'it isn't. The lock went wrong a couple of years ago, and it's never been put right.' Bland raised his eyebrows. 'I know it sounds careless, but really the wall's so low – only about six feet – and anyone could get over it in a few seconds if they wanted to come in that way.'

'So,' Bland said. He came in from the window. 'Do either of you recognize these? They were on the steps outside the French windows.' He held up a pair of lemon-yellow gloves. The two men looked at them curiously and shook their heads. Bland examined the right-hand glove carefully, and smelt it. 'Faint powder-marks and a distinct smell. The murderer has left us a present,' he said gravely. He put down the gloves and spoke to E. H. 'Was the light on or off when you came into the room, Mr Hargreaves?'

'Off. I snapped on the switch and saw – '

'Yes. Now correct me if I'm wrong. Next door to this room is the dining-room, and next door to that is the drawing-room which you were using at the party.'

'That's right.'

Two lines of worry creased Bland's smooth forehead. 'And you didn't hear a shot? Nobody heard a shot.' He said in a gently deprecatory tone, 'That seems to me very odd.'

Richard Hargreaves clicked his fingers. 'Not so odd. The walls of this room are soundproof.'

'Soundproof?' Bland's eyebrows went up.

E. H. said curtly, 'This is my library. When I come here to read or work I don't want to be disturbed by Richard's damned gramophone playing jazz tunes or by giggling servants. These walls and doors are lined with asbestos to exclude sound.'

'So that's why the shot wasn't heard. But in that case – ' Bland checked himself and nodded towards the French windows. 'How large is your garden?'

Richard Hargreaves answered. 'It's really hardly a garden – just a back yard. It's about twenty-five yards long by thirteen or fourteen wide. It leads on to Labriole Street.' He said tentatively, 'Of course the man must have come that way.'

Bland's chubby face was grave. 'There's no of course about it. There are two obvious possibilities. First, that Lionel Hargreaves was killed by one of your guests, who came in after him, shot him, opened the French windows and left a pair of gloves outside for us to find, and then returned to the party. In that case he's one of the people who left the party after half-past seven, to go to the washroom. Or he may have been killed by someone from outside who did all those things, and who came in and out through the garden door. If the murder was done by a guest, it's easy to see why the gloves were left – they'd be highly compromising. So would the revolver. If one of your guests is guilty we can expect to find the revolver – indeed we're bound to find it, since none of them has left the house.'

'Oh, but really,' Richard said, 'this is preposterous.' He took a blue silk handkerchief from his coat sleeve, and wiped his forehead.

'Is it? Can you tell me any reason why your son should have been killed, Mr Hargreaves?' Bland spoke impersonally, and looked at E. H., but Richard was included in the question. There was silence before either man spoke.

E. H. said harshly, 'I know of nothing. Every man makes enemies. I've made them myself in the way of business. Lionel made as many enemies as most men. But I know of nothing that would have caused anyone to kill him.'

'What about the servants?'

'Ridiculous. They had very little to do with Lionel.'

'In any event, surely they cancel each other out, as they were both on duty?' Richard said.

'Unless they were both concerned,' Bland said coolly. 'Very well. My men will go over this room for fingerprints, and they will search the garden. It will also be necessary to conduct a search of the house and everyone in it, for the revolver. And – '

The door from the passage opened, and a woman stood in the doorway. She said, 'They told me I should find him him here. Where is he?' She saw the body on the floor, put her hand over her eyes, and looked for a moment as if she were about to fall. Then she groped for a chair and sat down. E. H. and his son spoke at the same time. E. H. said in a voice more savage than Bland had yet heard him use, 'Young lady, are you accustomed to entering houses to which you are not invited?' Richard said in a quiet moan in which astonishment and some other emotion were equally mixed, 'Eve, what are you doing here?'

The woman took her hand away from her eyes, and stayed perfectly still for a few seconds. Bland, who was not particularly impressionable, thought that she was one of the most beautiful women he had ever seen. She was perhaps twenty-three years old, rather below medium height, with a slim figure: but it was her face that made Bland catch his breath. Beneath thick, black, shining hair dark eyebrows were outlined decisively against a rich creamy skin; below the eyebrows two magnificent dark eyes shone with an emotion that might have been anger, sorrow or fear. Her nose was short and straight above a small, rosebud mouth and a determined chin. She was wearing a white chiffon dress, that was very simple but obviously expensive. It revealed very clearly that she had a beautiful figure.

All this Bland noted while she was sitting in the chair, and such was the power of her beauty that when she raised her eyes to his he looked away for a moment.

E. H., however, was unmoved by her appearance – or if he was moved, it was merely to rage. He walked over and stood in front of her, apparently almost incoherent with anger. 'Who are you? What are you doing here?' She said simply, 'I am

Lionel's wife,' and the words brought Bland out of his spell; for
to his pained astonishment her voice was brassy and hard, with
a Cockney accent overlaid by a thin Kensington veneer. The
voice was so incongruous with the passionate and strange beauty
of her face that for a moment Bland thought someone else had
spoken.

The effect of her statement was curious. It seemed rather to
calm E. H., who stared at her for a moment, and then turned
his back on her abruptly. But Richard's face went very white.
'It's a lie,' he screamed. His voice had a feminine shrillness. 'I
don't believe it. Eve, you couldn't be such a bitch. You – ' He
lapsed into obscenity, and his father turned on him. 'Be quiet,
sir,' he said, in the tone men generally use for speaking to dogs.
Like a dog that had been struck, Richard shrank to silence.

'Have you any proof of this remarkable statement?' E. H.
asked. 'My son passed as a single man. Perhaps you can explain
why he was reluctant to acknowledge you as his wife?'

'Oh, really, this is the end,' the girl said. 'I come here and
find Lionel dead, and then I'm asked all these damned questions
by his stuffed-up pompous ass of a father. If you really want to
know, he said he couldn't acknowledge me as his wife because
his father was such a damned awful snob. He also said his father
wanted him to marry to improve the family position.' She put
a good deal of brassy malice into the last three words. 'He might
have added the family manners.' E. H. was about to retort when
Bland said, 'Excuse me.' He moved into the centre of the room,
and there was an edge to his manner that made all three of
them look at him. 'We've had enough of this. In future, Mr
Hargreaves, remember that I'm in charge, and I ask the questions. I should like you to come next door, while I ask some
now.' The girl shrugged her shoulders, but went with them into
the dining-room next door.

A long, dark oak refectory-table ran down the middle of the
vast dining-room, with chairs on either side of it. Bland set
down his hat carefully upon the table, took off his fawn raincoat
and laid it with the hat, and sat down on one side of the table,
indicating by a gesture that they should sit on the other. They

sat facing him with chairs conspicuously far apart, E. H. on the left with his hands on his knees, Richard in the centre not looking at his father, and the girl on the right. Light from a ceiling fitting gleamed on the girl's white face and blazing dark eyes, and on Bland's innocent expression and fair hair. It was very quiet in the room. Bland sat back and tapped his teeth with a pencil. He said, 'Mrs Hargreaves – ' She raised both hand in a curiously theatrical and unconvincing gesture, and said in her shrill voice, 'Don't call me that. My name's Eve Marchant – my stage name. I'm an actress. If you want me to answer any of your questions don't call me Mrs Hargreaves.' E. H. snorted and Richard looked wounded. Bland leaned forward, and his voice was soft and sympathetic. 'Do you want to talk about your husband now and get it over, or do you want to answer questions? I'd like you to tell me all about it – how you met him, why you married, how many people know you're married – the whole thing. It would be easier for you to talk to me, I think, and I should get a clearer story. But I can ask questions and you can answer them, if you'd prefer that.'

The girl looked down at her hands. 'They told me Lionel had been shot. Is that right?'

'Yes. Somebody killed him.'

She gave a short bark of laughter. 'You don't have to tell me Lionel didn't kill himself – he wasn't the suicidal type.' She stared at Bland for a few seconds, and this time his gaze did not drop. Then she smiled. 'I like you. I think you're a nice policeman. But I don't have to talk in front of them, do I?'

'Certainly not, if you don't want to.'

'Eve, darling,' Richard said, 'I think I ought to know anything – ' Both Eve Marchant and his father looked at him, and his voice trailed off. Then she frowned, with a curious air of indecision. 'Of course you're perfectly right, Dick. I know I've behaved terribly badly, but it's been so difficult. Oh well, really I couldn't care less. Let them both hear it – it may do the old bore good to hear what one of his sons was like.' E. H. shifted in his chair and Richard moaned. She said with no perceptible change in her voice, 'What the hell, Dick, I can't help it.' She ran a red tongue over her small mouth, and began to talk.

'Really, we're making all this to-do and you might think I had a great story to tell, but I haven't. Lionel and I met four months ago. I'm in a show at the Splendid – third chorus-girl from the left sort of thing. Of course it's not what I want to do, but there you are. I know some people think being a chorus-girl is the end, but maybe they'd change their minds if they had a living to earn. Anyway, Lionel sent round his card one night after the show, and we met. I thought he seemed nice enough, and he took me out to dinner.

'After that, if I do say it that shouldn't, he made a dead set at me, as dead a set as I've ever seen a man make at any girl. He used to come to the theatre every night, he sent me masses of flowers morning and evening, and we went out to dinners and dances almost every night. He was a wonderful dancer. Then he – '

'Just a moment. Did you know about this pursuit of Miss Marchant by your son, Mr Hargreaves?'

'I have never heard of Miss Marchant. And with regard to her statement that she has a living to earn, I suggest – '

'And you?' Richard did not reply, but Eve gestured impatiently. 'Oh, Richard didn't know anything. That all came later on. Except that he knew I went out with Lionel, didn't you, darling?' Richard still did not say anything, and a spot of colour showed on the girl's cheek. She went on talking.

'Within a week Lionel asked me to marry him. I refused. He asked me every day, rang up after I'd gone to bed at night and before I got up in the morning. He was mad to get married. But then I asked if I could meet his family, and he said his father wanted him to marry into society, and he thought it would be better if I didn't meet him just yet. He introduced me to Dick, but nothing was said about getting married in front of him. For a long time I stuck out that I should meet his father, and we should do it all properly. If I'd known what his father was like, I wouldn't have bothered. Then we had a row and I told him I couldn't care less whether I met his father or not, if he was too snobby to introduce me. And then we patched the row up – and one day we got married.' If there was a certain inconsequence in Eve Marchant's narration, Bland did not seem to be aware of it. He listened attentively, and made an occasional note. Richard was looking down at the floor, and his face was not visible. E. H. seemed to be bottling up something resembling a thunderstorm.

Bland said, 'How long ago did you get married?'

She looked down at her left hand, on which there was no ring. 'Two months ago, at Paddington Registry Office.'

E. H. sneered. 'So you held out for two months. Remarkable endurance!'

She turned to Bland, with her fists clenched and her fine eyes sparkling. 'My God, I won't put up with being insulted by this filthy old snob. If you want me to talk, make him keep his mouth shut. Christ, this really is the end.'

Bland's voice was suddenly warm with feeling. 'Mr Hargreaves, if you interrupt Miss Marchant again I shall have to ask you to leave this room.' He turned to her again. 'What happened after you were married?'

Her beautiful dark eyes met his frankly. 'What didn't happen? I found out inside about a week just what kind of rat I'd got married to. I married Lionel because I thought I loved him, and because I thought he'd give me a good home.' She repeated the words slowly. 'That's what I wanted, a good home. Lionel married me because he wanted me.'

E. H. thrust his head forward. He looked like a fine white-headed bull. 'I knew Lionel was a fool, but I didn't know he was that much of a fool – to marry a girl because she played hard to get. You married him because you found out that he was my son. You knew he was pretty well fixed. You – ' The girl jumped to her feet, and moved past Richard with the speed and grace of an animal. The anger in her face made her look more beautiful than ever. She slapped E. H.'s face with her hand, twice, hard. The second time E. H. caught hold of her wrist and twisted it, so that she cried with pain. Richard rose to his feet and stood irresolutely before them. From the other side of the refectory-table Bland said, without getting up, 'Mr Hargreaves, I think no good purpose is served by your remaining during Miss Marchant's interrogation. Let us have a talk later.'

E. H. let go of the girl's wrist and she began to rub it. He stood up. His eyes were like small blue marbles. He measured his words carefully, not looking at any of them particularly. 'If this story is true – and I can believe that Lionel would be fool enough for anything where a woman was concerned – I cannot stop you from obtaining what little money my son may have in his banking account. I doubt if there is very much, because he was in the habit of spending it all on women like you. I advise you, Richard, to give up your curious association with this woman who claims to be your murdered brother's wife. If you persist in it, the consequences will be unfortunate. Inspector, if you wish to ask me any questions I shall be available at my office tomorrow. No doubt, however, you will be able to draw your own conclusions from the information given you in the last few minutes.'

Bland tilted back his chair and stared at E. H. with something that looked like amusement. He said, 'How much money would you reckon your son Lionel had in the bank, Mr Hargreaves?'

E. H. seemed a little taken aback, but he replied without reluctance. 'I should be surprised if it were more than a few hundred pounds.'

'Not very much to provide a motive for murder.' His faint smile grew broader. 'That is what you're suggesting, isn't it – that Miss Marchant murdered him for his money?'

E. H.'s small blue eyes did not leave Bland's face. 'Crimes have been committed for as many shillings.' He turned on his heels and made an impressive exit, spoiled only slightly by the fact that at the door he almost collided with a tall, lean man with a narrow head, who looked down from his great height and addressed Bland. 'Are you ready for us next door, sir?'

'Yes, Filby. I want the room and the body photographed. Check the room for fingerprints. Pay special attention to the French windows. Check the steps leading out to the garden for footprints, and put two men on to a search of the garden.

They're looking for a revolver, and for anything else of interest they can find. If they don't find anything we shall have to make a search of the guests, and then of the whole house. Post a man on the front door. Ask the guests which of them went outside the drawing-room after 7.25 and before the discovery of the body. Then check their statements by those two servants, Jackson and Williams, who were on duty all the time. Make a note of any discrepancies – anyone who stayed out a long time, anyone who went out a bit before Lionel Hargreaves went out at 7.30, and didn't come back. Let me know the full result. If you have any trouble with the guests, let me know and I'll come and talk to them myself. And ask Dr McCullen to make an examination as soon as he arrives. All clear, Filby?'

'All clear, sir.' The narrow head disappeared.

'Well,' Bland said with a sigh. He turned to Richard Hargreaves and Eve Marchant, and gave them a smile so friendly that it transformed his face, and made him look almost boyish. 'One of the most disagreeable duties of a policeman is that he has to pretend to an inhumanity and callousness he doesn't feel. Believe me, I know you've both gone through a bad time, although officially I'm not permitted to allow that to have any influence on me. But I'd like you to finish your story, Miss Marchant, if you feel able to do so. Then I've got a couple of questions, and then your ordeal will be over.'

Eve Marchant smiled back at him, with a good deal of effect. 'You're very sweet. There really isn't a lot more to tell. After we married Lionel was as beastly to me as he could be. He paid the rent of my flat, but apart from that we might as well not have been married. I saw him about once a week. We never even had a honeymoon. He didn't so much as buy me a frock, and the ring was the cheapest he could get.' Her voice was brassily acquisitive, vibrant with desire for money. Bland glanced at Richard. He was gazing at her with his lips slightly parted and an expression of yearning in his eyes. 'There's no use pretending – inside a month Lionel was going about with other women, and wishing he hadn't got married.'

'And what did you think about it?'

Her voice softened as much as her voice could soften. 'Why, I'd met Dick. And I guess that was just a case of the old, old story – love at first sight, on both sides. Isn't that so, Dick?'

He wriggled uncomfortably. 'I don't like to – in front of the Inspector – '

She snapped at him and Bland had the feeling that a tigress was showing her claws. 'Oh hell, darling, don't be tiresome. You'll be lucky if you don't get asked anything worse than that.'

Richard's elegant toe moved on the carpet. 'Well, it's true, yes. Eve is so beautiful and understands me so well. But of course I didn't know – ' He stopped, apparently overcome by embarrassment.

'You did know she was married to your brother.'

She broke in, speaking excitedly, with quick gestures, and Bland had the fancy that the claws were being fairly clearly shown now. 'But you must see I *couldn't* say anything to you, Dick darling. I'd told Lionel I'd keep our marriage a secret and not tell *anyone* – and then I knew if I told you, Dick, I should have to stop seeing you. And I asked Lionel for a divorce.'

'But that would have meant publicity.'

'Exactly what Lionel said. He wouldn't agree to it because of the publicity. He thought his father would cut him off with the good old penny.' She laughed, not very pleasantly.

'You could have obtained a divorce, if he was unfaithful.'

She wagged a finger at him. 'My dear man, exactly what I was going to do. But I hadn't taken any steps about it – of course he was very unwilling – and now – ' She spread out her hands.

'So the position is that Lionel knew nothing of Richard, and Richard knew nothing of Lionel?'

She flushed. 'You're being perfectly beastly, but – yes.'

'And you confirm that, Mr Hargreaves?'

'Oh yes – yes. It was a terrible shock to me to learn this evening – ' Richard's voice died away and he waved a thin white hand.

'All right. Now, one or two questions to you both, just for

the record. You were out of the drawing-room after 7.30, weren't you, Mr Hargreaves?'

Richard Hargreaves took a cigarette from his silver case and tapped it reflectively. A certain alertness was apparent behind his languor. 'Yes, I was. Not for more than five minutes, though. Jackson and Williams can confirm that.'

'You didn't notice Lionel go out?'

'No. But there's no reason why I should have done.'

'No reason at all. Were you fond of your brother?'

Richard's air of alertness was a shade more noticeable, but he answered the question readily enough. 'I couldn't say that. In fact, we didn't get on well. Lionel was always the practical, hearty type, and I was always more artistic or aesthetic. At school he played Rugger, while I was secretary of the Dramatic Society. You know the kind of thing. And it went deeper than that.' He gestured faintly. 'I don't think Lionel was fundamentally a pleasant or generous person. He had an amiable manner, but he was really rather vicious. God knows, all the Hargreaves family are pretty vicious, but I think Lionel was the worst of us. But I know one shouldn't speak ill of the dead. You can put it that we were irreconcilable types.'

'Thank you.' Bland leaned back in his chair. 'Miss Marchant, where were you between 7.30 and 8.30 tonight?'

She said with some composure, 'I was in my flat in Catherine Street, Westminster.'

'Alone?'

'Yes.' She smiled and showed white, even teeth. 'I was reading a book. I'm afraid I've failed to provide myself with an alibi. But a funny thing happened this evening. Someone rang up about a quarter to six. They said they were speaking for Lionel, and that he wanted me to meet him here at half-past nine. So I got a taxi and came along.'

'Wasn't that a very unusual request?'

'Yes, it *was* unusual – because, of course, I'd never been here before – and I wondered what it was all about – but he rang off before I could ask any questions.'

'You don't know who telephoned you. You said "he". Are you sure it was a man?'

She looked doubtful, and for the first time a little frightened. 'You've got me there. I was bathing Binkie – my Peke, you know, such a sweet boy – and so I didn't pay all that much attention, until I came to think about it afterwards. And then it's easy to disguise a voice, isn't it? This voice sounded very deep and husky – it *sounded* like a man's voice. But why should anyone want to bring me down here? Do you think it was – the murderer?'

'Your guess is as good as mine. What's certain is that it's somebody who knows you were married. How many people knew that?'

'Nobody, I didn't tell *anyone*. I don't know if Lionel did – he always swore he hadn't.'

Bland had been making notes. His voice had a slight edge to it as he said, 'Thank you both for being so helpful. Will you leave me your address and telephone number, Miss Marchant, so that I can get in touch with you if necessary. I shall have to ask you to stay a few minutes, until we decide if a search of the guests is necessary, but I'll try to make it as quick as possible. No doubt you're feeling tired. And Mr Hargreaves, no doubt you're anxious to see Miss Marchant home.' Richard looked at Bland sharply, but his face might have been made of wood.

When they had gone out Bland stood up and stretched. He was walking towards the door when it opened and Filby came in. The tall detective was carrying a cloth-covered bundle rather as if it were a baby, but the jerk of his finger and the rolling of his eye clearly had reference to Eve Marchant. 'What a girl,' he said. 'Sex, and no mistake. Plenty of sex.'

'Oozing with it. And very effective it seems to be. She claims to have married one brother, and now he's dead she wants to marry the other, and finally she's got you under her thumb.'

'Take more than her,' Filby said indignantly, and pulled down the lower lid of his eye. 'See any green?'

Bland examined the eye. 'No green, but it looks very bloodshot. You should see an oculist.'

'I'd need my head examined if I fell for one like her,' Filby said. 'A dangerous woman. But I got something you'll like.' He laid the bundle on the refectory-table, and unwrapped it carefully to show a Smith and Wesson revolver. 'There's the revolver all right. No prints on it.'

Bland picked it up, broke it, sniffed and grunted. 'One shot fired. Where'd you find it?'

'In the garden. About ten yards from the library window. Foot or two off the path. Ground's hard. No footprints.'

'Good work. Any luck with the French windows?'

'Dozens of fingerprints. Can't get anything out of 'em. Nice, clean crime this one, if you ask me.' Filby always tried to make every crime a kind of sporting event, and he liked the criminal to have a fair chance. 'I've got that list of people who went outside, too. All went down the corridor, of course – they were going to the lavatory, or so they say. The two servants check it as OK. Nobody went upstairs or out the front door.'

'How many of them?'

'Five – six if you count young Hargreaves, the one who just went out – seven if you count the chap who was knocked off. All men. I've got 'em more or less in the order they went, too. Thought that might be important. Here we are. Half-past seven the chap who was murdered went out. Next was a chap called Bond, about five minutes afterwards he was. Then a squint-eyed one named Tracy. Then young Hargreaves. Then two young lads who went out together, and last someone named Sinclair, who must have come out just before the old man's speech started at ten to eight. Nobody dared to go out while that was going on.'

'Sinclair,' Bland said softly. 'Yes, of course, Sinclair. I was trying to remember.' He became conscious of Filby's startled gaze and said, 'Sorry, day dreaming. None of them tried to deny they'd been outside?'

Filby pulled at a protruding underlip. 'Bond didn't say he'd been out, but when the servants pointed him out he said he thought it was before 7.30. Nothing to it, probably.'

'Very likely not. All right, Filby. You can let the rest of them go home now. I've seen young Hargreaves, but I shall want to see these five.'

'You mean we can narrow it down to them already?' Filby breathed admiration.

'Not at all. Anyone may have come in from outside, and it may be nothing to do with any of these people. But it certainly can't have anything to do with those who didn't leave the draw-ing-room.'

'So we send them all home.' Filby leered, and the effect was cheerfully obscene. 'That girl with plenty of sex wouldn't be wanting an escort, I suppose?'

'She's got one already – Richard Hargreaves.' Filby raised his shoulders in a comic, exaggerated gesture of disappointment. 'But I've got a couple of jobs for you, in the way of checking up on her. Her name's Eve Marchant and she claims she was married to Lionel Hargreaves about three months ago at Pad-dington Registry Office. Check on it and get all the details you can. I have a feeling there's something fishy about it, from the way she told her story. And she says someone telephoned her about a quarter to six tonight at her flat in Catherine Street, Westminster, asked her to come along here, and that she took a taxi from her home at about a quarter to nine to come here. Check on those things too.'

'So she's in it, is she? She looked too good to be true to anybody.' He laughed at his own joke. Bland gave it a blank stare. 'No, this is just a routine check-up. Then you can go home. And now I'd better see these people. I'll take them in the order they went out – Bond, Tracy, then the two lads, and Sinclair last.'

'Oh ah,' Filby said. 'There's a woman called Mrs Rogers who's asking to see you. Quite a piece in a sly little way. Said something about information. Might be worried about some-thing.'

'All right. Keep her waiting. Let's have Mr Bond.'

# VII

*10.20 p.m. Wednesday to*
*12.35a.m. Thursday, January 16*

The room was dim, with patches of light round the refectory-table. Bland tilted back the dark oak chair in which he had been sitting and stifled a yawn. He said, 'So you went outside just about 7.30, Mr Bond?' He considered the man in front of him with impersonal distaste. His eye was offended by the smartness and newness of Bond's double-breasted dinner-jacket with its padded shoulders, and by the thin dark hair that was too smoothly sleek; his ear was offended by the strident assurance of Bond's voice. Thirty-five, he thought, or perhaps a young forty, working-class come up in the world and proud of it, strident perhaps to conceal an inferiority complex. The kind of man who is much too kind to his mother.

'Absolutely, old boy. One of those natural needs, you know. Wasn't out there more than three or four minutes. Didn't see a soul except those two chaps hanging about in the hall, and then I met old Tracy coming out of the drawing-room just as I went back to join the happy throng.'

'You didn't see Lionel Hargreaves leave the drawing-room, or any sign of him outside it?'

'Not a thing, old boy. Sorry.'

On the table lay the revolver and the gloves, covered by the cloth in which Filby had wrapped the revolver. Bland removed the cloth. 'Do you recognize either of these?' Bond shrugged. 'Not the revolver. The gloves might belong to anybody. Dick Hargreaves sometimes wears lemon-coloured gloves. So do I, for that matter.'

Bland made a note. 'What is your position with the Hargreaves Agency?'

'Production Manager. Look after blocks, make sure advertisements get in the papers to time and that the right ad goes in, generally act as head cook and bottle-washer looking after the production end.'

'How long have you been with them?'

'Nearly a year.'

'Have you any idea why Mr Hargreaves might have been killed?'

Bond rubbed the side of his face thoughtfully with his hand. His upper lip twisted in a grin, and his dark handsome face looked both malicious and sly. 'Well, there you have me. I don't want to tell tales out of school, wash dirty linen, all that sort of thing. But it's an open secret that Lionel was one for the ladies, and that he made a pass at Jean Rogers.'

'Jean Rogers?'

'Mrs Rogers – she's one of our copywriters. Women's angle, that sort of thing. Well, as I was saying, Lionel made a pass at her – quite unsuccessful, I gather. Nothing unusual in that – Lionel made a pass at anything in a skirt. *But* there was something special this time, because it's an open secret that Jean Rogers and Tracy, our Art Director, are – like that.' He twined two fingers. 'There you are. I don't say there's anything in it. If it's not that, though, you'll find it was something to do with a woman. There must be a hell of a lot of husbands in London who won't be wearing black because Lionel's dead.'

'You're implying that Tracy and Mrs Rogers are lovers?'

Bond laughed. 'Don't let's be technical. It's an open – '

'An open secret, yes. But if Tracy has been successful, would he have any motive in murdering an unsuccessful lover?'

Bond shrugged his padded shoulders. He clearly thought that Bland was too finicky. 'Maybe Lionel made another pass at her – he made at least two at most women. Maybe he had better luck the second time, and Tracy found out. *I* don't know. That's your business.'

Bland's face was blank. 'One more question. How well do you know the geography of this place?'

'Don't know it at all. Never been here before.'

Bland nodded. 'All right, Mr Bond. I can get in touch with you at the Agency if I want you?'

'Any day. Do I take it that I'm now free to depart?'

'Perfectly free. Ask Mr Tracy to come in, will you?' As Bond went out Bland noticed that he had a slight but perceptible limp.

When Bland looked at George Tracy he saw a very small man, with broad shoulders, an erect stance, and with dark hair standing up straight on his head. Vain, Bland thought, looking at the self-conscious handsomeness, the boldness of his strongly-marked features, the squint in the dark eyes that rather added to his attractiveness. Probably arrogant, he added after a moment's thought; and a strong personality. Tracy sat down in the chair on the other side of the table, and at once began to talk.

'Let me put my cards on the table, Inspector. I didn't like Lionel Hargreaves.' Tracy paused to give emphasis to the admission. 'And yet – life and death are astonishing things. Now that he's gone I feel as violent a shock as if I'd lost someone who was dear to me. When I think that less than three hours ago we were standing together next door, eating, drinking, talking – ' Tracy shook his head solemnly. An indifferent dramatic performance, Bland thought. 'I'm telling you this because I want to say here and now that, little though I liked Lionel, if there's anything I can do to send his murderer to the gallows – by God, I will.'

'The word gallows is obsolete,' Bland said rather coldly, 'but it will be helpful if you will answer some questions.' The balloon of Tracy's eloquence seemed to be a little deflated. 'You went out of the drawing-room about half-past seven tonight.'

'Certainly I did.' Tracy's squint became alarming. 'Are you suggesting – '

Bland's voice was weary. 'Lionel Hargreaves went out of the drawing-room just before half-past seven. He didn't come back. Therefore the movements of anyone who left the drawing-room after that time are a matter of interest to me. Is that clear? Now, how long were you out of the room?'

'I – ' Tracy was looking alarmed, and his speech now had no ornamental flourish. 'About ten minutes.'

'What were you doing?'

'I went to the washroom. Then I walked up and down the passage, and came out once or twice into the hall. Jackson and that other fellow must have seen me.'

'How do you know Jackson's name?'

'Well, really,' Tracy said, and laughed. 'I've been here a good many times to dinners and parties. What's the purpose of all these questions?'

'Did anyone pass you while you were walking up and down?'

'Yes. First of all Dick Hargreaves, and then those two young copywriters, Onslow and Mudge. They all went into the washroom and came out again.'

'They didn't go into the library?'

Tracy hesitated. 'I couldn't swear that one or other of them didn't open the library door and slip inside – they might have done so while my back was turned. But then they'd have had to slip out again while my back was turned, too. I should think it very unlikely.'

'You saw or heard nothing of Lionel Hargreaves? You didn't hear a shot?'

'No.' Tracy looked triumphant. 'But then I shouldn't. The library's pretty well soundproof, you know.'

Bland made no comment. 'You said you didn't like Lionel Hargreaves. How well did you know him?'

'Not very well. I'm Art Director of the Agency, and we were on the Board together. I might see him for an hour or so perhaps three days a week. But I was never intimate with him.' Tracy said it as though he had missed a chance of winning a sweepstake.

'Do you know of any reason why he should have been killed?'

Tracy's generous mouth tightened, and his manner became again that of a ham actor approaching a purple passage in Shakespeare. 'Perhaps I can tell you that, Inspector, if you'll tell me one thing. Do you think Lionel was killed by someone at the party tonight?'

'You do me too much honour. I've been here an hour and a half. I don't think anything yet.'

Tracy leaned back in his chair. His voice lost its tone of drama, and became deep, melodious, pleasant, and yet still not altogether natural. He might have been acting an altogether different part – that of the mature man-of-the-world delivering carefully his judgement on life. 'I think the most I should say is this – and I say it as one who, for his sins, has twenty years' acquaintance with the Hargreaves family. I came to this Agency twenty years ago as a junior copywriter, and I've known them, senior and juniors, ever since that time. God forbid that I should speak ill of them, and especially of the one who's dead.' Tracy's fine dark eyes looked hard into Bland's blue ones. 'But there are a lot of mysteries in that family, and I think you'll find the secret of Lionel Hargreaves' death in them. Look into the past, Inspector. Look into family history.'

Bland did not seem much impressed. 'I understand you are the creative Director. What does that imply?'

'It means that I organize all the creative work that goes out of the Agency, all the drawings, layouts, the whole of the Studio.'

Without any change in tone Bland said, 'You didn't like Lionel Hargreaves. Did your dislike of him have anything to do with his relations with Mrs Rogers?'

The man-of-the-world vanished, and was replaced by a furious John Bull, as Tracy's face became very pink and he thumped the refectory-table with a surprisingly large fist. The cast in his left eye was strikingly obvious. He got up from the chair and said with a deep bull's bellow, 'I refuse to have her name brought into this.'

'Just as you please. Have you ever seen these?' Bland whipped the cloth off the revolver and gloves, but the effect was disappointing. Tracy merely shook his head, with no sign of discomposure. 'All right, Mr Tracy. I'll bear your suggestion in mind.' After Tracy had gone out Bland stepped to the door and called, 'Filby.' A square-headed man appeared. 'Filby said you'd asked him to make some enquiries. Anything I can do, sir?'

'Yes. Ask Mrs Rogers to come in.'

Bland looked attentively at Jean Rogers. She was, as Filby had said, quite a piece: but it was true that she could not be called a beauty, and he noticed with some distaste the black and green sequins at the neck and hem of her evening dress. He said, 'You wanted to see me, Mrs Rogers.'

'Yes.' She was obviously ill-at-ease. 'It's not *certain* that someone here at the party had anything to do with this thing, is it? I mean, it could just as well have been someone from outside?'

'Why not?' Bland's voice was not encouraging, but Jean Rogers went on talking. She was turning and twisting an artificial flower in her hands. 'Then there's something I think you ought to know. There's a man named Carruthers who had a grudge against Lionel. He's a cousin of the family – the Hargreaves family, I mean – their only relation or something like that. He's a commercial artist who does work as a freelance. A lot of different firms call on him when they have something which is in his particular line. He's rather good on doing nice, decorative stuff for fashion books, and things like that. Well, about eighteen months ago he did a lot of work for us on an account for women's clothes – I know about it, because I wrote the copy on that account. Lionel Hargreaves was the director in charge of it, and he was very rude about the work Carruthers had done. Carruthers is rather a nice little man, very meek and mild generally, but he was really upset about this. They had an awful row, and Carruthers wasn't asked to do any more work for us for over a year.'

'That means he has done some recently?'

'Yes,' she said rather unwillingly. 'It's been patched up a bit in the past six months, because Tracy and Sinclair both know Carruthers is a useful man, and want to use his work. But he's not spoken to Lionel since they had their row.'

'I see.' Bland was playing with his pencil. 'And you think he may have murdered Hargreaves because of their feud?' There was only the faintest hint of irony in his voice, but Jean Rogers flushed.

'I'm not saying anything of the sort. I thought you would be interested to have information about someone who disliked Lionel. Apparently I'm mistaken, and the police aren't interested in things like that. I'm sorry to have wasted your time.' She tugged at her artificial flower and got up.

'Sit down, Mrs Rogers,' Bland said. His voice was not loud, but it was compelling. 'It is evident that you are an intelligent woman, and that you had a purpose in telling me this story. Are you seriously suggesting that Lionel Hargreaves was murdered because eighteen months ago he quarrelled with a man about some drawings – a quarrel which has since been patched up?'

'I'm not suggesting anything,' she said violently. She was nearly in tears.

'Or are you anxious that enquiry should be diverted from somebody else who had a quarrel with Hargreaves recently – and about you?'

She put down the flower, and, surprisingly enough, spoke in a tone of some composure, mixed with contempt. 'You don't waste time in digging for scandal, do you?'

'One doesn't need to dig when there are willing scandal-bearers.' His innocent blue eyes were sympathetic. 'And I'm here to listen to all kinds of stories – even stories like the one you've just told me. I try to deal with all those that involve emotional relationships as tactfully as I can, but all sorts of people are likely to be hurt in a case of murder. That's unavoidable. Try not to blame the police too much – they're only doing a job.'

Her eyes were wet. 'I know. I'm sorry. I'd better go.'

He leaned forward and spoke earnestly. 'If you like to answer some questions you may help me, and help yourself too. Let me tell you what's been told to me. I've been told that you and Tracy are in love, that Lionel Hargreaves made advances to you and that Tracy resented them. Is that true?'

'Yes, that's all true, but it doesn't really mean anything. George has a violent temper, and he simply told Lionel what he thought of him. It was all awfully foolish, because, of course, a lot of people in the firm heard about it – but it didn't really mean anything.'

'How long ago did this quarrel take place?'

She sighed and said, 'I think I'd better tell you the whole thing, though it's going to sound much more important than it was. About a fortnight ago I was in Lionel's office and he put his arm round me and kissed me. I told him not to be silly. He didn't take any notice, but just kept on kissing me and trying to make love to me. Then George came in and – lost his temper. He knocked Lionel down, and told him a few home-truths about himself. It was all over in five minutes, and half an hour later Lionel apologized to me. Needless to say George, like a fool, left the office door open, and the receptionist, Miss Peachey, passed by while the row was going on. No doubt Miss Peachey told her best friend, Miss Berry, and the whole thing was ridiculously exaggerated.'

'Did Edward Hargreaves know about it?'

She looked startled. 'Why, no. At least I hope not. He'd be dreadfully angry, because Lionel was the apple of his eye.' She chuckled. 'I think he'd have taken the view that absolute obedience should have been my role in obeying the instructions of a director.'

'Did Lionel repeat his attempt to make love to you?'

'Why certainly not. Did someone say he had?'

'It's been suggested.' Bland paused, and then said without emphasis, 'Now, Mrs Rogers – please believe that I don't ask this without a reason – what are your relations with Mr Tracy?'

Her gaze met his quite frankly. 'We're in love with each other, and if it were possible we'd get married.'

'Why isn't it possible?'

She sighed again. 'I married five years ago, when I was twenty-five. I left my husband after six months. He was a rat – a mental pervert. He was never unfaithful to me, but he had a mean, perverted mind. He thought up the most outrageous explanations for the simplest actions. If I bought some clothes he would make up a tremendous fantasy about my reasons for buying them – he'd say I wanted to attract men, and make all

sorts of awful insinuations.' She drew a deep breath. 'I'm not
telling you all this because I like it – simply to show that it
would be terribly difficult for me to divorce him. I've asked him
to divorce me, but he won't even consider it – he's a strict
Catholic. When I left Alan, I had to get a job, and after knocking
about for a bit I got one with Hargreaves as a copywriter. I
don't like any of the family much except Dick, but they pay
fairly well, and Sinclair, who runs the Copy Department, is very
nice.'

'And then you met Mr Tracy?'

'That's right. It's vitally necessary for both our sakes that
E.H. shouldn't know about us. He may have been a rake in his
youth – everyone says he was – but he's a puritanical, cold-
blooded old devil now.' She spoke with some warmth.

'And what do you hope to do in the future?'

'God knows.' She got up and walked about the room. 'I've
often wondered. I hope that one day Alan will divorce me, but
I really don't know – ' She stopped suddenly, and looked at him
almost with hostility. 'I can't see that my private troubles have
anything to do with you.'

'I hope you're right. Have you ever seen these before?' Bland
showed her the revolver and the gloves, but she shook her head.
'Have they got something to do with it all?'

'Rather more to do with it, I think, than the story you told
me when you first came in. But thank you for what you told me
afterwards – it may be very helpful. Good night, Mrs Rogers.'

She stood with her hand on the door and a frown on her
forehead, as if she were about to ask a question. Then she said,
'Good night,' and closed the door.

Onslow and Mudge had heard nothing, seen nothing, and said
that they had gone to the washroom together and returned
together. They showed a purely malicious interest in the murder
('To me,' Onslow said loftily, 'it's simply one exploiter the less,
though not such a dirty one as E.H.'), and by the time he had
finished with them that slight edge of exasperation had returned
to Bland's voice. He was smiling, however, when he said to one

of the detectives in the hall, 'Ask Mr Sinclair to come in,' and he was smiling still when he made a gesture for Sinclair to take a seat. The chief of the Copy Department was a tall man in his middle thirties. He had a mass of curly fair hair, a big straight nose, and a firm mouth and chin, and his face, as he looked across the table, was puzzled. Bland said, 'You don't remember me?'

'Why, yes.' Sinclair was hesitant. 'But I don't just place – '

'Charles Sinclair, isn't it? And you were at Beldham Grammar. Captain of the School, leading light in the Dramatic Society, captain of the cricket team. Remember the boy who went in number nine and tried to bowl slow leg-breaks?'

'Good *Lord*,' Sinclair said. The firm mouth broke up into a laugh, and the effect was charming. 'Wily Bland. Remember we always used to call you that because you were always convinced of your cunning even when you'd been hit for four fours in an over. You always thought you should have been kept on for one more over. I remember you were always a wily lad at school, but I never expected – ' He checked himself.

'Go on, go on, don't mind me. I know nobody regards a policeman as a human being, and I'm inclined to agree with them. I'll tell you one day how I happened to become one. It isn't a bad story. Do you still play cricket?'

'I turn out occasionally for the Banks. And you?'

'Haven't tried a leg-break in fifteen years. And I used to think I was England's answer to Clarrie Grimmett. Smoke?' He pushed across a packet.

'Thanks.' Sinclair busied himself with a lighter. Bland puffed reflectively for a moment, and then spoke in a voice that was less official and carefully controlled than usual.

'I recognized you when I arrived, and that's why I kept you until last. I've asked everyone here the routine questions about motive and opportunity, and in most cases I've got routine answers. There are one or two things that may lead somewhere, but it's very clear to me that I shan't get to know anything about these people personally unless I know something about the general set-up. How well do you know these people and this place?'

'Place – I've never been here before. Lionel was being rather catty about that earlier this evening. People – well, I joined the Agency about three years ago as chief of the Copy Department. Been in advertising since I was twenty-one. I know them all reasonably well, and naturally I know the way an advertising agency works.'

'Fine. How would you like to lend a hand by giving me an insight into the way in which these people are related to one another, both personally and in the Agency? It might help me a lot – and at the same time you'd see a murder investigation going on from inside. Enlarge your experience as an advertising man.' He grinned.

Sinclair's answering grin was enthusiastic. 'Nothing I'd like more. Just tell me where and how to start.' He blew a perfect smoke-ring.

'First of all, the routine questions. Did you see anyone else when you went outside at about a quarter to eight?'

'I saw a couple of servants hanging about in the hall. Went into the washroom and came straight back into the drawing-room.'

'You didn't hear anything while you were outside? Any noise that might have come from the library?'

'Sorry, I didn't. Should I have done?'

'It would help if you had – though, as the library walls were lined with asbestos, it's not likely anyone will have heard anything. Have you ever seen this before?' Bland took the cloth off the revolver once more, and it gleamed in the lamplight. Sinclair looked at it in apparent fascination. 'The weapon? No, I've never seen it.'

'We can't be sure it's the weapon yet, but someone left it lying about in the garden. Nor these gloves?' Sinclair shrugged his shoulders. 'Impossible to say. Two or three people in the firm wear gloves like these. Bond, our Production Manager, for instance.'

'All right. It's disappointing, but I didn't expect anything better. Nobody recognizes the gloves or the revolver. Now, the question of motive.' Bland made a faint gesture of irritation. 'In the last hour some of the least adequate motives for murder I've ever heard have been suggested to me. What do you know about Tracy, for instance?'

'He's a good chap, and a damned good advertising man – too good for the other directors. Damned rash and tactless, though – always bashing his head against a wall.'

'And about Mrs Rogers?'

'Oh, I see.' Sinclair looked for a moment as if he had tasted some unpleasant medicine, and then grinned again. The grin, Bland thought, made him look very much like the Captain of the School. 'I hadn't realized the kind of things you might want to know. But you've obviously been told about them already. It's all a pretty open secret – I should think half a dozen people in the firm must know. I believe they can't get married. It's a damned shame.'

'Did you know that Lionel Hargreaves had made a pass at her, and had a row with Tracy about it?'

'I'd heard some rumours flying about. But I'm not a bit surprised. Lionel would make a pass at any woman.'

'Well, that situation has been suggested to me as a motive for murder. A singularly stupid one, I must say, since Mrs Rogers powerfully repulsed the attack. It's also been suggested that he may have been murdered by a man named Carruthers, who was annoyed because Hargreaves had a row with him eighteen months ago about some drawings.'

'Oh, I say.' Sinclair laughed aloud. 'They have been picking out some corny ones for you. That's too ridiculous – though it's true that Carruthers doesn't like – didn't like – Lionel very much. Carruthers is a cousin of the family, you know.'

'So I've been told. What kind of man is he?'

'Mild, inoffensive, rather slimily pleasant. Not at all my idea of a murderer. He'll probably be in the office tomorrow, if you want to see him.'

'It's also been suggested to me, vaguely, that the secret of the case lies in the past.' Bland held up his hand as Sinclair began to speak. 'There's a résumé of what has been suggested to me in the way of motive. Now, if you can add anything to it, I'll be very glad. If you feel you know of any *possible* motive, don't hesitate to tell me – I'm grateful even for the things that have already been suggested, improbable though they are. I'm fishing in deep waters of the infinite at the moment, and I'll be grateful for any bait. And if you can give me a sketch of the principals, that will help too.'

In the dim light of the dining-room Sinclair's strong face looked oddly irresolute. 'I can hardly know where to begin. That suggestion about the past – who told you about the past?'

There was the faintest pause before Bland replied, 'Tracy.'

'E.H.'s second wife died two years ago,' Sinclair said slowly. 'At the time there were rumours that her death was not accidental.'

Bland snapped his fingers and said with uncharacteristic excitement, 'Of course – I remember. A yacht. Possible suicide. Not that I had anything to do with the case.'

'Perhaps I'd better tell you the tale the way I heard it. When I joined the Agency I knew that E.H. had a reputation for being hard as nails, and tough to get along with. I soon found out that he was a mean, hard, vicious old autocrat who won't be told when he's in the wrong. And although his publicity sense is pretty good, he frequently *is* wrong, or a bit old-fashioned, in his approach nowadays. But all that's by the way. I was saying that E.H. is tough – and he prides himself particularly on his toughness in personal matters. I don't believe he's got a spark of feeling in him for anyone but Lionel. He's certainly fond – *was*, I should say – of Lionel, although he hasn't much use for Dick. And that's odd when you think of it, because although Dick's a pansyfied type he's really not a bad chap, whereas there was something pretty nasty about Lionel. But perhaps it was the vicious element that appealed to E.H. – sort of case of Lionel doing all the things he'd repressed in himself, getting tight, chasing after all sorts of women, particularly other men's wives. Yes, E.H. was fond of Lionel. And of course he was in love with Lily – that was his second wife – as far as he could be in love with anybody. But I'm rambling. Sorry.'

'You're doing very well. Don't worry about rambling.' Bland lighted another cigarette. 'How many of the people who came out of the drawing-room tonight after Lionel came out were with the firm then?'

'Bond wasn't, nor Mudge, nor Onslow. Tracy was there, Creative Director with a much better advertising brain than Lionel or Dick, always having rows with them, and E.H. always backing them up. Well, to get back to this story. One day after I'd been there six months E.H. came in and said he was going to get married. It took us right back, I can tell you. And when we heard that she was only twenty-two, and when she came up to the office and we saw her – well, that took us back even more. She'd been a nurse-companion at the house of some friend of E.H., and she was pretty and unsophisticated – very unsophisticated, I should say. E.H. treated her with a kind of kindly courtesy that he has always on tap, and that she obviously found very fetching. And of course he had money. I suppose that was why she married him.

'They were married at St Margaret's, Westminster – I remember that I got awfully tight at the reception – and went away for a month on the honeymoon on a yacht E.H. had hired. They decided to stay on, and Lionel and Dick joined them, and a chap named Weston, E.H.'s solicitor. After they'd been out a week at sea, it happened. She went out on deck one night and never came back. The accepted explanation was that she had fallen overboard.'

'Was E.H. upset?'

'Very much upset. I wouldn't have believed that anything external to himself could upset him so much. Lionel was upset too, curiously enough – it took a lot to upset Lionel. And so was old Weston, I believe. He's the chap who could tell you anything there is to know, if he liked to open his mouth. He was very fond of Lily. In fact, I think everyone liked her. She was a nice, simple girl.'

There was silence in the room for a moment after Sinclair

finished his story, a dead, heavy silence in which the two men sat in their chairs, with the table separating them, and looked at each other. Then Bland said, 'Do you play chess?'

Sinclair was startled. 'A little.'

'I have an uncomfortable feeling that the death of Lionel Hargreaves is the opening gambit, as it were, in a game of chess. Consider, for instance, the revolver and the gloves. No attempt is made to conceal the revolver – it is thrown in the bushes, as though the murderer had disposed of it in fright or hurry. But the gloves were placed carefully on the steps outside the French window, and the person who coolly took off those gloves and placed them for us to find was not suddenly overcome with fright about the revolver. That's assuming of course, as I think we can, that the same person left both. It seems to me that everything that has happened this evening has happened to plan. Everything has proceeded logically and clearly, according to somebody's intention, and it doesn't seem to me that any end has yet been achieved. Then there are several minor queries. For instance, what was Lionel's appointment?'

'Appointment?' Sinclair stared.

'Certainly an appointment, or why did he go into the library? Everything shows that the murder was premeditated – the revolver, the gloves, the fact that it took place in the library, where a shot wouldn't be heard. Clearly, Lionel had an appointment with somebody in the library. Who was it? Did someone come up to him at the party and say, "Can I have a few words with you about such-and-such?" That seems very improbable, or they'd have walked out of the room together. Surely Hargreaves would have been surprised and suspicious if this someone had said, "You go out and I'll follow you in a few minutes." The only person he might possibly make an arrangement like that with is his father.'

Sinclair shook his head. 'No, E.H. came in looking pretty angry, and told Lionel in ringing tones that he wanted to see him later.'

'In any event, he didn't leave the room until he went out to look for Lionel. Now, let's put that problem in another way.

Suppose someone said earlier in the day, "I must talk to you this evening. Step out from the party at about half-past seven, and I'll slip out after you." That would imply that this problematic person – let's call them X – and Hargreaves were on pretty intimate terms. Now, is there anyone, except his brother Richard, who's on sufficiently close terms to say something like that?'

'No. But it might be that this X had a piece of news or information so confidential it transformed the whole situation, and made Lionel treat him as an intimate. Isn't that so?'

Bland nodded. 'Surely. But we haven't any indication at present that such a piece of news existed. Until something like that turns up – something it was important for Lionel Hargreaves to know or to keep secret – we can hardly theorize on it. If there *was* anything, it's a fair bet that it had something to do with his wife.'

'Lionel's *wife*?' Sinclair looked astonished. 'I didn't know he was married.'

'Neither did anyone else, but she turned up here this evening saying somebody had telephoned her at home and told her that Lionel wanted her to come here. Since their marriage was supposed to be secret, either somebody else knew about it or she's telling lies. There's something fishy about her. She says now that she's in love with Richard Hargreaves, and he certainly seems to be in love with her.'

'What a wonderful woman. What's she like?'

'Enough sex and beauty to sink a battleship, common as copper and hard as stone. First sight of her bowled me over, I must say. Now – if we suppose that Hargreaves had arranged to meet her in the library – '

'But why should he do that when the marriage was secret?'

'God knows.' Bland passed his hand across his forehead. 'It's too late for my brain to function properly. Let's have a talk tomorrow – I mean, at some decent hour today. Will you be at your office in the morning – say ten o'clock? Good. I'd like to have a look round.' He gripped Sinclair's hand firmly.

'Are you coming away now?'

Bland's fresh-complexioned face looked tired. 'Not just yet. I've got a few notes to make and things to think about.' When Sinclair went out the detective was tapping his teeth with a pencil and looking abstractedly at the wall.

## I

### *12.30 to 1.30 a.m.*

E.H. moved restlessly under the linen sheet. His eyes, wide open, stared into the darkness patterned by vague shapes never quite revealed as bookcase and dressing-table. He thought about his son Lionel and about his other son Richard, and his thoughts were not pleasant. He thought about the early days of his life, of the towns he had left in a hurry because of his skill with cards, of the cheap chisellers' tricks played on old women. These were thoughts that rarely oppressed him. He thought about other women, the women he had met and used and sometimes slept with in his twenties and thirties, the wife who had borne him children and to whom he had been coldly and monotonously unfaithful, and the second wife whom he had come as near to loving as it was in his nature to love anyone. These, too, were not comfortable thoughts.

He belched suddenly, and switched on the bedside light. 'Indigestion,' he said. 'Indigestion, on a night like this.' He felt vaguely aggrieved as he walked over to the dressing-table to get the tablets.

Richard Hargreaves' bedroom was decorated in green and silver. The ceiling was green, the low divan bed was green, the carpet was green, and the walls were dull silver. The curtains were silver edged with green. A light green chest of drawers with silver handles stood in one corner of the room. A green telephone stood on a silver-lacquer bedside-table. Richard Hargreaves sat on the bed and pulled off his dark shoes. His mind was still stunned by the thought of Eve's marriage to Lionel. How could she do it, he thought, how could she do it? Her marriage appeared in his thoughts as a move directed against him, a move taken by the hostile brother who was part of a hostile world. He had a feeling of injury that Eve should have joined the conspiracy against him. His thoughts flickered vaguely over the other events of the evening, the police inspector whose name he could not for the moment remember, and the loathsomeness of his father. He thought again about Eve, and then suddenly remembered the look of Lionel's body on the floor. He shivered, got into a pair of Cossack style green pyjamas, walked over to the mirror, and began rather half-heartedly, to dab cold cream on his face.

When Bond returned to his house in Highgate his wife was waiting up. She was a big-boned, morose woman, and she did not greet him cheerfully. 'You're late,' she said. 'I wondered what had become of you. The baby's got spots on his forehead – I think it's chicken-pox.' Bond left his leather attaché-case in the hall, and went into the sitting-room. He let his wife go on talking for a few seconds, and then cut brutally across her words. 'Lionel Hargreaves was murdered tonight,' he said. 'Shot. At that stupid party of the old man's.' She stood with her mouth open, looking at him. 'Mr Lionel?' she said. 'The old man's son?'

'Did you think it was his daughter? So now you know why I was late – and it's the first evening in a week I've been late – I don't know what you're moaning about. I want my slippers.' She got his slippers from under the sofa and gave them to him without a word. 'I shan't be coming up to bed yet, and I've got more important things to think about than chicken-pox. So if you want to stay down here keep your mouth shut.' She went upstairs without saying anything. For half an hour Bond sat staring into the dying fire.

Eve Marchant sat at her dressing-table and looked at herself in the triple mirror, with critical approval. She began to talk to herself aloud, which was one of her bad habits when she was alone. 'No wonder you bowled over that Inspector, my pet. He certainly fell like a load of bricks.' She wagged her finger at the mirror. 'But he's not such a fool as he looks. Rather sweet, I must say. My God, what an evening.' She sighed and took out of the top drawer of the dressing-table a big book, bound in red morocco tooled in gold. She headed a page 'Wed. Jan. 15' and began to write in it, in a round, sprawling hand:

*My God, what an evening. Mysterious telephone call, taxi to see Lionel, and then I find him murdered. And then a grilling from a rather nice police inspector. But before I put it all down, let's be quite honest, I'm not sorry Lionel's dead I'm glad, glad, GLAD!! And I simply couldn't help hinting as much to the policeman. Was that foolish? If it was, I just couldn't help it.*

*Poor old Dick, I'm afraid it was all an awful shock for him. He was very cold and deeply injured at first, but, after he brought me home I got the fluence to work, and it was all right again. Dear Dick – he really is a pet – couldn't ask for anyone sweeter.*

*I feel quite shattered. But before I get into bed I simply must put down an account of the whole awful day. It started badly – the water in the bath was half-cold because the geyser went wrong –*

Her pen scratched on the thick paper.

Sinclair let himself into the flat which he shared with his brother. I shall never be able to sleep, he thought. He took off his clothes, put on his pyjamas, got into bed, and began to read *Why Was Lincoln Murdered?*, a biography of John Wilkes Booth. Within five minutes he was asleep.

Jean Rogers found Tracy waiting for her when she came out of the house in Redfern Square. They were silent all the way back to Hampstead in his Morris car. The tyres crackled on gravel as Tracy turned in the drive. When he cut off the engine they sat there a moment. He said, 'This is a terrible thing about Lionel, Jean. Terrible. I don't mind telling you that it's really shaken me.'

'Yes,' Jean Rogers said in a flat voice. 'It's a terrible thing, George. You're quite right.' She got out of the car. Still in the same flat voice she said, 'I shall go home tonight. I have rather a bad headache. Don't bother to come with me.' The flat which she had rented, but rarely stayed in, was a few doors up the road. Watching her walk slowly away, with her shoulders sagging a little, Tracy felt quick desire for her. He walked after her to the end of the drive, and placed his hands upon her shoulders. She turned with a little start. 'No,' she said, with a kind of horror in her face.

'Not tonight. My headache is too bad. Please.' Something in her expression made him let her go.

Mudge was staying the night with Onslow in his unfurnished room in Camden Town. They brewed some strong tea and after Onslow had given Mudge a brief lecture on the reactionary nature of advertising agencies, they began to discuss the murder.

'Who d'you think it was?' Mudge asked. 'All joking apart, who was it? Who d'you think, Jack?'

Onslow turned his lean, handsome, supercilious face towards his friend. 'I'm not much interested in the private reasons for which a member of the boss class gets knocked off. I'm more interested in the system which permits so transparently worth-less, stupid and lecherous a specimen of humanity as Lionel Hargreaves to lord it over you and me. But if you want my opinion' – here he paused, and Mudge leaned forward to show by the urgency of his attention how much he *did* want it – 'I should say that the two most likely candidates would be the people nearest to him, who had most opportunity of knowing what a rat he really was – his father and his brother.'

# II

In a small room with bare walls distempered an unpleasing shade of brown a man sat behind a desk on which were placed neatly two inkwells, a blotting-pad and a paperweight shaped like a monkey. The place was Scotland Yard, and the man was Inspector Bland; he was looking at a file of newspaper clippings. The door in the room was opposite his desk, and he did not look up when he said 'Come in' to a knock. Filby's narrow head looked round the door. The tall detective was excited.

'Beginning to look as if he's slipped up somewhere. We've traced the weapon.' Filby repeated with ghoulish satisfaction, 'The murder weapon.'

'Well,' Bland said. His voice was noticeably sharper in this congenial air.

'Man bought it secondhand four days ago in a shop off the New Cut,' Filby said. 'We checked it through the number. God knows why he didn't file it off. And when I say a man bought it, I mean a man. And what a man. Flaming red hair, bushy eyebrows, rasping voice. Wouldn't take it away – asked to have it sent to him – gave the name of Jones. Do you know what I think?' Filby leaned across the desk.

'You think he was disguised.'

Filby was disappointed. 'How did you guess?'

'I'm gifted that way. It's not the disguise that impresses me as odd, though, but the fact that he should buy a revolver at all.'

Filby stared. 'If he was going to shoot the man, wouldn't he want a revolver?'

'Yes. But would he buy it in an obvious disguise just four days before he decided to murder somebody, ask to it sent to him, and then forget to file off the number? There's no doubt this is the revolver?'

'It's the one all right. Ballistics checked on the bullet.

Anyway, we've got the address of this chap Jones. Probably a phoney, but shall I go down and check on it?'

Bland hesitated, and then said, 'I'll go myself. You can send back these cuttings on Lily Hargreaves to Records. Reading between the lines, and looking at the report Chappell, who worked on the case, sent in at the time, there doesn't seem much doubt that she committed suicide, although nothing could be proved.'

Filby sat on the desk and swung his leg. 'I've not had time to check on the vamp's marriage lines, but I have checked on the phone call she received, and it's OK. Made at a quarter to six from a public box in Piccadilly. We're looking for the taximan who picked her up, too. I think that's all.'

'Let me have that address, will you?' Bland said. He took the slip of paper Filby rather unwillingly gave him, and read 114 Willington Street, Borough, S.E.1. He said thoughtfully, 'It's a very special sort of murderer that has red hair and bushy eyebrows and leaves his address in the shop where he buys a revolver. Do you know what sort of murderer?'

Filby's mouth was slightly open. He closed it with a snap. 'What sort?'

'A murderer with an alibi,' Bland said. He closed the door.


# III

### *10.0 to 10.30 a.m.*

A large beautifully polished brass plate on the outer pillars said 'Hargreaves & Hargreaves. Ground Floor'. Bland pushed open the swing doors and stepped into a hall that breathed money. A commissionaire in uniform said, 'The lift, sir?' and looked critically at Bland's raincoat. The detective shook his head and walked through more swing doors straight in front of him. Inside these doors was another hall, and a reception desk, which was unattended. A door to the left said PRODUCTION, another said

STUDIO. The air was warm and heavy. To the right ran a long corridor with doors opening off on either side. Bland's cough broke into air that was padded and quiet. The door of the Studio opened and Onslow and Mudge came out. They seemed not to have changed their corduroy trousers, sports jackets and knitted ties of the previous evening. They were deep in conversation.

'Something quite simple,' Onslow said, 'perfectly functional, to express their character as architects.'

'Quite,' said Mudge.

'The name alone surrounded by a thick rule would be enough. No copy. But what chance is there of doing anything simple – anything good – ' He broke off and stared superciliously at Bland, seeming to see him for the first time. 'The sleuth on the track. Good morning.'

'Good morning. Is Mr Sinclair in?'

'I'll take you along to him.' They walked down the corridor. 'I've always felt rather sorry for murderers,' Onslow said. 'Not that I approve of murder – but in the stinking capitalist world we live in it seems very hard that one man, who probably had some good reason for killing another, should be chased around by a lot of people who haven't the first idea of all the psychological subtleties involved, the whole complex of motives that drive people to commit crime.'

'Speaking as a policeman, I'd say that most murders aren't committed from a subtle motive. The chief motives for murder are two – money and sex. Anything else, believe me, is rare.'

Onslow raised his eyebrows. 'Is there anything subtler than sex?' he asked, and before Bland had time to think of a reply said 'Here's Sinclair's room,' and walked away. Bland knocked and went in. The room was panelled in oak, Sinclair's desk was a lighter shade of oak and the carpet was green. Sinclair looked pale and worn this morning, but his greeting, as he got up from behind the desk with hand outstretched, was warm. Bland accepted the cigarette he was offered, and sat down in an easy-chair.

'You seem to have something about Lily Hargreaves' death,' Bland said. 'Our man on the case had suspicions of suicide at the time, but we were never able to trace anything definite. I'll take your tip, I think, about seeing Weston. Where shall I find him?'

'I'll get his address for you. He's by way of being a personal friend of E.H. – known him for some years, anyway. Handles any legal work we have here.' Sinclair dialled a number on a house telephone and said, 'Let me know Mr Weston's address, will you? 27 Lexington Square, E.C.4. Thank you.' He made a note on a piece of paper and pushed it across the desk. 'That's his office – they haven't got his home address. Anything fresh on the case?'

'We think we've traced the purchase of the gun. And the purchaser.'

'No!' Sinclair breathed admiration. 'Quick work. How the devil did you manage it?'

'It wasn't difficult. The number was left on the gun, and it was bought only four days ago. The man who bought it kindly left his name and address. The name was Jones, and the man had flaming red hair and a husky voice. I'm going down now to check up on the story, and see if I can find Mr Jones. Would you like to come along? Or am I taking you away from something important?'

Sinclair waved his hand at two papers that lay on the desk. 'There's nothing that can't wait – and I'd certainly like to see you in operation. I thought you wanted to have a look round here?'

'I do – and I want to see Edward Hargreaves. But I think those things will have to wait on this.'

Sinclair opened the door of the adjacent room and said, 'Hang on to anything that turns up, Onslow. I'm going out with the Inspector. He's a bright lad is Onslow,' Sinclair said as they walked along the corridor. 'Damned good young copywriter. Red, of course, as they all are.'

'He seemed anxious to impress me with his sympathy towards the murderer.'

Sinclair laughed. 'He never knows when to stop talking –

though you'll have gathered that nobody liked Lionel. What do you make of the case?'

Bland smiled broadly. "I may be able to tell you after we've been to 114 Willington Street, Borough. Do you remember that day when Towser put carbide in the inkwell, and old Squiffy said – '

The swing doors closed behind them.

## IV

### *11.0 to 11.30 a.m.*

A dirty lace curtain hung at the small ground-floor window. Outside an optician's shop opposite a dog was chasing its tail. A small boy sat in the gutter throwing fivestones with one hand and picking his nose with the other. Bland's knock was answered by a small woman with hard black eyes and a dirty face. 'It's a pint today,' she said, and then stopped and said accusingly, 'You're not the milkman.'

'Not the milkman,' Bland said gently. 'The police.'

The woman did not show surprise or any other emotion. Her black eyes grew a little harder, and she ran her hand quickly across her nose. 'You've come to the wrong shop, then. This is a respectable place, there's nothing wrong goes on here. And how do I know you are a copper, anyway?'

Bland showed his badge. 'You've got a lodger named Jones, I believe?'

'Then you believe wrong. He left yesterday.'

'Perhaps you'd be good enough to answer a few questions about him.'

'P'raps I would and p'raps I wouldn't. I don't like narks, not even when they're dressed respectable. Why should I answer your questions?'

'It's a case of murder,' Bland said mildly, and her self-possession left her. 'My Gawd, murder. All right, you'd better come in.' She led them into the room with the lace curtain. Almost all the available space on the walls was filled with plates in wire frames, and brownish reproductions of Victorian paintings. The leather chairs squeaked protestingly as they sat down. 'Mrs Lacey, my name is,' the woman said, 'and ten years I've been here and never a word of complaint from anyone. You can ask all of 'em up the street,' she added triumphantly.

'What about Mr Jones?'

She ran her hand across her nose again. 'I thought he was an odd one. But it's not my business, you know, to pry into my lodgers' doings.' Her black eyes looked hard at Bland, and he leaned forward and said persuasively, 'It's just Mr Jones that interests me, Mrs Lacey. What did he look like?'

Quite unexpectedly Mrs Lacey hooted shrilly with laughter. '*Look* like – he looked like a bloody scarecrow, that's what. I've never seen a man with such real tomato-red hair. Real flaming red, not just carroty. And thick eyebrows and a big red nose – yes, he certainly looked like a scarecrow. And gloves.'

'Gloves?'

'*Always* wore gloves. Yes, he was a funny customer altogether – only came 'ere half a dozen times all told, and never stayed the night. Booked up for a month, paid his rent in advance, left after a fortnight – yes, he certainly was a funny customer. I never saw him but he was wearing a pair of yellow gloves, and he wore 'em inside and out of his room. I know that because once I 'ad to go up there for one thing or another, and he opened the door with the gloves on.' Mrs Lacey's little eyes sparkled, and she lowered her voice. 'It's my belief that there was something wrong with 'is 'ands, and 'e wore the gloves to hide it.'

'Any idea of his height? Do you think you'd recognize him again?'

'I'd know that 'ead of 'air anywhere,' Mrs Lacey said. She was becoming quite gay. ''Eight – well, I don't know, didn't notice it specially. But I'd know 'is voice – it was sort of deep and thick, if you know what I mean.'

Bland sighed. 'Yes, I think I do know. Now, is there anything special you associate with Mr Jones? Did he ever say or do anything that you particularly remember?'

Mrs Lacey pondered, and drew her hand across her nose again. 'You must excuse me,' she said. 'No, there was nothing. 'E just came one day with a suitcase that 'e kept locked all the time – not that I tried to look inside,' she added hastily. 'And then 'e went a fortnight later – I don't suppose 'e spoke half a dozen words to me all told.' She paused and then said slowly, 'But there *was* something else. I've just remembered it. A telephone call. Yesterday, just before 'e left, 'e made a telephone call.'

'Did you hear what he said?'

'I never listen,' Mrs Lacey said with dignity. 'Though the phone's in the hall, and generally you can't 'elp 'earing. But as it so happens he spoke very soft.'

'I noticed the telephone as we came in,' Bland said. 'Excuse me.' He went into the hall. Mrs Lacey fixed Sinclair with a nasty look. 'I don't want to get into any trouble over this.'

'No, of course not,' Sinclair replied politely. He was feeling rather uncomfortable.

'Because I 'ad nothing to do with any of it. Does 'e think this Jones did it?'

'I wouldn't say that. These are just routine enquiries.'

'What are you – a sergeant? You don't look like a copper to me.' Sinclair was glad when Bland came back and said that he would like to see Mr Jones's room. Mrs Lacey nodded, although she muttered under her breath as she led them up the stairs. The room contained an iron bedstead, a wash basin, a cupboard, and very little else. Bland gave it a not very thorough examination. He opened the cupboard, looked at the bed, walked over to the window, stood there a moment, and nodded. Within five minutes they were out in the street again. The small boy was still throwing fivestones and picking his nose. He stopped for a moment to stare at them, and then resumed both activities with increased concentration. 'A citizen of the future,' Bland said gravely as they walked past him, and Sinclair could not tell whether or not he spoke ironically.

# V

### *11.30 a.m. to 12.15 p.m.*

'It's Blackfriars we want,' Bland said, 'and this tram will just do us. What could be better?' He seemed almost gay as they mounted to the upper deck. 'Have you ever heard of Joseph van Dieren, Art Agent, 183 Old Bridge Street, Blackfriars?' Sinclair shook his head. 'Because that's where we're going now. What exactly is an art agent, by the way?'

'Roughly speaking, someone who has a number of advertising artists on his books, and handles their work. He may have one artist who's good at figure work, another who specializes in whimsical drawings, and so on. He sells their services to advertising agents like ourselves, and sometimes to advertisers direct, and gets his commission. Perfectly legitimate and often profitable business. We know most of the big agents, but Joseph van Dieren is a new one on me. Why are you interested in him?'

'Because the telephone call made by Mr Jones was to van Dieren's number. Don't the activities of Mr Jones strike you as very curious?'

Sinclair hesitated. 'He certainly seems a remarkable figure. That touch about wearing yellow gloves all the time sent a bit of a chill up my spine.'

'I didn't mean quite that. I meant the way in which Mr Jones advertised his actions.'

Sinclair seemed momentarily fogged. 'I don't get you.'

'Just consider his activities. Let's assume that Mr Jones equals X – that is, the murderer. For some reason unknown to us he takes a room with Mrs Lacey and adopts what would appear to be disguise. But what sort of disguise does he use? A self-evident one – a disguise which *calls attention to him.* Nobody would be likely to forget that red hair and the deep voice. And then the gloves. It shows very praiseworthy caution to wear gloves continually so that you will leave no fingerprints – but why *yellow* gloves? It's possible that Mrs Lacey might not have noticed a pair of dark brown or grey gloves, but she couldn't fail to notice yellow. And then calmly to leave what were presumably the very same yellow gloves outside the French windows last night. And why leave the number on the revolver? We should have traced it eventually, but he certainly made things easy for us. If our ballistics expert hadn't said quite definitely that the bullet that killed Hargreaves *did* come from that revolver I should suspect that we were being led up the garden path.'

'I see what you mean. And what do you think about this telephone call?'

'God knows. I'm inclined to think that in some obscure way Mr Jones and the telephone call are being used to provide an alibi. But what sort of alibi is it that you establish four hours before a crime?'

A frown creased Sinclair's brow. Suddenly he grinned. 'It would be funny, wouldn't it, if after all this there were a real red-headed man named Jones who'd killed Lionel just because he disliked him?'

'Very funny,' Bland agreed without enthusiasm.

The building was a small office block, decayed and worn. A small wooden board outside said, 'Joseph van Dieren, Art Agent – Down Corridor'. Inside the door it was darkish, and there was a smell of cats. They walked down the corridor past a flight of stairs until they saw a door which said in black lettering. 'Van Dieren – Art Agent. Knock and Enter'. They knocked and entered, and found themselves in a kind of cupboard, with another door to the left and in front of them a hatchway and a bell with a note above it, 'Please ring.' The hatchway shot open before they had time to ring the bell, and a voice said 'Yes.'

Framed in the hatchway was a woman's head, small and round. Beneath hair taken up in tight golden curls, her face looked like a doll's face. There were two patches of colour on her cheeks, and her mouth was shaped with lipstick into a perfect Cupid's bow. She wore large bracelets on her arms, with silver coins on them and they jangled when she moved. She said

in a shrill voice, 'If you want Mr van Dieren, he's out.' Her
eyes, large, round and blue, with very black lashes, looked
suspiciously at Bland but meltingly at Sinclair. 'If there's anything I can do – ' she said, and simpered.

'I am a police officer,' Bland said, 'and I should like to see
Mr van Dieren.'

'*Perlice*,' the girl said. She looked at Bland with unconcealed
dismay for a moment, and then said, 'But I've *told* you he's
out.' Her voice had gone up a tone in shrillness. 'He won't be
in till after lunch.'

'Perhaps you can help me. I'm trying to trace a call that was
made to this office yesterday, between 4.15 and 4.30. Do you
take the incoming calls?'

She seemed suddenly more composed. 'Course I do. There's
no one else here.'

'And was there a call about 4.15 to 4.30?'

'As a matter of fact,' she said, 'there was. Though I don't
know that I can tell you much about it. What d'you want to
know for?' She looked down at her red-stained fingernails, up
at Sinclair, and said with no very obvious relevance, 'My name
is Polly Lines.'

Bland gave the impression of someone with an immense store
of time and patience. His round face smooth and untroubled,
he said earnestly, 'I'm afraid I can't tell you that, Miss Lines.
But if you can tell us anything about the telephone call I shall
appreciate it very much.'

She considered the question with some care, and after a few
seconds she decided to smile. The smile revealed very small,
white, even teeth. 'Won't you come in – both of you.' She
flashed another smile to include Sinclair, got up and opened the
door they had seen to the left. When they went through this
door they saw that what had looked like a block of offices was
really two rooms. One of them bore the name 'Mr van Dieren',
and the other, 'Secretary'. This room was about ten feet square
and contained a small knee-hole desk, a typewriter, a telephone
and a wall switchboard, a small electric fire and two chairs. Miss
Lines tapped across the room on high heels, sat on one of the

chairs and crossed her legs with a rustle of silk. Bland sat on the other chair and Sinclair leaned against the wall in an attitude which he hoped was appropriate to a plain-clothes policeman. Miss Lines started to talk.

'Really, there isn't much to tell. A call came through about twenty past four, and I thought it might be Mr van Dieren himself – he'd been out since before lunch, and I thought he might have phoned to say he'd been detained. When I took off the receiver someone said, "Is Mr van Dieren there?" It was a deep, gruff sort of voice, and there was a sort of excitement about it. I said he wasn't and the voice gave a – well, a sort of sigh, it might have been relief.' She broke off suddenly, and looked at them both coyly, with her head on one side. 'But d'you *really* want to know all this? I'm not just being silly, am I?'

Bland assured her gravely that she was not being silly. She giggled. 'Well then, I said, "Who is that speaking?" or something like that, and *he* said, "My name is Jones." So I asked if there was any message I could take, or if it was any particular Mr Jones – because, after all, Jones is a common name, isn't it?' She appealed to Sinclair, and he said, 'It certainly is.'

'*Then* he said, very quietly but still in that deep husky sort of voice, "He'll know who I am. Just say Mr Jones called, and that I'll be getting in touch with him – and pretty soon too." I wouldn't swear to the exact words, but that was more or less what he said, and he spoke in a rather nasty way, if you understand what I mean.'

Bland and Sinclair both nodded encouragingly. 'And did Mr van Dieren come back?'

The black lashes fluttered over Miss Lines' blue eyes like two tiny machines. 'That's the funny thing. Mr van Dieren *did* come back, soon after five o'clock, and he didn't know anything about this Mr Jones. We have a Mr Jones on our books, an artist, but I should know *his* voice. So Mr van Dieren said it must be a practical joke of some sort, and not to take any notice of it.' She finished triumphantly on a high note, and her two listeners nodded approval again, with a slightly comic unanimity.

'And when are you expecting Mr van Dieren?'

Miss Lines became confidential. 'There you have me. Sometime he doesn't come in till after lunch, but usually he telephones in the morning. He hasn't been in touch today so far. It's been a dead-and-alive morning – until you gentlemen came.' Her eyes fluttered again at Sinclair, and Bland noticed suddenly that Sinclair was looking fixedly at something on the wall. Bland turned round and saw that a whimsical sketch of two children playing with a ball much bigger than themselves hung there, and at the same moment Sinclair spoke.

'I wonder if you can tell me who made that sketch?'

Miss Lines looked astonished, but not displeased. 'Yes, it's one of the artists we have on our books. His name's Carruthers.'

Sinclair nodded to Bland. 'That's the man I was telling you about. You remember, the cousin. It's odd that he should be on the books of – ' His voice melted away.

Miss Lines looked warmly and invitingly at Sinclair. 'I didn't know policemen were interested in art,' she said.

Bland stood up. 'Will you give Mr van Dieren this card and tell him that I'll call round here at 2.30 and that I'd like to see him.' They were at the door when he said, 'Just one other thing, Miss Lines. How long have you been here?'

She considered, looking at her fingernails. 'Just on a year now. Soon after Mr van Dieren opened the business.'

# VI

## 12.35 p.m. to 2.15 p.m.

It was half past twelve when they got back to the Hargreaves office. Sinclair had accepted an invitation to lunch from Bland, but even the chief of the Copy Department, he explained, must make a pretence of doing some work, or at least of seeing what work had been done. In the reception office they met Richard Hargreaves and Eve Marchant. Richard was dressed with some care in perfectly plain dark clothes, with a cream shirt, red tie and handkerchief, and black suede shoes. Eve Marchant, wearing a bottle-green man-cut suit, greeted the detective with the enthusiasm of an old friend.

'Don't you think I'm brave, Inspector, to invade the holy of holies? It's the first time I've been here, and I'm terrified the old man's going to jump out at me from behind a corner. Is there any news? Or is that something I shouldn't ask in a flippant tone? Dick's great on tones – he's always telling me I'm using the wrong one.'

Before Bland could reply Richard Hargreaves said, 'Did you want to see me? Eve and I are just going out to lunch, but that can wait if there's anything you want me for.'

'Just one question. I expect it's wasting my breath, but – have you ever heard of an art agent named van Dieren?'

'Van Dieren?' Hargreaves teetered nervously from one foot to the other. 'No, I don't know that I have. But Tracy's really the man to ask – I don't have much to do with our artists. Is he something to do with the case?' He suddenly turned to Sinclair. 'Been the most damnawful row going on this morning. Just as well you were out, so that you didn't get involved in it.'

Sinclair raised his eyebrows. 'The old man on the warpath again?' Richard Hargreaves nodded. 'My God, yes. All about money this time. Production costs too heavy, art costs too heavy. Poor old Tracy's been in with him for the last half-hour, and I had a lecture for an hour on the errors of my ways.' With a curiously girlish gesture he waved goodbye to them. Eve placed her hand in his arm and they went out through the swinging doors.

As Bland followed Sinclair down the corridor, a door to their left suddenly shot open, and Tracy was in the doorway with his back to them. E.H.'s voice, heavy with power, came through to them. 'Understand, Tracy, I will not tolerate this kind of waste. An advertising agency is not an art gallery, it is a commercial concern, and its purpose is to make money, not to support unsuccessful artists. Do I make myself clear?'

'Perfectly clear.' Tracy slammed the door and turned round.

His face was red with anger. He said, more, as it seemed, to himself than to Bland or Sinclair, 'I hope that bastard dies,' and walked across the corridor to a room opposite Hargreaves'. Sinclair looked after him unhappily. 'He takes it too hard. This sort of thing happens once a week and Tracy certainly gets his fair share of kicks. But it's a mistake to – '

The door of Tracy's room opened again suddenly, and his head was framed in the doorway. 'Could I see you for a moment, Inspector?' Sinclair waved a hand and moved on down the corridor. 'Pick me up in the Copy Department when you're ready. No hurry.'

There was plenty of fake panelling in Tracy's room; Bland reflected that it acted as a kind of keynote for these offices. A cigarette was offered and accepted, and he sat waiting for Tracy to begin talking. The Art Director was not looking well this morning. His colour was bad, and he had apparently cut his face while shaving. He seemed to find the silence uncomfortable, and yet to be at a loss for words. He said at last, in a tone of reluctant apology: 'Blew off the handle last night I'm afraid – about Jean Rogers. Sorry. But frankly, I find this whole damned thing a strain. I'm a sensitive man, and I hate anything to do with violence.' Bland merely inclined his head. There was another silence. 'Is there anything fresh?' Tracy asked, in what seemed a kind of desperation.

'One or two things. But you had something you wanted to say to me?'

Tracy ran his hand quickly through his thick hair. 'Well, damn it, yes I have. You know what I told you last night, that I thought you'd find the key to all this in the family history. Have you followed up that line?'

'I'm thinking about it. An art agent named van Dieren wouldn't have anything to do with the family history, would he?'

'Don't know the name,' Tracy said irritably. "I was thinking about the death of Lily, E.H.'s wife, two years ago. Know anything about that?'

'Suppose you tell me.' Bland was looking at his fingernails. 'I know she was drowned in an accident.'

'Accident, hell. She committed suicide.' Tracy wagged a finger. 'I met the captain of the yacht afterwards, and he told me. A sea like glass, a part of the ship where there wasn't the remotest chance of her going overboard. No doubt in the captain's mind about it. And I'll tell you another man who knew more about it than he said, and that's old Weston, E.H.'s lawyer. He's a close-mouthed old devil, but he can tell you a lot – if you get him to talk.' The Art Director thumped the desk in front of him. He was impressively earnest. 'Find the reason for Lily Hargreaves' suicide, and you'll find Lionel Hargreaves' murderer.'

'What was Lily Hargreaves like?'

'Charming,' Tracy said emphatically. 'Young, fresh, pure. Innocent – you might almost say ignorant. God knows why she married E.H. But the Hargreaves family have always had a fascination for women.' There was another silence. Tracy sat in a revolving chair with his face to the light, and the cast in his eye was distinct and disturbing. Bland said, 'And that's all you have to tell me?' His eye was caught by a picture on the wall opposite, an oil painting of two fishermen in reds and greens, the paint laid on thick. Tracy noticed the direction of his look, and smiled. 'A genuine Tracy. And don't tell me you like it, because I know it's bad. I used to think I might be an artist twenty years ago, but I became an advertising man instead. That's the trouble with creative advertising work – it takes the energy out of you for anything else.'

Bland said again, 'That's all you have to tell me?'

'I thought you should know that,' Tracy answered absently. When Bland went out he was still standing looking a little wistfully at the painting. His large, firm hand was tugging at his hair.

Bland stepped across the corridor to E.H.'s door, knocked, and went in without waiting for an answer. He said while he walked across the room, 'I called on Joseph van Dieren this morning.' E.H. stared at him from behind a desk that was noticeably bigger in a room that was noticeably bigger, than Tracy's. 'Should I know that name?' he asked. He looked genuinely perplexed.

'I don't know. I'm trying to find out where he fits in the picture.' Bland sat down without being asked, and held his hat on his knees. 'He's an art agent. He was telephoned by the man who bought the gun with which your son was shot.' E.H. bent forward eagerly, and Bland said, 'No, we've not found the man. He took a room for a few days in the name of Jones, and the two things we know about him are that he bought the gun and that he telephoned this man van Dieren. Van Dieren was out, so he didn't talk to him.'

'You think you're on the track of something?'

Bland shrugged. 'It could be that Jones is the murderer, and then again it could be all a sideline.' He paused and added carefully, 'We might be doing better if you were quite frank with us yourself.'

''What do you mean?'

Bland said, still speaking carefully, 'What happened to your second wife, Mr Hargreaves? You know as well as I do that her death wasn't an accident.'

The red face turned purple and then the blue eyes bulged. Then E.H. said, with a restraint that was at the same time dignified and reproachful, 'Somebody has been telling you lies, Inspector. My wife's death was an accident.'

'Oh, come now, Mr Hargreaves,' Bland said, in a tone that was not less than insulting. 'When the sea was like glass, and when she was in a part of the ship where she couldn't possibly have fallen overboard? Of course nothing could be proved, but the captain had no doubts, and neither had our man on the case. Don't think that we're *too* simple, Mr Hargreaves.' He waited for the explosion, but it did not come. With a wounded dignity that was not less than admirable, E.H. said, 'I can only repeat what I said, sir. My wife's death was an accident. If you will not believe that, you must disbelieve it. The subject is too painful for a discussion.' Bland was rising to go when E.H. said, 'Stay a moment.' Behind the big desk E.H.'s gaze was sincere and appealing. When he began to talk, phrases rolled from his mouth easily, and with a curious falsity.

'I am anxious to make my position clear, Inspector. Lionel's death is a serious blow, both to me personally and to the business. Personally, because he was my eldest, and my favourite, son. In the business, because he was a man who it will not be possible to replace. So that both as father and as a businessman I shall not rest until I see his murderer apprehended.' He paused for a moment. Bland was looking at his hat. 'I say this partly because – very wrongly, I fear – I failed to pass on to you last night what may be an important piece of evidence.' He pushed over the desk a letter and an envelope. 'This arrived by post yesterday morning. I was going to speak to Lionel about it last night. I held it back after his death, thinking – God knows why – that I might be able to do something with it myself. But it should be in your hands. I must have been almost insane with rage ever to think anything else.' Perhaps it was because E.H.'s general appearance was so coldly calculating, Bland reflected, that the things he said sounded so improbable. He looked at the letter and the envelope.

The envelope was addressed in amateurish typing to E. Hargreaves, Esq., The Hargreaves Agency, 18 Boxeter St., W.C. The letter was also amateurishly typed, on flimsy paper. It read:

*Your son Lionel is married to a girl named Eve Marchant, a tart who shows herself off every night half naked in the chorus of the Splendid. Go and have a look at her and see how you like your daughter-in-law. Not quite a society marriage, is it, Mr Snotty Hargreaves?*

'Is it true that you wanted a society marriage for your son?'

E.H. said calmly, 'It would have been for the advancement of the family.'

'Was it generally known that you wanted a society marriage for him?' E.H. nodded. Bland put the letter and envelope in his pocket. 'I'll keep these. Anything else?'

'Nothing else,' E.H. said. 'I'm glad to have got that off my chest. It was worrying me.' He gave a sudden, dramatic picture of an executive type looking worried, and shot out a hand. 'Let me know progress, Inspector. My thoughts are with you.' He stood up, and Bland stood up too. E.H. said with every appearance of sincerity, 'I shan't rest until Lionel's murderer is found.'

When Bland returned to Sinclair's room he found the Copy Chief talking earnestly to a dapper, baldish man with a soft voice and a ready smile. He gave Bland a limp handshake. Everything about him, indeed, was a little limp, the defeated droop of his shoulders, the casual drabness of his suit and tie, the handkerchief dropping from his coat sleeve, and the rather down-at-heel shoes he wore. Sinclair was beaming. 'This is Carruthers – you know, I was telling you about him, Lionel's cousin – I've just been asking him about van Dieren. I told him that I'd spotted one of his things on the wall of that office.'

Carruthers uttered a deprecatory cough. 'I hope there's nothing criminal in that, Charles. Really, all this questioning terrifies me.' He spoke with an uneasy jocosity.

Bland introduced himself and said, 'Tell me, what do you know about van Dieren?'

'I don't know him well at all, not really, at all.' Carruthers seemed for some reason very nervous. 'You know, of course, that he's my art agent. Not that he's ever done anything for me – a pretty poor agent. I only stay with him because I'm too lazy to change.'

'What does he look like?'

'I suppose he's about fifty – might be a little more. He's got a lot of grey hair and shouts a bit. But there's something else about him.' Carruthers seemed to reach in the air for a word, and finally brought it down out of space. 'Something – funny. He doesn't ring true, somehow. It's as if he had a secret past in which he'd been quite a different person from the man he is today. That's as near as I can get.' He looked solemnly at Bland.

'How long have you known him?' asked the Inspector.

'About a year. He hasn't been in business much longer than that.' He wriggled again, and blew his nose. 'But I really – ah – hardly know him at all, in the real sense of the word. I doubt if I've seen him more than a dozen times.'

There was a little silence. Carruthers consulted an enormous turnip-shaped watch. 'I'm sorry to be so little helpful. I've got an engagement for lunch. Is there anything else you wanted to ask, Inspector?'

Bland said slowly, 'Not just at the moment. I'd like to have your own address, though. Just in case I need to get in touch about van Dieren,' he added, seeing Carruthers' look of alarm. Carruthers gave him an address in Balham. 'I have a little flat there. And now if there's nothing else – I must fly.' He smiled uneasily, and wriggled himself out of the room. Sinclair stared after him in unaffected surprise. 'I wonder what's the matter with him. He seems to have got the wind up about something. This van Dieren sounds an odd fish.'

'Perhaps when I see him I shall find out what's worrying friend Carruthers so much. In the mean time even a policeman must eat – and frankly, I'm very hungry. Shall we see what Soho has to offer?'

At lunch Sinclair chatted easily and rather maliciously about all the people in the case. He contrasted E.H.'s determination to appear unaffected by Lionel's death, which must have hurt him badly, with Richard's attempts to simulate a sorrow he did not feel. It would be pathetic if it weren't comic, or comic if it weren't pathetic, Sinclair said, to watch the two of them together. Indeed the whole place was like a Freudian study-circle of psychopathological cases, from Tracy mooning away after Mrs Rogers, whom he could never marry, to Richard steering himself into the arms of somebody who would serve as a substitute for his mother – or would it be his father? Or look at Carruthers. A nice quiet little chap, who had sex on his mind because he could never get off with girls.

'Bond?' Bland suggested.

'Bond,' Sinclair said. A glance at him showed that he was a mass of frustrations, and probably perversions. Frustrated ambition chiefly, leading to malice, envy and all uncharitableness.

'What do you know about the office boys?' Bland asked, and Sinclair gave his dazzling smile.

'Now you're having fun, and you're quite right not to mind my chatter. After all, aren't we all psychopathological cases? I'm sure all policemen must be.'

'And you?' Bland asked, and Sinclair smiled again.

They had paid the bill and were just outside the door when Bland suddenly felt a pain in his eye. He put his hand to it, and pulled down the lid.

'What's the matter?'

'Something in my right eye.' Sinclair clucked with concern. They stood in the street, and poked about with handkerchiefs ineffectively. The eye was watering, and when Bland tried to look out of it he was blinded by a mist of tears. 'A chemist, or better still, a doctor,' Sinclair said, but Bland, handkerchief to eye, was looking at his watch. 'I'm late now, and I don't want to miss this man. I'll call in at a chemist afterwards, if I don't get it out in the taxi.' He hailed one, and it swerved to the kerb. With the handkerchief to his eye, Bland called 'Good-bye.' In the taxi he pulled the eyelid down and dabbed at the eye with a corner of his handkerchief. He succeeded in shifting what he took to be the piece of grit so that if he kept his eye half-closed it did not water.

# VII

## 2.30 to 3.0 p.m.

The hatchway opened and Miss Lines' head appeared. 'Oh, it's you.' She seemed disappointed. 'Where's your friend?' Without waiting for a reply, she added, 'Mr van Dieren's in now. I'll tell him you're here.' Her head popped out of the hatchway for a moment, and then back. 'Go in, will you.' Bland turned the handle of the door which said 'Mr van Dieren'.

Mr Joseph van Dieren was a surprising, and indeed theatrical figure. He gave an impression of extreme size and extreme disorderliness, and yet he was neither very big nor, really, very disorderly. Through his half-closed eyes Bland saw that his hair was grey and extremely thick, his eyebrows bushy and his face florid. He had a large handlebar moustache, of a kind that Bland had thought to be long extinct, and he wore a rather shabby suit of rich, ginger-coloured Harris tweed. There was a great deal of this suit; it billowed around him like a wave, and was the most conspicuous thing about him as he stood up and waved Bland to a chair. His voice was a deep and manly roar, varied occasionally by a querulous higher note, as he said that he was sorry to have been out, and asked what he could do for the Inspector.

'Do for me,' Bland said vaguely. He looked round the room, and as he did so his right eye gave a twinge, and he was obliged to use his handkerchief. In his brief look he noted the general air of disorder and decay, the files bursting with papers and covered with dust, the empty inkwells and the extraordinary mass of oddments on the desk. He saw on the desk a litter of papers, a quarter-full bottle of port, a mass of cigarette-butts, an empty bottle labelled 'Phosferine', a torch battery, an old black shoelace, half a sandwich, a watch key, and a number of books on art. He noticed also that Mr van Dieren, no doubt a reader of detective stories, had given him a seat in the light, while his own chair and face remained in shadow. Bland turned his chair so that the light did not fall on his eye, and said, 'What can you tell me about Mr Jones?'

'That telephone call?' Van Dieren guffawed loudly, in what seemed an unnecessary gale of mirth. 'That's a funny thing. You're going to have a hard time believing this, I know – but fact is, I can't tell you anything. We've *got* a Jones on our books, right enough. Who hasn't?' he asked, and went off into another fit of laughter. 'But nothing to do with the chap you want. I know because I rang him up and asked him.' He was silent for a moment, fingering his coat sleeve idly. He produced an enormous handkerchief from his pocket, blew loudly on it, and said abruptly, 'Glass of port?'

'No, thank you. Have you ever met Edward Hargreaves?'

There was another silence from Mr van Dieren's darkish

corner – a silence with a quality of strain about it. Then Mr van Dieren said, 'Don't mind if I do?' and, with a hand that seemed not to be quite steady, poured out most of the port in the bottle into a dirty tumbler. He drank half the port at a gulp and said, 'Knew him in America a long time ago. Not seen him for years. Saw in the papers he lost his son. Sad thing.'

'That's what I've come about,' Bland said placidly. 'This man Jones who telephoned you bought the gun that killed Lionel Hargreaves.'

There could be no doubt that Mr van Dieren's hand shook now, as he put down his glass of port on the dusty table. He fidgeted again with his coat sleeve, and finally settled on a button, which he tugged viciously. The deep roar of his voice was almost completely replaced by the querulous tone, as he said, 'They can't fix it on me. They're trying to fix it on me.'

'How could they fix anything on you?'

Mr van Dieren seemed genuinely upset, and yet his dismay retained that curious theatrical flavour of which Bland had been conscious since the beginning of the interview. It was, as Carruthers had said, as if he were two men – as though he were pretending to be frightened, and yet had some real fright, which was still concealed. He began to talk now, very fast, and as though the words were dictated. 'Let me tell you a story.

'Thirty years ago I was a good-looking young man.' He stared at Bland as if he expected contradiction, but the detective had his head back and his eyes almost closed. 'And ambitious too. Had visions of myself as a big business man.' He laughed again, not loudly but a little pathetically. The edge of a curtain seemed to lift on a picture of frustrated ambition, to make clear some of the odd things about Mr van Dieren, his loud voice and ginger suit among them. 'Real estate. I was in real estate. In the Middle West in America. I've done most things in my time.' He poured the rest of the port into his glass. 'And though I say so, I was a damned good salesman.

'Well, there I was, eating my heart out in a little town named Abingdon, working for a couple of old boys who just about knew the motor-car had been invented. Then I met Eddy Hargreaves, and we cottoned to one another at once – at least that's the way I thought it was, though I realized later on I'd made a mistake. Anyway, I cottoned to him. He was smooth as paint was Eddy, a good talker, and a great mathematician too. I told him about my idea of starting up a real estate agency in Abingdon – it was a growing town, expanding fast – and I showed him my list of contacts. I knew I could take a lot of them along with me if I had my own agency. The difficulty was – money. I hadn't got any money. Eddy told me he could put up the money, and we agreed to split fifty-fifty on profits. We started in a small way, of course, but we both worked like niggers, and we showed a profit right from the start.

'After we'd been going three months Eddy made a suggestion. We were having difficulty because our capital wasn't enough to cover the outlay we had to make, and Eddy said he could arrange for us to become the local agents for the Nation-Wide Loan and Investment Corporation, a big firm in Philadelphia. What this meant in simple language was that they loaned us money for the purchase of real estate, and we passed the loan on to the chap who bought the real estate, taking a small percentage out of it. It meant that we made a bit less profit on each deal, but our turnover rocketed up, and we sent the two old boys out of business. Profits went up too, and we were both well in the money.

'Now, there was another side to this business we did for the Loan and Investment Corporation, and that was sale of the Corporation's stock to anyone who was interested. There were 100–dollar, 250–dollar and 500–dollar bonds, and they were easy enough to sell, because the Corporation was offering pretty good interest. I used to go around selling the bonds with my real estate, and Eddy did all the bookwork and handled our affairs with the Nation-Wide people. It was a very useful sideline, and I had more money than I'd ever had in my life. I used to sell the stock, and give them their stock certificate, and interest was paid every six months. We paid them their interest, and the Nation-Wide people paid us. Everyone was happy. That went on for a year.

'Then one day an old man named Schwartz called on me. We'd sold him a thousand dollars' worth of stock, and he hadn't received his half-yearly interest. Instead of speaking to me or to Eddy about it, he'd written off direct to the Nation-Wide people. He showed me their reply. Their letter said that they had no record of any shares held in his name, and that they had sold none of their stock through us, they had simply loaned us money for real estate deals.

'I had it out with Eddy that night – if you can call it that. First of all he denied the whole thing, said Schwartz must have made a mistake. Then he admitted it. I think that was my worst moment. I'd hoped against my good sense that it might have been some sort of mistake. And when he admitted it he changed his tactics entirely, and suddenly became furiously angry. I was taken aback for a bit by that, as he knew I would be. He was always smart, was Eddy Hargreaves.

'What did I think he'd been doing, he asked me. Where did I think the money had come from, the money I'd spent as well as him. Gradually I got the whole story out of him. He'd simply played me for a sucker all along the line. He'd had fake share certificates printed, and kept the money. I worked it out that the total sale of stock was something round about 30,000 dollars. All of it had been sold by me, all of it was worthless, and Eddy had had pretty well all the money. When I asked him where it was, he simply laughed. Finally, he promised to meet me in the morning. He said we could pay back most of the money out of profits.

'I was a fool, I see that now. I should have taken him to the police immediately. In the morning when I went round to the hotel he'd gone. I never saw him again.'

Bland had been scraping a small black scab off the back of his hand while he listened to the story. He said, without looking up, 'And you?'

Mr van Dieren gulped the rest of the port, and made a wry face. 'I'd sold all the stock, taken all the money. They gave me two years for embezzlement. It was a light sentence.'

Bland remained silent for a moment, thinking about this ghost from the past. 'Who would be trying to frame you?'

Mr van Dieren fingered his coat sleeve uncertainly and then blew his nose again nervously and loudly. 'How should I know?'

Bland said patiently, 'You've told me a story about Hargreaves and yourself thirty years ago. You say somebody is trying to fix his son's murder on you. If you're right, that could only be somebody who knew the story. Who would know it?'

The red-faced man glared at him and said querulously, 'Eddy Hargreaves would know it, wouldn't he?'

'So you think that he killed his son and tried to plant it on you. Why should he do that?' Bland held up his hand. 'You can't tell me? All right – I can't tell you, either. Who else might have known that story? It's not one Hargreaves would spread around, is it?'

Mr van Dieren looked sly. He looked at the dirty window and at the port bottle on the table and at the worn carpet on the floor. 'How do I know who knew the story? When you find that one, you'll find the man you want.'

'Maybe,' Bland said. He opened his eyes wider and they began to water immediately. He dabbed at them, half-closed them again, and said, 'Do you know anyone else connected with Hargreaves?'

The art agent shook his head. He was looking straight ahead of him, and smirking slightly. Then he clicked his fingers. 'Carruthers.'

'Hargreaves' cousin. Could he be trying to fix you? Would he know the story?'

The smirk became more pronounced. The art agent fiddled with the watch key on the table, looked at it absently, and put it down. 'He's not the one who's trying to fix me – I doubt he'd know that story – but he might know something else. Might be interesting to have a chat with him.' Mr van Dieren had recovered his early jauntiness. 'Somebody's trying to frame me,' he said. 'But they'll have to get up early in the morning to frame Joseph van Dieren. And I think I know who it is.'

'Why do you want to see Carruthers?'

Van Dieren got up, grinning. 'Because he might be able to give me a bit of information about – *somebody* – that I'd be very pleased to have. He doesn't know what this bit of information is, but he'd give it in spite of himself, if you see what I mean.' Bland didn't see, and said so, but this statement provoked one of van Dieren's loud, artificial guffaws, that followed him outside. Slanting rain fell on Bland's shoulders as he looked up and down New Bridge Street. 'A chemist,' he said to himself, 'I must find a chemist.' He found one after three minutes' walk. A small brush dipped in oil and run across his eyelid removed the pain magically. Bland and the chemist looked at the brush afterwards, and the chemist pointed out what he said was a speck of dirt. Bland put a shilling in a collecting-box for Dr Barnardo's Homes, and took a taxi to 27 Lexington Square.

# VIII

## *3.15 to 4.0 p.m.*

William Weston, the Hargreaves' lawyer, was a man in his late sixties, with a domed, bald forehead, jaws that drooped like a bloodhound's, and honest blue eyes. His voice was as decorous as his clothes, when he said, 'I don't know that I can do anything for you.' Bland raised his eyebrows in surprise. 'I mean,' the old man explained, 'I don't think I can tell you anything that will help you. You know that I am not permitted professionally to disclose any of my clients' legal secrets.' He smiled briefly, revealing a complete set of very white false teeth. Upper and lower set clicked emphatically as he finished speaking.

Bland said, 'I came to you chiefly because you've known Edward Hargreaves for a long time. I'm told that you're his oldest friend. I want you to tell me anything you can about his personal life that might give us a line on his son's murderer. From what I hear he must have made some enemies. Are there any of them who might have something to do with this case? Is there anyone who might want to strike at Edward Hargreaves through his son?'

The lawyer was silent for a moment, looking down at the papers on his glass-topped desk. Then, with a decisive click of his teeth, he got up and stood with his back to the fireplace, in which a large coal fire was burning. His hands were joined together behind his back. 'Your request, sir, is a curious one, and not the least curious thing about it is the form in which it is put. I should not describe myself as Edward Hargreaves' oldest friend – I should hardly describe myself as a friend at all. It simply happens that I have known him for several years. If you ask my opinion, I should say that Edward Hargreaves is a man who has no friends.'

Bland made a sound that might have indicated despair at the lawyer's loquacity, or surprise at his statement. Mr Weston, however, seemed to take it as an expression of discontent, for his immediate reaction was to offer Bland, with some apologetic clicking, a gold-tipped Turkish cigarette. Bland took it, settled back in his leather armchair, and half-closed his eyes. He seemed to be falling asleep. Mr Weston's measured voice went on:

'I am surprised also, sir, because such knowledge of human nature as I have gained during sixty-seven years does not lead me to suppose that the kind of business enmities I might know of would afford cause for murder. There was, for instance, a man named Morton. He came to Hargreaves from another advertising agency, and he brought with him an advertising account for the Monotone Electric Corporation – an account worth £100,000 a year. This account meant a profit of £10,000 a year to Hargreaves, and because Morton was able to bring it with him he came to Hargreaves at a salary of £1,500 a year, on a three years contract. Within eighteen months Hargreaves had ingratiated himself personally with the Monotone people, broken Morton's contract on a technicality, and forced his resignation. You will hear many such stories. But they are not reasons for murder. And if they were,' Mr Weston's tone was faintly ironic, 'they would be reasons for the murder of Edward Hargreaves, and not his son.'

Bland stirred in his chair, but if he had intended to speak, he was not permitted to do so. Mr Weston's teeth clicked again and he gave a bloodhound's sad but knowing smile. 'My professional experience leads me to suppose that there is a concealed motive behind your questions. Could it be, I wonder, that you are anxious to discover the relations that prevailed between Edward Hargreaves and his sons?'

'It could be,' Bland said. 'What were they?'

Mr Weston sucked air through his false teeth. 'They were not good. Edward was fond of Lionel, but his affection manifested itself oddly. He has an overweening family pride, coupled with a passionate family jealousy, and these warred with his personal avarice. He was alternately severe and indulgent to Lionel, who had a certain superficial dash and glamour. I should say that he had little but contempt for Richard.'

'What about the cousin, Carruthers?'

'Carruthers?' the lawyer said on a note of surprise. 'He was brought up with Richard and Lionel at Redfern Square, but he hasn't lived there since he was thirteen or fourteen. I shouldn't say Edward had any feeling either way about him.'

Bland looked with some distaste at his Turkish cigarette, and laid it down. 'Would the fact that Lionel Hargreaves had married a chorus girl have upset his father and caused a quarrel?'

The lawyer's bloodhound jaws drooped. His blue eyes fixed Bland with a hard, calculating stare. 'Do I understand that Lionel did in fact contract such a marriage?'

'Yes.'

'Then that would certainly have precipitated a quarrel. A very violent one. It might have caused Edward Hargreaves – ' Mr Weston stopped, and clicked his teeth loudly.

Bland leaned forward. 'To alter his will?'

Mr Weston was cautious. 'Possibly.'

A kind of mist mingled with the electric light in the room, and made a halo round Bland's fair head. He said, 'What can you tell me about the death of Lily Hargreaves?' The lawyer was badly shaken. He took out a silk handkerchief, apparently from somewhere in his buttocks, and patted his gleaming forehead as Bland went on, 'I know that she died on a cruise. I know that the sea was calm, and that she was in a part of the ship where she couldn't possibly have fallen over-board. I know that you were a guest on that cruise.'

Above the bloodhound jowl the blue eyes were grave. With less than his usual sententiousness, the lawyer said, 'There are some things about which one would rather not talk.'

Bland said sharply, 'There are things about which one has to talk. Did Lily Hargreaves commit suicide?'

'Her death can have nothing to do with this case.'

Bland tapped his teeth. 'It is an offence to withhold information that may lead to the discovery of a murderer.'

With comic serenity Mr Weston said, 'I am well aware of that, sir.' He looked at the red and yellow flames of the coal fire and went on abruptly, 'Lily Hargreaves committed suicide.'

'Why?'

Still looking at the fire the lawyer said, 'She was disappointed in her husband. He was over sixty and she was twenty-two. She found out that he valued her simply as a possession. He loved her in his way, perhaps, as much as he could ever love anybody or anything – but it was a hard, inhuman way. She was delicate and easily hurt, and it was a mortal hurt to her when she found out the kind of vicious, bitter, ungenerous man she'd married.' He spoke with passion.

'Was that all the reason?'

Softly the lawyer said, 'She was frightened of her stepson.'

'Her stepson?' Bland frowned. 'I see – you mean Lionel and Richard.'

'They were her stepsons legally.' Mr Weston's voice was still soft. 'She was twenty-two and they were in their thirties. A curious situation.' Bland said nothing. 'It was Lionel who frightened her. Richard was never anything more than a cipher. You will have heard, perhaps, of Lionel's reputation with women.

'Lionel and Dick and I all joined the party at the same time. On the second night we were aboard Lionel had too much to drink. It didn't affect him in the way that drink affects most people. He lost all his surface friendliness and became unpleasant, tried to pick a quarrel – I had seen him drunk once before, and I kept out of his way when he was drinking. That night Lily had gone to bed and we were playing a rubber of bridge, when Lionel practically accused Richard of cheating. We left the rubber unfinished, and about half past ten we all went to bed. Edward Hargreaves had received a wire from Tracy, and had gone back to London – it was something that needed his urgent personal attention. At half past eleven I heard a knock on my cabin door. I opened it, and there was Lily Hargreaves.

'She was panting with fear. There was a bruise on her arm and her neck was badly scratched. She told me that Lionel had entered her cabin, and that he had tried to make love to her. She was much distressed. I soothed her as best I could, told her that Lionel had been drinking, and promised to speak to him.'

Bland was tapping his teeth with a pencil. 'Why didn't she get off the yacht, go to her husband and tell him about it?'

Weston pulled at his bloodhound jowl. 'My dear sir – I don't think you fully realize the situation. Edward Hargreaves is not a man to brook such a thing. He might have done violence to his son.'

'Would that have worried her?'

'Besides, we – or rather, I – did not regard the matter with such seriousness. After all, Lionel had been drunk. It seemed that the reasonable and sensible course was to speak severely to Lionel, and to try to smooth the whole thing over. At least I thought so at the time. Perhaps I was wrong.' He sighed. 'I have been bitterly sorry since then that I did not take her off the yacht that night. But the fact remains that I took her back to her cabin, and advised her to lock the door. On the following morning I spoke to Lionel. He called me a meddling old fool, and said it was none of my business. He cooled down a little when I threatened to tell his father, and he promised to apologize to Lily. She stayed in her cabin all day, and would see nobody – she said that she had a bad headache. After tea Lionel, Richard and I went ashore. I left them together – they said they were going to drink all the evening – and went off to look at the antique shops. Half an hour after I left them Lionel told Richard that he had left something important on the ship. He went back there alone. That night Lily committed suicide.'

There was a brief pause before Bland spoke, and his voice was much gentler than usual. 'You were fond of Lily Hargreaves?' The lawyer suddenly struck the desk in front of him, so that Bland thought the glass of it would break, in a gesture that fitted oddly with the placidity of his manner. 'I loved her. Nobody could help loving her. She was sweet and gentle, innocent and shy – it was a black day for her when she met Edward Hargreaves and his sons. I tell you, Inspector, she was killed by Lionel as surely as if he had thrown her overboard. I was sure of that at the inquest  I am sure of it now. And yet – what could I do, what could I say?'

'Did you say anything about her coming to your room at the inquest?'

'I didn't. It would have been simply my word against Lionel's. And what good would it have done her?'

'And you never told Edward Hargreaves?'

With a determined click of his teeth Mr Weston said again, 'What good would it have done her?'

'Are you sure that neither Edward nor Richard Hargreaves knew anything? Did they accept the theory of accident?'

In the last few minutes, Bland noticed, the lawyer's face seemed to have sunk in, the hard lines become accentuated. He did not answer the question directly. 'They're a bad family. I'd not trust any of them.' Then his head jerked up, and he looked at Bland. 'I beg your pardon. Both of them guessed that it was suicide, but I'm sure that Edward, anyway, never guessed the cause. About Richard – I'm not so sure. I've sometimes thought that he must have guessed his brother's secret – but if he did he never betrayed it to me.'

'And – supposing neither of them knew – what do you think would have happened if they'd have found out?'

Mr Weston's teeth clicked. 'Who knows,' he asked sententiously, 'the workings of the human heart? I have known murder committed by a girl of thirteen because of her infatuation with a man of fifty. I have known a criminal who had spent years in prison, and yet he fainted at the sight of blood.'

'I know a little about the actions and motives of criminals myself,' Bland said mildly. He made a mental note that the lawyer's pomposity made a good cover for evading awkward questions, and got up to go. 'Just as a matter of form, where were you between 7.30 and 8.30 last night?'

Mr Weston laughed and his heavy cheeks moved up and down. 'I am honoured to be on the list of suspects – but I fear I have an alibi. I dined at the Reform Club with a friend of mine who is a solicitor. His name is Geoffrey Matthews. We went into the dining-room at 7.15 and came out about a quarter to nine. Here is his address.' Still chuckling, he unscrewed a fountain pen and wrote a name and an address on a notepad in a firm, angular hand. Bland noted with faint surprise that, in spite of his decorous appearance, the lawyer was so dandyish as to use green ink. He asked abruptly: 'Do you know a man named Joseph van Dieren?' The look that Mr Weston gave him out of his blue eyes was remarkably shrewd, and his reply remarkably brief. "I don't. A suspect?'

Bland admired again the unobtrusive skill with which a question was turned aside. 'Hardly a suspect. A ghost.'

'Like Lily Hargreaves?'

'Like Lily Hargreaves. Except that, so far as I can see, they are two separate ghosts. It would be nice if one could find some connection between them.'

# IX

Bland sniffed appreciatively at the air as he came out of Weston's offices. The rain had stopped, and a damp, thick mist was hanging about Lexington Square. *Fog*, he thought, thick, delicious, soupy London fog, and he clicked his heels on the pavement. For some reason the dank mist made him feel more cheerful. Was it, he wondered, that it bore a relation in some way comforting to the fog that was settling down on this case? And was that fog really impalpable? Wasn't there rather a discernible pattern which narrowed down the suspects to two – or at most three people? He frowned. 'But what about Jones?' he said, and a taxi-driver who had moved noiselessly to the kerb in answer to Bland's raised hand looked alarmed. 'What's that, guv?'

'New Scotland Yard,' Bland said briskly, and stepped inside. Back in his office he called Filby, who said eagerly, 'What about old Jones's alibi?'

Bland tapped his teeth with a pencil. 'God knows. Jones only visited the place he was staying at half a dozen times, and never stopped the night. He left it just after four o'clock yesterday afternoon, after making a telephone call to an art agent named van Dieren. Then he vanished. He made himself a nice alibi for a time before the murder, and then abandoned it when it might have been useful. You can make what you like of that.'

'Maybe the murderer wasn't Jones, and it's all a red herring.'

'Then what was Jones doing with the gun?'

Filby shook his head, and his long, melancholy face grew longer. 'Beats me. But here's something for you. We gave Lionel Hargreaves' office a look over this morning, and what should we find but this, on his blotting-pad. I brought it away with me.' He showed Bland a yellow blotting-pad with the words 'Jones 7.30' written in pencil in one corner. Lower down, in ornamental lettering, as if the writer had been doodling while listening on the telephone, was the word 'Eve'. 'I've checked with Lionel Hargreaves' handwriting and this is his all right. So he had an appointment with Jones.'

'It looks that way,' Bland agreed. 'And presumably it was made on the telephone. Did you check on that?'

'I tried to, but no luck. The girl on the switchboard couldn't remember any calls particularly.'

'All right, Filby – good work. I've got some more news for you.' Bland recounted the results of his interviews that day. 'Now – will you check this alibi of Weston's. He was very glib with it, but that's nothing against him. And find out all you can about van Dieren. Where he was last night particularly, but I also want to know where he lives, where he came from, how long he's been in business, how much money he's got – anything you can find out. Concentrate particularly on any details about his past linking him with the Hargreaves family or with anyone else at the house last night. Check whether he's a Dutchman – he's got a Dutch name – and try to find out whether he really was in America, as he claims to have been. You might get something out of that girl of his, Polly Lines. If you're looking for adventure, I think she may be interested.'

'Is that so?' Filby's eyes gleamed, and he went off at a tangent. 'This Lionel was a bit of a lad if what old Weston says is true. I mean, hang it all, she was his – '

'Precisely.' Bland sighed, and tipped back his chair. He looked worried, and almost boyish. 'There's no means of checking Weston's story, but if it's true, and the old man found out about it, he'd have a good motive for murder. And there's quite certainly something fishy about van Dieren. And Carruthers was as nervous as a kitten when I talked to him this morning – quite genuinely nervous – I wonder why.' He tapped his teeth gloomily. 'Too many suspects.' He drew the anonymous letter from his pocket. 'And there's this, too. Get a check made on it, and see what comes out – make of typewriter, characteristics, and so on.'

'It could be,' Filby said, 'that this van Dieren rang himself up on the telephone to put you off the scent. After all, why shouldn't he ask for himself in the name of Jones? Who'd expect him to do that?'

Bland brought the legs of his chair gently to the ground. 'Who would? If he wanted to call attention to himself and get himself suspected of murder, he certainly couldn't find a better way of doing it. We shouldn't have heard of the name van Dieren unless Jones had telephoned him.' He walked over to the window, and stood looking out. 'It's going to be a foggy night. I'm going to the theatre – I'm anxious to see what Eve Marchant looks like in the chorus of the Splendid, and she's sent me a couple of tickets. I shan't be back till morning.' He picked up his fawn-coloured raincoat.

'I hate fog,' Filby said. 'It's dangerous. My aunt was knocked over one night in a fog. I wouldn't be surprised if there was another murder in this fog.'

'Dangerous,' Bland said thoughtfully. 'I wonder if you're right.'

Voicing Bland's own earlier thought, Filby said, 'Looks as if we're in a fog, too, eh?'

Bland stopped with his hand on the doorknob. 'Not altogether. Here's a couple of tips that may help you to see your way through it. The first is that marriage is a beautiful institution. And the second is that it's always nice to know you've got asbestos between you and the guests when you're shooting someone.'

# X

## 7.15 to 7.45 p.m.

'Just a snack,' Sinclair said cheerfully. 'Something to enable us to face the glories of the Splendid. I shall look forward to seeing this girl – Marchant, you said her name was? She must have something quite special to be able to hook *both* the Hargreaves lads – such different types too. I trust you're not going to put anything on those Whitstables? Pepper and salt – my God, what a barbarian.' They sat on the high, uncomfortable stools, and looked at their reflections in a mirror. Bland thought that his companion seemed a little merrier than was justified by their three drinks. 'How did you get on with the mysterious art agent?'

'He told me a curious story about E. H. in his early days in America. It seems E. H. did van Dieren a very bad turn, and van Dieren landed in prison. Have you ever heard about that?'

'News to me, old boy, but I could believe anything bad about E. H. Anyway, why would the man lie about it? I hope you didn't let Miss Lines seduce you – from your duty?'

'She's more interested in you.' And not surprisingly, he thought, as he regarded their images in the mirror: his own, well-brushed, blond, boyish, but a little insignificant; Sinclair's full of dash, and with a ready smile, like a film star. Which film star? Bland searched for a name and, while he rolled an oyster down his throat, settled on a fair-haired Robert Taylor. Taylor-Sinclair, and Van Heflin-Bland, he thought, with an inward chuckle – and doesn't Taylor-Sinclair know it! The Copy Chief had, indeed, looked rather smug at mention of Miss Lines' interest in him. The captain of the XI, Bland thought a little nastily, still accustomed to conquests. He swallowed another oyster, and as he did so Sinclair gave him a Robert Taylor smile, and said, 'How about old man Weston and Lily?'

'He told me an extraordinary story too – one that reflects no credit on anybody. But I think I must regard is as confidential, even from my Watson.' He smiled amiably, and Sinclair looked almost embarrassed.

'Good Lord, yes. I'm interested, of course, but don't think I want to pry. Anyway, it's better that I shouldn't know secrets. I'm a tremendous gossip.' He looked at the clock. 'Just time for some lobster, and a glass of indifferent Graves on draught to wash it down. Suit you?' The tone was masterful, and one would hardly dare to say, Bland reflected, that it *didn't* suit. Was this perhaps still the captain of the cricket team regarding Bland as a boy trying, not very successfully, to bowl leg-breaks? Or was this the real and characteristic Sinclair? As these questions passed through Bland's mind Sinclair smiled again, and said, 'Think I've changed?' Without waiting for a reply he went on, 'I have, you know. In one way at least. I aspire to be an author. Detective stories. Tell me honestly, now, what do you think of them?'

Bland picked tentatively at half a lobster in its shell, and put a piece of firm white flesh into his mouth. 'Delicious,' he said, and then, 'Not very much like life.'

Sinclair pointed with a fork. His face was bright and enthusiastic. '*Exactly*. The essential thing about the detective story is that it's not very much like life. It doesn't set out to be like life – that isn't its function. The detective story is decidedly a romantic affair – something that brings a world they don't know, a world of romantic violence quite alien to their own lives to the sickly young men who spend their days in front of a ledger, the overworked and underpaid shop girls, the colonels in the clubs and the dowagers in their boudoirs. It isn't reality that these people want from detective stories – it's fantasy. The future of the detective story is in the field of fantasy.'

Bland drank some of the Graves. It was, as Sinclair had said, indifferent. 'You've written a fantasy?'

Sinclair swallowed a large piece of lobster quickly. 'A detective story to end all detective stories. It opens when the hero goes into the flat one day to find a dead man on the floor, and a girl, naked beneath a black mackintosh, standing over the body with a smoking pistol in her hand. An exciting opening?'

'Very exciting. Of course the girl didn't really kill the man?'

'Of course not. He'd been poisoned. The girl had been taking a bath in her hero's flat, and heard a prolonged ringing the doorbell. Slipping on a black mackintosh, she went to open the door – '

'Why a black mackintosh?'

'She was a fetishist with a penchant for black mackintoshes,' said Sinclair imperturbably. 'She opened the door with a gun in her hand, and the body fell in. She was so startled that she fired the pistol.'

'What was she doing in the flat?'

'I'm not sure yet. I'm only in the third chapter, and I'm clearing up things as I go along. But the germ of it is that there are ten characters, including the detective and the hero, and they're killed off one by one.'

'Including the naked girl?'

'Certainly. She is found, naked again, frozen to death inside a refrigerator. Finally, only the hero and the detective are left, and the hero realizes with horror that the detective must be the murderer. At that time they're having a drink together. He sees the detective looking at him with peculiar fixity, and understands suddenly that the drink is poisoned.' Sinclair paused dramatically, with the last piece of lobster on his fork. 'And *then* – the detective drops dead. The drink was poisoned – but the hero has poisoned it. He's a schizophrenic, and has murdered them all in his other personality. That's the end.' Dabbing his lips with his napkin, Sinclair looked at Bland. 'What do you think of it?'

'A little unsaleable.'

'Nonsense. You talk like a policeman. Of course it will be a terrific success. Let's go.' Before Bland had got down from his stool, Sinclair was half-way out, and looking at his wrist-watch. 'Just late enough. I'll get my car.' A swirl of fog met Bland at the door, and he groped in the thick white blanket in which Sinclair was hidden. He heard Sinclair's voice saying 'This way,' and then became conscious of two or three things at once: a violent jolt in his back that sent him reeling off the pavement into the road, the steady throb of a car engine, and a sudden feeling of danger and isolation. Then he heard a voice shouting, saw bright lights advancing terrifyingly towards him, and became conscious of the cold, hard road. When he picked himself up the car was not more than three yards from him. Sinclair jumped out of it, full of concern. 'Good Lord, old man, what happened? It's a good job my brakes are functioning.'

Bland picked himself up, brushed his hat carefully with his raincoat sleeve. 'It certainly is. Somebody pushed me.' He looked thoughtfully into the fog. 'Not much good going after him. Might have been a nasty accident.'

'Do you think it was an accident?'

Bland put his arm round Sinclair's shoulders. 'It's only in your detective stories that the criminal tries to kill the detective. Let's go to the Splendid.'

# XI

## 8.0 to 8.45 p.m.

'There she is.' Eve Marchant danced just where she had said she danced, three from the end at the left-hand side. Like the rest of the girls, she wore a black brassière, pink knickers and black stockings. She did not dance very well or very badly. She was in no way conspicuous in the chorus.

Sinclair seemed disappointed. 'She must have what it takes, but I can't see what it is, can you?' Bland did not reply, and they watched the show in silence, while the leading girl in the chorus sang:

> 'My disposition's for loving,
> And though my intention is pure
> My disposition's for loving
> And there isn't any cure. . . .'

Sinclair was using a ridiculous pair of opera-glasses which he had obtained by putting sixpence into a slot in front of him. 'My word, there's the old man.' Bland followed the direction of his gaze and saw E. H. sitting in a box, with another figure just behind him. When this figure leaned forward a little, it revealed the baldish head and snub nose of Carruthers. E. H. was sitting upright in his chair, staring down at the stage with an expression of complete disapproval. Bland whispered to Sinclair, 'See you at the interval.' As he tapped on the door of the box he heard the girl on the stage finishing her song:

> *'So darling, although I may tell you*
> *I'll love you and always be true,*
> *Still my disposition's for loving*
> *And the lucky man won't always be you.'*

Carruthers came to the door. He looked startled, and almost apprehensive, when Bland beckoned him outside. E. H. did not turn round.

'The old man's in a pretty surly mood. He certainly doesn't like this girl. Do you want him?'

'Both of you. How do you happen to be with him?'

'I was in the office this afternoon, and as a mark of high favour was asked to share his box. Dick, as a mark of high *dis*favour, wasn't asked. What do you want to see me about?'

'I saw van Dieren today.'

Carruthers' look changed to one of positive alarm. 'He's been on the telephone to me at home, saying he wants to talk to me. He rang me up this evening. He seems very amused about something or other, as though there was a huge joke – and he asked me to go and see him tomorrow.' He paused and twiddled at a button. 'What did you think of him?'

Bland's fresh-coloured face was ingenuous. 'He seems a very odd character, and he's mixed up in all this affair somehow. There's something about him that's a fake – that's my feeling, I think.'

Carruthers nodded emphatically. 'I shall certainly take my work away from him.' He coloured suddenly, and for no apparent reason.

'Will you ask Mr Hargreaves if I can see him in the interval.' Carruthers turned, but before he could go back into the box the door opened, and E. H. appeared. He stopped short when he saw Bland and Carruthers, and said to Bland, 'You want to see me? We'll sit in the box. Do you mind, Arnold?' With an exaggerated deference that might have concealed annoyance, Carruthers said, 'Not at all. I'll go and have a drink.'

They went into the box. On the stage a man was throwing clubs in the air. Below them gleamed a hundred boiled shirt-fronts. Still looking at the stage, E. H. said, 'You see, that postcard wasn't far wrong. She shows herself half-naked. A delightful daughter-in-law.'

'She's not your daughter-in-law now.'

'She has been once, and if my son Richard has his way she will be again. I find her fondness for my family distressing. I am not impressed by either her occupation or her talent.' E. H. fixed his cold blue eyes on Bland and said, 'Have your investigations led to any conclusions regarding that anonymous letter?'

'Not yet. I've seen van Dieren – he says he knew you in America. And I've seen Weston. He seems to think your second wife committed suicide.'

E. H. was still looking at the stage, where the juggler was now balancing three of the clubs on his chin. 'None of Weston's business. Anyway, it's all lies. Why should she commit suicide? She was happy enough with me.'

'You don't know of any other reason?'

'I don't know *any* reason.' E. H. rapped on the ledge in front of him with his knuckles. 'Don't try to be smart with me, young man. I've dealt with smart people all my life, and I've always been a little too smart for them.'

'Were you too smart in America, when you handled the affairs of the Nation-Wide Loan and Investment Corporation?'

Bland saw with some admiration that Hargreaves took this question without any sign of emotion other than a muscle twitching in his jaw. He said, almost to himself, 'Joe Riddell. I thought he was dead.' Then he looked at Bland. 'I suppose you got this story from the man you call van Dieren. What does he look like?'

'Seedy, thick grey hair, might be a wig, big moustache, about five feet eight inches, deep voice, ring-mark on third finger left hand but no ring. Theatrical manner. Looks in his late fifties.'

E. H. shook his head. 'That's not Joe Riddell.'

'This would be thirty years ago.'

'Joe Riddell was six feet tall. And he's dead. I thought he was dead. What story did he tell you?'

'He didn't mention the name Joe Riddell. He told it about himself – and you, of course.'

'What story?' E. H. had his voice under better control than his breath, which was coming in jerks.

'Something about embezzlement. He said you were responsible. He got two years. Did Joe Riddell get two years?'

'Yes. The rest of it is lies. I had no responsibility. That was made clear in court.'

Bland tapped a cigarette thoughtfully on his thumbnail and lighted it. 'Naturally not. Did your Joe Riddell have flaming red hair?'

'No. Why?'

'Just trying to fit Jones in the picture. But then Jones's red hair was probably a wig. How long since you last saw Riddell?'

'Nearly thirty years. I've never seen him since we parted. I had some threatening letters once – God knows how many years ago.'

'Was he a man who would bear malice that long – supposing he's still alive?'

'He was a fool. No, I don't believe he'd hate me for thirty years. Anyway, man,' E. H.'s voice was impatient, 'if he hated me why should he kill Lionel?'

Bland leaned forward. Neither man was now watching the stage. 'Why, indeed? Let's not worry about Riddell. Who else knew this story about him?'

'No one outside the – ' E. H. stopped and stared at Bland thoughtfully. He said, 'I don't recollect that I've ever told anybody.'

Bland pulled on his cigarette, and was silent for a moment. 'You didn't tell Weston? He's acted as your lawyer for a good many years.'

'Why should I tell Weston about something that happened before I knew him?'

Bland stood up. His face was a little pinker than usual. 'Well, if Joe Riddell's dead and if you've never told anybody about this thing, I suppose it must be Joe Riddell's ghost come back to put a spoke in the family wheel.'

E. H. stood up too. He was a little taller than Bland. 'I don't like – '

'*You* don't like,' Bland said furiously. 'You've tried to make a fool out of me from the time the investigation started. You held out over that anonymous letter until you thought it might pay to show it to me. You're holding out over your wife's death. You're holding out over Joe Riddell. I can't make you talk, but I'm telling you now that you're being too smart for your own good. You may be a good businessman, but this isn't business. It's murder. It's not smart to play against murder – it's stupid, because the murderer's got no hesitations or compunction. Think it over, and if you want to come out from behind your barricade let me know. Until then, it's pointless for me to talk to you.'

Bland walked out of the box and went straight to the bar. Sinclair was sipping a pink gin and talking to Carruthers, who looked rather depressed. He brightened when he saw Bland.

'May one buy a policeman a drink? You look as if you need one.'

'Thanks. Whisky.'

'The old man a bit trying? It's something that comes naturally to him, doesn't it, Sinclair?' Carruthers seemed to be talking to hide his nervousness. 'Sinclair's had more recent experience of E. H. in his awkward moods, but my experience is of longer standing. I remember him as pretty trying ever since I was a kid. The old man paid for my schooling, and sent me to the same school with Dick and Lionel. He was really very decent about all that, although he wouldn't do anything for me afterwards. He wanted me to come into the firm and I wanted to stay on my own and do freelance work. I got my way in the end, but there were some awful scenes when he reminded me that he'd paid for my schooling, and so on.' Carruthers gave a mock shudder. 'He's never loved me much since.'

'Did you ever hear him talk of Joe Riddell? Years ago, I mean when you were a boy.'

'Joe Riddell?' Carruthers looked earnest. 'No, I don't seem

to remember that name. I'm pretty sure I've never heard E. H. mention him. Who is he?'

'Just another mystery man,' Bland said gloomily. 'The case is full of them. What do you think of the show?'

Sinclair grinned. 'I should have thought our presence at the bar was sufficient comment. I can dispose of it in one word: wet. I'm looking forward to meeting the glamorous Eve at closer quarters, though. Is that on the programme?'

'She's sparing us ten minutes of her time after the show, at her flat. I think Richard will be there too, so you'll see him if you're coming along.'

Sinclair's fine eyes flashed, and Bland was reminded again of the Captain of the School. 'Good Lord, yes – I'd like it more than anything.'

'How about you Carruthers?'

Carruthers consulted his turnip-watch. 'I'd like to, although I've got some work to finish at home.' He hesitated. 'But I'm all agog to meet this charmer. I think I *will* come – if you're sure it's all right.'

Striving to catch some recollection, Bland said, 'Oh Lord, yes – she said bring anyone along. Sinclair and I must be getting back to our seats – Eve Marchant sent us complimentary tickets, and I'm willing to bet she'll be keeping an eye on our seats between kicks.'

Sinclair raised his glass. 'Back to the funeral.' The chorus was dancing again when they got back. This time they were wearing blue brassières, black knickers, and no stockings. 'Expanse of knickers in a waste of shame,' Sinclair murmured. They settled down in their seats.

# XII

## *10.15 to 11.30 p.m.*

'How do you *do*?' Eve Marchant asked, raising her eyes to Sinclair's and then dropping them, with a revolting and yet somehow dreadfully attractive demureness. 'I've heard so much about you from Dick – and Lionel, too.' She shook hands with Carruthers with no particular interest, turned to Bland and spoke with a coyness that managed to be catty. 'Did you enjoy the show? I noticed that you'd abandoned us once or twice.'

'Duty called,' Bland said solemnly. 'I was talking to Edward Hargreaves, who was in a box.'

She clasped her hands in an affectation of pleasure. 'What an honour. Did you know that the old man is my prospective father-in-law, Mr Sinclair?'

Sinclair moved uneasily. 'Congratulations.'

'Don't say that – he loathes me, although I'm sure I couldn't care less. But what *will* you think of me – I'm forgetting my manners. Will you have a whisky or gin? Really, though, I'm dying to hear what he said about the show.' While she was pouring a whisky Bland pondered again her curious sexual attractiveness, something distinct from her beauty. How could one define it? Something in the way she moved her shoulders, a contrast between the demureness of her manner and her brassy voice – what was it? He moved the base of his glass on the chair arm. 'You want me to tell you what he really said, Miss Marchant?'

Her colour heightened a little. 'More than anything.'

Bland sipped his drink. 'He said he was not impressed either by your talent or your occupation, that you showed yourself half-naked, and that he found your fondness for his family distressing.' He saw Sinclair and Carruthers looking at him in pained surprise, he saw the slightly increased rise and fall of

Eve Marchant's breasts, and he saw that she was looking rather fixedly at a point beyond him. Richard Hargreaves was standing in the doorway, with a black Homburg hat in his hand.

For a moment nobody said anything. Sinclair and Eve Marchant began to speak together, and stopped together. Richard came into the room, walked over to the cocktail cabinet and poured a drink. When he turned round his face was smooth and unworried. Bland turned the stem of his glass again, and wondered if this was the best time to ask his questions. Then he thought with faint impatience that it was no use being finicky, and dropped his words like stones into the troubled waters. He spoke to Richard. 'I'm sorry to seem officious, but I've come here to ask some questions.'

'Certainly. But that reminds me – I've got some information for you about this chap van Dieren. It seems that Bond, our Production Manager, had some dealings with him about a year ago. It was before Bond came to us, so that explains why no one else knew anything about him. Bond seemed to think he was a rather unsavoury figure, and I told him to get in touch with you.'

'Many thanks.' Bland asked Carruthers, 'Did you know that Bond knew van Dieren?'

'Well, I don't think I've ever met Bond. No, I didn't know.'

Richard Hargreaves stared at Carruthers with surprise. 'But do *you* know this van Dieren fellow, Arnold? I thought you didn't like to have anything to do with art agents.'

Carruthers wriggled. 'Well, I don't usually, but he was – ah – very persistent that he could do something with my work and I – ah – let him handle it. He hasn't been very successful.' There was a silence, while Richard still stared at Carruthers, who looked down at the floor. Then Bland said, 'Have you ever heard of Joe Riddell, Mr Hargreaves?'

'Joe Riddell? Good Lord, yes. Don't tell me that Joe Riddell comes into this?'' Hargreaves looked at Bland with what seemed to be quite genuine amusement and astonishment.

'Just tell me what you know about him.'

'It dates rather a long way back, and really I don't know

much, except that Lionel and I used to use the name of Joe Riddell as a kind of magic charm when we were kids together. He used to write threatening letters to my father – they came in the post regularly every week at one time, and I remember they were from all sorts of different countries. My father told us a bit about him when he was in a good humour. He often talked about the past to us then, and told us about adventures in America in which he'd been the hero – these last few years he's found it more convenient to forget all that. He told us about this Joe Riddell. It seemed they'd been partners in business together – some kind of real estate, I think it was – and in some way or another the old man was too smart for Riddell. Riddell went to jail for a term – I forget how long – and swore undying vengeance against the old man.

'That's the story, and that's really all there is to it. Nothing ever happened, and none of us ever saw Joe Riddell. These letters, and one or two postcards, came every week for some time, and then they became more infrequent. Finally they stopped coming. I should think, all told, they came for about a year. The reason it stuck so much in my mind was that we were all of us kids at the time, and we built up Joe Riddell into a sort of bogey-man, a kind of O'Grady. You know: "Joe Riddell says you've got to do it" – that kind of thing.'

'Did any of you ever see Joe Riddell?'

'Oh no. That was the essence of the whole thing – that he was a sort of invisible man. When the letters stopped coming it all died down, and pretty soon we stopped talking about him.'

'Now, I want you to think before you answer this question. Do you know if your father ever met him – after the anonymous letters were sent, I mean?'

'I'm inclined to say no, but I can't really be certain.' He looked up at the ceiling. 'I'm just trying to remember whether there *was* any ending to it at all – whether I've forgotten something. All I can say is that to the best of my belief and knowledge the old man never saw Joe Riddell – but I don't absolutely *know*.'

'Was your father alarmed by these letters? Did he ever take precautions of any kind?'

'Good Lord, no. He treated the whole thing as a kind of joke. If he'd thought of it as anything serious, he'd never have told us about it.'

'Would it surprise you to learn that Mr Carruthers doesn't know the name of Joe Riddell?'

'Why, not particularly. Though I should have thought you'd remember the story, Arnold. You must certainly have heard it at one time.'

'I suppose I must, Richard, if you say so.' Carruthers was apologetic, but he did not sound altogether convinced. 'It's really rather odd that I shouldn't remember at all. My memory's not usually as bad as that. But still, I suppose it's passed out of my mind with the years.'

'It must have done,' Richard said, more emphatically than usual. He looked down at his long, elegant fingers. 'Perhaps the explanation is that even as a boy I was always rather exceptionally sensitive, and things like this always had a great deal of significance for me. Arnold probably wasn't influenced so much – and so he doesn't remember the name.'

'H'm.' Bland looked at Eve Marchant. 'I'm sorry – I know I sound like the Grand Inquisitor. But doing this sort of ferreting is one of my penalties of being a policeman – and now I've got to go on doing it with you.' She fidgeted with a glass ornament on the occasional table by her side. 'Yesterday morning Edward Hargreaves received an anonymous letter. I won't repeat the terms of it to you, but it stated categorically that you were married to Lionel, which was news to him and everyone else at that time. Now, we don't know whether Lionel told anyone of your marriage, but it doesn't seem probable that he did, from what you've told us. Last night you said you'd not told anyone. Now, I want you to think – are you absolutely sure of that?'

There was a moment's pause – an almost imperceptible pause – before Eve Marchant replied. Then she spoke, with a bright emphatic air of sudden recollection. 'I'm too silly – Myrtle Montague.'

'Myrtle Montague?'

'My best friend. Well, she *was* my best friend. I mean – '
She seemed for a moment embarrassed. 'In the show business
you generally make friends with someone in the show, and when
I met Lionel I was playing at the Follies in "Ladies, Let's Love".
Myrtle Montague was a girl in the chorus and I saw a lot of her.
Since I've been in this thing at the Splendid we've lost touch.'
With a slightly artificial brightness, she said in her metallic voice,
'That's show business.'

'Yes, indeed,' said Bland. 'And you told Myrtle Montague?'

She talked fast and loud. 'We were friends at the time and
it was really *before* Lionel had told me that I mustn't say anything to anybody. And I felt I absolutely *had* to tell somebody.
But Myrtle said she wouldn't tell anyone, and I'm sure she
didn't.' Richard was looking at her rather oddly. She continued
breathlessly, 'If you say I shouldn't have done it, I simply
couldn't agree more, but I do hope you won't hold it against
me.' She looked at Richard and then at Sinclair, and her face
puckered appealingly.

Bland said pleasantly, 'It's a good thing you remembered.
Do you know Miss Montague's address?'

'No, I don't – yes, I do, though. She lives in a teeny-weeny
little flat off Shepherd's Market – I've got it down somewhere.'
She fumbled in a suede bag with a claw clasp on it, and produced
a small black and red diary. '86 Carteret Street, just off Curzon
Street,' she said triumphantly, rather as if she were handing
Bland the murderer on a plate. She looked at him with an air
of guilelessness that he found very attractive, and said, 'I do
hope *you* won't hold it against me, Inspector.' Her legs were
crossed, and Sinclair was gazing ardently at her knees.

Bland got up and looked at her quizzically. Under the lamplight the skin of his face showed fresh and pink. 'You're sure
there's no one else you've forgotten to tell me about? '

She met his quizzical gaze with one of her own. 'Quite, quite
sure, Inspector.'

'Then I think I should be getting along.' When he was at the
door Richard Hargreaves said, 'Oh, by the way – just a minute.'

He was tracing a pattern on the carpet with one pointed suede shoe, and he looked – it was odd, Bland thought, how often a theatrical simile seemed appropriate in this case – like an actor struck suddenly with stage fright. When he began to speak, it was with a slight stammer. 'I don't know – I expect you all know – Eve and I are engaged to be married, and E. H. has been pretty beastly about it all. Well, we don't feel that's the kind of thing that ought to be put up with and so we're – going to get married pretty soon. That's all.'

Nobody spoke for a moment. Then Carruthers wished them both joy, with politeness, but a certain lack of enthusiasm. 'You know, this is going to make the old man awfully wild.'

'Damn the old man,' Richard said, in rather a high-pitched voice. Eve Marchant said nothing, but she smiled like a cat.

Sinclair came forward and said with his ready smile, 'Congratulations – and especially to you, Richard. I've only met Miss Marchant this evening, but I've seen enough of her to know that you're a lucky dog. Do you know, I have only one regret.'

'What's that?'

'That I didn't see her first.' As soon as he had spoken the words, Sinclair flushed a bright red. Carruthers said, with a malice that Bland had not seen revealed, 'No, Lionel saw her first.' Richard looked up angrily, but Eve saved the situation by saying in her metallic voice, 'I think that announcement deserves a drink, Richard. And I'm intent that the great analytical mind should congratulate us. You haven't done that, Inspector.'

With a pleasant impersonality, Bland said, 'Of course I congratulate you. I hope you will be very happy.' He raised his glass and drank. They all drank.

'But what do you *really* think?' she asked coquettishly, and Richard moved unhappily, and said, 'For God's sake, darling.'

'You don't want to know what a policeman thinks. But the fact that you were Lionel's wife is bound to be known, and a good many people will say that you marry too often into the same family.' Richard made an angry, ineffectual movement. 'If it's any satisfaction to you, I think you're bringing things to a head – which, from my point of view, is a good thing.'

Richard Hargreaves looked puzzled. 'You mean you think our marriage is connected with all this?'

Bland picked up his hat. Sinclair and Carruthers moved towards him at the door. 'Directly – perhaps not. Indirectly – yes. I think you may be in some danger.' Richard looked at Bland with his mouth slightly open. 'Good night.'

## I

*9.30 to 10 a.m.*

'Well, what do you know?' Filby said. 'She certainly is a cool one, that girl. Only ten minutes in the grave, and she's marrying another. And the same family, too.' He tapped his nose, and looked at Bland with a terrifying expression of low cunning. 'Let's hope she don't need to marry this one the same way as the other.'

'What do you mean?'

'She got him tight,' Filby said dramatically. 'Blotto. Stinking. One over the eight. Half seas over. The registrar was doubtful whether to marry 'em, he was so tight. But he could just about make the responses, and said he knew what he was doing. No difficulty in checking it, because of another thing. *She* got the licence – they remembered that. Enterprising girl, ain't she?'

Bland played with the paperweight shaped like a monkey which stood on his desk. 'Enterprising enough, yes. And far more intelligent than you'd think to watch her prancing about in the chorus. A good head, with her heart always at its service. You can get almost anything in this world, Filby, if you've got a sufficiently hard head and an equally hard heart.'

'She must be bloody Cleopatra and the Queen of Sheba rolled into one.' Filby's long, melancholy face looked indignant. 'By the way, I've found the taxi-driver who picked her up from her flat Wednesday night and took her to Redfern Square – so that's all OK.' He brooded again. 'Marrying two in the same family. What's she doing it for? She can't be in love with this one, too.'

'Money, partly. Don't forget the father's pretty well fixed.'

'But couldn't the old man cut her out of his will? He's mad at her, isn't he?'

'Perhaps she thinks he'll get used to her. He's very keen on his family. But I agree there must be something else driving her on to marriage – and I've got an idea what it is.'

Filby raised his eyebrows and whistled. 'A bit more mystery?'

'It might be very simple.' Bland leaned back in his chair with his trilby hat on the back of his head. Fog and damp hung about the room. Outside the window a thick creamy blanket had been placed over the world, dulling even the sound of traffic. He coughed, and the dry noise was odd in the quiet room. 'Any luck with that anonymous letter?'

'What you'd expect. No fingerprints, except Hargreaves' own. Typed by an amateur, or someone who was trying to look like an amateur, on an old Remington 12. Small letters "e" and "l" slightly out of alignment, small "d" badly worn and "n" a bit worn. Conclusive enough, if we could fix the typewriter. Shall we check on all the typewriters at that advertising agency?'

'Not yet. I don't want to alarm them at the moment. What about Weston's alibi?'

'Watertight. This chap Matthews was with him all the time between 7.15 and 8.30 except for ten minutes soon after 7.30 when Weston went outside to wash.'

'Yes, simple but efficient. The first alibi we've come across.'

'Suspicious,' said Filby. He pulled his lower lip, raised his eyebrows and looked like a horse. 'After all, he's the family lawyer. And he told you that tall story about Hargreaves' wife.'

'I wouldn't say it was a tall story – or if it is, Weston believes it himself. What did you get on van Dieren?'

'Mystery again.' Filby shook his head. 'He's been running this art agency for less than eighteen months. Dropped vague hints occasionally to various people that he used to know old man Hargreaves a long while ago, and that he's an old scoundrel. Can't trace any connection between him and Hargreaves, and can't trace him farther back than that period of eighteen months. Nobody knows where he came from, nobody seems friendly with him. Doesn't come into his office much, business is in decline – he bought it when it was a fairly good concern. Lives alone in a little place out Earls Court way. Can't find out whether he stayed there last night or not. That's all.'

'Little enough. And yet there's a germ of something important in it. Consider, Filby: the study walls were lined with asbestos. Somebody sent an anonymous letter to Hargreaves about Eve Marchant. Edward Hargreaves' wife died two years ago, and he's shown no inclination to remarry. Joe Riddell is a figure out of the very distant past. Doesn't something about those things strike you?'

Filby's mouth was open. He closed it and said firmly, 'No.'

Bland's face looked white and a little strained. 'But I simply can't understand about Jones – I don't see where Jones comes in, and why. I sat up half the night thinking about it.'

'You think too much,' Filby said pityingly. 'What's the next move?'

'Eve Marchant's friend, Myrtle Montague. I hope she'll have something to tell us about the anonymous letter. I have a feeling it came from or through friend van Dieren.'

'You mean he did the murder?'

Bland paused at the door with his forehead puckered. 'If he did, he was acting for someone else. But don't ask me how that could be, for I don't know.' He put on his trilby hat, flipped the brim, and grinned. 'I'm off to see Myrtle.'

'Perhaps she'll give us a clue,' said Filby hopefully.

Bland looked at him seriously. 'Perhaps she'll be Mr Jones.'


## II

### *10.0 to 10.30 a.m.*

Sinclair was invariably punctual at the office. Or almost invariably: for this morning he was held up by the fog, and arrived half an hour late. His faint feeling of annoyance was not dispelled by Onslow, who came into his room and stood with his hands in his pockets. 'The old man's been asking for you.

He's in a hell of a stew. Got in at 9.30 on the dot, and been asking where everybody's got to.'

Sinclair nodded, and vented a little of his annoyance. 'Right. Next time you come in here, knock on the door.' Onslow raised his eyebrows and went out without saying anything. His manner showed clearly that he classed Sinclair among the capitalist exploiters. Sinclair rang through to E. H. on the internal telephone. A voice at the other end said, 'Yes?'

'Sinclair, Mr Hargreaves. You wanted me?'

E. H.'s voice was smooth but bitter. 'Oh, you've arrived.' He paused, but Sinclair saw no occasion to reply. 'I've been waiting to see you since 9.30, but I'm busy now. Come in at 10.30.' There was a click. Sinclair replaced his own receiver, just as the door opened and Bond came in. There was a gleam in the Production Manager's eye which Sinclair could see meant no good. He was not wrong.

'Spot of trouble, I'm afraid,' Bond said, with a hypocritically sympathetic look. 'Something seems to have gone wrong with the works somewhere.' Sinclair raised his eyebrows, rather like Onslow. With the same sympathetic look, Bond unfolded a copy of that day's *Daily Express* and pointed to an advertisement for one of their clients, Quickshave Shaving Cream. 'See anything wrong with that?' he asked with intolerable smugness. Sinclair looked at the advertisement, which showed two men shaving, one with a look of disgust on his face, the other beaming happily. Above the first was written in a bold script, '*He* used "Shaving Cream",' above the second, '*He* changed to Quickshave.' There was nothing wrong with the blocks, or the headings or the copy. He put down the paper and said, 'Well?'

Even more smugly, Bond said, 'Price.' He pointed to the bottom of the advertisement – *In Tubes 9d.*, *In Jars 1s. 6d.* 'Isn't it 7½d. and 1s. 3d. now? Remember the price reduction a couple of weeks ago? And we agreed it should be corrected on all proofs?'

Sinclair remembered it perfectly. He said sharply, 'Who passed the proofs?'

Bond produced from under his arm a proof, and said with

what seemed to Sinclair obviously mock reluctance, 'It looks as if you did.' Sinclair bent over the proof and saw that it was perfectly true. He remembered also that the proof had come up when he was talking to Onslow about a new scheme for Flowspeed Airlines. He had been told that it was wanted urgently, and checked it for literals and initialled it. The mistake was certainly partly his responsibility: but it was also partly Bond's, for the Production Department had been informed of the change in prices, and had been told to alter copy accordingly. He said with no decrease in sharpness, 'I thought you were going to alter all proofs.'

. Mock reluctance was replaced by mock sympathy. 'Sorry, old man. We altered all the rest, but the stereo for this had already been made.'

'Is that any reason why you shouldn't have altered it?'

Bond was imperturbable. 'Well, old man, I suppose it isn't. But it *is* up to the Copy Department to check copy points, isn't it?'

With an effort, Sinclair controlled himself. Privately, he believed that Bond had noticed the price mistake, and let it through from pure malice. But he said pleasantly, 'OK. I'll deal with it. Thanks for pointing it out.'

'That's all right.' Bond hesitated in the doorway. 'What's happened to that friend of yours – the Inspector chappie? I believe he was asking questions about a lad named van Dieren.'

'Do you know something about him?'

Bond laughed. 'Do I not. I don't suppose it's important, but he'd probably like to know.'

'He's coming along here later this morning – I'll ask him to talk to you.' Bond went out. Left to himself, Sinclair walked up and down on his green carpet. The mistake was annoying, but not serious. He pondered whether he should let it slide, or forestall criticism by telephoning Magee, the Advertising Manager, and tell him about it. He decided to telephone, picked up the external telephone and said, 'Get me Mr Magee of Quickshave.' The internal telephone rang. Tracy's voice said, 'Sinclair? E. H. wants to see us both in his office. Will you come in.' Sinclair picked up the external again, and said 'Cancel that call.' He was feeling thoroughly sour when he walked down the passage and entered E. H.'s office.


# III

### *10.30 to 11.10 a.m.*

'Well, the police,' Myrtle Montague said. 'This *is* a surprise. You don't look a bit like a policeman. *Do* come in.' She led him into a tiny sitting-room where a coal fire burned brightly, and photographs of male film stars lined the walls. 'Do let me have your hat,' she said. 'And your coat. You'll pardon my négligée, won't you? You see, I wasn't expecting you – I've never had a policeman come to see me before.' She said it as brightly as though Bland were a District Visitor. She was a small, blonde girl with china-blue eyes, and he wondered for a moment if she could possibly be as ignorant as she appeared. She was wearing a bright red dressing-gown, and it was clear that she had only just got out of bed. Bland offered her a cigarette. 'Well,' she said, 'State Express. *Super*. I don't think I can resist one, though I really shouldn't.'

Bland paused with a cigarette half-way to his mouth. 'You have a cough?'

'Oh no. I mean my voice – of course I'm resting now, but I have to look after it. Though with this *beastly* fog I don't think it matters about smoking, do you? Poor you,' she added suddenly, and Bland was amused.

'Why poor me?'

'Having to be out in the fog. It's quite true what the old proverb says, isn't it – a policeman's lot is not a happy one. Would you like a cup of coffee – my coffee really *is* something, though I say it myself'

'I won't have anything, thanks,' Bland said a little

desperately, and plunged in before she could say anything else. 'Miss Eve Marchant sent me here to see you.'

Myrtle Montague's china-blue eyes widened. 'Are *you* a friend of *Eve's*? And she asked you to drop in and have a chat when you were passing by? Well isn't that – '

'Super,' Bland said quickly. He had decided that her appearance told the truth. 'I'm here on business, Miss Montague. You were very friendly with Miss Marchant, weren't you?'

She bridled slightly. 'I *am* very friendly. We just haven't seen each other for a few weeks, that's all. She's in this new thing at the Splendid, and I'm resting. That's show business.'

'I'm sure. Now, did Miss Marchant tell you anything about a man named Lionel Hargreaves?'

'She certainly did.' Miss Montague tried to look crafty. 'But I don't know what I ought to tell *you*.'

'Then supposing I tell you. They were married, weren't they? You may as well say yes – Miss Marchant told me so herself.' She nodded. 'And you know what's happened to Lionel Hargreaves.' This time she shook her head, and he said a little impatiently, 'Don't you read the papers?' He was quite taken aback, when she said simply, 'No.'

'Oh,' he said weakly, and then pulled himself together. 'It doesn't matter. The important thing is that Miss Marchant says she told you about the marriage before anything was announced. Is that right?' She nodded again. 'And she says she told nobody else. Is that right too – as far as you know?'

She seemed to have become suddenly impressed with the seriousness of the whole thing. 'I don't think she told anybody else.'

'Did you tell anybody?'

She shook her head happily. 'I wouldn't tell anybody about a thing like that, when it was told me as a secret.'

'You're sure you didn't tell anybody?'

'Certain sure.'

'Not even your father and mother?'

'Haven't got a father and mother.' She put out a hand to her mouth. 'I'm a liar. I'm ever so sorry. Of course, I told my sister,

Pauline. But that's the only person I did tell, cross my heart on it.'

'Pauline Montague,' Bland said thoughtfully. 'Or is your sister married?'

'Oh no, she's not married, but her name's not Montague, I mean my name's not Montague. It's just my stage name – I took it because it sounded distinguished.' She blushed. 'My name's really Ella Lines, but I wanted a super name for the stage, so I took Myrtle Montague.'

Bland realized why there had seemed to be something familiar about her face. 'So your sister's Pauline Lines – Polly Lines?'

'That's right.'

'And she works for a man named van Dieren.'

'Well, this is a surprise,' Miss Montague said. 'Fancy you knowing that. Do you know Polly?'

'We've met. Do you know anything about her boss? Does she talk about him?'

She pulled her dressing-gown about her, and frowned with an effort of concentration. 'That's a funny thing too. And it's why I told Polly, though I shouldn't have done. Her boss is ever such a funny man. Of course Polly's a bit of a fast one.' She nodded sagely. 'She likes the men. Well, so we all do, but Polly's a bit naughty – if you know what I mean. But that's neither here nor there, except that I think her boss's business isn't quite straight, in some way or other. The real thing I was going to say was that I told Polly because her boss often talked about old man Hargreaves – that's Lionel's father – and how he'd cheated him over something or other. So naturally when Eve told me she'd got married to Lionel, I told Polly. I never breathed a word to anyone else.'

'And Polly might have told her boss. Is she friendly with him?'

'A bit *too* friendly, if you ask me.'

'I see.' Bland paused a moment and stubbed out his cigarette. 'What do you think of Eve Marchant? I'd better tell you why I'm asking all these questions. Lionel Hargreaves has been murdered, and now Eve Marchant's discovered that she wants to marry his brother, Richard.'

Her reaction to this was not quite what he had expected. 'Is she going to marry him?'

'She says so.'

'Good for her,' she said simply. 'She told me she'd met Richard too, and he was ever so nice. What a pity about Lionel, though.'

Bland blinked. 'But doesn't it seem to you a bit odd that she should marry again – and her husband's brother, too – so soon after her husband's death?'

Miss Montague looked at him, and giggled. 'Lionel wasn't very nice to her. And there's a very good reason, too, but wild horses wouldn't drag it out of *me*. You'll have to ask Eve about that. She's ever so nice, don't you think?'

'Very attractive indeed,' Bland said hollowly.

'Well, she's in show business. That's enough to explain anything. We're awfully funny people, you know, Inspector.' She looked at her watch. 'You'll pardon my saying it – it's been super meeting a real live policeman, but I've got to see my boyfriend at the Savoy Grill at twelve, and I'm not dressed yet.' They moved towards the door, and she gave him a parting smile. 'I think you're ever so nice,' she said.

Bland walked slowly up Curzon Street inhaling great mouthfuls of fog. It was now so thick that he could hardly see the edge of the pavement. So van Dieren sent the anonymous note, he thought – or van Dieren had told somebody else, who sent it. All the trails led back to van Dieren – a man who had not the slightest reason for wishing Lionel Hargreaves dead, but who might have borne a grudge against his father. If van Dieren was acting merely as an agent, was not his employer taking a tremendous risk, in view of the fact that he must know all about the murder? Bland stood on the kerb and said aloud, 'It all depends on Jones.' A girl standing just by his side looked at him coldly, and moved a step or two away. 'I beg your pardon,' he said.

# IV

E. H. looked at the three of them with an apparent urbanity that, Sinclair thought, presaged the worst. 'I should like to read you this letter, gentlemen,' he said. He read it. The letter was from Mr Ian Gordon, Managing Director of Furnishings Limited, and said that they regretted that they were unable to place their advertising with the Hargreaves Agency. The scheme submitted to them, the letter went on, was no doubt a sound one, but the Board of Directors felt that somehow it had not quite the tone they were looking for. In his, Mr Gordon's view, a view with which the other directors had concurred, it lacked, in a phrase, the spark of inspiration. He thanked them for the trouble taken in preparing the scheme and remained, with kind regards, theirs sincerely. E. H. read the letter in an impersonal voice, clasped his hands, looked at them, and said, 'Well, gentlemen?' Sinclair breathed in deeply and looked across the room, out of the big French window, at the people passing in the street. Richard Hargreaves stared at his suede shoes. Tracy looked straight at E. H., his head thrown back a little self-consciously, the squint in his dark eyes very plain. Nobody said anything. Without any apparent loss of urbanity, E. H. tapped the letter and said, 'I want your observations.'

Richard's toe moved in a circle on the carpet, and he spoke in a low voice. 'Just one of those things. I don't see that there's anything much to be said about it. We've put up schemes before and had them turned down. So has everyone else. I can't see any point in holding an inquest.'

'I don't agree,' Tracy said, in his rich voice. He stared defiantly at E. H. 'This scheme was always an abortion. But maybe Richard's right, and there's no point in holding an inquest on an abortion.'

'Just what does that mean?' E. H. asked.

Tracy flung out his arm in the fine eloquent gesture that had so impressed so many advertising conventions. 'I mean that an advertising man is a creative artist. Or at least he should be. *I* am a creative artist. And no creative artist can do good work when he is hampered at every turn by pettifogging restrictions about spending a few pounds. We lost the Furnishings Account because I wasn't allowed to use the artists I wanted on it – they were too expensive. We lost it also because the original ideas I presented were altered and blotched about by everybody who had anything to do with the account and especially by – ' Tracy stopped suddenly.

E. H.'s lips were set in a thin line. 'I don't know why you should be affected in your speech by the fact that my son Lionel is dead. As I understand it, you put the blame for the loss of the account chiefly on my dead son, who interfered with your ideas – '

'Really, I protest.' But Tracy said it weakly, a little cowed by the unmistakable note of menace in E. H.'s voice.

' – and my own refusal to allow you to spend an unlimited sum of money in indulging your desire to obtain the most expensive art work obtainable.'

Tracy got up. His squint was terrifying. 'I won't stay here to be insulted.' He lurched, rather than walked, out of the room, and slammed the door behind him.

During this altercation E. H. had not raised his voice, nor had Richard looked up from the floor. With almost an increase in urbanity, E. H. said, 'Have you anything to say, Sinclair? Do you attribute our loss of the account to interference with the work of the Copy Department? I hope that you will take a less purely departmental view than Tracy.'

'I don't think my view's departmental. Do you really want me to tell you, sir, why I think we lost the account?'

A shade of acerbity touched E. H.'s voice. 'I hoped I had made it plain that that was my purpose.'

Sinclair said bluntly, 'We lost it because Mr Gordon doesn't want to be mixed up with a firm that's involved in a scandal. Stupid, no doubt, but that's the truth.'

E. H. stared at him, and then ran his hand through his white

hair. 'But how could I have been so stupid? I should have
realized that. You'll forgive me – I have been much upset by
Lionel's death. I really am not myself.' It was typical, Sinclair
thought, that the evident distress shown by E. H., which in
anyone else would have seemed pathetic, appeared in him
simply a little unreal and disgusting. The telephone bell rang.
E. H. picked up the receiver. 'Yes. Hargreaves here. Who is
that? Who? Van Dieren – oh yes, van Dieren. I should like to
see you.' He looked at a diary on his desk. 'Two o'clock would
suit me. I shall expect you then. Goodbye.' As he hung up the
receiver, the clock above his head struck eleven times, with a
silver tinkling note. E. H. rose and walked slowly over to a
cupboard which stood in the wall opposite the window. He came
back with a bottle and three glasses. When he spoke, his voice
was as urbane and portentous as ever. 'You must drink a glass
of wine with me, Richard, and you too, Sinclair. It is eleven
o'clock.' It was E. H.'s invariable habit to drink a glass of sherry
at eleven o'clock in the morning and at five o'clock in the
evening. The habit was known to all the senior members of his
staff, but it was very rarely that they, or even his sons, were
invited to drink with him. The glass of sherry was to be interpreted as a kind of discreet apology for the Furnishings episode,
Sinclair thought, but also as a mark of high good humour. As
though to confirm these thoughts, E. H. spoke again, with a
touch of ponderous archness. 'I wonder if we should ask Tracy
to come in here. I think not. He is so impetuous that I fear he
might take the invitation in the wrong spirit.' He poured sherry
into the three glasses. 'You will find this is a very decent Amon-
tillado.' The liquid was pale amber against the electric light. As
they sipped it E. H. said casually, 'A man named van Dieren is
coming to see me this afternoon – he tells me that he has some
information which may be relevant to Lionel's death.' Below
the halo of white hair the small blue eyes looked at them both,
keen and hard.

# V

Bland walked a few hesitant steps in the fog, wondering whether the information he had just received need affect his next move, which had been to speak to Bond about van Dieren. Was it perhaps more immediately important to check on what Ella Lines, or Myrtle Montague, had told him, and find out whether Polly had spoken to van Dieren about the marriage? He decided that it was, turned round and padded softly through the fog towards Piccadilly. The fog tickled his nose, and he sneezed. 'Damn,' he said, and stopped to light a cigarette.

He stood in front of the small hatchway that was now becoming familiar, and was about to ring the bell when the hatch popped open, and Polly Lines' round doll's head appeared. The physical resemblance between the two girls was a marked one, but there was a viciousness and intelligence in Polly's face quite absent from her sister's. She stared at Bland, and said immediately, 'He's out.'

'It's not Mr van Dieren I want to see. It's you.'

'Me?' Her blue eyes opened wide.

'Yes. May I come in?'

'I suppose so,' she said grudgingly, and opened the door to her room. 'I don't know what you want me for,' she said, and patted her hair. 'I've told you everything about that telephone call.'

'It's not about the telephone call. It's about your sister.'

'My *sister*.' She stared. 'What's she got to do with it?'

'Did you tell your employer anything about the marriage of a friend of your sister's named Eve Marchant to Lionel Hargreaves?'

Either she was a first-class actress, or her surprise was genuine. 'Why not? Yes, I did. He was always going on about old man Hargreaves, and saying he'd done him down and he'd get even one day, and I thought he'd be interested to know about this. It was just a bit of gossip, that's all. I haven't done anything wrong.' It was unpleasantly warm in the little office, and of necessity they were close together. One of Miss Lines' crossed legs was almost touching Bland's and he could not help seeing the sharp points of her breasts jutting out of her black jumper.

He leaned back in his chair. 'Cigarette?' She giggled. 'I don't mind if I do.' Her eyes, as he lighted the cigarette for her, were watchful. 'Damn,' she said. 'It's out.' She held his hand as he relighted it, with her small, rather pudgy hand, the nails tipped with scarlet, and she recrossed her legs, so that one of her knees was touching Bland's. 'Suppose you tell me what this is all about?'

'All right. Lionel Hargreaves has been murdered. His marriage to Eve Marchant was secret. Lionel didn't tell anybody, Eve says she only told your sister, and your sister says she only told you. Lionel's father received an anonymous letter before the murder, telling him that his son was married to Eve Marchant. That's the story in a nutshell.'

'And you think my old man here had something to do with it?'

'I know he had *something* to do with it, but I'm not sure what it was.'

'And you think I can tell you something else?' Bland shrugged his shoulders. Her voice was shrill as she said, 'I can't. It's nothing to do with me, and I don't know anything about it.' It seemed to Bland that the pressure of her knee against his increased slightly.

'And you didn't type that anonymous letter?'

'Typed,' she cried. 'You didn't say it was typed. I had nothing to do with it.'

He looked round the room. 'Where's your typewriter?'

'Mr van Dieren sent it away for overhaul.'

'What make is it? A Remington? She nodded. 'A Remington 12?' She nodded again. 'Where was it sent for repair?'

'I don't know. Mr van Dieren sent it while I was out.'

'Did it need repair?'

She said reluctantly, 'Not much. Some of the letters were out of alignment.'

'Small "e" and "I"?' Her eyes were wild with alarm as she nodded a third time. 'All right. If you've nothing else to tell me – ' He stood up.

She came close to him, and took hold of his coat. Bland was not a tall man, but she was so small that she was a head below him. 'Listen,' she said. 'I had nothing to do with this, nothing at all, d'you hear? I don't want to get into any trouble.' She pressed herself against him, and he disengaged her, not gently. Her cheap scent was strong in his nostrils.

'What do you know about van Dieren?'

'I don't know anything,' she cried. 'Not anything.'

'Have you ever stayed at his place in Earls Court?'

She stepped away from him, her face contorted with rage. 'Get out. Go on, get out. Before I throw something at you.'

Bland looked round critically. 'There's very little to throw. But I'll go. You're being very stupid, Miss Lines. If you change your mind, and decide you've got something to tell me, ring me up at once, or come to Scotland Yard.'

'Get out,' she screamed. 'Get out.'

He turned and went out. The last sight he had was of her china-blue eyes staring at him with hatred. Outside in the street he ran his fingers round his collar. 'Good Lord,' he said. 'The things I do for law and order.'


# VI

### *11.45 a.m. to 12.15 p.m.*


'Darling, I thought we'd agreed that we shouldn't see each other alone in the office,' Jean Rogers said. 'It's really awfully tactless. You know how people talk.'

'I had to see you,' Tracy said, 'I simply had to see you. I just can't stand it.'

Her voice was not impatient, but rather elaborately patient, as she said, 'What's the matter now?'

'It's that bloody swine – the old man. He as good as told me I waste the firm's money. Well, by God, I only need to be told that once.' His face was very red. 'I shall hand in my resignation.'

She laid her hand on his shoulder. 'Don't do anything you'll regret.'

'I'll hand in my resignation,' Tracy said obstinately. 'I won't stand it. He's not the only pebble on the beach.'

'But he's a very good one. You'll not find anyone else who'll pay you what Hargreaves does.' As he started to protest she said hurriedly, 'Darling, I know you're worth every penny of it. But he *does* pay well.'

Tracy got up and walked about. 'So you think I should put up with it?'

She stood close to him. 'Just for a little while. You know I'll be seeing Alan again soon, and this time perhaps I'll really be able to make him agree to a divorce.'

'And then we'll get married?'

She said in a doubtful voice, 'Then we'll get married.'

His face broke into the fresh, attractive smile she knew so well, and he tossed back a lock of hair from his forehead. He took her into his arms and kissed her. 'Of course we will. Forgive me, darling. I suppose I shouldn't forget that Lionel was killed the night before last. I'm just a bad-tempered impatient devil, I know I am.' Since he was holding Jean Rogers in his arms he could not see the sudden change of expression on her face as he said these words: but he could not help seeing the door of the room open after a perfunctory knock, and Bond put his head round it. Neither could he miss the long, malicious look Bond gave them before he said 'Sorry,' and closed the door.

Bond closed the door gently and stood in the corridor for a moment, his dark face happy with malice. He walked along the corridor to Sinclair's room, and looked in. He found Sinclair in the Copy Room next door, looking critically at a piece of

Onslow's copy. Onslow was standing by his side, looking, if possible, even more critical than Sinclair.

'These two are all right,' Sinclair said. 'But this third piece – I can't quite lay my finger on what's wrong, but somehow it doesn't ring the bell.' Onslow nodded. 'Have another shot, will you?' Sinclair said curtly to Bond, 'I've spoken to the Quick-shave people, and settled that point.' But Bond was not so easily shaken off.

'Can I see you for a moment?'

Sinclair paused with his hand on his door, and said, 'I'm very busy.'

'This won't take a minute,' Bond said, 'and it's most interesting.' As they went into Sinclair's room the door from the corridor opened and Miss Peachey, the receptionist, said, 'Inspector Bland.'

Bland was looking wonderfully fresh and unruffled, and he beamed at Bond. 'The very man I've been looking for. I understand you have something to tell me?'

'I certainly have. You were asking some questions about a man named van Dieren? Well, before I came here I was working with a firm of art agents myself, and believe me, I learned something about friend van Dieren.' He raised his eyebrows. 'Dirty work.'

'What kind of dirty work?'

'Dirty drawings – and photographs. It's not unknown and it's not unprofitable. Very few people, even inside the trade, know about it, but we had some dealings with him, and I called round once or twice. Devil of a queer cove he was, and his little bitch of a secretary too. Met her, Inspector?'

'Yes,' Bland said.

'*She* certainly knows what's what,' Bond said with a grin. 'And I'd lay a bet the old man's taught it to her, queer though he does look. One day when I was up there he asked me if I was interested in art studies – and then he showed me some of the filthiest photographs I've ever seen in my life.'

'And were you interested?' Sinclair asked. Bond laughed

loudly. 'Another crack like that from you, my lad, and I'll tell the Inspector about your little slip-up on Quickshave.'

'You think van Dieren was making a good thing out of it?'

'If what I heard afterwards is true, he certainly was. He didn't do a lot of legitimate business, that I do know.'

'All right,' Bland said. 'Thank you, Mr Bond. That may be very useful.' Bond paused at the door and grinned again. 'I'm honoured if I've told the police something.' He said to Sinclair, 'I've got a titbit to tell you, but it'll keep.'

Bland breathed deeply when Bond had closed the door. 'As a policeman I try to feel no prejudices, but I must admit that I've taken a dislike to that man.'

'A dislike that's shared by almost everybody here.' Sinclair looked at Bland a little quizzically. 'Isn't your department falling down a bit – I mean, not knowing about these activities of van Dieren's?'

'No, I don't think so. He's never been in prison, and there's no special reason why the man I asked to make a check on him should have looked to see if he was running a separate pornographic business on the side.' He tapped his teeth with a pencil. 'You notice that every trail we have leads back to van Dieren. Jones telephoned him, I've found out this morning that the anonymous letter came from his office, that curious story which should have been told by Joe Riddell came from him. And yet it's clear enough that he's merely acting for somebody else, or else he wouldn't move so openly. Bond's story would explain why Polly Lines was alarmed on that first day when we called, when she heard I was from the police, and why she was almost relieved when she found it was a case of murder.'

'You mean – she knows about these – other activities?' Sinclair flushed.

'I should think that almost certain.' Bland chuckled. 'She tried to seduce me this morning – at least I think that was her intention – but my purity remains untouched. I was going to say, though, that we have no proof whatever that Bond's story is true. I'm inclined to believe it because I can't see why he should invent it, but it's always possible that he's trying something on. In a murder story any character as obviously unpleasant as Bond would be clear of suspicion automatically, but in real life he's as likely as anyone else to have committed murder.' His unusually long speech was interrupted by a tentative knock on the door. It opened, and Carruthers' round face appeared. He spoke apologetically. 'I'm so sorry – I came straight in to see you about some work that Richard's given me to do – I didn't mean to disturb you.'

'Not at all,' Bland said casually. 'We were only chatting. I'm sorry to tell you, by the way, that your friend van Dieren seems to be in this up to the neck.'

Carruthers' Adam's apple moved up and down. His alarm would have been comic had there not also been something unpleasant and furtive about it. 'Are you going to arrest him?'

'Why, not at the moment, I think.'

'He's coming up here this afternoon,' Sinclair said, and Bland and Carruthers both looked startled. 'To see E.H. I don't know what it's about, but he telephoned this morning and made an appointment. Richard and I were in the room at the time. It's something to do with Lionel's death, I think. So if you want to arrest him, he'll be here at two o'clock.'

'He'll be much more useful laying the trails somebody has carefully designed for him,' Bland said. 'If Mr van Dieren's given enough rope, I feel he'll hang – not himself, but somebody else. I think I'll pay another call on him this afternoon myself – some of the points in his story can be checked now. I feel the time has come to play what you, Sinclair, used to call a forcing game, when we were at school together.'

# VII

The hands of the clock above the reception desk pointed to two o'clock exactly when the disorderly figure of Joseph van Dieren pushed open the swing door and said to Miss Peachey, the platinum-haired girl who sat behind the reception desk, 'I want Mr Edward Hargreaves.' She noticed a general smell of drink that surrounded him. She could not help noticing also the frayed sleeves of his big raglan overcoat, and the great moustache and bushy eyebrows that gave a fierce expression to his face.

'I'll see if he's in.' She dialled a number on an internal telephone. 'Mr Hargreaves? Mr van Dieren here to see you. Certainly, sir.' She put down the telephone. 'Mr Hargreaves will be free in a moment, Mr van Dieren. Will you take a chair.'

'No, I won't take a chair. I had an appointment at two o'clock and it's two o'clock now. Why doesn't he keep it, eh?'

Miss Peachey said nervously, 'Mr Hargreaves will see you in a moment, sir.'

'He'd better.' The man in the big coat began to walk up and down the reception-room with a ferocity which was somehow rather comic. 'I'm not hanging about for him. I've been waiting on this day for twenty years, and I'm not going to be done out of it now.' Two or three people came through the reception-room, and looked at van Dieren curiously. The internal telephone rang. Miss Peachey answered it, and said with relief, 'Mr Hargreaves will see you now.'

'And about time too.' He followed her along the corridor with a gait that was just perceptibly not straight. The last thing she saw before she closed the door was E.H.'s face, grim and with no trace of customary benevolence, staring at his visitor.

Ten minutes later she heard a sudden crash, a sound of breaking glass, and E.H.'s voice raised in anger. A series of large French windows with balconies outside them ran from the offices on this side of the corridor to the street. She opened one of these windows, and heard E.H. yell into the thick fog, 'There he goes. Catch the little devil. Catch him.' Following the direction of E.H.'s finger, she saw a small boy running. E.H.'s injunction to catch him was a vain one; visibility was not more than a few yards, and in a few moments the small boy had vanished.

'God damn and blast,' E.H. said. 'I'd like to wring that boy's neck.'

'What happened, sir?'

He held out for her inspection a large stone. 'Little devil threw this and broke my window, that's what happened.' By this time other French windows had opened, and Onslow, Mudge and Mrs. Rogers had come out on their balconies. They stared at E.H. and the stone, and at the window, which had lost a good deal of glass. E.H. became suddenly conscious of their gaze, and stepped back off the balcony into his room. Miss Peachey carried back with her the smell of fog which, thanks to her incautious opening of the French window, had now pervaded the reception office. Miss Berry, her particular friend from Accounts, came in, and they agreed that the weather really was too vile, and that there was nothing worse than the English climate.

They were just speaking wistfully of the joys of Torquay in January when the door of E.H.'s room opened, and van Dieren shot out of it, head down, scuttling along the corridor in his big overcoat. E.H.'s voice followed him: 'And don't bring me any more cock-and-bull tales. When you've got something to say, I'll listen to you.' Van Dieren did not reply. With his head well down, without a glance at Miss Peachey or her friend, he charged out through the swing doors into the street. E.H. stood glaring down the corridor for a moment, and then slammed his door. Miss Peachey said to her friend, 'The old man certainly sent *him* off with a flea in his ear.'

# VIII

Miss Peachey, the receptionist, liked her job. 'You see life,' she said, and she meant by the phrase that she preferred to sit at a reception desk, watching people pass by, swapping jokes with the boys from Production, and using her upper-class tone in the presence of upper-class visitors, to sitting in the unquestionably less lively but perhaps more discreet social atmosphere of one of the typists' offices. But although she talked to the boys from Production, although she kept her eye open for that Very Rich Young Man who would surely arrive one day and ask her out to lunch as a preliminary to marriage, Miss Peachey was an alert and conscientious receptionist. It turned out that this fact was of some importance; or at least it was of some importance that she sat at the reception desk all the afternoon from the time Mr van Dieren left, until five o'clock, with the exception of a brief five minutes, when her place was taken by her friend from Accounts.

At ten minutes to three Mr Weston arrived. He had an appointment with E.H. at three o'clock, and although he hardly came into the category of Very Rich Young Men, and she did not expect him to ask her out to dinner, Miss Peachey was pleased to see him. There was something – she hardly knew how to put it even to herself – something very trustworthy about Mr Weston. Whenever she saw his drooping jowls, his honest blue eyes and his respectable bowler hat and overcoat, she was reminded of a gentle St Bernard dog, and the portentiousness of his manner somehow added to this impression. When she rang through to E.H. he told her to ask Mr Weston to come in at three o'clock. She put down the telephone, and gave Mr Weston what she classified as one of her genuine smiles, something quite distinct from the mechanical smile with which she greeted everyone, as part of her job.

'And how is our Miss Peachey in this vile weather?' Mr Weston's teeth clicked. 'Still breaking all the hearts?'

'*Some* people,' Miss Peachey said, 'have got no hearts to break.'

'If I were twenty years younger, I should know what answer to make to that.' Mr Weston twirled his rolled umbrella in a way that might have surprised Bland had he seen him. 'And how is our lord and master?'

'If you ask me, he's in a pretty bad temper, and has been for a day or two. But then he's had enough to make him. Wasn't it a terrible thing about Mr Lionel?'

'Terrible.' Mr Weston's teeth clicked again.

'And today some lad threw a stone and broke his window, and then ran away in the fog.'

'Tch, tch,' Mr Weston clucked.

'And then a man named van Dieren called – rather seedy looking, not quite a gentleman really, I think – and *he* seemed to rub up Mr Hargreaves the wrong way too.' Miss Peachey paused, conscious suddenly that she had said rather more than she should have done, even to so thorough a gentlemen as Mr Weston. And indeed the lawyer, although he said nothing looked uncommonly thoughtful when he received this information. After a moment he looked at the clock. 'It is three o'clock,' he said. He rose and, carrying a fine leather dispatch-case in his left hand and the rolled umbrella in his right, walked down the corridor with a step remarkably springy for his sixty-seven years. He stopped at the first door on the left, knocked, and went in. Miss Peachey returned to her invoices with a slight, nagging itch in her mind that she shouldn't have made that remark about another caller.

It was almost half an hour before Mr Weston came out, looking even more sober than usual. He settled his bowler hat on his head, and then thoughtfully lifted it to say good day to Miss Peachey. She noted it with pleasure as a mark of his absolute gentlemanliness, and she followed his tall, slightly

stooping figure in its progress out of the swing doors with something like affection. She noted also the other visitors to E.H.'s
office during the afternoon, and was able to name them with
perfect confidence later on, as Bond, Sinclair and Richard Hargreaves, in that order.

At about four minutes past five o'clock, when Miss Peachey
was thinking that it was time to spend a few minutes in the
washroom, she was startled by a sound which she took to be a
strangled cry, coming from E.H.'s room, followed by a heavy
thud. She hesitated for a moment, but only for a moment, and
then walked up to the door, and knocked on it lightly. There
was no reply, but it seemed to her that she heard a scuffling
noise, the kind of sound that might be made by a large rat. She
pushed open the door. Fog was thick in the room, because of
the broken window, and for a moment she thought that there
was nobody there. She noticed a bottle and a glass standing on
the desk, and then, while she stood with her hand upon the
door, she heard a groan. Miss Peachey was a girl of common
sense and courage, and though she jumped, she did not scream.
She advanced cautiously towards the desk, and when she had
taken two steps she saw a brown shoe and sock sticking out
beyond the desk edge. The shoe and sock moved, and then
suddenly were still. Then Miss Peachey screamed.

# IX

## 4.0 to 5.15 p.m.

The fog was very thick, and it took Bland and Filby half an
hour to get to New Bridge Street. As they turned the corner
from Fleet Street, Bland gripped Filby's arm. 'What's that?' A
moment later the sound became unmistakably the clang of a
bell, and a fire engine moved slowly past them in the fog. The
two men looked at one another. In Filby's eyes there was merely
bewilderment, but in Bland's there was alarm. 'It's no use trying

to hurry in this fog,' Filby said in a soothing voice, as Bland moved forward, and became entangled with a burly man's umbrella. For all that, they quickened their pace when they saw in front of them a patch of brightness glowing through the fog. The bright patch became an orange glare, and Bland began to run. He pushed through a crowd of people, and came to a stop in front of van Dieren's office block. The building was on fire. Flames leaped from the ground-floor and first-floor windows, and the sharp smell of smoke mingled with the odour of fog in their nostrils. Two fire engines were at work, and Bland walked over to the officer in charge, and spoke to him urgently.

'Inspector Bland, CID. Did this fire start on the ground floor?'

The man looked at him oddly. 'Certainly did. Someone pretty well soaked a couple of offices down there with petrol and set light to them – or that's the way it looks. Something else, too – we found a dead girl in there. Had a job getting her out. Our chaps thought the fire had made her unconscious, but I'm not so sure. You'd better have a look at her.' He led the way over to a spot away from the fire engines, and pointed to a tarpaulin. 'Under there.' With Filby just behind him, Bland lifted the tarpaulin, and the face of Polly Lines looked up at him, hideously burned and distorted, but still recognizable. He pulled the tarpaulin right back, knelt by her side for a moment examining the body, and then got to his feet. 'There's a lump on her head,' the fire officer said. 'She could have been hit.'

'I saw it.' Bland's round face was grave and sad, and he spoke to Filby almost with a note of tenderness in his voice. 'Poor fool. If she'd talked to me this morning – if I'd known then what danger she was in – but I didn't.' He stood looking down at the tarpaulin for a moment and then said, 'You've seen no sign of van Dieren, I suppose? Theatrical-looking figure with grey hair and a big moustache? He's the man who rents those offices that are on fire.'

The officer shook his head. 'No one else. A girl on the first floor noticed the fire soon after it started – smoke coming under the door – or we might not have recovered her body at all. Had to break down the door, and no key inside. It's dirty work all right. Thanks to that girl who reported it, we've got the fire under pretty well.'

'Is there any chance of getting a look at the offices?'

'Not yet. Maybe in another half-hour. But everything will be pretty badly burnt – there won't be a lot left to look at.'

Bland turned to Filby. 'Will you take a look at the offices and salvage anything you can in the way of papers, files, metal objects – anything you can lay your hands on. If van Dieren comes, I want him at Scotland Yard for questioning. And let me know the result of the examination of that girl, and how she died.' Filby nodded without saying anything. Bland said, 'By God, I'll see somebody pays for this.'

When he got back to his office he found a note on his desk saying that Edward Hargreaves had been found dead in his office, and that poison was suspected as the cause of his death.

# X

## 5.45 to 6.30 p.m.

The little group of people gathered together round the reception desk met Bland with a cold hostility which he did not fail to notice. They are blaming me for this death, he thought. And in a way they are not wrong to blame me, because a policeman's job is primarily the prevention of crime, and not the discovery of criminals. A detective who is engaged on a case, holds the threads of it in his hands, and yet fails to prevent a crime, has failed. Yet that is a hard thought, for the detective starts at a great disadvantage against that very rare type of criminal who plans a crime, or a series of crimes, well in advance, and then carries them out methodically. In such cases the detective, even when he knows the name of the criminal, has no choice but to wait for a slip to be made.

These thoughts moved at the back of his mind while flash-light photographs of Hargreaves' room were being taken, while he was kneeling at the side of E.H.'s body and looking at the dead face with its crown of white hair, and while he was listening to Dr McCullen telling him that Edward Hargreaves had been poisoned by hyoscin, and that the hyoscin had certainly been contained in the sherry. Such disturbing and unsatisfactory thoughts remained with him while he was told that the glass containing the sherry had no prints except those of E.H., and that the bottle had apparently been recently wiped, and bore no prints other than those of E.H. His face, when he went out into the reception hall again, was stony.

'You probably know something of what has happened. I may as well tell you now that Mr Hargreaves has been killed by drinking sherry loaded with poison. Now, I want to know – '

'Just a minute.' It was Tracy, unexpectedly bellicose and unfriendly. 'We may not be detectives, but we can see what's in front of our noses. We could see that E.H. had been poisoned, and we've found out who did it. And God knows it's hard for a plain man to understand why this murderer's not under lock and key already. Of course it was this man van Dieren that you've been asking so many questions about. It's about time to stop asking questions. Let's get some action.'

Bland's voice was harsh. 'All right. Since you've constituted yourself the cheerleader, let's hear what happened.'

Tracy ticked off the points on his fingers. 'First, E.H. always has – had – a glass of sherry at eleven o'clock in the morning and five o'clock in the afternoon. It was a custom as regular as clockwork – something that several people in the office knew about, and that he never missed. Next, we can check that the sherry was all right at eleven o'clock this morning, because Dick and Sinclair here were in the room with E.H., and drank with him.' Richard Hargreaves and Sinclair nodded. Tracy looked uncomfortable for a moment, but continued, serious and oratori-cal. 'So someone put poison in the sherry after eleven o'clock. It wasn't done during lunchtime, because he had sandwiches in

his room, and no one came in to see him. His first visitor, at
two o'clock, was this man van Dieren, who had telephoned
this morning to make an appointment.' Tracy looked round,
conscious that he was holding his audience. Sinclair was gazing
rather anxiously at Bland, Richard Hargreaves looked almost
as pale and shaken as Miss Peachey, Bond was staring sullenly
in front of him, and Mrs Rogers was looking at Tracy. A little
apart from the rest of them, Mr Weston listened intently, with
one hand occasionally cupped to his ear. 'We don't know what
happened between the two of them. Probably we shall never
know. What we do know, thanks to the alertness of our receptionist here, is that E.H. turned van Dieren out after twenty
minutes, saying that he wouldn't listen to his cock-and-bull
stories.'

Miss Peachey interrupted. 'He didn't say exactly that, Mr
Tracy. He said that if van Dieren had something to say, he'd
listen to him.'

Tracy waved the remark away. 'But we know something
more than that. An odd thing happened while this man was in
the office. A little boy threw a stone, broke E.H.'s window, and
ran off in the fog. There was very little chance that he'd be
caught on a day like this – and he wasn't caught. E.H. came
out on to his balcony and stayed out there for a couple of
minutes. During that time he had his back to the room. That
two minutes gave ample time to the murderer. The bottle of
sherry always stood in the same place, on the sideboard – the
murderer simply had to distract E.H.'s attention. And that was
the only time during the afternoon when his attention *was* distracted. Miss Peachey was at the reception desk all the afternoon, and we have her word that E.H. didn't once leave his
room. The conclusion is obvious. This man van Dieren put
poison into the sherry. The case against him is cast-iron.'

Bland's face was not friendly. 'There's one flaw in that case
– only one, but it's big enough to break it wide open. You make
a great point of the fact that Hargreaves took a glass of sherry
at eleven o'clock in the morning and five in the evening. It's
obvious, therefore, that the crime was premeditated, and that

the murderer brought poison with him, dropped it in the sherry and walked out.

'But that means that you can pretty well exclude van Dieren from the list of suspects. Yesterday, I described his appearance to Hargreaves, who said he'd never met him. He'd never been in the offices.' He turned to Miss Peachey. 'Had you ever seen him before?'

She shook her head decidedly. 'Oh no, sir. I shouldn't have forgotten him, I'm sure of that.'

'Quite so. His manner and dress would not be easily forgotten. Now – since van Dieren had never been here, since he had never met Hargreaves, how did he know about the bottle of sherry? Where did he get the information about Hargreaves' habits?'

There was silence. Tracy said lamely, 'He got it from somebody here. Somebody told him without knowing it was important. They must have done.'

'All the people here who would know Hargreaves' habits deny any knowledge of van Dieren, except Mr Bond here, and Carruthers, who's not here at the moment. Did you give van Dieren this information, Mr Bond?'

Bond laughed. 'Certainly not. Last time I saw van Dieren I'd never put foot inside this place, and never seen the old man.'

'We can also ask Carruthers. But if he didn't give this information,' Bland shrugged, 'where's your case against van Dieren?'

Tracy stuck out his jaw. '*Somebody* told him.'

'Not at all. Even if Carruthers did tell van Dieren, there's no cast-iron case against him – he's simply one of the suspects.' Bland spoke with a vicious pleasure, addressing himself particularly to Tracy. 'The trouble with amateurs is that they theorize from prejudice, not from facts. Let's work from the facts. There was only one door to Hargreaves' room. There was also the French window leading on to the balcony, but as it only fronts on the street, it's obvious that nobody entered that way to put poison in the sherry. Whoever came in must have had the chance of distracting Hargreaves' attention for sufficient time to poison the sherry. Either van Dieren did it – in which case he must have been told the exact geography of the room, position of the bottle of sherry and so on – or it was done by one of the other people who came in the room between eleven o'clock in the morning and five in the afternoon. You say you were at the reception desk during that whole time, Miss Peachey?'

'Except for the lunch hour, when Miss Bellamy was here, and she says nothing happened during that time.'

'She didn't know anything,' Tracy said. 'We sent her home.'

'So you sent her home. That was very kind of you. No doubt you thought you were assisting the investigation. If she didn't know anything, she could hardly have known less than somebody who sent home a witness who would obviously be needed. It's no use blustering, Mr Tracy, your interference and stupidity are both inexcusable.' The anger of men who are generally calm is always impressive. Bland's manner was normally so soft and placid that they were all to some extent cowed. Sinclair almost jumped when Bland said in the same tone, 'And you, Sinclair, you've seen enough of this case to know Miss Bellamy would be needed for questioning.'

'Really, I – she said no one went in during the lunch hour.'

'And did you make absolutely sure that she hadn't left the desk for ten minutes of that time? Of course you didn't. And you, Miss Peachey – are you sure that you really remained at your desk the whole time?'

'Quite sure,' Miss Peachey said with composure. 'Except when the stone was thrown – then I looked out of the French windows, but I didn't leave the reception hall. I should have seen anyone walking along the corridor.'

'All right. Who else did you see go in there during the afternoon?'

Miss Peachey was conscious of the importance of her answer. Her voice had a hollow sound. 'Mr Weston, Mr Bond, Mr Sinclair and Mr Hargreaves.'

'In that order?' She nodded. 'Can you remember the times? Don't say you're sure of them if you're not.'

'I am sure – within a minute or two, anyway. Mr Weston went in at three, and came out just before half past. Mr Bond went in just after half past three, and stayed about five minutes. Mr Sinclair was in for about a quarter of an hour, and I should think he came out about four o'clock. Mr Richard was in there from about ten past to half past four. And then, of course, I went in just after five o'clock, and saw – '

'All right,' Bland said. 'Now, would you swear to those times?'

She nodded. 'Within a minute or two, yes. I always notice people going in and out of Mr Hargreaves' room, because he hates to be disturbed when he's engaged, and I used to tell people if anyone else was in there.'

'Thank you very much. You've done extremely well, and that's very helpful. Now, Mr Bond, do you agree that you went in for five minutes?'

'That or less. I went in to give him the price of a printing job. He queried one or two details about it – asked if it wouldn't be better done in colour lithography, rather than half-tone. I told him it wouldn't be so suitable.'

'Did you notice the bottle of sherry?'

'Can't say I did. Wouldn't say it wasn't there, though.'

'Did Hargreaves seem just as usual?'

Bond pursed his lips. 'He was pretty short with me. But then he was a man who'd often be pretty short.' He looked at Richard, and added, 'If you don't mind my saying so.'

'Mr Sinclair, why did you go in to see Mr Hargreaves?'

Sinclair's handsome features were set in a sulky expression. It was clear that he resented his reprimand. 'He'd asked me in the morning to come in sometime to show him the copy and layouts on a new scheme for Flowspeed Airlines. He asked me to come in between three and four o'clock. It was a custom of his to look at absolutely everything that was going through, so that he kept his fingers on every account. I didn't notice the bottle of sherry, but then I don't suppose I should have done, if it were on the sideboard.'

'He didn't offer you a drink?'

'No, he didn't drink with his staff – unless it was a special occasion of some sort. We had a drink this morning, I know, but that was unusual.'

'*We* is Mr Richard Hargreaves and yourself, I gather. What was the special occasion?'

Sinclair moved uneasily. 'Nothing much. E.H. got upset – he was very worried about Lionel, I think – and blew off the handle about our losing an account.'

'Who did he blow off the handle, as you put it, against. You?'

Sinclair moved again. 'Really, it's – it was all over in five minutes – '

'It was me,' Tracy said in a deep voice. 'Make what you can of it, Inspector. I walked out of the room before the olive branch was extended and the sherry bottle produced.'

'It was all over in five minutes,' Sinclair repeated. 'And we had a drink because it was eleven o'clock. That's all I meant by a special occasion.'

'Mr Hargreaves.' Richard Hargreaves was scuffing the carpet with his pointed shoe. 'Why did you go in to see your father?'

'A private matter.' He did not look up.

'We'll talk about it later. Did your father offer you a drink?' Richard shook his head. 'Did you notice the bottle of sherry?'

'I've been trying to remember.' Richard wearily passed his hand over his eyes. 'I *think* – I'm almost sure – it was standing in its usual place on the sideboard.'

'You couldn't swear to it?'

'No-o, I don't suppose I could.'

'All right. Mr Weston, I'd like to talk with you privately, and you too, Mr Hargreaves. Mr Tracy, if you'll leave Miss Bellamy's address, I'll be grateful. Then the rest of you can go.'

*

Bland sat at Lionel Hargreaves' old desk, and looked over it at the lawyer. 'I didn't question you out there, because I think I know part of what you've got to tell me. But I'll ask you the routine question. Did you notice the bottle of sherry?'

'Yes.' Weston nodded, and his jowls moved. 'It was on the sideboard when I left just before 3.30. I'll swear to that.'

'Why did you notice it?'

The lawyer's jowls shook a little as he laughed. 'Because I always look at it expectantly, in the hope that he'll offer me a drink, and he never has yet.' He stopped laughing, and added solemnly, 'And never will now, poor fellow. But let me tell you what I have to say, Inspector. I came along to see Hargreaves by appointment at three o'clock today, about a case the firm has against a man named Fairbrother, who has refused to pay for some display work done for him. At that time he seemed rather gloomy, but fairly calm and reasonable. Just after 4.30 he telephoned my office and said he wanted to see me as soon after five o'clock this afternoon as possible, for a specific purpose.'

'Let me guess,' Bland said. 'He wanted to make a new will.'

Weston's teeth clicked. 'Now, how did you know that?'

'Not very difficult. One, Richard told me last night that he was going to marry Eve Marchant very soon – you remember, I mentioned her to you yesterday. Two, his father strongly disapproved of the marriage. Three, E.H. telephoned you just after he saw his son. It might have been something else, but a new will seemed a good bet. Did he say anything to you about this will, its provisions, and so on? And what was his old will?'

'The existing will,' Mr Weston said portentously, 'shares the estate equally between Lionel and Richard. There are a few minor bequests of a hundred pounds here and there – I am myself beneficiary to the extent of a thousand pounds, which is more than I deserve, as I said to him at the time.' He coughed.

'What about Carruthers? Does he come in the will?'

Mr Weston's eyes were raised in surprise. 'He is one of the small beneficiaries. He is left a thousand pounds. I do not imagine he expects more, because he was down and out two years ago and E.H. gave him two thousand pounds, and told him then that he should not expect to be remembered in his will.'

'And the will means that when Lionel was murdered the estate went wholly to Richard, with the exception of those few items?'

'There was a clause to cover the death of either brother, in which case the other brother inherited. On the death of Lionel, Richard became the sole legatee.'

'All right. What about the new will?'

The lawyer spread out his hands. 'I wish I could tell you. All he said on the telephone was that he wanted me to come along to his office – he wanted to make a new will. I was surprised – not particularly by the request but by the urgency of it – and I asked him if it was really essential for me to come along this afternoon. He said, in a tone that indicated annoyance, that it *was* essential. No word passed between us about the provisions of the new will.'

'He didn't say anything to indicate what changes he had in mind?'

'Nothing at all. He merely said he wanted to make a new will, and said nothing at all as to its nature.'

'So that, for all you know, he may merely have wished to change a few minor bequests?'

Mr Weston pursed his lips. The effect was to make him look remarkably judicial. 'It is not likely that he would have asked me to come along here at such very short notice to change a few minor bequests.'

Bland stayed for a few moments staring into space, and then gave Weston a mechanical smile. 'One more thing. What is the size of the estate?' As the lawyer pursed his lips again, Bland said, 'I don't want anything more than a general idea.'

'In general terms,' the lawyer said solemnly, 'between ninety and one hundred thousand pounds.'

Bland whistled. 'As much as that? All right, Mr Weston. Thank you.' When the lawyer had gone, Bland sat still for a few moments, and then walked out of the room and across the corridor. Richard was standing in E.H.'s room, looking at the men who scurried about the room like ants. On his face was an expression of sullen despair. 'Come now,' Bland said, and his voice was kind. 'Things are not as bad as they seem. This routine activity must be endured. And after all – you were not so very fond of him.'

The young man looked up. An expression of surprise was on his face, and his voice was high-pitched and hysterical, as Bland had heard it once before. 'I hated his guts. But don't you understand what's happened?'

Bland steered him gently into Sinclair's room, and said, 'You tell me. Or would you prefer that I told you, and you can correct me when I go wrong. First of all – this afternoon you told your father that you were going to be married. He threatened to cut you out of his will, and you told him, I imagine, that he could do what he liked, but that you intended to marry Miss Marchant.'

Richard struck the desk with his fist. 'Why should I put up with everything all the time? I've been bullied all my life by him and Lionel.' His voice was shrill.

'Precisely. Now – can you tell me in detail what happened when you went in this afternoon? And what are – and were – your plans for the marriage?'

'I told him that I'd arranged to get married to Eve next week, by special licence. Now – I just don't know – I haven't seen Eve.' He flapped with his hands in the air. 'He asked me to forget it, and then at least to wait, and I wouldn't. That was what really upset him, I think – the fact that I insisted on holding out against his will, for once. He said all sorts of awful things about Eve – hateful things about her character, and about her being at the Splendid. He said she was nothing better than a prostitute, and that he'd send for Weston to alter his will. He said he'd wished I'd died instead of Lionel. In the end I walked out of the room.' Richard gave a curiously ladylike nod of the head.

'Did he say anything about the change in the will?'

'Yes – he was leaving his money to charity. He said, "I'm leaving my money out of the family now, Richard, so you can

cease to worry about it. It won't be of interest to you any more."
Then he said something about selecting a charity.'

'He didn't have time to make a will. He telephoned Weston,
but he died before seeing him.'

'Yes, I know.' Richard stared at Bland. 'You mean – you
can't mean – oh, this is too much.' Suddenly he put his head in
his hands and began to sob. There was no doubt that the sobs
were genuine. Bland stood looking at him thoughtfully until
they had subsided, and Richard looked up, revealing a tear-
stained face. 'I'm sorry. It's not that I was fond of my father,
or of Lionel for that matter. But all this happening in a couple
of days – I'm afraid it's upset me.' He wiped his eyes with a
fine linen handkerchief. 'I swear to you that I had nothing to
do with all this.'

Bland was a little impatient. 'I didn't say you had. Are you
sure you've nothing else at all to tell me? Either about your
conversation this afternoon with your father, or about anything
else?'

Richard shrugged his shoulders with a girlish and appealing
gesture, and spoke with what seemed to be complete sincerity.
'Before God, Inspector, I swear to you that I've nothing else to
tell.'

# XI

## *6.30 to 7 p.m.*

Filby's face was rather red. 'It seems a bit hard to blame me for
not finding out about the dirty pictures, I must say, sir. After
all, you never said anything about – '

'I didn't say I blamed you, Filby. Don't be so sensitive. Let's
have a look at these drawings you've found. I'm a bit puzzled
about them. Tell me again, and carefully, how you came to find
them.'

'Well – it's a bit of a funny thing at that. These drawings

were out in the passage. Fire had burned pretty well all the papers in the rooms – wooden filing cabinets make beautiful firewood.'

'No indication of how they had got into the passage?'

'None at all. Fire was in the rooms, so they're only a bit singed.'

Bland went over to a side table and carefully unwrapped the tissue paper in which Filby had put the drawings. He studied them for some time without expression, while Filby stood by his side with his hands on his hips. 'Filthy, aren't they?' Filby said with relish.

'They're competent, too – that's the thing that interests me. And another thing that interests me is the signature.' Bland pointed to the bottom of two of the drawings, where the letters ARTES were printed neatly. 'All the same, aren't they?'

'Yes, all signed like that. What d'you make of that?'

'It gives us a lead. Put someone on to watch van Dieren's place at Earls Court and bring him in if he turns up there. And pack up these drawings and bring them with you – I want you to come with me on these calls tonight.'

'What, me? I'm tired. Haven't had any sleep since this thing started. What d'you want *me* for?'

'Witness to things said and done,' Bland said curtly. 'Now tell me about Polly Lines.'

'She was murdered. Hit on the head first, and then suffocated. If the girl had given the alarm a bit later, we might never have known about it. But now what do we know, what have we got?'

'No word of van Dieren or anyone else having been on the scene this afternoon?'

'Not a word or a sign. How did you get on over the old man being popped off? Any clues?'

'There are a few things, but nothing important or decisive. Tracy made a lot of fuss about van Dieren – he was there this afternoon and behaved suspiciously – but I don't know. I'm being led to a conclusion I don't like at all, Filby. I don't believe it's true, either, but I can't get away from it.' He stared at Filby. 'I wish I could understand about Jones.'

'If you ask *me*, Jones was an absolute and complete red herring,' Filby said. He fumbled for a handkerchief in his coat sleeve, failed to find it, and wiped his nose with the back of his hand. 'I can't see he links up with anything. He's been put in simply to exercise your brains.'

Bland was still staring at Filby, with his eyes wide. 'My God, I wonder if that's it.'

'What's what?' Filby asked, bewildered by the fact that his remarks were taken so seriously.

'Shut up, Filby. I must think.' Bland sat down at his desk, and put his head on his hands. Filby looked at him with complete incomprehension. When the Inspector looked up two or three minutes later, his eyes were shining. 'I believe it is,' he said softly. 'I believe that's the way it's being worked. Talking to you does me good, Filby.'

Filby beamed. 'Talking to you does me good, too,' he said handsomely, and Bland was momentarily disconcerted.

'I don't know that it's necessary to pay those calls now – but perhaps we'd better. After all, I may be wrong.' He walked over to the window. 'The fog is lifting.'

'Who are you going to call on?'

'As many people as we have time for – Bond, Sinclair, Carruthers, Tracy, Mrs Rogers, pretty well everyone connected with the case. And we must certainly pay a visit to van Dieren's house. That may be useful.'

'We shall never get round London tonight.'

'We certainly shan't if we don't start soon,' Bland said cheerfully. 'I'll pay a call on my friend Sinclair first, and you wait downstairs – I shan't want you with me for that interview.'

# XII

'I must say,' Sinclair said, 'I think you were awfully rude.'

'That was partly tactical, and partly that I felt sour,' Bland said. 'It did seem to me that one of you should have put a spoke in Tracy's wheel, and that you could have done it. But it also seemed to me that it would ease a difficult situation if I got a little tough.' He sipped reflectively, and looked at the amber liquid in his glass, then at his surroundings. His eyes moved from the early Picasso and Rouault reproductions, to the Finnish wood tables and chairs, the plain maroon carpet, and finally came to rest on the flickering glow of the fire. 'This is a pleasant flat. Do you look after yourself?'

Sinclair laughed. 'I'm not so industrious, or so domesticated, as all that. These are service flats – a woman comes in and does for me. This is her evening off. And my brother lives here with me, and lends a hand. My elder brother,' he said, as Bland raised eyebrows in surprise. 'Ten years older than I am – before your time at school. He's a stock jobber.' With no change of tone, and with his usual bright smile, Sinclair said, 'I'm in the top class of suspects now, I suppose?'

'Why?'

Sinclair's grin was engaging. 'It seems to me that in what may be called the Case of the Poisoned Sherry there are only five starters – the people who went in the room and had a chance to poison the sherry. Van Dieren, Weston, Bond, Sinclair, Richard – you pays your money, gentlemen, and you takes your choice. And since you seem to think it's not van Dieren, can you wonder that my collar feels uncomfortably tight, especially when you snap at me because I didn't stop one of our directors from sending home a member of the staff?'

'I didn't say it wasn't van Dieren – in fact, I'm prepared to agree that he seems to have had the best chance of dropping the poison in the sherry. I simply pointed out that there's no cast-iron case against him.'

'Have you seen van Dieren – has he offered any explanation?'

'If he explains, it will be at Scotland Yard,' Bland said grimly. 'His so-called art agency was a cover for selling dirty drawings – but, somehow, I don't feel we shall see friend van Dieren again until we look for him.' He told Sinclair what they had found at Old Bridge Street. 'Now, he may or may not have killed this girl, but he almost certainly knows the game is up at Old Bridge Street, and he won't go back there. There are only two explanations of his conduct – either he's the murderer, in which case we've got to find a genuine motive and link between him and the Hargreaves family – or he's acting for the murderer, without knowing what he's doing. If we adopt that second idea, then the window might have been smashed deliberately, and the fire started deliberately, to throw suspicion on van Dieren. But if that's so, I wouldn't be much inclined to take out an insurance policy on van Dieren's life – from the murderer's point of view, he'll have served his purpose, and can now be eliminated.'

'What about these drawings – is there any clue in them?'

'They're signed ARTES. Does that suggest anything to you?'

Sinclair pondered. 'Not unless the artist's initials are R.T.S. Is it an anagram or something?'

'Something like that, I think. But I don't know that it has anything to do with the murder.'

'So we're left with the problem of the five suspects,' Sinclair said. He poured more sherry in Bland's glass. 'It's narrowed down now, isn't it, to one of the five people who, if Miss Peachey is telling the truth, went in the room and had the opportunity of poisoning the sherry. Or do you think there was an unseen person? – like someone in a John Dickson Carr locked-room mystery?'

'There was no unseen person.'

'Then it was one of those five people?'

'It was one of those five people.' Bland drank his sherry at a gulp, under Sinclair's disapproving eye, and stood up. 'Look for the question of motive – and remember that the obvious is very often the true.' As Bland put his hand on the door, the handle turned from the outside, and a man came in. He was an older edition of Sinclair, with the same tall, graceful figure, the same fair hair and bright blue eyes, but with a gravity that contrasted sharply with Sinclair's air of slight irresponsibility. 'I beg your pardon, Charles,' he said. 'I had no idea you were engaged.'

'This is my brother Edgar – genius of the Stock Exchange. Edgar, this is Inspector Bland, who was at school with me, but is none the less just about to arrest me for poisoning my employer's sherry.' With a friendly grin, Sinclair said, 'Have a drink?'

Bland's last impression was of Edgar Sinclair saying, in a voice that sounded as if he had a plum in his mouth, 'I do trust you are joking, Charles. Thank you, I do not think I will have a drink.' When he got outside, Bland saw with some pleasure that visibility had improved. After lending its assistance to the murderer during the afternoon the fog, he reflected, was now obligingly giving the police a hand. He got into his car, and sat for a moment at the wheel. 'Carruthers,' he said. 'Yes, next, I think, Carruthers. But I must pick up Filby.'


# XIII

## *8.0 to 8.30 p.m.*

Mansfield Court was a small block of flats in dirty red brick, just off Balham High Street. It had an air of genteel dinginess, the hall was badly lighted, there was no porter and no lift. Rows of numbered doors ran along either side of an uncarpeted corridor. Number 73 was on the first floor. When Bland knocked there was silence for a moment, and then he heard a key turn in a lock. It might have been half a minute afterwards that the door opened and the figure of Carruthers, collarless and a little flustered, stood in the doorway. He took a step back when he saw Bland and Filby behind him, and an expression of dismay showed on his face. He said, with an attempt at composure, 'I was just having supper. Come in.' He waved apologetically to a table where bread and cheese and half a beetroot lay like a still-life. 'I should like to ask you to share it, but you see my meal is simple. If you'd care for some bread and cheese – or some coffee – ' He began to flutter towards a door. 'This is my little kitchenette – '

'No thank you.' Bland's tone was not pleasant. He took from under his arm the drawings Filby had found in van Dieren's office, and put them on the table. 'I believe these are your work.'

'Mine?' Carruthers gasped. He almost danced round the table in his excitement and alarm. After a first horrified glance he made no attempt to touch or look at the drawings. 'Not *mine* – you must be mistaken – these have nothing to do with me.'

'Come now, do not be ashamed of your handiwork. I am no art expert, but these seem to be competently done.' Bland's voice was menacing. He pointed to the signature, and said softly, 'ARTES. Doesn't that mean anything to you?'

'Certainly not.' Carruthers' eyes were wild.

'Next time, use another pseudonym. It doesn't need a cryptographer to discover that the letters A-R-T-E-S in that order are alternate letters of your surname, beginning with the second and ending with the tenth. If further evidence is needed, I imagine our art experts can provide it.'

'Further evidence.' Carruthers sat down suddenly, and his face was white. 'You don't mean you're going to prosecute me?'

'You acknowledge that these are your work? I'm asking you in front of a witness.'

'I – I don't know – you must realize my position, Inspector – '

'Do you admit it?'

'Yes,' Carruthers said, and looked away.

'All right. You understand that the dissemination of this kind of stuff is punishable by law? If you want to avoid that, you'd better answer some questions. Truthfully, this time.'

Carruthers' voice was muffled. 'Anything. I've been a fool, I know, but – '

'When did you start doing these things? Who put you in touch with van Dieren?'

'It all began eighteen months ago – '

'Just about the time van Dieren set up in business, in fact?'

Carruthers seemed disconcerted. 'I don't know. Was it? It may not have been so long.'

'Did you know him before he took over this business?'

'No, no.' He shook his head emphatically. 'I think it was soon after he'd started up. I was very hard up at the time – you see the style in which I live.' He waved a hand round the tiny flat with its worn blue carpet and hideous furniture. 'It's not easy to make a living and stay free and independent. It's an important thing to be independent,' he said, and looking at his wistful, weak blue eyes, Bland recognized him as a type of the defeated artist, the sensitive man who has not the capacity or the strength of will to produce a work of art.

'Did you ask Hargreaves to help you?'

'I'd rather starve,' Carruthers said, and the detective was surprised by the violence of his tone. 'You know what they saw about him – he throws his money about like a man throwing fly-paper. My God, no. I asked him for money once, and he gave it me, but the way he did it – I'd never ask him for money again.

'It was while I was on my beam ends that someone told me about this man van Dieren, and that he'd pay good money for stuff like this. I – '

'Who told you?'

Carruthers said readily enough, 'Somebody named McGillivray, in an advertising agency. But he died last year, so you can't ask him about it. Well, I started working for van Dieren, and he paid me – not very much, but a good deal more than I'd been getting. He always paid me by cash – said it was better that way. I used to take the things up, wrapped in brown paper, and give them to that girl Polly Lines – she knows all about it, of course,' he said spitefully. 'Van Dieren tried to browbeat me, and I wouldn't stand for that. You've got to preserve your independence – it's what I've been trying to do all my life.' His mouth set in a weak but obstinate line.

'You choose a queer way of doing it,' Bland said coolly. 'Did van Dieren ever ask you anything about the Hargreaves offices?'

'The Hargreaves offices?' Carruthers echoed, on a note of surprise. 'Why, no; he said something about how badly E.H. had treated him – I told you about that.'

'He didn't ask about a bottle of sherry, and where it stood in Edward Hargreaves' room? You didn't tell him anything about that?'

'Good Lord, no.' Carruthers was staring in astonishment. 'What on earth made you think so?'

Bland did not answer. 'When I saw van Dieren he chuckled, and said he was going to see you. Last night you told me he'd telephoned you, and you were seeing him today. What did he talk to you about?'

'I never saw him. He sent a telegram, telling me not to come. Here it is.' Carruthers took down a telegram, still in its orange envelope, from the mantelpiece, and handed it to Bland. The detective read: CANCEL ARRANGEMENT THIS AFTERNOON SOMETHING CROPPED UP UNEXPECTEDLY GOING OUT LONDON FOR A FEW DAYS VAN DIEREN. The telegram had been handed in at 9.30 that morning. 'I had an appointment for half past three this afternoon. But what's the matter – what's all the trouble about?'

'This afternoon Edward Hargreaves died in his office from drinking sherry that had been doctored by hyoscin. There is a strong possibility that your friend' – Carruthers made a movement of protest – 'your *employer* van Dieren was responsible for the insertion of the hyoscin. This afternoon also van Dieren's offices were burnt down, and this girl, Miss Lines, found dead, under conditions which make us suspect that she had been murdered. Your works of art were salvaged from the fire.'

Filby stuck his neck forward and spoke for the first time. 'Where were *you* this afternoon?'

'I was at home here, doing some work. But I can't prove it. I haven't an alibi, I'm afraid.' He smiled weakly. 'My best alibi is that I only benefit to the tune of a thousand pounds. E.H. told me that a long time ago. Not much reward, is it? But, my God, what a terrible thing it is. Poor E.H. – what an end, after a life like his, to die from drinking doctored sherry.'

'When did you last go up to van Dieren's office?'

'Three or four weeks ago, I should think. I haven't been there since you said he was mixed up in Lionel's affair. I didn't want to have anything to do with all that.' An earnest, pleading look was in Carruthers' eyes, and he made a motion towards the drawings on the table. 'What are you going to do about those things? For God's sake give me a chance. I swear I'll never touch this kind of thing again.'

Bland stood staring at the floor. Then he picked up the drawings, walked over to the small coal fire, and put them on the red coals. He held them there with the poker until they were ash. When he turned round there were tears in Carruthers' eyes. He started to speak, but Bland stopped him. 'There's no need to say anything. I've burnt those drawings because I'm looking for a murderer, not a petty crook, and some of the things you've told us may be useful. But if I find you playing about with this kind of thing again I'll crack down so smartly you'll be in prison inside twenty-four hours.'

When they were outside Filby said, 'It's something to have got those things cleared up, but you were too easy. He's a slimy little devil – why did you let him go?'

'He'll do us more good outside prison than in it. I think, with what we know now, we can really forget our other calls, but perhaps a visit to Bond may be useful.'

# XIV

Bond's house in Highgate was a semi-detached two-storey house
in a row of semi-detached two-storey houses. A step up, Bland
thought, on Mansfield Court in social solidity, but still nothing
very impressive – hardly a house that justified the air of a
successful man that Bond maintained. The small iron gate
creaked a little, and a light came on in the front room downstairs. A tall woman, running to fat, appeared in the doorway
in answer to Bland's ring.

'Is Mr Bond in?'

'Who wants him?' Her voice was shrill. 'Anyway, he's not
in. You'll find him at the Crown if you want him.'

'I'm a policeman,' Bland said, and she took a step backwards.
'There's nothing at all to be worried about, Mrs Bond. May we
come in for a moment?'

'All right,' she said grudgingly, and Bland walked into a
suburban sitting-room, filled with knick-knacks and photographs. Two armchairs were placed symmetrically in relation to
an electric imitation coal fire. Lace curtains were at the window,
and two pink basket chairs stood on a maroon carpet patterned
in yellow. Bland sat down in one of the chairs, and Filby sat
opposite him on the edge of another. Bland said enthusiastically,
'What a charming room. Have you lived here long?'

'Ten years.' In the light Mrs Bond was revealed as a big
sulky-looking woman in her late thirties. She might have been
handsome in a hard way ten years ago, but now she had a
pronounced middle-age spread. She wore no make-up. 'What
do you want him for? Is anything wrong?'

'I simply want to ask him a question. Is he usually out at this
time in the evening?'

She drew herself up. 'He certainly is *not*. Tonight's his night for going to play in the darts team, otherwise he's home as regular as clockwork every night. My old man may have his faults, but he's always regular coming home, though I won't say he's always in a good temper when he comes. But what's the question you want to ask?'

'After all, which of us hasn't got his faults?' Bland laughed pleasantly. 'Your husband was a bit late home tonight, though, wasn't he?'

She nodded. 'And his dinner in the oven for an hour and a half. But what did you want – ' She paused as the front door slammed. 'There he is now. They must have got the darts over quicker than usual.' They heard the clatter of a stick in the hall.

Bond was neither pleased nor surprised to see them. 'What's the trouble now? It's bad enough to be mixed up in a lot of bloody murders at the office without having them brought into your home. What do you want?'

His wife interpreted his mood correctly. 'Did you lose at darts?'

'Yes, I did. And who wouldn't lose at darts when they've been put on edge by a lot of people being shot and poisoned? And everyone asking questions about it down at the Crown. I wish I'd never gone down tonight.' He sat down and began to unlace his shoes.

'There are just two questions, and the first one is personal. Why do you use a stick for walking?'

Bond looked up with a startled and furious face, and then decided to laugh. 'Well, I don't know. Don't tell me you've got around to suspecting *me*. That's a bit too much of a good thing.'

'Why don't you tell them – show them you've got nothing to hide,' his wife said anxiously. She turned to Bland. 'He's always had – '

Bond turned on his wife. 'Shut up. I'll tell them all right, and in my own way. I've had one leg shorter than the other since birth.'

'That's true.' His wife nodded solemnly. 'That's absolutely true. He should wear a surgical boot, but he won't.'

'You look a little doubtful, Inspector,' Bond said sardonically. 'Perhaps this will convince you.' He took off his sock and stood up. His left leg was smooth and white, and it was immediately apparent that it was a little shorter than the right.

'Thank you. Just one more question. When you went in to see Hargreaves at half past three, was he smoking a cigarette?'

'I don't have to think much about that one,' Bond said. 'He wasn't. He was a non-smoker.'

'Thank you.' Bland got up and put on his hat. Filby got up, and put on his hat too, looking absolutely bewildered. 'I'm sorry if I've been a trouble to you.'

Bond stared at him. 'Do you mean to say you came out here to ask those two questions? You must be crazy. I always thought the police force wasted a lot of public money, but this beats everything.'

'There *was* another reason, but I hardly like to mention it,' Bland said. 'We came here because I never can resist your sweet smile. Good night.'


# XV

### 9.30 to 10.30 p.m.

'I can't make head or tail of all this,' Filby said. 'I understand why you wanted to know about his leg – to make sure he wasn't Jones – but what the devil was all that about a cigarette? What does it matter whether Hargreaves was smoking or not?'

'It doesn't matter – I just said that to give him something to take his mind off the other question. But it might matter that Bond is a good family man, who comes home punctually in the evening. I didn't care much for his wife, but I don't think she was lying about that. What are the other names on our list?'

'Tracy, Mrs Rogers, Richard Hargreaves, Eve Marchant, van Dieren, Weston. Shall we go and see Eve Marchant?'

'I think not. Telephone the Yard, and see if there's any news of van Dieren.'

'OK.' Filby returned in five minutes. 'Not a trace,' he said cheerfully. 'They're keeping a watch on his flat in Earls Court, but he's not turned up. Smelled a rat all right.'

'Let's have a look at his flat, and then call it a night.' He put the car into gear, and then swung away from the kerb.

'Why don't we call on Tracy?'

'If you tell me how he could have poisoned the sherry, we'll go along and see him.'

'Then the murderer *did* go into the room?'

'Of course he did.'

'I don't see why you can't simply tell me who it is, if you think you know.'

'I don't tell you, because this is still all purely theoretical. I'm still in need of proof. If my ideas are right, this story is so astonishing that nobody will believe it without proof. It's possible that I shall find some of the things I'm looking for at van Dieren's house. Or I may find that I'm making a big mistake – but I don't think I am.' Filby lapsed into a sulky silence which he preserved until they reached Earls Court. There, in a narrow street of small shabby houses, Bland stopped the car, and they got out. 'Where's – oh, there you are, Hemming.' A man who had been concealed in the shadow said, 'Evening, Inspector. Good thing the fog's cleared. Couldn't see much before that.'

'But you're sure no one's been in the house?' Bland's voice was sharp.

'No doubt about that. It's the second on the right, dirty little place it looks. No back entrance and no garden.'

'Did you make enquiries about van Dieren in the neighbourhood?'

'Ridley did that, sir. Seems nobody knows much about him – bit of a mystery man, and they didn't see much of him. Used to come home late, and go out early. One thing that may be interesting – a girl used to come home with him sometimes – somebody saw her leave about two o'clock one morning.'

'What did she look like?'

'Only a vague report, but they say she was short and fair.'

'Polly Lines,' Bland said thoughtfully. 'Good work, Hemming. Filby and I are going in now, and we shall probably be half an hour. Who's on with you?'

'Peplow, sir. He's down the road.'

'If anybody approaches while we're in there follow them and stop them from coming in. Then let me know.' They moved silently along the pavement, and turned in at the second house on the right. Even in the dim light of a street lamp they could see that the windows were dirty, and that paint was flaking off the door. Bland produced a bunch of keys and fiddled with the lock. Behind him Filby was breathing heavily. 'Shall I do it?'

'If you'll stand to the left so that I have a little light,' Bland said rather irritably, 'I may be able to – ' He stopped, for one of the keys had unlocked the door, and it had swung open with a slight creak. 'Now, first of all let's make sure there's no one here.'

'Dead, you mean?'

'Dead, drugged, or alive and kicking.' They searched the house. There were two small rooms and a scullery on the ground floor, and two rooms on the first floor, and it did not take them long to discover that there was certainly no one in the house. When they had finished, Filby pushed his hat to the back of his head and looked at Bland, with an expression of astonishment. 'This is a damned rum go if you like. What the devil does it mean?'

'Let's have another look at these rooms downstairs.' The sitting-room was decorated with a dark blue paper covered with magenta flowers. A piece of dirty hair carpet was on the floor, and the furniture consisted of a small dark wooden table, an old padded easy-chair, and a bookcase containing some dozen books in brown-paper wrappers. The bedroom contained a divan bed, with the bedclothes made, an inset cupboard, and a chest of drawers. Both cupboard and chest of drawers were empty. In the scullery they found crockery on a small dresser, stale bread in a bin, and some liver sausage in a small blue safe. The upstairs rooms were covered in dust, contained no furniture at all, and were plainly unused. The small table in the sitting-room and the chest of drawers in the bedroom looked remarkably clean among the surrounding dirt. Curtains that were almost black with dirt covered the windows in sitting-room and bedroom, screening them from the road.

'What a bloody awful place to live,' Filby said, and shivered. 'And what an empty one too. No secrets here.'

'No bodies, you mean.' Bland's eyes were gleaming. 'The place is full of secrets. One, the mystery of the missing clothes. Two, the mystery of the polished furniture. Three, the mystery of the paper-covered books. Why did he put those books in paper covers?'

'Perhaps he was fussy about them.'

'If you can judge by the dirt, that's the last thing he was. But let's have a look at them.' Bland opened one, and his eyebrows went up. '*Justine* – the Marquis de Sade.' He opened another. '*The One Hundred and Twenty Days of Sodom* – more de Sade. *Miss Smith's Torture Chamber*. There's one mystery cleared up – anyone would want to keep these in brown-paper wrappers. But it's curious that van Dieren's own tastes should be pornographic, like the things he sold, don't you think?'

'I can't see anything curious about it. If he wasn't interested in the damned stuff he wouldn't have started selling it, or asked that little pip Carruthers to do it for him in the first place.'

'You're perfectly right, of course.' Bland tapped his teeth. 'And yet I feel it's suggestive. Doesn't it suggest anything to you, Filby?'

'No.'

Bland sighed. 'Then take the most mysterious thing. Where are van Dieren's clothes? It's clear that since he lived here he must have kept them here. Did he take them away himself this morning, with the intention of skipping – or did someone else remove them, and why? For that matter, why did van Dieren do it? What could his clothes tell us about him that we don't know already? And then the polished table and chest of drawers, and the neatly stacked washing-up, compared with the surrounding dinginess. Don't those points add up to something?'

Filby pushed his hat to the back of his head. 'They add up to a headache. The whole case adds up to a headache.'

Bland opened the front door. 'I want men kept on here in case van Dieren should turn up, though I don't think he will. And get the place fingerprinted in the morning. We may get something out of that.'

'Did you find what you wanted?'

'I found what I expected, but I don't know that it does any good. We need our small piece of luck now to clinch the case.'

## SATURDAY, JANUARY 18 TO SATURDAY, FEBRUARY, 1

Bland's attitude and activities during the next fortnight bewildered Filby, who became doubtful at times whether the Inspector was not losing his grip on the case. At first he was keen, and nervously anxious for news; as days went by without any dramatic development, it seemed to Filby that he became gloomy about the case – though he seemed less to show gloom than an apathetic lack of interest in what was happening. Nor did some of his enquiries seem to Filby to make very good sense.

The first of these activities, which Bland put in hand with a good deal of enthusiasm, was to issue a warrant for van Dieren's arrest on a charge of murder. 'Murder?' Filby said. 'So it was van Dieren – I said so all the time.' Bland was non-committal. 'We've certainly got enough evidence to call him in, and if he's innocent this may make him show up. I want a special watch kept on ports – it's most important that he shouldn't get out of the country. And the papers can splash it as much as they like – but perhaps I'd better see to that myself.' And he did see to it, so that headlines like HUE-AND-CRY FOR VANISHED ART AGENT and ADVERTISING MURDERS: POLICE WATCH PORTS appeared in the *Howl* and *Shout*. 'He'll not get out of the country,' Filby said confidently. But he was not so confident when some days had passed without anything being seen of van Dieren. Dozens of reports of people seen 'answering the description of the wanted man' (a description provided by Bond and Carruthers, and checked by Bland from his recollection of the art agent) were followed up without success.

Nor was there any success with the fingerprinting of van Dieren's little house. There were very few fingerprints, and it became obvious that the table and chest of drawers found in the cottage, and some of the kitchen utensils, had been carefully cleaned and polished so that there were no prints at all on them.

A few prints were found elsewhere, some of them on the books in the brown-paper covers: but these proved to be the prints of Polly Lines. No other prints were found in the cottage. This worried Bland more than Filby. As the tall man very reasonably said, why worry about prints when they hadn't got van Dieren? And when they got van Dieren they would hardly need the prints. But this argument did not make Bland less depressed.

It was on the first day of this dreary fortnight that Bland, to Filby's surprise, put a man on to trailing Richard Hargreaves. 'I told him a couple of days ago that he's in a dangerous situation,' Bland said, and when Filby asked why, the Inspector merely smiled and said facetiously. 'Isn't marriage always a dangerous project?' The reports of the men who trailed Richard, however, made dull reading. His days were fully occupied at the office, where, they learned from Sinclair, he was working surprisingly hard, and with surprising enthusiasm, to fit himself for the post which he now occupied as head, and in fact owner, of the Agency. Where he had been lackadaisical he was now energetic; where he had once confessed ignorance with a shrug of the shoulders, he now showed himself keen to learn. His evenings were spent with Eve Marchant, in a round of dinners, cinemas and theatres. He did no entertaining, and drank very little.

Most of the other instructions Bland gave him seemed to Filby very curious. The telegrams to New York, Paris and Amsterdam, asking whether anyone answering the name or description of Joseph van Dieren was known to them, were, of course, more or less routine matters: and Bland seemed even slightly cheered when they were answered in the negative. Further enquiries to New York produced information regarding the mysterious Joe Riddell whose story van Dieren had told to Bland as his own. The Inspector did not seem particularly pleased or surprised when he learned that Joe Riddell, who had indeed served a sentence of two years imprisonment for embezzlement in an affair in which a young man named Edward Hargreaves had been mixed up, died in 1933. He had been in prison several times on charges of embezzlement and fraudulent company promotion.

A mysterious line of enquiry which produced surprising but hardly useful results was an attempt to obtain some traces of van Dieren's past activities. About these it seemed to Filby that Bland was unnecessarily and uncharacteristically fussy and irritable. He insisted, for example, on an elaborate investigation being made among all van Dieren's neighbours in Earl's Court to discover whether any of them recalled his personal habits, or remembered details of the visits of Polly Lines. Had anyone noticed van Dieren smoking a pipe or a cigarette when he came out in the morning? Did he carry an umbrella? How many times had Polly Lines been seen entering and leaving the house, and was there any indication whether or not she had stayed the night? How much milk did the milkman leave? Where did van Dieren get his groceries, and how often were they delivered? These were some of the extraordinary questions to which Filby found answers. The answers were all of them what might have been expected, and they did nothing to lift Bland's gloom. Very few people remembered van Dieren leaving his house – they had other things to think about – and nobody recalled him smoking a pipe or a cigarette, or using an umbrella. Polly Lines (or somebody answering her description) had been seen to enter the house some half-dozen times, and twice had been seen to leave in the early hours of the morning. Nobody remembered other visitors, and van Dieren was known as a man who kept himself to himself, and never talked about his business. The milkman left half a pint of milk every other day, and was paid at the end of the week. The groceries, delivered weekly, were such as it might have been expected a single man would order.

One curious thing was discovered when Bland ordered an investigation into the length of time that van Dieren had lived in the house, and occupied his office, and asked Filby to obtain the agreements. There was no agreement for the office, which had been rented monthly, but the house had been taken on a year's tenancy, and the house agent had a copy of the agreement. It was not, however, made out in the name of van Dieren, but in that of Polly Lines! Filby saw the house agent, who was able to remember quite clearly the letting of the house. Van Dieren had called on him, had inspected the house, and agreed to take it. He had paid a year's rent down, so that the agent, very pleased to let the place that was in a poor state of repair without doing any work on it, had made no enquiries about his financial status. And when the time came to sign the agreement, he had telephoned and said that for private reasons the agreement was to be made out in the name of Miss Lines. This had been done, and although the agent thought this a curious thing, he had thought it wise to ask no questions.

Bland received the news with more annoyance than he had yet shown over the hold-up in the case. 'He's a cunning devil.' He walked up and down his small office with furious impatience. 'If something doesn't break soon, Filby, I shall have to do something to make it break, and I don't want to do that.'

'I've got an idea about this agreement,' Filby said, and although Bland's raised eyebrows were not encouraging, he proceeded to unfold it. 'What's to have stopped them getting married?'

'Who?' Bland asked. He sounded quite startled.

'Van Dieren and Polly Lines. *There's* a reason why the agreement was made out in her name. She had some sort of hold over him, made him marry her, insisted on the agreement being in her name, so that she kept hold on his affairs. In the end he had to kill her to break the hold – some form of blackmail maybe, mixed up with the Hargreaves family. How's that?'

'Out,' Bland said, and laughed when Filby looked annoyed. On the same day the Inspector, who had spent a good part of the past two days sitting at his desk in what appeared to be a trance of inaction, got up and went out. When he came back he looked a little happier. 'I've been to see Myrtle Montague,' he said, 'to ask some more questions about her sister.'

'Did you ask whether she'd ever said anything about getting married?'

'I did, and she hadn't. Myrtle says she wasn't the marrying kind.' Filby looked disappointed. 'What she did say was that

her sister told her once or twice that she was frightened of van
Dieren, and that he did ever such funny things. When Myrtle
asked what kind of things she giggled, and wouldn't say. Once
she said she thought he was mad. Polly didn't tell her sister
anything about staying at Earls Court, although Myrtle knows
she went there, from remarks she dropped at odd times. But
Myrtle's quite certain that Polly never married van Dieren – she
was too much afraid of him for that.'

Filby was not dismayed. 'It was an idea, anyway,' he said
rather nastily, and it was certainly true that Bland had contri-
buted nothing in the way of ideas lately. 'And here's another
one, that's been going round in my brain for a day or two.
Suppose van Dieren's dead.'

Bland was playing with his monkey paperweight. He did not
say anything.

'If those early ideas of yours were right – and he's *not* the
murderer after all, but some sort of – ' Filby reached for a word,
and discovered it with some pride ' – *scapegoat*, then he
might have been bumped off. It's funny he's not turned up by
now.' This was a week after the news had been splashed in the
papers.

'Not so funny,' Bland said rather absently. 'Don't forget that
there are indications that he planned a getaway, eliminated
traces by which he thought we might follow him, and so on. It's
one thing to go into hiding when you've made no preparation
for it, and another to proceed according to an elaborate and
well-laid plan.'

Filby was irritated. 'You don't seem to have any constructive
suggestions.' Before Bland could reply the telephone bell rang,
and he picked up his receiver. 'Sinclair? Show him in.' He
turned to Filby a more cheerful face than he had shown for a
couple of days. 'Prelude to action, I hope,' he said. 'I'll see him
alone.'

Sinclair's bright handsomeness illuminated the drab room. 'So
this is your cubby-hole,' he said, as he sat down. Bland laughed.

'Not quite so impressive as an advertising executive's office,
I'm afraid.'

'But socially much more useful. I came in, like a faithful Watson, to see if there was any news on the case, and to give you one or two snippets, if you're interested. We've not seen you around the office lately.'

'I've been busy,' Bland said vaguely. 'Thinking and worrying. And I find this is the best place to do that. As for news, if you mean news of van Dieren, there just isn't any. He's vanished into thin air for the moment, but it's only a matter of time before we get him.'

Sinclair looked at him curiously. 'I suppose you're quite sure he's the murderer? But you're bound to say yes to that – after all, there's a warrant out for his arrest. But there are some pretty queer rumours floating round the office. I don't know if you're interested – '

'I'm always interested in rumours.'

'I don't know where to begin,' Sinclair pondered, frowning. 'And I hardly know where the rumours started. But it's about Dick Hargreaves. Should I be right in thinking that there's a hell of a strong circumstantial case against Dick?'

'You might be. Let's hear it.'

'Point one – as Bond said to me a couple of days ago – *cui bono*? And Richard certainly profits, whereas it's hard to see that van Dieren or anyone else does, or did. From being a humble younger son, rather out of the limelight, he's become sole owner of a big advertising agency, and worth a hell of a lot of money.

'Next – this is a bit intangible, but it's been noticed by most of the people who come in contact with him – there's been a change in Dick since E. H. died. He's much more pleasant, works harder, even seems a bit less of a pansy. I dare say that's partly the influence of Eve Marchant, and it's certainly all to the good. But somehow – so soon after E. H.'s death – although nobody loved E. H., people don't like it.'

'I see.' Bland was looking at the paperweight on his desk. 'There's nothing else – nothing more tangible?'

'Only the fact that Dick is going to marry this girl very soon.

Nobody likes that – it leaves a bad taste in the mouth. But he seems to have been completely under her thumb.'

Bland was looking depressed. 'Any other developments?'

'Only a bit more marriage news. Tracy and Mrs Rogers. Her husband's agreed to divorce her at last. I'm very pleased – they're both nice people.' Sinclair's forehead crinkled as he leaned forward. 'Look here, it *is* Dieren, isn't it? I've been puzzling my brain trying to work out what you told me a few days ago. You as good as said you knew the name of E. H.'s murderer.'

'I do.' Bland's voice was impersonal.

'And he was one of the people who went into E. H.'s room that afternoon?' Bland nodded. 'Then it *must* have been van Dieren. I can't see that anyone else had a chance to do it.'

'I haven't said it wasn't van Dieren. There's a warrant out for his arrest, you know.' Bland got up from his desk, and took his hat and coat. 'Thank you for the news. I've got to pay a call now.'

'Something to do with the case?'

'A call on Eve Marchant.'

In the sitting-room of the flat in Catherine Street two tall French windows reached almost to the ground. The thin January light came through them and showed the furniture that was too new, the china dogs standing on the mantelpiece, and the gay chintz curtains. Eve Marchant stood by the French windows and said, 'When are you going to catch this wretched man, Inspector? Not, personally, that I could care less.'

'You aren't interested in the arrest of your husband's murderer?'

She waved her hands. 'I don't think of him as my husband any more. Dick and I are going to be married soon, probably next week.' In her shrill voice she said, 'I don't see why we should put it off. Let people talk – I don't care what they say.'

'Don't you think you should tell him?'

'Tell him what?'

Bland looked at her unlined, smooth white neck, where a

muscle was throbbing. 'About the little stranger. I know he's a nice chap, and you think you've got him taped, but he won't be very pleased if he finds out afterwards.'

She stared at him without saying anything. An ormolu clock on the mantelpiece ticked through the silence. He said, 'If you're wondering how I know, let's be frank and say that I don't. But anyone can make a guess. You wouldn't have got Lionel tight and made him marry you unless you had some very good reason. Your friend Myrtle Montague used those exact words – a very good reason – and giggled over them. She didn't give you away – she told me she couldn't say what the reason was, because it was a secret, but one doesn't have to think very long or hard to discover it. You knew Lionel wasn't the sort of man who would give you what you wanted, you knew he'd never live with you or give you a home, but you thought you might be able to use the fact that you were married to him and that you were going to bear his child as a lever to work on his father. When you saw the way in which Lionel behaved you saw it was no use hoping for anything from him, and you turned to Richard. After Lionel was murdered and you saw what E. H. was like, you saw that you could never convince him of the truth of your story. It became imperative then that you should marry Richard as soon as possible.'

He thought that he had never seen her look more beautiful. She stood facing him, with her dark eyes staring, her hand gripping and twisting a paper spill, and the pulse throbbing in her neck. When she spoke she made no attempt to deny his assertion, but said simply, 'What business is it of yours?'

Bland's voice was quiet and friendly. 'It's not my business, and I'm sorry to hurt you by talking about it. But it's a piece of the puzzle, and I want you to tell me that it's true.'

'You're a good guesser. But not quite good enough, Mr Police Inspector.' I've lost another friend, Bland thought. She doesn't love me any more. 'I've told Dick already. He knows about it, and it doesn't make any difference. I told him, if you want to know, on the day he announced that we were going to be married.'

'I'm glad,' Bland said. 'Will you believe me when I say I'm sorry – '

She put her hand on her hip and struck a pose reminiscent of any bad actress playing the part of outraged but contemptuous virtue. 'No, I won't. It's no use trying any of your smarmy civility on me, do you understand that? I don't like insignificant little police sneaks. There's the door, and you can get outside it now. I don't want to see you again.'

'I couldn't care less,' Bland said. At least, he thought, when he was out in the street, she had given him an exit line. Unfortunately, it was one that was not quite true.


Bland told Filby about this visit to Eve Marchant, and the tall man was incredulous. 'But what's he marrying her for? Do you think she's telling the truth, and she *has* told him about it? Are you going to ask him and find out?'

'I don't think she'd try to bluff by saying she had told him when she hadn't. Too dangerous. And as to the reason for why he's marrying her, don't forget that she's a very beautiful woman. This guess helps to get a bit of the puzzle out of the way, that's all.'

Filby was disappointed. 'You don't think it's got anything to do with van Dieren or the murders, then?'

'Not directly. Is there any news on van Dieren, by the way?'

'Nothing, and if you ask me there won't be. Somebody's knocked him off.' Half an hour later Filby was dumbfounded when news came through that a man answering van Dieren's description, and giving that name, had been arrested in Liverpool, while boarding a ship for New York. Bland took the news coolly, but he left for Liverpool on the next train. While he was away, Filby read with some disgust more reports by the detectives put on to trail Richard Hargreaves, who was still living a blameless and uninteresting life, read the answers to *The Times* crossword puzzle on the previous day, compared them with the clues and still failed to understand them, disposed of several false reports of people who claimed to have seen van Dieren, and received another negative report from the men who were trying, so far unsuccessfully, to trace the purchase of the hyoscin. His spirits were maintained, however, by the thought that van Dieren had been taken and they were even raised during the afternoon by a visit from Myrtle Montague. He received her in Bland's office, and she seemed disappointed not to see the Inspector.

'He's away today,' Filby said easily. 'But anything you can tell him you can tell me. I'm his right-hand-man.'

She looked a little doubtful, but she said, 'It's simply that I've remembered something. I mean I forgot to tell Mr Bland something, and as I thought it might be important, I thought I'd drop in. I've never been at Scotland Yard before, you see.'

Filby beamed. 'What do you think of it?'

'*Super*.' She looked round. 'But this is a poky office. Yours, I suppose?'

'Certainly not.' Filby was more indignant than if it had really been his own office. 'This is the Inspector's room. What was it you wanted to tell him?'

'He came round to see me the other day – I must say he's *ever* so nice – and he was asking me what poor Polly said about that beast who killed her.' Filby took in suddenly the significance of her demure black dress, with its edge of white at the throat. 'And I told him that she said van Dieren sometimes did funny things and had funny habits, and then he asked me if she ever said *what* things and *what* habits, and *I* said she'd never mentioned any.' She paused to take a breath. 'That wasn't right. She *did* mention one thing.'

'Is that so?' Filby affected a little indifference, and pushed the Inspector's chair on to its back legs, as Bland did.

'She said he was so much afraid of soiling his hands that he always wore gloves at home.'

'Gloves.' Filby let down the chair with a bump that certainly was not typical of Bland. 'He wore gloves.'

'That's what Polly said. Is it so important?'

Filby's eyes were bulging, and he rubbed a slightly bristling cheek quickly with his hand. 'I should think it is.' He said craftily, 'She didn't say anything about the colour of the gloves.'

'I don't – think – so. She was always hinting that she could tell me terrible things about him, but she never said what they were. I'm sorry.'

'Not at all. You've been most helpful.' Filby showed her out with a vast and uncharacteristic beam spread over his features, and she stared at him as if he were a lunatic. Then he sank back into Bland's chair and began to tap his teeth with the Inspector's pencil. This, he thought, will certainly be something to ask van Dieren when the Inspector brings him back.

But he was wrong, for when Bland came in next day, as neatly dressed and as gloomy as ever, it was to say that the arrested man was not van Dieren, or not the right van Dieren. He was a perfectly respectable Dutch commercial traveller, who bore a slight resemblance to the wanted van Dieren in height, age and build, and who had booked a passage in the name of van Dieren for the very good reason that it was his own name. He was furiously angry that he had been detained and had missed his ship, and complicated explanations and elaborate apologies had been necessary. The Dutch Embassy had been called into the matter, and further explanations had been made to them. All this had not made Bland lose his temper, but it had not made him happy.

He listened to Filby's excited description of Myrtle Montague's recollections without visible pleasure. At the end of them he said only, 'It's a pity she couldn't remember that before.'

'But don't you see what it means,' Filby cried. 'It means van Dieren and Jones are the same person after all.'

'It doesn't necessarily mean that, I'm afraid. It only shows that van Dieren had something to hide, and that was plain as soon as we found that there were no prints in his flat. It's obvious that he must have taken good care that they should be eliminated. But we can't deduce from this that there's any *proof* of his identity with Jones. Remember, if van Dieren *isn't* guilty, then someone's been framing him as the murderer from the word go. If he *is* guilty, and if he masqueraded as Jones, you still have to explain his apparent foolishness in drawing attention to himself by making that telephone call.'

Before Filby could reply, a policeman brought in two letters and put them on Bland's desk. The Inspector looked at one of them, after he had opened it, with such an expression of concentrated attention that Filby asked. 'What is it?' Bland passed it over without saying anything. It was an invitation to the wedding reception of Richard Boynton Hargreaves and Eve Marchant, to be held at Johnson's Hotel at one o'clock on the following Wednesday, the fifth of February. Filby was surprised to see that the Inspector's eyes were sparkling with an eagerness that had been missing from them for a few days. 'I think this is what we've been waiting for, Filby.'

'You mean that there's something special about this wedding that will bring van Dieren out of hiding?'

Bland laughed and then nodded. He was looking out of the window, and from beneath his lips came a singularly tuneless and dreary whistle. 'He must alter the place of the wedding reception. It must be at the house in Redfern Square.'

'Where his brother was killed?' Filby's eyebrows went up. 'He'll never do that.'

'He must do it. The solution of the case may depend on it.' Bland brought his fist down with a crack on the table. 'I must go and see him. We're on the last lap now, Filby.' He put on his trilby hat and his raincoat. When he went out he was still whistling.

## WEDNESDAY, FEBRUARY 5

### I

#### 9.30 to 12 a.m.

Early on Wednesday morning Miss Berry left the sham-Tudor house in Pinner where she lived with her mother and father, and went round to the almost identical sham-Tudor house where her friend Miss Peachey, the receptionist, lived with *her* mother and father. The Peachey family stood on a rather higher social level than the Berry family, because Miss Peachey's father was a bank manager whereas Miss Berry's father was an electrical engineer, who worked with his hands; but Miss Peachey and Miss Berry did not allow these social differences to influence their friendship. They had already gone over pretty thoroughly the ground of Richard Hargreaves' marriage, canvassing it from almost every possible aspect, but it was the kind of subject that can never really be exhausted, and when Miss Berry had admired the rather startling fur-trimmed coral coat and matching dress that Miss Peachey was wearing (though privately she thought that her own sober black coat and neat pale blue crêpe dress with the lace collar was far more appropriate to the occasion) they settled down happily to a half-hour's gossip before catching the train up to town.

'It's easy enough,' Miss Berry said, 'to see that *she's* just after his money, but what I can't understand is how *he* can be so taken in.'

Miss Peachey, it has already been indicated, was a girl of shrewd common sense, and she now made a common sense remark, which she had made several times before. 'There's more in this than meets the eye. I don't mind telling you, Rhoda, that if we hadn't been given the day off and practically ordered to attend the reception, I shouldn't be going.'

'What *do* you mean, darling?' Miss Berry asked, although she knew very well what her friend meant.

'Why do they want to get married when his father and brother are only just in the grave? And she married to the brother, too. And then to hold the reception in the very house where his brother was killed. It's a regular scandal, Rhoda, and you know it.' Miss Berry shrugged her shoulders to imply that, after all, it was the way of the world, but she made no attempt to contradict her friend. Miss Peachey turned round from the mirror in which she was putting the finishing touches to her complexion, and waggled a powder-puff at her friend. 'I shouldn't wonder if they *have* to be married.'

'Do you really think so?' Miss Berry breathed. It was a fascinating speculation.

'Indeed I do.' Miss Peachy drew a delicate Cupid's bow over her upper lip. 'She was married to Lionel, we all know that – but suppose she was carrying on with Richard all the time.'

Even the gravity of the speculation could not prevent Miss Berry from giggling. 'I've never thought Richard was that kind of a man.'

Miss Peachey scraped a fleck of lipstick off a tooth. 'Every man is that kind of man.' She pointed dramatically at the window. 'Look, it's beginning to rain.' The day was indeed exceptionally dark, and a few heavy drops of rain were falling out of the lowering sky. 'That's a bad sign,' Miss Peachey said with relish.

Mrs Bond regarded the whole affair as a nuisance, and her husband's insistence on pressing his dark blue suit when she wanted to use the electric iron provoked her to say so. When she complained that he was making a lot of fuss about nothing, Bond hummed to himself, and went on pressing his trousers. At length he laid down the iron and spoke with what was, for him, extreme good humour. 'Look here, old girl, just keep your nose out of this, will you? I know what I'm doing.'

'I wish I did. I don't believe you're up to any good.'

'I'm not up to anything except trying to look smart so that the new Managing Director will notice me, and give me a rise.' Bond put on the trousers, still humming. 'Not but what it might be useful to find out how this marriage is linked up to the murders – it must be linked up somehow.'

'You mean so that you can tell the police?'

'*That* for the police.' Bond spat accurately into the fire. 'You get nothing out of telling the police, and there's no taste in nothing. Besides, why should I tell that little rat anything, coming here and asking questions about my leg, and whether old man Hargreaves smoked cigarettes? No, my dear, anything I find out will be used for the exclusive benefit of yours truly. And I *have* found out one or two things already – or at least

I've got my suspicions. I told you about Tracy and Mrs Rogers, didn't I?'

'But they're going to get married.'

'Ah, but they weren't going to when I spotted them – and old man Hargreaves wasn't dead then, either. I don't say there's anything in it, but you never know. And if I could find out anything about the reasons for this marriage – well, it might be useful.'

'Take care you don't burn your fingers.'

'Have I ever burnt 'em yet?' Bond asked jauntily, as he pulled on his pointed patent-leather shoes.

Sinclair spent the morning at the office. Richard had announced that his wedding-day was to be a holiday, but Sinclair had a good deal of work to do, and took this chance of making up arrears. As he was one of the few people invited to the register-office ceremony, he had dressed with a good deal of care, in a sober suit of clergyman grey, a white shirt and dark tie. The effect of these clothes was to make him look more like a film star than usual.

Soon after eleven o'clock he was surprised to hear footsteps moving down the corridor of the deserted offices. They stopped outside his door, and Bland came in, looking dapper and conventionally respectable. A keen eye might have noticed that his hair was brushed with particular care, that his nails had been recently manicured, and that his eyes were exceptionally bright and sharp. Sinclair greeted him with a smile, and slipped the papers he had in front of him into his desk. 'How did you know I was here?'

'Your brother told me when I telephoned this morning.' Bland sat down and looked at the flower in Sinclair's buttonhole. 'I've been invited to the reception, but not to the wedding. I see you've been more greatly honoured.' Sinclair nodded. 'And what do you think about it all?'

'I think they're damned fools not to wait a bit. I must have heard pretty well everyone in our office express shocked surprise about the way the marriage is being hurried through, or the fact that she's marrying again into the same family, or the holding of the reception at Redfern Square. The three put together – well, I must say it does seem a bit steep, even to me.'

'Are there any rumours about the fact that the reception's not being given at a hotel?'

'The general view is that she's keen to hold it at Redfern Square, and that Richard's putty in her hands. Though I heard Carruthers the other day saying it was the family home, and perhaps that was why Richard wanted to hold it there. He's best man, you know – nearest relative and all that. By rights, of course, it should be *her* family that arranges the reception, but I gather there's no question of that – she prefers to forget her father and mother.' Sinclair leaned back in his chair. 'But what was it you wanted to see me about?'

'Partly to discover what you're telling me now – the way that people are thinking and feeling about it. Partly to tell you that I hope to break the case today. There may be some surprises at the reception.'

'Really.' Sinclair's face showed his pleasure. 'Do you mean that some fresh evidence has turned up? I was beginning to think you'd come to a dead end. Have you got van Dieren yet?'

'Not yet. But I'm hoping that this marriage may bring him into the open.'

'Out of the place where he's hiding, you mean?'

'You might put it that way.'

Eager and enthusiastic, Sinclair leaned across the desk. 'Tell me one thing – I can see you've come to a conclusion, in some way I can't fathom. Do you believe that van Dieren was responsible for E. H.'s death?'

'Yes,' said Bland.

Carruthers got up late, and moved about his Balham flatlet humming the 'Wedding March'. He ate some toast and marmalade, drank three cups of coffee and read the morning paper until, looking at his watch, he discovered that it was a quarter past ten. He dressed in a hurry, telephoned Richard and apologized for being late, and set out for Redfern Square at a quarter to eleven.

Jean Rogers and Tracy had also been invited to attend the register-office wedding. 'What I can't understand,' she said, as they set out from Hampstead in the car, 'is what Richard sees in her. I grant that she's attractive and all that, but then she really is *such* a tarty piece. I shouldn't have thought Richard would have cared for a tarty piece. But there – I suppose he's just bowled over.'

Tracy grunted from behind the wheel, and then said, 'She's very beautiful.'

'And has such a delightful voice,' said Jean Rogers, who was not without malice. 'And no doubt equally delightful parents – except that nobody has ever seen them.'

'You know what she says – her mother divorced her father, and then married again. Mother's in India, father's in South Africa. No particular reason to doubt it.'

'It's wonderfully convenient. Father and mother in East End, daughter in West End, is more likely, I should think.'

He pulled at his stiff collar. 'Really, you're uncommonly catty this morning. Don't forget what people might say about us. He that is without sin, you know.'

She put her hand on his arm. 'I know. I'm sorry. But I do dislike that woman.'

Mr Weston tapped the top of his egg and looked seriously at the elderly housekeeper who was pouring out his tea. 'Young Richard Hargreaves is getting married today.'

'I know, sir.' She pursed her lips. 'Saw it in the papers. Scandalous, I call it.'

'Rarely, I am bound to agree, can nuptials have been celebrated under less auspicious circumstances.' Mr Weston fished behind him, produced a large coloured handkerchief, and blew his nose with a honking noise. 'And you see also, Mrs Harrison, that Jupiter, or whoever rules upon Olympus, is concerned, like yourself, to express disapproval. In other words, it is raining.

But let us hope, none the less, that this youngest member of an ill-fated house will contract a happier marriage than his brother.' He neatly sliced off the top of the egg and ate it. 'Perfectly done. I shall be attending the wedding reception, Mrs Harrison, and perhaps I shall bring back a piece of cake.'

'I don't believe I could eat it, sir – it'd choke me. It's my belief the two of them did in his poor father and brother. A scheming hussy that girl is, if half what they say is true. I believe she's been behind all these murders.'

Mr Weston dived further into his egg, and looked profoundly shocked. 'Such sentiments, my dear Mrs Harrison, should hardly be voiced within the privacy of these four walls.' He waggled his spoon at her. 'If I were to repeat them, now, to Mr Hargreaves or Miss Marchant, who knows but that they might bring a suit against you for slander in which I should be regretfully compelled to testify against you.'

This elephantine playfulness was lost on his housekeeper. 'I don't care about any of that. And what's more, I shall always believe that that Richard – nasty effeminate young man he is – had something to do with the death of that poor Lily Hargreaves.'

There was a clatter. Mr Weston dropped his spoon on the floor. Mrs Harrison stooped and picked it up for him.

'Thank you,' he said. 'That will do, Mrs Harrison.'

And the actions and emotions of the bride and bridegroom on this momentous morning? They shall be left in obscurity with the hope that both Richard and Eve entertained all the feelings appropriate to a wedding-day.

# II

Richard Hargreaves slipped the ring on Eve Marchant's elegant third finger, and took her into his arms. Both of them were smiling happily. Carruthers tapped Richard on the shoulder and said, 'Best man's privilege – after you, old boy.' Richard, still smiling, relinquished his wife, and Carruthers kissed her – not on the cheek, but on the mouth. Tracy, Mrs Rogers, and Sinclair gathered round to offer congratulations, which Eve accepted with a demure smile. The registrar beamed. They went outside in an atmosphere of rather forced heartiness and good fellowship, Eve, Richard and Carruthers walking ahead together, arm in arm, and the others following a few steps behind.

The day was still dark, with a thin, penetrating rain falling. They ran to get into the cars. Richard waved a hand, shouted 'See you later,' and they drove off in turn. Richard and Eve first in the new Lagonda that he had given her as a wedding present, Carruthers and Sinclair in a hired Buick, and Tracy and Mrs Rogers in Tracy's Morris. None of them saw a man sitting in a Ford V8 on the other side of the road, reading a newspaper, who put in his clutch when the Lagonda had gone a few yards, and moved after it.

Neither Richard nor Eve spoke for five minutes, and then he said, 'Thank God that's over. It will be wonderful when we can leave all this, and get away by ourselves.' She simply looked at him, and placed her hand on his knee. 'Arnold seemed to kiss you rather enthusiastically.'

She laughed. 'Do you blame him, darling?'

'It's in the family tradition that you should marry a jealous husband,' he said, and then quickly put his hand on hers as he saw her flinch. 'I'm sorry. I'd really forgotten for the moment about Lionel, and everything else. But don't worry – it will be over soon, and we shall be by ourselves.'

'I know. You're very sweet to me.' A genuine, incongruous

tenderness sounded in her brassy voice, and she hesitated before she said, 'Darling – you know, I couldn't care less what people say – but do you think we shall have to stay long at this reception? I know it's going to be fiendishly difficult, and that all the women will be awfully catty. I really am dreading it.'

'I know.' Richard sounded a little hesitant. 'But I suppose I shouldn't dash off too quickly, now that I'm in sole charge at the office. You can disappear after half an hour, if it's too great a strain. Our plane for Paris doesn't go until six, you know.'

'There's no doubt she's a beautiful woman, but I wish Richard joy of her all the same. She's too beautiful to be true.' Carruthers laughed at his own joke. Sinclair was silent, and Carruthers said reflectively, 'It's certainly remarkable, the whole affair, and most imprudent. I advised against it, but I think she hurried Dick into it. It's certainly odd that she didn't bring any relative along to the wedding, isn't it? Of course, we all knew she wasn't out of the top drawer, but it rather looks as if she were out of the bottom.'

Sinclair was looking out of the window. He said without turning his head, 'Malicious,' and Carruthers coloured slightly, and stopped talking.

In the third car Jean Rogers was talking to Tracy. She had changed her mind about Eve Marchant. 'Do you know, I believe she'll make him a good wife.' She said this as if surprised by her own daring. 'I saw her looking at him in that certain way, and I think she's fond of him.' Tracy grunted. 'She's too beautiful for any other woman to look at her without feeling jealous – and I suppose a woman can't help being jealous in a sort of way of the fact that she's carried off this rich young man and is dashing away with him to a honeymoon in Paris – and she *has* got the most awful voice – but I believe she's fond of him, and I'll be prepared to throw my old shoe with a good heart when they drive away.'

'I suppose she's leaving the stage?'

'I doubt if Dick wants her to go on doing that act in the

chorus at the Splendid. In fact, I doubt if she wants to go on doing it herself.'

Tracy dexterously steered his way through half of a traffic jam. 'I wonder why the devil they're holding this reception at Redfern Square? There's something queer about that. Sends a bit of a shiver up my spine, I must say, when you remember what happened there last time.'

'I dare say that it was just the most convenient place.'

Tracy spoke emphatically. 'Whatever the reason, it's in damned bad taste, and I don't like it.'

## III

### *1 to 1.45 p.m.*

From the first, the reception did not go well. Perhaps it was partly the day, heavy, cold, dark, with the thin rain persistently falling and a faint threat of snow in the whipping east wind; partly the fact that, by what seemed to be, as Tracy said to Jean Rogers, the very peak of bad taste, the reception took place in the very drawing-room in which the party had been held on the night of Lionel's death, with the folding-doors into the dining-room thrown open; perhaps the guests were disturbed by the fact that the newly married pair seemed very obviously to find the occasion a severe strain on their nerves. Not all the people present, of course, had been there on that earlier occasion, but the uneasiness felt by the people from the Hargreaves Agency who had attended the other party communicated itself to the whole company. It seemed to spread even to the additional servants who were helping Jackson and Williams on this occasion, causing one of them to drop a tray of drinks, and another to spill a glass of sherry over Tracy's suit. Conversation was uncertain and uneven, with silences punctuated by bursts of laughter like the clatter of gunfire before a battle.

Among those people, almost all of whom seemed to be waiting for something to happen, Richard and his wife moved with a discomfort that grew steadily with the uneasiness of their guests. Richard was not, indeed, an inattentive host, but he seemed to be conscious that he moved in an atmosphere of disapproval and coldness which in one or two cases was hardly concealed. This hostility was even more apparent towards Eve, who had only one or two acquaintances in the room. The men were altogether too friendly to her, while some of the women, who had known Lionel Hargreaves and his father, were barely civil. Sinclair, who had seen nothing of what was going on, said to her, 'Can I get you a drink? I'm afraid all this must be rather a strain.'

'Nothing to drink, thank you.' She clasped her hands. 'Strain isn't the word. I never knew women could be so catty. It's these friends of the family who're the worst. Some awful old spinster sister of an advertising man who just had to be asked said to me that it must be interesting to be married so often. I told her it was more exciting, no doubt, than not being married at all.' Her large eyes looked pathetically at Sinclair, and her voice was almost a wail. 'But it's not very nice, is it, to have things like that said to you on your wedding-day? Oh, here's Dick.' She went up to him and took his hands. 'Dick, darling, I'm having such an awful time I could cry. This really is the end, darling, the dreaded end. Can't we go away now, and leave these people to themselves?'

Richard looked pale, but determined. 'I don't think we ought to go away quite yet. We've only been here half an hour.'

'Then for God's sake let's start on our cold buffet, and stop talking. It's driving me crazy.' The long refectory table in the dining-room was laid for a meal. Richard looked miserable. 'I don't think everything's quite ready yet.'

'It *must* be ready.' There was a touch of hysteria in Eve's voice.

'And people keep coming in and out. I said they could have a look over the house, and a lot of people are doing just that.'

'Dick, I can't stand much more of this.' The hysteria could

be heard plainly now. 'I wish I'd never let you alter the arrangements, and hold the reception here. I wish – '

'Here's Bland,' Sinclair said, and she swung round and stared
at her husband.

'You didn't say he was coming.'

'Why, darling – ' Richard protested when Bland, in the doorway, saw her hand swing up and slap Richard's cheek, as it had
been raised to strike his father in the next room three weeks
ago. Her hand left a shaped red mark on Richard's white face.
Everybody in the room heard the sharp report, and looked at
Richard. He stood motionless, while his wife walked away with
a firm, quick step which became almost a run as she neared the
door. She went past Bland without a word or look and ran
upstairs, quite plainly sobbing.

Something had happened at last, and the hum of excited
voices testified that it was for an incident like this that the guests
had been, perhaps half-unconsciously, waiting. 'Isn't she *awful*,'
Miss Peachey said to Miss Berry. Onslow and Mudge, both of
them wearing their sports jackets, corduroy trousers and knitted
ties, exchanged significant glances. Jean Rogers, standing next
to Tracy, suddenly gripped his arm tightly, and he looked down
at her in surprise. Richard Hargreaves walked away from Sinclair and across to Bland, straight through the crowd of people
who looked at him, some of them with sympathy, and others
with satisfaction. He said to the Inspector with some bitterness,
'You saw that?'

'I'm sorry,' Bland said, with a warmth that seemed hardly
warranted. His eyes were watchful. 'I know this is an inappropriate moment, but I offer you my congratulations.' Richard
seemed hardly to have heard. He was looking up the beautiful
curve of the stairway after his wife. She disappeared at the head
of the stairs, without looking back. Bland placed his hand on
Richard's shoulder, and spoke gently. 'Do not expect too much
of marriage, my friend, do not imagine that the rose is without
its thorns. And don't forget that your wife has had a great deal
to endure in these last few days.'

'I don't forget anything.' Richard made an impatient gesture, and suddenly swung round to show Bland a face distorted by fear and passion. 'If Eve's come to any harm because of this crazy notion of yours, I'll – '

Bland was not listening. 'There are some people I do not see here. Where are – '

They were standing in the doorway, and there was suddenly a good deal of noise and commotion in the hall. Out of this noise Filby emerged, with his lean long-nosed face excited, and his hat on the back of his head. Two of the assistant menservants were following him. 'Downstairs,' Filby said, and Bland jumped into action. 'Come on,' he said to the two assistant servants, and went after Filby, down the staircase to the servants' quarters. Richard Hargreaves looked again up the staircase, and then followed them like somebody in a dream. Sinclair followed Richard.

They went down the narrow winding staircase, and were in a long corridor with doors leading out of it on either side. 'Servants' quarters,' Filby said. 'But they're upstairs now, of course.' He led them along the corridor, to a door at the end of it, outside which another man was standing. This man said, 'In the cellar, sir,' and Sinclair gaped. He whispered to Bland, 'These are your men?'

'Of course,' Bland said impatiently. Then to Richard, 'Is the door of the cellars left open generally?'

'No, locked. The key hangs in the pantry just along the passage.'

'How far do the cellars extend?'

'Right underneath the house and almost into the road. There are six of them – wine cellar, a couple of empty rooms and then three lumber rooms with all sorts of odds and ends. Can't think what anyone would want down there.'

Bland said to the man on guard, 'Do you know which cellar, Burke?'

'Somewhere up the other end, sir. Not in those first two, anyway.'

'Is there any way out the other end?' Bland asked Richard, who shook his head. 'Good. All right, let's go. No torches if you can help it. Ready for anything, but I don't think there'll be much trouble.' He raised his eyebrows at Richard and Sinclair. 'What about you two?'

Sinclair's eyes were shining. 'Yes, of course I'll come. Who is it – van Dieren?'

'Yes, van Dieren.'

'You've lured him out at last.'

Bland did not answer this, but said impatiently, 'You, Hargreaves?'

Richard swallowed, and said simply, 'Yes.'

'Right.' Bland spoke with a note of command in his voice that Sinclair had not heard before. 'Take off your shoes and let's go down.'

While Sinclair was unlacing his shoes, Richard whispered, 'It's awfully dark down there, but there's a light switch in every cellar, and I can show you where they are.'

'No lights unless I give the order,' Bland said sharply. 'We need surprise. Open the door, Burke, and then stay at the top of these stairs. The rest of us will go down.'


# IV

## 1.50 to 2.5 p.m.

When Burke opened the door they saw at first nothing but darkness. Then Sinclair's eyes became a little accustomed to the gloom, and he made out the dim outline of two or three stone stairs, and a rail at their side. Filby went down first, followed by Bland, Richard and Sinclair himself, the two detectives following behind. As they went down the steps Sinclair lost the sense of identity of other people, as one does easily in darkness. He knew that Richard was before him on the stone staircase, and that one of the detectives walked behind, but so silently did they move that until he put out his hand and touched Richard's jacket he could have believed himself to be descending the stairs

alone. When they had gone down six steps the staircase curved
sharply to the right. He heard in front of him a hoarse whisper,
'How many more?' and Richard whispered back, 'Seven or
eight.' It seemed minutes later, but was no doubt only a few
seconds, that Sinclair reached the bottom of the stairs, and was
conscious of bodies near him. Bland said to Richard, 'What's
the geography?'

'We go straight through to a door at the other end. This is
the wine cellar and there are racks about everywhere. I think
you'll need the torch.'

'Torch, Filby,' Bland said. 'But no longer than you need.'
The yellow torchlight cut slices of darkness, and revealed in
flashes the steel racks in which bottles presented themselves like
guns. There were paths between racks and Bland said, 'The one
to the left.' Filby put out the torch and they moved again, so
quietly that Sinclair was painfully aware of somebody, he supposed one of the detectives, breathing heavily by his side. He
could just make out the shapes of the racks on either side. When
he put out his hand he felt the cold touch of the neck of a wine
bottle. Ahead he heard a voice which he recognized as Richard's
say, 'The entrance to the next one is just ahead on the right.
The next two cellars are empty. The others contain old boxes,
trunks, and so on.'

'Doors to the cellars?'

'Yes, but they're usually left open.'

'Flash your torch at the entrance of each cellar, Filby, and
see that there's no one in it'

'OK,' said Filby hoarsely, and flashed the torch. An open
door stood in front of them. Beyond it the second cellar
stretched, square, clean and empty, just a little more than Sinclair's six feet in height, so that he had to bend a little in passing
through the door. The torch played round, and made it plain
that there was no place in this cellar for anyone to hide.

While they were passing cautiously through the second and
third cellars Sinclair lost the sense of time so that he could not
have said within minutes how long they had taken to walk
through them. There was no sound in the cellars except the

occasional drawing-in and sharp expulsion of breath, and Sinclair found himself moving like a careful automaton, while he wondered what they would find in the fourth, fifth or sixth cellars. Van Dieren, Bland had said, but how had van Dieren got there? And why was he there? What possible reason could the art agent have for coming out of hiding on Richard's wedding-day, and entering the cellars? Had he simply walked in as van Dieren, or in some disguise? Disguised, perhaps, by the red wig of that Mr Jones, who had never appeared in the case since his first dramatic entry. Suddenly Sinclair touched Richard Hargreaves, who moved in front of him. Richard was trembling.

Richard's whisper, however, was clear enough when he replied to Bland's question: 'Old boxes in this cellar, but I can't remember where they are.' Bland spoke to Filby and the torch played again, on books and files, cases filled with papers, a bicycle with broken spokes standing against the wall. At the same time they all saw a gleam of electric light in the next cellar. Richard drew his breath sharply, and Sinclair felt a coldness in his stomach. Bland said to the last man, 'Stay here and cover this door. The rest of us across – and quietly.' They moved towards the gleam of light slowly and noiselessly, in an atmosphere of growing tension. Once there was a rustle of paper, and Sinclair could have cried aloud with hysteria, and then with relief as something scurried over the floor and away. At last they were near the half-open door and could see the interior of the fifth cellar.

One dirty electric lamp threw a dim light in the cellar, and by this light they saw that the middle of the room was piled high with cases, trunks, boxes and all sorts of household odds and ends. Behind this pile somebody was bending down, apparently turning out the things in one of the boxes. The face and body of this person were invisible, but as a hand came up and took from the top of the pile of cases what looked, in the dim light, like an article of clothing, Sinclair saw something – and saw it with a shock of surprise that made him feel slightly sick.

Whoever was behind the pile of cases was wearing lemon-yellow gloves.

They stood behind the door, while the yellow gloves appeared again, and took something else – again it seemed to be an article of clothing, but Sinclair could not be quite sure – from the top of the pile. Then Bland stepped forward, flung the door into the cellar wide open, and called, in a voice which contained a tone of mockery. 'You can come out, Mr van Dieren.'

The rustling behind the pile of boxes stopped at once, and the image came suddenly to Sinclair's mind of an enormous frightened mouse running back into its hole. But there was no hole here for the mouse – the trap had fastened on it. Or was that thought too dramatic? Bland called again: 'It's no use. I know what you're doing down here. You may as well come out.' There was a scuffling noise, and the figure darted into the last cellar, and slammed the door. They heard a key turn. Bland said sharply to Richard, 'You're sure there's no way out?'

Richard shook his head. There was sweat on his brow, and he seemed unable to speak. They advanced into the cellar, to the spot where the figure had been, and saw that a number of trunks and cases had apparently been moved to reach an old box at the bottom of the pile. This box had been opened, and its contents scattered around. Old shirts and pillowcases, a pair of dirty green curtains, a hairbrush, a camera, bits of lace, some broken picture-frames – these had been placed haphazardly on the floor. But they noticed these things afterwards, for they looked first at what lay at the bottom of the trunk. This was a rather worn and frayed ginger-coloured suit. Bland bent down and lifted it. 'Van Dieren's suit,' he said. 'Quite unmistakable, to anyone who'd seen him wear it.' He ran his hand through the pockets. 'Nothing here. I should have thought – ' He bent down to look at the box again and picked up from the bottom of it a piece of paper with typewriting on it. He read this, and said to Richard with a grim smile, 'This seems to be addressèd to you. I'll read it. It has van Dieren's address at Earls Court on the top, and it reads:

'Dear Richard, I cannot go on with this. You have made me act as your dupe through this whole affair, because of what you know about me, and I have always suspected your motives. But now your father is dead, they say he has been poisoned, and I hear that the police suspect me. You have forced me to do a lot of things for you, but I can't be an accomplice to murder. I shall go to the police and tell them I have acted as your tool, because of your hold over me. I know what the consequences will be for me, but I am prepared to face them. I write to you so that you shall have a chance to get away – '

Bland stopped and said, 'The letter is torn off there, at the end of a line, and there is no signature. An incriminating document.' He put it in his pocket.

Richard's face was white with terror. His voice was high, and the words tumbled out. 'I didn't do it – I swear I didn't. I don't know anything about that letter. I've never met van Dieren.'

Bland said sharply to Filby, 'Break that door down.'

Filby and Hemming put their shoulders to the oak door. It shivered, but did not move. 'All of us,' Bland said, and attacked the door with Sinclair. Richard Hargreaves stood with his hands hanging at his sides, and his eyes staring into space. The third time they attacked the door there was a sound of tearing wood, the lock gave way and the door opened. One of the policemen was taken off balance and slipped over on his side. There was no sound from inside the room, and Bland snapped, 'The torch, Filby.' Before the tall detective had time to take the torch out of his pocket a figure in a dark coat and yellow gloves rushed head-down out of the darkness, and butted him in the stomach. Filby said 'Ouch', and went sprawling, with his torch clattering on the stone floor. Richard Hargreaves made no move to stop the advancing figure, but in order to reach the door it had to dodge round the boxes, so that Sinclair and Bland had time to make an intercepting move. Sinclair caught hold of the dark coat from behind, but with an astonishing quick movement the figure wriggled out and away so that Sinclair was left with the coat in his hands. But Bland was coming fast and straight from the other side of the room. The other swerved to avoid him, a little too late. Bland's rush carried them both to the ground. There was a flurry of arms and legs, and then Filby and Sinclair joined them, and the struggle was over. Bland got up from the floor and dusted his suit carefully, his face impassive. It was then that Sinclair saw the face for the first time.

## SATURDAY, FEBRUARY 8

### 3.0 to 4.0 p.m.

In a room on the first floor of the Richard the Third Restaurant, that last resort of the witty and beautiful, where all the men speak in epigrams, and all the women smile as if they understood them, Detective Inspector Bland was giving a luncheon party.

There was a particular reason why this luncheon party, which was a celebration of the end of a difficult case, should be held at the Richard the Third Restaurant – for this restaurant had seen the successful end of another case in which Bland had been engaged. Now, as the six of them sat sipping liqueurs at the end of a luncheon in which everything, from pâté Richard the Third to cheese soufflé, had been chosen with some care, Bland's smooth, round face was beaming with a pleasure not quite unmixed with smug satisfaction at a job of work completed. They had talked during luncheon of English, French and American police methods, of ways of cooking turbot, and the possibility of another war ('There won't be a war this year, or next year either,' Filby, who was a reader of the *Daily Express*, had announced confidently): but now Sinclair, his face bright and handsome, looked across from the other side of the round table at which they were sitting.

'What I can't understand, and what we'd like you to explain more than anything, is how you solved this case.'

Bland moved the stem of his glass between his fingers, and said with an affectation of coyness that Filby found altogether intolerable, 'It won't sound very impressive, but if you're interested, I'll be pleased to run through the way in which things worked out.' Filby covered his mouth with his hand to hide a yawn. It was pleasant to have been asked to lunch, and an honour, of course, and the food – and especially the drink – had been grand, but it was really a little too much to expect him to listen again to something that he had heard two or three times already. He rested his head on his hand, for Bland was already speaking in his pleasant, monotonous voice.

'Let me give you first of all the facts about the murder of Lionel Hargreaves, as I formulated them on that Wednesday evening. He had been shot through the back from close range, by somebody who had presumably worn a pair of yellow gloves, which were left behind as a present. Nobody heard the shot fired because the library, where he was killed, was soundproof. The murderer could have come from outside, through a door in the garden wall, or he could have entered the room by walking out of the drawing-room, where a party was going on, down the corridor and into the library. We were able to prove, thanks to the presence of servants in the hall, that there were only six people who walked out of the drawing-room during the relevant times – Bond, Sinclair, Richard Hargreaves, Tracy, Onslow, and Mudge. The last two went out together, and vouched for each other, and although it was theoretically possible that they might have committed the murder together, in practice we were soon able to clear them from suspicion, since they had absolutely no motive for committing the joint crime. This left, therefore, these four people – or someone from outside. Anyone else at the party was automatically excluded from suspicion, although the possibility of some sort of complicity between two people couldn't be ignored. Suppose, for example, Mrs Rogers had made an appointment with Lionel to meet him in the library – and it had been kept by Tracy. That kind of possibility had to be kept in mind.

'But as soon as the possibility of two people being concerned is mentioned, we come across another question which was generally ignored – why did Lionel go into the library? Since the library was a soundproof room, it was essential that the murder should be committed there, if the shot was not to be heard. The fact that the murder took place in the library indicated strongly that it was premeditated, and the presence of the gloves and gun made this almost certain. But if the murder was premeditated, the murderer must somehow have arranged that Lionel should be in the library. How? The obvious answer was that he met him there by appointment.

'Accepting this answer, I was brought up against the inherent improbability of anyone actually at the party being able to make such an arrangement without making Lionel suspicious. It *might* be that Bond, Sinclair, or Tracy would be able to say, 'I've got something awfully important to tell you, old man – can I have a chat about it in the library?' – but that didn't seem at all likely. It was more likely that Richard, as Lionel's brother, could say such a thing – but more likely still that the appointment had no connection with the party at all. This was confirmed the next day when we found on Lionel's blotting-pad the note "Jones 7.30" and the word "Eve". The obvious conclusion to be drawn was that "Jones", who soon appeared in the case, had telephoned and made an appointment which referred to Eve Marchant.

'A further point was immediately apparent. If the murder was premeditated, and if the murderer had chosen the library deliberately, as a soundproof room, that could be done *only by someone familiar with the house*. By questioning I discovered that neither Sinclair nor Bond had been inside the house before. For the time being, therefore – unless something new turned up – they were eliminated from suspicion.

'The dramatic entry of Miss Marchant on that evening, her statement that she was secretly married to Lionel, the fact that Richard was obviously in love with her, the mysterious telephone call made to her to ask her to come along at half past nine – all this added further complications and possibilities. Her statement provided Richard with a motive. He said that he knew nothing of her marriage to Lionel – but supposing he had found out about it suddenly? If Miss Marchant's story was true, however, who had telephoned her?

'Later on various suggestions about the murderer were made. Bond made one out of pure malice, Mrs Rogers made another to try to lead suspicion away from Tracy, because she feared he might have committed the murder. Sinclair suggested that I should investigate the death of Lily Hargreaves two years before, and this idea proved useful. That ended the investigation on Wednesday evening.'

Mrs Rogers looked meltingly across the table at Tracy. Delicious, she thought, a delicious lunch, and delicious the candlelight and the drawn curtains, the candles now guttering, so that one could see faces dimly and softly. It was good of the Inspector to have given them this wonderful lunch, and of course his account of what had happened was fascinating. If only his voice were a little less monotonous! If only she had drunk a little less wine! She blinked quickly, to overcome the feeling of drowsiness that had almost made her close her eyes, and lit a cigarette. Bland was talking again.

'On the following morning the case unfolded, and presented its central problem – a man called Jones.

'You all know now that Jones bought the gun with which the murder was committed, that he made himself as conspicuous as possible with his red hair and yellow gloves, that he vanished at four o'clock on the day of the murder, and was never seen again. One could easily enough understand that the murderer would wear a disguise when buying the gun, but why should he wear such a conspicuous disguise. and go to the lengths of hiring a room and living in it – though the landlady said he never stayed the night? Why, why? I thought at first that Jones was used to create an alibi for the murderer in some way – but since he disappeared *before* the murder, what kind of alibi could possibly be created? Or perhaps he was simply an accomplice, a red-haired herring designed to lead us off the trail? I couldn't dismiss this altogether, but it seemed unlikely, because the accomplice would know too much of what went on. I considered the possibilities that Jones might be part of the pair Richard Hargreaves-Eve Marchant, or part of the pair Tracy-Mrs Rogers, working in collusion, but I couldn't see what they gained by such an elaborate fandango. Throughout the case, when incomplete and partial solutions were suggested, I went on asking myself the question "Why Jones?" – and when I answered it the case was solved.

'The other action of Jones we knew about, apart from his

purchase of the gun, was his telephone call to Joseph van Dieren. When I called on van Dieren I found that he was an eccentric figure who denied all knowledge of Jones, but told me an extraordinary tale about E. H. having got him into prison in America many years before. I noticed, without paying any special attention to it, that van Dieren had a curious habit of plucking at his left coat-sleeve. When, later on, I asked E. H. about van Dieren's story he did not deny its truth, but denied that it had anything at all to do with anyone who looked like van Dieren.

'With the help of Mr. Weston I was able to clear up the mystery of Lily Hargreaves' death. But although her death was an indirect cause of the murders that followed two years later – I think, indeed, that her death put the whole idea into the murderer's head – it had nothing directly to do with the case, and I don't propose to talk about it.

'I began to build up a case – or rather it built itself up – against van Dieren. The telephone call had been made to him, he had known of an episode in E. H.'s early life that was known to very few people, and I discovered that an anonymous letter received by E. H. about Eve Marchant had been typed on van Dieren's machine. It was clear that there was something wrong, and even criminally wrong, about him – his secretary shivered when she knew I was a detective, and Carruthers, the sole link I could find between van Dieren and the Hargreaves family, shook with terror whenever I mentioned his name. At the same time I had nothing like sufficient evidence to arrest him – a fact which I mentioned to Sinclair and Carruthers on the day that van Dieren was to call on E. H. As it turned out, if I *had* arrested him then – even though I had only an inkling of the truth – I should have saved two lives . . .'

Below that domed brow Mr Weston's small, intelligent eyes were heavy. A good chap, Bland, he thought, a *very* good chap. Look at this lunch he had provided for them. And then such an excellent cigar! He took the giant Upmains from his mouth, and looked at it appreciatively. Delicious fragrance! Through the blue smoke he looked at Mrs Rogers – a fine figure of a woman,

and how pleasant it was that everything had worked out well
for her and Tracy. What a good world it was altogether, Mr
Weston thought; but when he closed his eyes he saw behind the
lids an image of Lily Hargreaves. He opened them again, and
it seemed that Bland's voice was coming from far away.

'We have reached the time of E. H.'s murder. I don't need
to recapitulate the circumstances of it to you, except to point
out that it shortened our list of suspects, which in the first
murder was Richard Hargreaves, Tracy here, or an outsider. In
the second murder we could reduce the suspects quite definitely
to van Dieren, Richard Hargreaves, Sinclair, Bond and Mr
Weston. You won't fail to notice that one name appears on both
lists – Richard Hargreaves. Two other names, those of Weston
and van Dieren could be added, because both might have filled
the role of "outsider" in the first murder, but Weston had an
alibi for that murder which we were unable to break, and van
Dieren could presumably have no knowledge of the asbestos-
lined library.

'The cases against both Richard and against van Dieren were
strengthened by this second murder. Against van Dieren,
because he had been sent away by E. H. "with a flea in his ear",
having apparently told "a cock-and-bull story", and because he
was the person who most obviously had an opportunity of adding
poison to the sherry, because in the thick fog a small boy broke
a window in E. H.'s room while van Dieren was there and
E. H.'s attention to what was going on inside the room was
relaxed for some minutes. Against Richard, because it appeared
that E. H. had been in touch with Weston that afternoon with
the object of changing his will, cutting Richard out of it and
leaving his money to charity.

'On the same afternoon van Dieren's offices were burned
down, and his secretary found murdered. At the same time,
although everything in the office was burnt, some pornographic
drawings were found just outside the office, signed ARTES. I soon
saw that this was a code name for Carruthers, consisting of
alternate letters of his name. I had already been told by Bond
that van Dieren carried on this kind of business, and the

drawings provided an explanation for Carruthers' cold sweat of fear whenever van Dieren's name was mentioned. But why were the offices burned down? To conceal the fact that a murder had been committed? Hardly – why bother to do that when two unmistakable murders had been committed already? To conceal, then, something in the offices? It looked like it. And if this had been done by van Dieren, or by his order, then it was likely van Dieren would disappear. But one could argue, then, that anything left lying about on the premises, as those drawings of Carruthers were, was left for us to find, as a red herring.

'All this added to the conclusion that was slowly and inescapably being built up. That there were *two* murderers, one the executant, and the other the guiding hand. The executant – the person who appeared always in a suspicious light – was van Dieren, who seemed almost to go out of his way to court suspicion. The guiding hand was obviously the younger son, the person who stood to gain overwhelmingly by the death of a brother of whom he was jealous, and a father who had always behaved to him ungenerously, who was to be cut out of his father's will because he threatened to make an unsuitable marriage – Richard Hargreaves.

'That,' said Bland, drawing breath, 'is what we were meant to believe. I might have believed it, but for a trivial incident in which Filby was the central character. It was a gesture of Filby's that led me straight to the truth.' A sigh went round the table, passing from Filby to Mrs Rogers, from Mrs Rogers to Sinclair, on to Weston and Tracy, and back to Bland. A sigh of suspense – of anticipation – or merely of boredom? In the gathering dusk faces were almost invisible, and it would have been hard to say. But Bland, at least, was interested in the story he was telling, and was obviously determined to pursue it remorselessly to the end.

'When Filby was talking to me about the case he made a gesture as if to take a handkerchief out of his sleeve. But he had mislaid his handkerchief, as men sometimes do who carry them in their sleeves, and he quickly – and rather inelegantly – wiped his hand across his nose instead. Now, the point is this –

I had seen van Dieren make an identical gesture towards his sleeve, not once, but two or three times during our short interview. But he had restrained himself, and drawn back his hand quickly or fiddled with a button on his coat-sleeve, so that I had not realized that he was looking for a handkerchief. Was it that van Dieren, like Filby, had no handkerchief? No – for he produced a handkerchief from his jacket, and blew his nose on it loudly. Had he changed over from keeping his handkerchief in his sleeve to keeping it in his pocket? Possibly – but that could not account for my impression that he did not want me to know the meaning of his gesture, that he had drawn back suddenly and avoided putting his hand into his sleeve. Was it possible, then, I asked myself, that van Dieren when he saw me was playing some kind of part? And when I had asked myself that question I asked myself another: *was not one impersonation involved, but two*?

‘When I had answered that question I had solved the case. I understood what really happened, and – most important – what the murderer was trying to do. And I saw that the clues did not lead to two persons but direct to one. I knew then that the murderer could be nobody but Arnold Carruthers.

‘If one looks at the whole thing through those distorted eyes,’ the detective continued, his own blue eyes looking dreamily into an unfathomed distance, ‘one can recognize that the idea probably came into his mind when Lily Hargreaves died. He had been brought up with Lionel and Richard, on terms of comparative equality, had gone to the same school with them – and then he had been suddenly transformed from an equal to a poor relation. He reacted to this treatment as many young men might have done – he determined to be independent, and to be an artist. He was lonely, poor, sexually frustrated (as I learnt from Sinclair), and it must have become plain for him after a time that he wasn’t, and never would be, a serious artist. Like all frustrated people he found compensation in a daydream in which he was free and rich, with unlimited opportunities for enjoyment. For he was not moved by one frustration only, but by two. He was shy and uneasy and unsuccessful with women – and he compensated himself for this by making pornographic drawings.

'But the further a compensation is removed from reality, the less satisfactory is it as a substitute for reality. And there is a time when the substitute altogether ceases to satisfy, when the heart cries out for reality, whatever the cost of obtaining it. Carruthers reached the point when, to obtain what he conceived as reality, he was prepared to commit murder. He became what we can call, for convenience, mad – but not certifiably mad. The scheme which entered his head was highly complex and hardly sane. Its purpose was nothing less than to inherit the Hargreaves fortune by eliminating everybody who stood between the fortune and himself. I suggest that Lily Hargreaves' marriage put the idea of inheriting the Hargreaves money out of his mind. Her death, in curious circumstances, with a strong hint of suicide, brought it back with a rush.

'His first step was taken six months after her death, when van Dieren first appears on the scene. An existing, moderately successful art agent's business was bought, with the aid of a loan from E. H., who did not know, of course, what he was lending the money for – a neat ironical touch that must have touched Carruthers' sense of humour. The character of Joseph van Dieren was created. Van Dieren had, of course, no background and no history. Instead of trying to provide him with a false background, Carruthers very sensibly set to work to create a real one. One suspects an impersonation when a man suddenly appears and disappears, but hardly when he had been in physical existence, with a business of his own, for eighteen months.

'It was not very difficult to create and maintain the separate character. Carruthers lived alone in Balham. Van Dieren lived alone in Earls Court. Their acquaintances were different, their appearances different. Physically, van Dieren was composed of a large false moustache, a fairly obvious wig – so obvious that nobody guessed it was meant to conceal anything – a suit of clothes that was too big, a deep bass voice and a bit of make-up. About half of Carruthers' time was spent in the character of van Dieren, and through the art agency he was able to find an easy market for his pornographic drawings. For eighteen months he bided his time and perfected his scheme. He might have been prepared to wait even longer, but for the coincidence – the only one in the case – that Eve Marchant's friend in the chorus was the sister of van Dieren's secretary. Eve told her friend that she'd been secretly married to Lionel, and, of course, the news came through to Carruthers in his role as van Dieren. It must have decided him to act – because if there were a child of the marriage it would inherit legally when Lionel died. So Mr Jones appeared on the scene.'

Bland paused and looked round in the dim light at the assembled company. Filby was looking at his pipe with a disgusted air. He had, of course, heard all this before. Sinclair's customary bright look was somehow blurred, as if there were a film over his eyes, but he was staring at the detective with what might be thought flattering attentiveness. Tracy's head was in his hands, Mrs Rogers seemed to be looking at the ceiling, and Weston was frankly nodding. Not an altogether satisfactory audience, Bland reflected, and thought rather wistfully of Eve and Richard, who had sent a cable from Paris where they were honeymooning, "CONGRATULATIONS TO SLEUTHERY". Perhaps they would have improved the standard of listening. Perhaps the lunch had been too good. He plunged on, like a swimmer in difficult water.

'Jones was a bold and successful conception, who again helped to conceal the truth by appearing to reveal it. He flaunted his red hair and yellow gloves – he was concerned to give an address to which the revolver he bought could be sent – he positively advertised himself as the murderer, and also as somebody wearing a disguise. He made a quite unnecessary telephone call to van Dieren's office, which he made sure that his landlady would overhear – what landlady wouldn't listen to the telephone conversations of a red-headed man who always wore yellow gloves, and who never stayed overnight in his lodgings? The gloves were really necessary, of course, so that no fingerprints should be left in Mr Jones's room. If fingerprints were left, and

found later to check with Carruthers', the fat would really be
in the fire. This question of fingerprints worried Carruthers all
along, and he went to extravagant lengths to eliminate them, as
we shall see. The purpose of Mr Jones was to create the character of van Dieren even more firmly – since nobody expects, nor
was there any obvious reason for, a *double* impersonation. But
his subsidiary purposes were to cast suspicion on van Dieren,
for reasons that I'll explain in a moment, and to make it quite
clear that Jones, whoever he might be, was *not* van Dieren.
Filby once suggested that the two of them might be identical,
and I remember that I answered caustically that if van Dieren
really wanted to draw suspicion on himself he couldn't have
done it better. But van Dieren (it's easier to keep the names
separate than to call them all Carruthers) *did* want to draw
suspicion to himself. Why?

'There lies the key to the whole plot. If Carruthers had gone
about eliminating everybody who stood between him and the
Hargreaves fortune in a straightforward and simple manner he
would (as he realized) very soon have been caught. By arranging
this elaborate build-up he thought he stood no chance of being
even suspected. For in his plan he did not mean to kill Richard
Hargreaves – he meant to arrange things so that Richard should
be hanged as the murderer of his father and brother, so that he
should inherit as the next in line. In Carruthers' plan van Dieren
was to be used to cast suspicion gradually on Richard. Gradually
– for it would never do if Richard were arrested for murder of
his brother alone. Carruthers' role as van Dieren was to draw
suspicion on himself, and to show at the same time that van
Dieren could be only a pawn in somebody's hands. Since Richard was the person who profited by the crimes the conclusion
was that he must be a pawn of Richard. Incidentally, he was
used to make it absolutely clear that Carruthers himself had
nothing to do with the crime, by various remarks and innuendoes
and by the picturing of Carruthers as a tool of van Dieren. Jones
was probably intended to have a final unveiling as Richard by
the discovery of his red wig in Richard's possession, or something like that; but if he remained for ever unexplained, that

would do almost as well. Jones served the purpose of drawing attention to van Dieren, but here and elsewhere Carruthers overplayed his part a little – Jones was rather *too* palpably a figure in disguise, so that one asked awkward questions about him. When he vanished from the scene at four o'clock on Wednesday, the stage was set for Lionel's murder.

'The mechanics of that were simple. Lionel was telephoned by somebody calling himself Jones, who said he knew about Lionel's marriage to Eve Marchant, and wanted to see him about it. Lionel was, we know, anxious to keep the marriage secret, and agreed to meet Jones that night at 7.30. Jones must have threatened to tell E. H. if Lionel would not agree to see him, and then no doubt said something like, "You won't need to leave the house – I'll come up through the back entrance and see you in your library." When Lionel entered the library he may have found "Jones", but I should think it more likely that he found Carruthers, from the fact that he was shot in the back. He would hardly have turned his back on a stranger, especially so odd a stranger as Jones.

'On the same day, to thicken up the plot a bit, Carruthers telephoned to Eve Marchant, to say that Lionel wanted to see her, and he typed on van Dieren's machine an anonymous letter about the marriage, which he sent to E. H.

'Then came one of the most difficult things he had to do – to face me as van Dieren. He couldn't have looked forward to that, especially when he was unlucky enough to meet me by chance for the first time as Carruthers, a couple of hours before he was due to meet me as van Dieren. He seemed, and no doubt was, frantically nervous. But he got away with it all right as van Dieren, partly because of a piece of good acting but chiefly because by bad luck I got a piece of grit in my eye, which was watering so badly that I had to keep it half-closed. He very wisely sat half in the shade, so that I could see him only dimly. He spun me this tale about E. H. in America, which was meant to link van Dieren up with Richard who knew the story, but linked him up with Carruthers just as effectively. He was guilty of another piece of over-subtlety here, because when I asked him as Carruthers if he remembered the story he said he didn't whereas Richard remembered it at once. If Richard had been guilty one would have expected that he would deny the story.

'He was over-subtle about his drawings, too. When he burned down the offices – '

'Why did he do that?' Sinclair asked. The words fell start-lingly in the thick and hazy twilight.

'Fingerprints again. He was terrified of a fingerprint verifi-cation. And because of another of his mistakes – Polly Lines.'

'How much did she know about it all? And why did he kill her? And, by the way, who pushed you in the road that night when I nearly knocked you over? Or was that really an acci-dent?'

Bland laughed. 'Of course it was. I told you at the time that it's only in books that the murderer tries to kill the detective. Polly Lines knew about the pornographic racket, but of course she wasn't an accomplice in the murders. He was madly foolish to let himself get mixed up with her, but he was a sexually frustrated man, and Polly Lines was no doubt one of the few women he could get. But she must have learned that he made up. I doubt if we shall ever know what story he told her to explain that, but the fact that he was in such a shady business made it possible for him to tell one of half a dozen plausible tales. When she heard talk about murder she became suspicious and frightened, and he killed her because of that, and burned down the offices to avoid any chance of fingerprint recognition. He also destroyed all the letters and correspondence of the firm, including samples of van Dieren's handwriting. He was extremely careful about handwriting – she signed all the letters, and he even got her to sign the agreement for his house. After the offices were burnt we couldn't find a scrap of paper signed by van Dieren, so that we could compare his handwriting with Carruthers'. He made a big mistake, though, in leaving those Carruthers drawings outside the office for us to find. His idea was to confirm once again that van Dieren had Carruthers on his books, and that they weren't intimate friends, and the drawings were left to give a plausible reason for their tie-up.

Carruthers' reasoning probably went something like this. It might be dangerous to conceal the fact that van Dieren and Carruthers were linked in some way. All right then, let's admit it. Let Carruthers appear frightened when he hears van Dieren's name. And then, at the right moment, give evidence to show *why* Carruthers was worried – because he was afraid that the business about the pornographic drawings would come out. It's an old trick, to admit responsibility for a minor offence to avert suspicion about a major one, but it's still an effective one.

'In this case, however, the trick was spoilt by the signature. What pornographic artist in his senses would sign his work – and with a signature consisting of alternate letters of his own name, at that? And it was only a step from wondering about the signature to wondering how and why these particular drawings happened to escape the fire, and if they'd been left deliberately.

'Before I realized the significance of the handkerchief, I was just working by guess and by God, trying to separate what was genuinely important from the trails that, I could see, had been laid by the murderer. I even played around for some time with the idea that Jones had been invented to conceal a non-existent physical defect – if Bond's limp wasn't real, for instance, he might create Jones just to give himself an alibi. I tried to make something, too, of the fact that Jones never stayed overnight – if he were a married man, of course he probably wouldn't be able to do so. And all the while I saw this case building up against Richard, through van Dieren – a case which puzzled me because it was too obvious. If Richard was the murderer, then he'd behaved with astonishing stupidity.

'E. H.'s murder of course, was done in the obvious way, by van Dieren dropping poison in the sherry while E. H.'s attention was drawn away by the small boy who'd been engaged to throw the stone. The beauty of this was that it was made absolutely clear that Carruthers couldn't have committed this murder, because (as Carruthers) he'd never entered the room. After that van Dieren vanished, and Carruthers hoped I would arrest Richard, because of his obvious motive. But by that time I knew exactly what was happening, and I was determined to force

Carruthers to make a further attempt to incriminate Richard, which might allow us to catch him in the act. I put a man on to watch Richard, simply to make sure that no attack was made upon him, because that couldn't absolutely be ruled out. In the meantime I tried to find some link that would identify van Dieren and Carruthers as the same person. I failed in that – he'd covered the two main tracks of fingerprints and hand-writing too carefully. Since his arrest, however, we've found, by advertising for them, some receipts signed incautiously by "van Dieren" in the early days of his agency, which present the same characteristics as Carruthers' hand.

'Carruthers must have been disappointed by my failure to arrest Richard, but he was prepared for it. He couldn't produce van Dieren's body, so his last and most ingenious idea was to show unmistakably that Richard had killed van Dieren, and by extension, therefore, must have committed the two other murders. I was prepared for this, and while Carruthers was playing cat-and-mouse with Richard, I was playing cat-and-mouse with him. I asked Richard to alter the place in which his wedding reception was held to his house in Redfern Square, because I thought it certain that Carruthers would think that too good a chance to miss planting incriminating evidence. I had men watching Carruthers from the moment he left home that morning, and when he went down into the cellars they knew what he was going to do. That was the only way we could catch him – as we had to catch him – red-handed.'

The room was almost dark as Bland stopped speaking, and there was no sound in it but the gentle rhythmical breathing of five people. They were all asleep. With a sigh Bland got slowly to his feet, raised one of the wine bottles and poured the few drops of it down Filby's neck. With a horrified look on his face Filby opened his eyes and shook himself. 'All over?' he said.

'All over. They can't take drink, I'm afraid.' Bland stood up. 'We must go.'

'The Jones case is closed?'

'From the point of view of investigation it's certainly closed. Finished. I don't want to hear about it or him any more.'

'Neither do I,' said Filby handsomely. 'But aren't we going to say goodbye to those people?'

'We'll just get our coats, and then say it.' They met a waiter at the door, who peered at them both. 'Inspector Bland? There's somebody to see you downstairs. Something to do with some criminal case, he said it was.'

'Oh yes. Who is it?'

The waiter said, 'A man called Jones.'

# THE THIRTYFIRST
# OF FEBRUARY

*To Kathleen*

Who Lac'de and Fillitted the earth so fine,
With Rivers like green Ribbons Smaragdine?
Who made the Sea's its Selvedge, and it locks
Like a Quilt Ball within a Silver Box?
Who Spread its Canopy? Or Curtains Spun?
Who in this Bowling Alley bowld the Sun?

*Edward Taylor*


Mine Heart's a Park or Chase of Sins: Mine Head
'S a Bowling Alley: sins play Ninehole here.
Phansy's a Green: Sin Barly-breaks in't led.
Judgment's a pingle: Blindeman's Buff's plaid there.

*Edward Taylor*

# CONTENTS

# THE FOURTH OF FEBRUARY

On Monday February the fourth, in one of the years following the second of our great wars, the wife of a man named Anderson died. Her life ended at the comparatively early age of twenty-eight; and the circumstances of her death, as recounted at the inquest, were curious without being remarkable. She had been preparing dinner in their flat when she had suggested (her husband told the coroner) that they should drink a bottle of wine with the meal. They debated which wine they should drink with the fillets of sole she was preparing, and decided on a bottle of Chablis. The Andersons kept their modest stock of wine in a cellar below their ground-floor flat; and Mrs Anderson had left the sitting-room where her husband was reading the evening paper, to go down and fetch the bottle. He sat reading for a few minutes, until it occurred to him that his wife was a long time in the cellar. He got up (Anderson told the coroner), went to the head of the cellar stairs and found, to his surprise, that although the outside switch which gave illumination to the dark twisting stairway was switched on, the cellar was in darkness. He turned the switch on and off, as a man will do in such cases, but no light appeared. (It was found afterwards that the fuse had blown.) He called his wife, but there was no answer. Anderson, now a little alarmed, went back to the sitting-room for a box of matches, and with their aid groped his way down the steep, narrow stairs. At the bottom he found his wife, dead. She was, in fact, quite decisively dead, for she had sustained a fractured skull and a broken neck. Anderson made sure that there was no hope of her revival, and then went upstairs and telephoned doctor and police. He made a favourable impression at the inquest by giving this evidence in a composed manner, but with a subdued voice.

Why did Mrs Anderson fall? A box of matches lay near her body, so that when going down the stairs she had presumably, like her husband, the benefit of their light. Perhaps her match had blown out and she had not troubled to strike another; perhaps she had slipped on one of the steps, which was very uneven. One conjecture seemed as idle as another, after the event. The only awkward question that Anderson was asked came from a little juryman, wearing a stiff collar and a made-up bow tie. 'Whose suggestion was it that you should drink this bottle of Shablees?' the juryman asked.

'My wife's,' Anderson said in his low voice.

'And she made it while she was cooking supper?'

'Yes.'

'And then – while *she* was doing the cooking – *she* went down to the cellar to get the Shablees?'

'Yes.'

The little juryman cocked an eye up to the ceiling. 'Did she ask you p'raps to keep an eye on things while she was gone?'

'No.'

Tugging at his stiff collar, the juryman pounced. 'Why didn't *you* go down to the cellar, if she was busy with the supper?'

The look of absentminded resignation on Anderson's face did not change. 'My wife always liked to choose herself the particular bottle of wine we drank. It was one of – it was something she liked doing.'

The little juryman cast a look of triumph round the court and sat down. The Coroner expressed sympathy with Anderson. The verdict was accidental death.

After the funeral, Anderson went back to his job as an advertising executive. During the following weeks the quality of his work, and his ability to concentrate, were poor; but that was not surprising, since they had been poor for some time before his wife's death.

# THE TWENTYFIFTH OF FEBRUARY

## I

At a quarter to ten on Monday morning a brisk regiment of black Homburg hats marched down Bezyl Street. Beneath the hats advertising men were to be found, respectably overcoated, equipped with briefcases, wearing highly polished shoes: the younger faces among them alert, with pushing doglike noses, the maturer ones lined and yellow or red and sagging like overripe tomatoes. These older faces wore, beneath their outward cynicism or bursting good humour, a look like that of men hurrying for a train. Then the hats shot into offices, right and left, and in five minutes Bezyl Street was clear of them.

One of the hats, concealing a face that had graduated from dogginess to a lined and yellow maturity, turned into a corner building. Above the first floor of this building was a sign that ran round the corner into Vale Street and said VINCENT ADVERTISING VINCENT ADVERTISING VINCENT ADVERTISING VINCENT ADVERTISING. The word VINCENT was on the corner, so that if approached from Vale Street the sign read ADVERTISING VINCENT ADVERTISING VINCENT ADVERTISING. The Homburg hat tilted upwards, looked at the sign and above it at the watery grey February sky, and disappeared inside the building.

The swing doors closed with a faint hiss. In the reception hall the air was warm and slightly sweet. A body as soft as a cushion moved behind the reception desk.

'A cold morning, Mr Anderson.'

'But seasonable, Miss Detranter.'

Framed advertisements reviving the glories of past campaigns lined the corridor. Anderson walked slowly between them, came to a small square landing with three doors set into it, turned right down another corridor and opened a door. Within it were the apparatus of a life – kneehole desk, revolving chair, hatstand, oak cupboard, green carpet. He took off his dark overcoat

and put it on a hanger, hung above it his black silk-lined hat
and sat down in the revolving chair. The watch on his wrist said
eleven minutes to ten.

A typewritten note was propped against his desk calendar.
It said: *9.20 Mr Bagseed rang. Please ring him back. J. L.*
Underneath it was another typewritten note: *VV has called a
conference at 10.30. He would like you to be there. J. L.* He
turned the pieces of paper face downwards, and looked at the
morning's mail. A letter from Artifex Products about next year's
advertising for Quickies, the lightning pick-me-up; some proofs
of new advertisements for Crunchy-Munch, the tasty chocolate-
covered mixture of toffee and biscuit. He picked up one of the
telephones and said: 'Mr Bagseed of Kiddy Modes, please.'

The switchboard girl's name was Miss Vine. She had a clinging voice. 'Mr Bagseed's ringing you, Mr Anderson. He's on
the line now.'

'Put him on.'

Bagseed came on as always with a rush, as though he had
been talking for some time and was taking up a point made in
the middle of a conversation. 'I say, you know, this won't do,
Mr Anderson. We can't let this appear.'

'What won't do, Mr Bagseed?'

'I've been on to you once already.' The voice was nasal,
querulous, accusing. 'We must stop this advertisement at once.
It just won't do.'

'Which advertisement, Mr Bagseed?'

Impatiently the voice said: 'Why, the one for tomorrow's
*Gazette*. Just look at it yourself. Are you with me, Mr Anderson? Are you there? Have you got a proof of the advertisement
there? Are you with me?'

He held the telephone between left ear and shoulder and
flicked over the contents of a folder marked *Kiddy Modes
Proofs*. He stopped at an advertisement showing a little girl
wearing a Kiddy Modes frock and looking rather anxiously up
at her mother.

'I'm with you, Mr Bagseed.'

'Well.' The voice laughed nasally. 'Do you know what Mr

Arthur said when he saw that proof this morning? He said – I can't repeat his exact words, because they're not polite – but the gist was that he said the little girl looks as if she's asking to go to stool.'

'But Mr Bagseed – ' He picked up a pencil and began to draw on his blotter.

'Mr Arthur asked if we were trying to make Kiddy Modes a laughing-stock. I said of course not; I said it's only if you look at it in a certain way. But he said – ' Anderson put the telephone down on the desk and drew a man's head with a wide-open mouth. Occasionally words came out from the receiver: 'But I said – but he said – and I had to admit – '

The pencil point snapped. Anderson threw it across the room, picked up the receiver again and spoke in a deliberately gentle voice.

'This advertisement had already been approved by you, Mr Bagseed, as Kiddy Modes' advertising manager. Isn't that so? And we agreed then that the drawing was excellent? Isn't that so?' The door opened and a face followed a pipe round the opening. 'Just to keep the record straight,' Anderson said amiably.

The nasal voice changed to a whine. 'I know, I know. The fact is sometimes Mr Arthur's simply – unpredictable. It makes life difficult.'

'It makes life difficult.' Anderson raised a hand in greeting, pointed to the telephone and turned down the corners of his mouth. The newcomer sat in the visitor's chair, placed one leg over another, and looked at his beautifully polished black shoe. 'But now that we've got it straight, let's see what we can do to help you. I've got two advertisements that we can substitute – the one with the teddy bear and the one with the doll's pram. The paper won't be pleased, but to hell with the paper. Which do you want? The teddy bear?'

Whining apologetically, the voice said: 'The teddy bear will be fine. You can't imagine, Mr Anderson, what a weight that is off my mind. You've no idea – '

'Not a bit, Mr Bagseed. I'll make that substitution right away.

'Bye.' Anderson dialled a number on the house telephone. 'Production. This is Anderson. Kiddy Modes. Scrap B18 for the *Gazette* tomorrow and give them E21 instead.' There were protesting noises. 'Yes, I know it's late. Complain, hell – let them complain. Who pays for the bloody advertisement anyway?' He put down the house telephone and sighed.

'Swear words so early on a Monday morning,' said the man with the pipe. He was a big man with a square face, in his early forties, who looked both friendly and dependable. His name was Reverton, and he was one of the three directors of Vincent Advertising, who were housed in the three rooms facing the square landing. 'What's the matter with the Bagwash?'

Anderson mimicked the nasal voice. 'Mr Arthur's looked at one of our advertisements and Mr Arthur wants it changed.'

Reverton puffed at the pipe. 'We could do without that account. Can't have important executives getting hot under the collar over penny numbers. What's it worth – thirty thousand a year?'

'Twentyfive.'

'They get more than that in service.' He looked reflectively at his black shoe. 'How's it going? Getting you down at all?'

'No. Why?' Anderson found it difficult to meet Reverton's straight enquiring gaze, and stared at the desk. But there was something wrong with the desk, although he could not have said just what, and his gaze shifted to the broken-pointed pencil lying on the carpet. He saw that Reverton was also looking curiously at the pencil, while his square-nailed fingers tamped down tobacco in the pipe. Reverton picked up the pencil and put it on the desk. The match flame flickered above his pipe.

'The best thing to take a chap's mind off worry is work. Like to handle a new account? Something big?'

Anderson put both arms on the desk and stared keenly at the wall. 'Try me.'

'This is really something, Andy. I wanted you to have it. I told VV as much.'

After keenness, gratitude. 'That's damned nice of you, Rev.'

'Nonsense. We've all got our plates full. Besides, it's just up your street.' Anderson's eyes followed blue smoke on its way up to the ceiling. 'Appeal to your sense of humour, too.'

'Sense of humour?'

'It's something rather' – puff puff, went the pipe – 'special. VV's absolutely sold on it. You know the way he gets. That's what the conference is all about.' Reverton rose, a square head and thick neck running into a stiff white collar, belching smoke like an engine. 'Thought I'd put you in the picture.'

'And are you sold on it?'

Reverton paused at the door and grinned, man to man, not director to executive. 'Not necessary. If VV's sold on it we're all sold on it.' The door closed. His steps faded along the corridor.

What was wrong with the desk? Blotter, letters, engagement pad, calendar. Calendar, he thought, calendar. The calendar was made of brass, and you turned the small and inconvenient knobs at the back of it to alter the day of the week, the date, and the month. Anderson stared at the calendar and then looked at his morning paper. The paper said Monday, February 25. The top slot in the calendar said Monday, the slot to the right said February. The slot to the left said 4. It was simple enough. The calendar was showing a wrong date. But Monday, February 4, was a very special wrong date. It was the date on which Anderson's wife had died.

The house telephone rang. A plummy voice said: 'This is Mr Pile. Can you – h'm – spare me a few minutes?'

'Right away, Mr Pile.' Mr Pile was another director.

He sat staring at the calendar, then picked it up and turned the knob so that it showed a correct date. Then he got up and walked further down the corridor, away from the directors' offices, to a large room where half a dozen girls sat in front of typewriters. He stopped before one of them. Her name was Jean Lightley, and she was Anderson's secretary. She was a plain girl of about nineteen, who wore horn-rimmed spectacles and had a great fund of embarrassment. She said with a slight gasp: 'Oh, Mr Anderson, did you get the messages?'

'Yes, thanks.' He said casually: 'Jean, did you change my calendar this morning?'

'Why, I always do, Mr Anderson.'

'And what's the date today?'

'*Today*, Mr Anderson?' She gasped again. 'Monday, the twentyfifth.'

'Quite sure that's what you changed it to this morning?' She nodded, beyond speech, and he turned away, out of the room and back along the corridor to the square landing where the three doors bore the names of the three directors. Anderson knocked on the door which said in gold letters *L. E. G. Pile* and opened it without waiting for a reply. He said 'Good morning' to a small man in his early sixties who sat behind an enormous desk.

Mr Pile wore a plain dark grey suit of an old-fashioned cut, a decorous striped tie and forbidding pince-nez. He was looking at some papers and said 'Good morning' without raising his head. Anderson remained standing in front of the desk. In Reverton's room he would have sat down without being asked. In Vincent's the chairs would have been covered with magazines, which Vincent would have thrown on the floor. But Pile was one of the elder statesmen of advertising, a man who believed in emphasising social and administrative distinctions. However important an executive might be, he was less important than a director. In Mr Pile's room an executive stood up until he was told to sit down, and it was perhaps thirty seconds before Mr Pile looked up from his intensive study of the papers on his desk and said in a surprised tone: 'Sit down, Anderson.' Then Anderson sat down. Mr Pile stared at him, a little wizened old man with small hard eyes behind the pince-nez. Below the hard shell of his exterior was a layer of soft, warm shyness and embarrassment. And below the shyness, Anderson guessed, was solid rock. Now he seemed to have difficulty in forming his words.

'Did you – have a pleasant weekend, Anderson?'

'Quiet, thank you.'

'Did you – spend any time in the garden?'

'My flat is in town,' Anderson said. He had conducted this conversation many times, in half a dozen variations. Which would it be this time, he wondered – the Beauty of Getting Away From It All or Town Mouse and Country Mouse? As Pile talked behind the immense desk in the sombre room the electric desk lamp flashed every so often upon his rimless pince-nez, so that the eyes behind them were almost invisible. '. . . So that in some ways,' he was saying, 'the country cousin, ignorant and foolish as he may be in the way of the world, has an advantage over the – ah – more sophisticated town mouse. But I mustn't push my little joke too far. All we advertising men are town mice, are we not?' Anderson covertly looked at his watch. 'Are you an admirer of the immortal Walt? I refer,' Mr Pile said with a slight cough, 'to Disney, not Whitman.'

Wasn't this preamble more than usually lengthy? Was there a slight uneasiness behind the pince-nez? 'I admire the early films very much,' Anderson said, and added: 'I'm due for a conference with Mr Vincent in a few minutes.'

Mr Pile regarded him, apparently sightlessly. 'You know of – ah – Sir Malcolm Buntz?' Anderson nodded. Sir Malcolm Buntz was a director of South Eastern Laboratories, one of the firm's largest accounts. 'Sir Malcolm has a nephew who contemplates' – Mr Pile coughed – 'a career in advertising.' Anderson said nothing. 'He is, I am sure, an amiable young man, but amiability is not, as I remarked to Sir Malcolm, the sole, or perhaps even the chief, requisite for a successful career in advertising. Sir Malcolm, however, has been insistent.' He sighed to indicate the degree of Sir Malcolm's insistence. 'And it is difficult to refuse him. In short, the young man is coming here to serve a brief apprenticeship. I have agreed with Mr Vincent and Mr Reverton that he shall begin it under your watchful eye in the Copy Department.'

'We're very busy.'

'So much the better. It will be a baptism of – ah – fire for him. Let me have a report on him, and do not,' Mr Pile smiled with wintry shyness, 'spare Sir Malcolm's feelings.'

'When does he begin?'

'He begins this – ah – morning,' Mr Pile said. Light shone on his pince-nez. 'His name is Greatorex.'

## II

Reverton and Anderson sat in armchairs in VV's room. Wyvern, head of the Art Department, a thin dyspeptic man who wore a sports jacket and dirty grey trousers, sat staring out of the window into the street. The time was twenty to eleven. Wyvern said suddenly: 'Here he is.'

There was a commotion outside, and then a little man rushed into the room. 'Boys, boys, I'm sorry,' he said. 'But wait a minute. This'll kill you. Just wait a minute, that's all I ask.' He flung on to the floor a briefcase stuffed with magazines and papers, whisked off hat, scarf and overcoat, and darted out of the room again. There was the sound of a lavatory flushing, and then he was back. 'Well,' he said. 'Well. What's all this on my desk? Books, magazines, papers, nothing but junk.' He threw a handful of art magazines to the floor and beamed round at them. His hair stood on end and his thick eyebrows stuck out. 'I suppose Rev's told you two boys what this is all about?'

Placidly puffing at his pipe, Reverton said: 'Only hints, VV. I thought you'd like to explain.'

'Well,' said VV, delighted. He uttered an indistinct exclamation, and darted at a bell push. A girl appeared. VV smacked his hand on the desk. 'My hot milk and my tablets, Miss Jones.' The girl vanished. VV sat back in his chair and looked round at them as thought they were an audience of three hundred, instead of three. 'There's one thing,' he said, 'that every one of us has done this morning. Do you know what it is? Not only every one of us in this room, but every man in these offices.' His hands fluttered, his triangular gnome-like face shone with pleasure. 'It's not what you're thinking, Jack my boy,' he said, pointing at Wyvern, whose face gave no indication that he was thinking anything. 'We don't do *that* every morning – not even the biggest rams among us.'

Reverton took his pipe out of his mouth. 'There are no statistics on that, VV.'

'Statistics? We've got the whole history of the human race.' He rocked with laughter. 'And we don't all evacuate every morning either, unfortunately. What *do* we do, then?' Miss Jones returned with a glass of milk and three green tablets which she placed at his side. He waved them away impatiently. When she had gone out he repeated: 'What *do* we do?' His voice dropped to a whisper. 'I'll tell you, gentlemen. *We shave.*'

Reverton went on blowing smoke from his pipe. Wyvern continued to look out of the window. Anderson sat forward, looking, he hoped, keenly interested. In his mind he saw the calendar which said *Monday, 4 February*. What did it mean? VV jumped up and began to walk up and down the room among the piles of *Scope, Verve, Vogue* and *Printers' Ink* on the floor.

'Every morning modern man crawls out of his warm bed, stretches, faces a mirror and assaults his face with cold steel for anything from five to thirtyfive minutes. He cuts and scrapes and hacks away, fighting the unending battle against the growth of Nature. Every morning he gains a victory – but at what a price. Bits of sticking plaster, after-shave lotion, cooling powder – he calls them all into play; he has a row with his wife and catches the eight-fifteen feeling very much the worse for wear.' VV's voice, which had risen to a pitch of histrionic excitement, changed suddenly to a mellifluous cooing. 'Now supposing we had discovered a means of eliminating this daily torture, supposing we could say "Hey Presto" and find ourselves shaved – wouldn't that be the greatest boon ever brought to twentieth-century man?' He stood for a moment with one hand stretched before him, and then slowly lowered it. 'Boys,' he said solemnly, 'this is something big. Really big. This is something more than just another advertising account. It's a national benefit.' He sat down, put one of the green pills on his tongue, and sipped the milk.

Wyvern shifted in his chair. Anderson looked down at his

legs. He had for a moment the extraordinary impression that the lower part of his body was separated from the upper half. Suppose that were really so? Suppose that the foot, the whole leg, failed to obey the instructions telegraphed from the brain. Suppose that one telegraphed such a message now, and – suddenly his right foot flickered on the carpet as though moved by a tic. He watched its performance dispassionately.

'Better get down to cases,' said Reverton. 'I've got it all down here in outline, VV. Shall I give it to them?' Drinking his milk, swallowing his tablets, glancing from one to the other of them, VV nodded. 'All right then. This is a new product, absolutely unmarketed. It's extracted from the tgojumba tree which grows in Central Africa, refined and specially processed.'

'The what?' said Wyvern.

'The tgojumba tree.'

'Any relation to the miraculous yam-yam you find on the shores of Coromandel?'

'I know, I know,' said Reverton. 'It's funny. Maybe it isn't the tgojumba tree; maybe it's simply a laboratory product. We'll have to know that – they mustn't think they can do any woolpulling with their advertising agents. But the important thing is that it works. You use it almost exactly as you use a brushless shaving cream – except that it's razorless as well as brushless. Smear it on your face, leave it on for a minute, wipe it off, and your face is perfectly smooth and stays smooth the whole day.'

'No five o'clock shadow?'

'No five o'clock shadow,' Reverton said solemnly. 'That's the product. Now, here's the set-up as far as this agency is concerned. Manufacture is beginning in South Africa and it's planned to market the product simultaneously here and over there. Negotiations are going on now in the States and on the Continent. Our first job is to suggest a name for the product. At present it's just called Preparation Number One, but the name the manufacturing company suggests is Nu-Shave. Both VV and I think that stinks. Next, we've got to think how we're going to handle a campaign, which may start by the end of this year. The sky's the limit for the South African company, Multi-African

Products, who're making the stuff. We've got to decide where we're going to pack our biggest punch. Press, cinema, posters – we've got a revolutionary product to advertise, and if we can find revolutionary means so much the better.' Reverton stuck his pipe back in his mouth, and then took it out again. 'One more thing, Andy and J. W. VV's called this preliminary conference to start you thinking. He'll handle the account from the creative side. I shall deal with administration. You'll be responsible for copy ideas, Andy, and you, J. W., for what comes out of the studio. Your boys are bound to know about it. Enthuse them, but tell them to keep it under their hats.' Reverton stuck his pipe back, apparently for good. VV swallowed the last of the green pills, got up and stood with his hands behind his back, staring at Anderson and Wyvern. 'Any ideas, boys? How does it seem?'

Sucking his pipe, Reverton said delightedly: 'Hold on now, VV; give the boys a chance to think.'

Anderson thought it was time he said something. 'The end of this year means it's not all that urgent.'

VV wheeled and confronted him, genial but admonitory. 'It *is* urgent. I want it treated as urgent. I want the sparks to fly. I want creation, boys, and no damned nine months' gestation, either.' Like a little dynamo he whirred between the three seated figures.

Wyvern said in a discontented croak: 'Does the stuff exist?'

Like a conjurer, Reverton produced from his pocket a small brownish jar, and passed it round. A label said *Preparation Number 1*; the top screwed off to reveal a white paste. Wyvern and Anderson looked at it curiously, and then Anderson said: 'Has anyone tried it?'

'This very morning.' Reverton tilted a perfectly smooth face for inspection. 'Worked like a charm. On, off, beard gone.'

'Nu-Shave,' Anderson said thoughtfully. 'You know, there could be worse names.'

'Or Razorless,' Wyvern suggested. 'Might be something in Razorless.

'Pa and grandpapa both bless
The day they changed to Razorless.'

VV's fist struck his desk. We're in for it now, Anderson thought;
he's got a scheme hatched out already. The little figure behind
the desk was bristling with annoyance, but when he spoke he
was not annoyed but histrionically grieved, humorously disappointed. 'You're not thinking right, boys.' The fist unclenched
and cupped his chin. 'This isn't a product for humour. You don't
sell a revolution with humour.'

It's foolish to contradict, it's foolish to question, Anderson
thought, as his foot moved to make circles and crosses in the
air. But he wants just a little opposition perhaps. He said, with
the right mixture of protest and conciliation: 'But other shaving
devices have been sold on humour, VV. We don't need to talk
about tossing our razors over the windmill, but surely there's
a case for being lighthearted. After all, it's an occasion for
celebration.'

VV's fine hands fluttered in the air, his voice beat like an
incantation, his eyes stared straight ahead of him, like the eyes
of a man in a trance. 'This is the way I see it, boys. Shaving is
one of the acts that bind us to a world of ritual, the world that
each of us secretly detests. The alarm clock, the toothbrush, the
razor, the railway timetable – they're all part of the pattern that
makes up the mechanical life of modern man. Take a thousand
jigsaw pieces, fit them together every day – and our lives are
the result. But what we are doing is to take away one of those
pieces. There's a hole in the jigsaw, the pattern's not complete.
Through that hole modern man can catch a glimpse of freedom.
It may be a small thing in itself, but my word it's a wonderful
symbol.

'Now, I want you to think in those terms, boys. Forget that
you're advertising men and remember that you're human beings.
We don't want humour here; we want humanity. I can see
one headline that says just FREEDOM FROM SHAVING. That's the
essential, simple human story.' VV's voice had dropped to a
low, reverent note. 'The whole day's changed – no more family

quarrels now Dad's in a good temper every morning. I can see another heading that says *I Threw Away My Razor* – and the story there is the symbolism of it; that it's the finest thing he ever did. I can see a sweet little girlie writing in her diary *Happy Days Began Last Friday*. I can see a little boy saying *Daddy Has Time to Say "Good Morning" Now*.'

VV's voice changed again. Reverence disappeared, and an easy conversational tone took its place. 'I'm just thinking aloud, you know. This is general direction, nothing more. I don't want to interfere with you boys. Think it out for yourselves. There's always another way of doing it. But don't miss the wood for the trees. There's a great human story here. Don't miss it through trying to be clever or scientific or funny. And don't get bogged in detail. The great thing is the tone. Once we've got that the details will arrange themselves.' He had talked himself into a good temper. He stood up and beamed at Wyvern. 'And don't try to find out about the tgojumba tree, J. W., so that you can draw it. Look for the secrets of the human heart instead. Go to it, boys.'

The audience was over.

Outside the door Wyvern said: 'Now we know it all. God has spoken. I need a drink at lunch. You?' Anderson nodded. 'See you in the *Stag*,' Wyvern said and shambled away down the corridor. His gait was equally unsteady, whether he was sober or (as was often the case) drunk. Anderson started to walk after him and then turned back and re-entered the room he had just left. The effect of his entrance seemed to him extraordinary. Reverton was bending over VV's desk, the heads of the two men were close together, almost touching. As he came in they almost sprang – it seemed to Anderson – apart. More than that, it was Anderson's impression that the two heads close together had worn expressions that were perfectly serious, and even sombre; but now, when they looked up, Reverton's face was set in his characteristic self-deprecatory grin, and VV looked eagerly amiable. Was the change, then, nothing more than a trick of light, or had their expressions been adjusted deliberately to receive him? He stood for a moment, while both men looked at him enquiringly.

'It's about Greatorex.' VV looked mystified. Anderson said with a kind of exaggerated self-conscious humour: 'The nephew of Sir Malcolm Buntz, you know.'

Reverton's mouth had clamped hard on his pipe. He took it out to say: 'Lad who fancies he wants to be an advertising man. You remember L. E. G. wanted to put him through the mill here and it was agreed he should start in Copy.'

'Oh ah,' said VV. He took no interest in such matters. 'What about him?'

'I understand he's started this morning. I think, as head of the Copy Department, I might have been told before today.'

Reverton said: 'Andy, old boy, I must plead guilty. We've been working like stink on this new account. Tried to stave off L. E. G., but you know what he's like when a client like Sir Malcolm wants a favour – never lets go. He asked me to let you know on Friday and I forgot. We've all been blowing our tops here the last couple of weeks.' His smile was an apology.

'Can't he start in another department? Lessing and I have got enough to do.'

Reverton looked unhappy. 'L. E. G. particularly wanted him to start in Copy. Brains of the place, you know.'

There was silence. Anderson said sulkily: 'If that's the way it's got to be, then.'

'Now now,' VV said. 'Don't take this too seriously, Andy. How long's this boy supposed to stay in Copy? A fortnight. All right, then, let's make it a week. Give him an idea how the wheels go round, see if there's anything in him; toss him out after a week if he's no good. How's that?'

'All right.' On the way back to his room Anderson thought that he should have been firmer; he should have said *No*. But it was not easy to say *No* to VV.

Charlie Lessing was waiting in the room when he got back. He was a donnish, soft-spoken, thirtyish young man with a small mouth and large horn-rimmed spectacles. 'Six pieces of Crunchy-Munch copy are on your desk. I have consumed a great deal of that nutritious and delicious sweetmeat to put me in the mood. I feel a little sick. What was the conference?'

'Somebody's found a way to end razoritis. VV's discovered the fifth freedom.' He explained. Lessing's small mouth made an O of surprise.

'Are you sure the End of the World League didn't dream this one up in the night?'

'That's what Wyvern thinks, but VV won't have any of it. He says it's all genuine. He's given a directive.' Lessing groaned. 'Humour is out. Science is out. Humanity is in. Regard this as a great human problem and you'll be thinking the way the boss thinks.'

'That's the way I always want to think,' Lessing said seriously. 'Life began for me today – it's a different man who says "Hallo" in the morning – is that the line?'

'That's about it. And don't forget how wonderful it is for the kiddies that Daddy can spare a minute to clip them over the ear after he has breakfast. There it is. You may as well ask Research to get out a competitive file on shaving, although I can't see that we shall need it. And a little bit of historical research won't do any harm.'

'What about the tgojumba tree?' Lessing squinted down his snub nose. 'I long to say something about that. We don't need any research. The sap's extracted by the natives and they anoint themselves with it – that's why they've been the cleanest-shaven tribe in Central Africa for so many years. But for the sensitive white skin the original treacly sap has been refined by our laboratory chemists and combined with an unguent derived from powdered hippopotamus testicles to produce a shaving preparation of a kind hitherto unknown.'

'I forgot to tell you,' Anderson said. 'That won't do'

'Won't do, sir?' Lessing looked comically offended.

'Shaving. This is anti-shaving, not shaving. We need a name, and it musn't be comic or smart. *Nu-Shave* and *Razorless* have received heavy frowns.'

'Depilo?'

'Too scientific.'

Lessing laughed. His laugh was surprising, a high-pitched scholar's giggle. 'You know, I can't believe this. Somebody's having a little joke.'

'Rev's tried it and he says it works.' Anderson dismissed the question, and Lessing with it. When the copywriter was at the door he called him back. 'I say, have you got a mother's only son in there? Nephew of Sir Malcolm Buntz, answers to the name of Greatorex?' Lessing nodded. 'What's he like?'

'Nondescript but harmless. I kept him happy looking at our old ads in the guard books.' Lessing giggled again. 'He kind of thought he'd like to do something creative. Do you want him?'

'Not now. I'll see him this afternoon. But get him to work making out a list of names, will you, Charlie? He can't break anything while he does that. And forage about a bit yourself.'

With a parody of VV's most cooingly persuasive tone, Lessing said: 'And don't be inhibited by anything I've said. Think for yourself.' He went out.

Anderson sat down to look at the new Crunchy-Munch scheme. The telephone rang and the switchboard girl said: 'Oh, Mr Anderson, Mr Bagseed's been asking for you. He said it was important.'

'Get him for me, will you?' He was frowning at the headline CRUNCHY-MUNCH SAVES SECRETARY'S JOB when Bagseed came through, nasal and anxious.

'Look here, Mr Arthur's on my back about those drawings. You know, the ones for our summer campaign.'

'Ah yes.' Anderson unhooked the house telephone and dialled Jean Lightley's number. 'Jean,' he said, 'drawings for Kiddy Modes that should have come in last week from Crashaw Studios. Find out what's happened. Quick.' Bagseed had been talking without a check. 'Yes,' Anderson said. 'Yes. Yes.'

'I simply must have those drawings for Mr Arthur this afternoon.'

'I'm right behind those drawings, Mr Bagseed.' He improvised. 'You'll have them today.'

Nasal complaint became nasal friendliness. 'Grand, Mr Anderson, grand.'

'Not a bit.' He improved the situation with a little invention. 'As a matter of fact, these drawings are a bit late because I asked the artist to make sure they were just right. And you can't hurry an artist. You know what artists are, Mr Bagseed.'

'I do indeed, Mr Anderson. I'm sorry to have bothered you.'

'It's what we're here for.' They both said ha ha. Anderson put down the receiver. He saw that Lessing's scheme was a series of strip stories, each containing four little pictures. In CRUNCHY-MUNCH SAVES SECRETARY'S JOB, Picture I shows a crestfallen secretary being reprimanded for carelessness by her employer. 'You're all right in the morning, Miss Jones, but every afternoon you make these silly mistakes.' In Picture 2, Miss Jones talks to her friend. 'The fact is, Sheila, I get hungry and we don't have time for a tea break.' Sheila replies: 'A Crunchy-Munch bar keeps you going. Tastes good, too.' Picture 3: Miss Jones, with typewriter in front of her, letters at side, is eating a Crunchy-Munch bar and thinking: 'Yum-yum, it *does* taste good.' Picture 4: Employer says: 'These letters are perfectly typed. Congratulations on snapping out of the depression, Miss Jones.' Miss Jones (thinks): *Congratulations to Crunchy-Munch, you mean*. Underneath the story was a slogan: CRUNCHY-MUNCH THE VITAMIN-PACKED CHOC-COVERED BAR OF ENERGY. The other pieces of copy exploited the same theme in strip form. The Art Department had made rough layouts that looked very neat and clean.

Anderson sighed, shook his head, and scribbled headings on a sheet of paper. After ten minutes he looked at them:

> AFTER LUNCH COMES CRUNCHY-MUNCH
> CRUNCHY-MUNCH ROUNDS OFF YOUR LUNCH
> LUNCH TIME'S ALWAYS CRUNCHY-MUNCH TIME
> ALL THE BUNCH EAT CRUNCHY-MUNCH

He sighed again. Jean Lightley coughed. 'Oh, Mr Anderson, Crashaw Studios say you can't have those drawings until tomorrow. The artist's away ill and somebody else is finishing them off.'

'Hell!' Anderson sat looking at the desk. 'Did you employ

all your feminine charms?' Jean Lightley went red. 'Did you speak to Crashaw himself?'

'To his secretary, but I don't think – '

'All right, all right. You go to lunch. If Bagseed rings up again I'm in conference.' He talked to Crashaw and by a mixture of wheedling and threats obtained a promise that the drawings would be sent that afternoon. He was about to go out to lunch when he noticed the calendar. It read *Monday, 4 February*.

Anderson sat down and stared at the calendar. Somebody had turned it back again to the three-weeks-old date. Why? But as he continued to stare at the neat '4' he felt an obscure uneasiness. Was he quite certain that he had made the alteration back to '25'? Was it not possible that he had forgotten? He said aloud: 'You know perfectly well that you altered it,' and the spoken words seemed to give some small reassurance. He put on his Homburg hat and dark overcoat, and went out.

## III

Wyvern said: 'What I like about you, Molly, is the way you pour it down. It might be the kitchen sink instead of your throat.'

'Pour it down fast and you don't taste it. Only way to drink beer.' Molly O'Rourke's hair was bunched in tight curls on her head, and her long nose looked as if it was made of chalk. She had once read sociology at the London School of Economics and now ran the Research Department of the firm. 'So I said to him you can take it or leave it. So he said if that's the way you feel I'll leave it. So I said all right, but don't come crying back for more tomorrow. That's original and good. It's not good, he said, but you've certainly got something about it being original. Original, I said, you don't know what originality means. If I – '

The *Stag* was crowded. Somebody dug Anderson violently in the ribs and he lost the end of Molly's story, as he had lost the beginning. 'So that was the end of a perfect romance.' She turned to Anderson. 'You seem a bit low, pet. What's up?'

'Nothing. Have another drink.'

'Thanks, another beer, beautiful chemical beer – how I love it. Wouldn't recognize real beer if I met it nowadays.' They were standing at the counter, and the rising and falling swell of people pushed their bodies against each other and then gently ebbed away from them. The glass behind the bar reflected back at Anderson a yellow face, deeply lined and folded, with melancholy bloodshot eyes and thinning hair. He ordered drinks.

'Let the man alone,' Wyvern said in his deep croak. 'He's got every right not to be cheerful.'

'Because of his wife?'

'Partly because of his wife.'

Molly stuck her long nose forward. 'So what? I never thought you were tied up all that tight to Valerie, pet.'

Anderson pushed over the beer. 'It's only three weeks.' He was annoyed that his voice sounded apologetic. 'February the fourth. Three weeks today.'

'You ought to snap out of it,' Molly said. 'In my time – if I may let my back hair down for your benefit – I've lost three husbands. Not to mention all those I mislaid before the ceremony. The first time I was young and innocent and went into it neck first. He used to beat me, but I didn't mind that. It was when he wanted me to beat him in front of his girlfriend that I stepped out. He was what you might call sophisticated.'

'You make it different each time,' Wyvern said admiringly. 'And I will say you make it better. What happened then?'

Molly gulped her beer. 'Then? Then I got a divorce and married again. This time *he* was young and innocent, looking for his mother. You wouldn't think I was the mother type, would you? But that's the way he used to think of me, and perhaps he wasn't so far wrong at that. He was sweet, always bringing presents – nothing valuable, you know, cigarette cases, powder puffs, silk stockings, everything you can think of. Then the police picked him up in a store. Turned out he was a kleptomaniac. That was the end of another perfect romance.'

'What about the third?'

'Oh, the third was a bastard. But what I want to show you, Andy pet, is that you've got to keep your chin up. Life's nothing but a succession of kicks in the jaw, anyway.'

Anderson joggled the beer in his glass. 'What else have I got to worry about?' he asked Wyvern.

'Eh?'

'You said partly my wife. What's the other part of my worry?'

Wyvern bent his narrow head forward until Anderson saw, fascinated, the small pock-marks and blemishes in the sallow skin. 'Somebody's whispering things in the office. Somebody's saying you're slipping and need a rest.'

'Who's saying that?' Anderson was surprised by the sharpness of his own voice.

'A little birdie told me.' Wyvern put his head on one side. 'I'd look out on this shave-me-quick account if I were you.'

'Rev suggested I should handle it.'

'Good old Rev, dear old Rev.' Wyvern's smile was lop-sided. 'Know what he said to me the other day, with his pipe sticking out of his mouth. "Andy's a good scout – puff puff – but he doesn't quite – puff puff – believe in his work." When Rev says you're not believing in your work, boy, that's a time to look out.'

'But how can you believe in your work?' Molly asked. 'You can only do it. Don't tell me VV and Rev believe the stuff that goes in their own advertisements.'

'I know what they mean,' Anderson said. He remembered Rev's head by the side of VV's, the sombre faces quickly changing to false geniality.

'You not only know what they mean; you know they're right.' Wyvern tapped a nicotine-stained finger on the dirty knee of his trousers. 'You want to be a successful advertising man. All right. You've got to be able to draw or write a bit. But that's not much. You've got to be intelligent, so that you see through advertising. You see it's all a lot of cock, you see it's parasitic, you see it's a bloody fleecing of the public. All right. But that's not all. In fact, that's not much. Because *then* you've got to be able to believe it all while you're working on it. You've got to believe that Crunchy-Munch is the most nutritious and delicious chocolate bar ever made, that Kiddy Modes really make the best baby clothes, that some stinking patent medicine which can be made for a penny a bottle is really a remedy for physical states that should be treated by a doctor, that this bloody little device for avoiding shaving in the morning is something that can revolutionize people's lives. And it's because he can see through advertising and be deceived by it at the same time that VV's a bloody perfect advertising man.' He ordered more beer.

'What about you?' Anderson said. 'I've never noticed you showing much belief in the blessing of advertising.'

'Don't talk about me,' Wyvern cried in a passion of delighted frustration. 'I'm no advertising man. I'm just a painter who took to commercial hack work because he had to keep his mother. And Molly is just doing a job. We don't have to believe; we aren't inside the charmed circle. I can afford a bit of irresponsibility, a few drinks too many, dirty trousers and an old jacket. But you're different, Andy boy; you're *it*. You're the next best thing to a director. You talk to clients and soothe them down. You're a big boy, not just a technician like Molly and me. You're all set for your directorship if Rev doesn't trip you up before you get it. You've got to wear that black hat, you've got to be serious. I can stay silent in a conference if I want to, but you've got to have an opinion about everything. In short,' Wyvern croaked happily, 'if you want to be saved you've got to believe.'

Anderson drank his beer, ordered another round, and argued it out as he was expected to argue it out. The same discussion, he reflected, was going on between hundreds of advertising men over lunch-time drinks. Dozens of commercial artists were blaming the mothers or wives or children who had made them take the road to commercialism instead of the road to high art, a herd of copywriters were busily biting the hands that fed them when they should be regretting their own lack of talent or toughness. But he had got beyond all that himself; he was reconciled to advertising, he was prepared to take it as seriously as anything else. The pub got more and more crowded. They ate sandwiches. Wyvern began to talk to a commercial artist named Harvey Nicols, Anderson found himself standing again thigh to thigh with Molly O'Rourke, who was telling him about her third husband. People all round them were talking so loudly that he heard only snatches of what she said, mixed with other fragments of conversation.

'– left Rayson, Jones and Johnson and went to Palefox, Wiggins and Grass – '

'– One of these schemes stinks, they said, and it's not your competitor's – '

'– He gave me a black eye.' That was Molly.

'– A new slogan, he said, so I told him – '

'– There's absolutely nothing doing down *that* alley – '

'– So she said, really I'm too Jung to be a Freud – '

'– Ask for a thousand and he'll offer eight fifty. Ask for twelve hundred and he'll offer – '

'– And we Adler good time together. Like it?'

'– So I gave him a black eye.' That was Molly again.

He had heard it all before. Wearily, he said he must go away and work. Molly went to talk to Wyvern and Harvey Nicols. When Anderson got outside, his head was slightly fuzzy with beer.


IV


After lunch Anderson interviewed Sir Malcolm's nephew, Greatorex. He was fair-headed, wore a neat brown suit, and was perhaps in his middle or late thirties. Anderson was surprised both by his age, and by the fact that he was not obviously a booby. Greatorex talked about himself readily enough, and with a pleasant absence of bumptiousness or embarrassment. He had travelled a good deal, and had been farmer, shorthand typist, journalist, factory worker, and a dozen other things.

'And now you want to be an advertising man. Why?'

'During the war I edited our regimental wall newspaper. That was fun.' For the first time Greatorex showed a trace of embarrassment. 'When I came out I took a course in advertising. I thought it would give me some background, but Mr Pile said advertising people don't think you learn much from courses.'

Anderson played with an ivory paper knife. 'Why advertising? Why not journalism? After all, you've got some experience there. By the way, what paper did you work for?'

Greatorex coughed apologetically. 'The *Herts and West Essex Reporter*. Dull. In advertising you're dealing with real products. I think that's a bit more worth while. The army gives you different ideas about things like that.'

'I wouldn't know – I wasn't in it. But you must talk to Mr Wyvern about advertising being worth while.' Greatorex looked puzzled, and Anderson regretted the remark. He explained something about the new account, and the list of names that was required. Greatorex listened with almost pathetic eagerness. When he had left the room Anderson grimaced, said 'Idealist,' and forgot him. But he began to think about what Wyvern had said in the pub. Was it true that he was slipping?

He recorded mentally the mistakes of the day. Bagseed's first telephone call had been handled well enough, but he should never have made that promise about delivery of the drawings on the second call. For that matter, he should not have forgotten the drawings. Then it had been a tactical error to adopt an even faintly critical tone to VV about the new account in face of his obvious enthusiasm. It had been foolish to make that remark to Greatorex reflecting on the sanctity of advertising. Above all, it had been foolish to ask Jean Lightley about the calendar.

Was any of this important? Anderson asked himself, and answered No. It was not important, but it was disturbing. A successful advertising executive should possess above all things the kind of mind that enabled him to know when to be judiciously angry, when to blurt out his thoughts with calculated ingenuousness and when to keep them to himself. Anderson had always regarded his own ability to judge the likely reactions of other people to any remark as his most valuable stock in trade. If he could no longer trust –

But it was foolish to meander on in this way. With determination Anderson brought back his mind to the new account. VV's instructions were always sketchy, but this time they had been more than usually inadequate. How was it possible to talk about this stuff at all without knowing something of its ingredients and history? Anderson decided that he had better talk to Reverton; and talking to Reverton, he reflected, might enable him to discover how he was regarded. He had always assumed that it would be only a matter of time, and a comparatively short time, before he was offered a place on the board. If Reverton had really made that remark to Wyvern (although Wyvern, who was malicious, was quite capable of inventing it), then he must be very careful in future.

Reverton's office was slickly modern, with bleached furniture and two abstract paintings on the walls; it offered a sharp contrast to the gloom of Pile's office and the disorder of VV's. Reverton sat behind his pipe at the desk and listened while Anderson talked in jerks, ticking off points on his fingers. One, before doing anything serious, they must have some dope about the secret process, not necessarily for use in the advertising, but for their own information and satisfaction. Two, they must think in terms of an educative campaign, as well as of the announcement of a modern miracle. They must remember that miracles were always greeted with incredulity. Three, they must test the product throughout the firm. Four, they must know the approximate price at which it would be marketed. Reverton nodded again and again.

'I absolutely agree, Andy. I'm damned glad you've brought all this up. Between you and me, the trouble with VV is that he rushes into these things half-cock.' He became suddenly solemn. 'VV's a great man. But when it comes down to practicalities he can be a bit of an ass, too.' Anderson said nothing. That was the kind of remark that it was dangerous to answer. 'Now, point one. We're fighting it out with the people in South Africa about the process. They're very cagey about ingredients and processing, but we'll get it out of them in the end. Meanwhile just for the present we must go ahead on the assumption that we'll have a story to tell on the manufacturing side, without making it the principal story.

'Point two, education. I agree entirely. We advertising men have a duty to the public. I know all the smart boys think that's funny, but it happens to be true. We've got a responsibility to society.' Puff puff. 'We've got power – and we have to be careful not to misuse it.' Puff puff. 'Think of this as an educative project, Andy, and you'll have me with you.'

Anderson still said nothing. Reverton took the small jar out of his desk. 'Point three. This is the only sample of Number One that we've got at the moment. So we can't test it out throughout the firm. I used it this morning, of course, but my beard's not much.' He looked at Anderson's blue chin.

'I'd like to take it home and try it out this week. Then I'll pass it on to Lessing.'

'Good old Andy. Getting right down to brass tacks. Glad there's another practical man in this organization.' Reverton tamped down tobacco, looked at the small pot in Anderson's hand and grinned. 'Chin chin, Andy. Let me know how the old white magic works.'

Back in his room again Anderson took off the cap and looked at the white paste again, then smelt it. There was an odour which faintly resembled eucalyptus. Anderson turned down his mouth in distaste and called in Lessing. Lessing sniffed, and shook his head.

'They'll have to find a way of getting rid of that smell. By the way, do you like the Crunchy-Munch scheme?'

Anderson hesitated and then said: 'Well, to be frank, I don't. It's too far-fetched.'

'Far-fetched hell. There really are vitamins in that stuff.'

'And I don't think we ought to try to sell a chocolate biscuit by a strip scheme. With rationing, it sells itself anyway. I roughed out some headings myself.' Anderson read them. 'What do you think?'

'Not much. I don't think we want to be comic about the

stuff. It's not a joke; it's got serious food value.' They argued for nearly half an hour. Lessing repeated the same points unweary-ingly, his eyes mild behind the large round spectacles. Anderson had difficulty in keeping the conversation on the friendly plane that generally existed between them. Suddenly Lessing broke off. 'Your calendar's wrong. It says the fourth. Today's the twentyfifth.' Deftly he twirled the little knob and altered the date. Anderson stared at him, and at the calendar.

'You want to scrap this strip scheme, then.' Lessing held out his hand for the copy and layouts.

'No,' Anderson with an effort. 'No. I'll present it to VV tomorrow morning and I'll put up my own headings and copy as an alternative. Both anonymously, of course. OK?'

Lessing grinned. 'Whatever you say. Let's go out and have a cup of tea on it.'

They went out and had a cup of tea and a piece of cake. Lessing told Anderson about the new words spoken by his two-year-old child, who said 'Eyeoo' when she wanted her right shoe and 'Effoo' when she wanted her left shoe. When they came back Jean Lightley met them in the corridor and gasped: 'Oh, Mr Anderson, Mr Crashaw says he can't let you have those drawings this afternoon after all.'

Molly O'Rourke opened the door of her room, marked *Research*. 'Thought I heard you. Bagwash is on the line, and he won't take "Out" for an answer. I think Mr Arthur's in the eighth month of an idea and he wants you to act as midwife.'

Pile's secretary came out of the typing pool. 'There you are, Mr Anderson. Can you spare Mr Pile a moment?'

Anderson telephoned Bagseed, apologized for the delay in delivering the drawings and listened to complaints that Mr Arthur was right on Bagseed's back. Mr Arthur wanted to see the drawings now. Mr Arthur thought they were not get-ting good enough service. Confidentially, Mr Arthur had said to him –

A pulse was beating in Anderson's forehead. He interrupted. 'Mr Bagseed, you're getting as much service from us as any other three clients put together.'

'Well, really – ' Mr Bagseed's nasal voice almost expired.

'And the moment your drawings arrive they'll be sent up to you. Now, there are six people on my back, and I'm going to try to shake some of them off. Good-bye.' He told the telephone girl that he was out to any further calls from Kiddy Modes. He talked to Crashaw, who was apologetic. The artist who had started work on the drawings was eager to finish them himself, and they thought that would be a good thing after all. The drawings were going to the artist that night, and would be delivered tomorrow morning. Anderson saw Mr Pile, who wanted to know how Greatorex was getting on. 'I may meet Sir Malcolm at the club tonight and he will be taking a – h'm – avuncular interest, you know.' Anderson said that Greatorex seemed rather old to be starting a career in advertising, and Mr Pile looked embarrassed.

'To make a clean breast of it, he has – tried several occupations without complete success.' Did the eyes twinkle behind the pince-nez? 'But can I – report back – to Sir Malcolm in a satisfactory sense on his first day?'

'He seems a bright enough chap,' Anderson said wearily. 'And eager. That's a great thing. He's been with Lessing most of the time.'

Mr Pile talked for another ten minutes. Back in his room once more, Anderson stared at the green carpet. He headed one sheet of paper with the words *Crunchy-Munch* and another with the words *Preparation Number One* and stared at them. What a way to spend a life, he thought: Crunchy-Munch, the shaving revolution, and Sir Malcolm Buntz's nephew. And for how many years now had that been his life? His triumphs had been a toothpaste, a chilblain ointment and a patent medicine, his disaster a breakfast food and a motor-car. Could a life be more meaningless?

He pulled up his thoughts again. That was the way Wyvern would think; those were not the thoughts of an executive who was looking for a place on the board and believed it to be almost within his grasp. There was a job to be done and you did it – well or badly. To give the job itself a moral value was nonsense.

And then he noticed the desk calendar. The date it showed was the fourth of February. He felt suddenly very angry at the idea that somebody was playing this kind of vulgar and unpleasant joke on him. But there was a simple way to stop it. He pressed the buzzer for Jean Lightley and kept his finger on it, so that she came running into the room. He asked her questions. Gasping, she reiterated that she had not touched the calendar since she put it to the right date that morning. She did not know who had been in the room. 'But nobody would alter your calendar, Mr Anderson.' She looked as if she thought he was mad.

'Somebody has.' He said it very gently. 'It's been altered three times today, Jean. Unless there's a magic spell on it.'

'A magic spell,' she gasped.

He articulated clearly, as one would to a child. 'Now I want you to take this calendar outside, and keep it in your room for the rest of the week. Then we shall see if the spell works when it's on your desk as it does when it's on mine. Do you understand?' She nodded, apparently incapable of speech. 'That's good, then. Off you go.' When she was outside the door Anderson sighed with relief and regret. Relief that the calendar was out of the room, and regret that again he had acted foolishly. It remained to be considered who would want to worry him – and who would choose that way to do it.

That remained to be considered. In the meantime, it was certain that he would do no work that afternoon on Crunchy-Munch or Preparation Number One. He put on his hat and overcoat and left the office. On the way out he passed Mr Pile, who looked at him sharply, but said nothing. Mr Pile did not approve of staff leaving before the office closed at five-thirty, not even men who had a place on the board almost within their grasp.

It is well known that, in our carboniferous era, managers and administrators frequently find their lives separated into two distinct parts which involve a division of the personality. Fiction and film have familiarized us with the capitalist who is a tyrant to his employees, but an emotional slave to his wife and children; with the gangster whose eyes well with tears at thought of the old folk while he is treating the young ones with summary brutality; or with the theme ingeniously reversed, of the executive unendingly patient in his office, but brusquely unpleasant outside it. The case of Anderson resembled this classic businessman's schizophrenia. In his capacity as advertising executive he had developed through years of training an incisive intelligence, and the ability to make quick and generally correct decisions about the people and problems confronting him; as a private citizen he was erratic, irresponsible and quite incapable of assessing the motives from which people act, or of maintaining a viewpoint for any length of time. This double nature was the cause of most of his misfortunes. A man of strong personality who wishes to achieve practical success in life will no doubt do so; a man of weak personality who recognizes his own limitations may batten very well off the strong or the rich; but Anderson's personality combined strength and weakness in ways of which he was quite unaware. Such a combination is dangerous both to its possessor and to those who come into contact with him. Anderson, who was not by nature inclined to investigation of his own character, had become vaguely aware of this fact in the past few weeks.

Anderson was the only child of a head book-keeper; and soon after his birth in 1909 his father and mother moved from a small terrace house in Wood Green to a new and more commodious establishment in Ealing. This house, in which the child grew up, was built in a modern Tudor style of architecture. It had an oak door with studs, imitation Tudor external beams and plaster, and leaded light windows. The fireplaces were modern with coloured tiles, except the fireplace in the lounge, which again was an imitation Tudor open fireplace in bright red brick. There was a wooden fence in front of the house protecting a neat small lawn, which Anderson's father mowed at weekends during the summer. At the back of the house was another small lawn with flowerbeds. The house was called 'Tudor Vista', and it was situated in a road of similar houses, each of which, however, differed from the others in some small architectural details. 'Tudor Vista' fulfilled the ambitions of Anderson's parents. It gave his father a garden, modern plumbing and a touch of the picturesque, all of which had been lacking in the house at Wood Green. His mother was happy to move into such a really nice neighbourhood, with really nice people in it. The importance of this achievement could be understood only in terms of the background from which Anderson's father and mother had escaped: on his father's side the family had been small, unsuccessful tradesmen struggling with a grocer's business; on his mother's they had been, even more humiliatingly, in service. Anderson's parents never spoke of these things; he learned of them through his maternal grandmother, who came to live with them when her husband died. When she talked to the child of the family in which she had been for many years second housemaid he was puzzled, and asked her why she worked for other people. 'To make my living, silly,' she said, and told him of the great house near Wimbledon Common, the six servants that were kept, and the two gardeners – her husband had been one of them. 'Like a park' – she said to Anderson – 'the garden was like a park', sniffing contemptuously at the little patches of lawn tended so carefully by Anderson's father. In the child's mind the garden was like Richmond Park, where he had once been taken for a picnic; great pies were eaten from spotless white cloths laid on the grass, fluid was poured from strange flasks into little metal cups, everyone always wore their best clothes, deer flickered in and out of the shade. He could see the park, but he could not visualize the great house she described with its wide stairway and splendid gallery nor understand his grandmother's contempt for the small rooms and funny windows of 'Tudor Vista', and for the dainty teas provided by his mother for the ladies of the neighbourhood. Sometimes his grandmother appeared at these teas, and at the social evenings when a nearby husband and wife came round for a game of whist or auction bridge, interrupted after a couple of rubbers by a long pause for refreshments, neat little sandwiches or fragments of sardine placed upon fingers of toast. Hers was an awkward presence upon those social occasions, however, for she would not sit quietly nodding in the ingle nook. 'I think I'll be clearing away now,' she would say, or 'I'll just be washing up while you play your hand of cards.' Mrs Anderson would say quite sharply, 'Sit down, mother, do,' and would add that she had made the necessary arrangements for the daily woman, Kitty or Mary or Bessie, to come in that evening. There was not the slightest need for anybody to stir. But somehow Anderson's grandmother would find her way out to the kitchen, and there could be heard among the rattle of plates, talking altogether too familiarly to Bessie or Mary or Kitty. It was a relief to his mother, Anderson thought years later, that Granny died peacefully in her bed when he was nine years old.

That was in 1918, just before the end of the war. His father had been upset when he was rejected for service because of his flat feet. A quiet little grey man with an inoffensive moustache, he said little, but after his rejection mowed and trimmed the front and back lawns with fanatical care. His mother was upset also; but his parents' distress seemed to Anderson, when he looked back on it, to have been more social than patriotic. It was the right thing to go to the war, the thing other people were doing, and it was an unpleasantly individual mark to be separated from service by flat feet. The flatness of his father's feet had always been a joke, but after his rejection for national service it was treated very seriously. 'He suffers from a disability in a manner of speaking,' his mother would say to visitors, adding with a sigh, 'It kept him out of the army.'

The war went on, there were shortages, Bessie was replaced

by Elsie, Anderson went to a local High School. And then the war was over, the cost of living was high, and there were thousands of people who kept it high by deliberately refusing to work. Anderson's father spoke about them with a passionate anger, an anger the more noticeable and impressive because he was usually so quiet. 'If they won't work let them starve,' he would say. 'It's not can't-work; it's won't-work. There's work for everybody to do that wants to work. Those miners.' And words would fail him to describe the treason of the miners, whose positive refusal to hew coal for the nation he compared with his own readiness to serve his country.

But the treachery of the miners was not sufficient to wreck the financial stability of 'Tudor Vista', although Mr Anderson pulled his small moustache upon occasion with more than customary vigour. When Anderson was twelve years old, an event occurred of some importance in his life. He won a scholarship, but did not take it up. Acceptance of the scholarship would have meant attendance at a public school as a boarder, and a financial strain upon his parents. It was, therefore, surprising that his father was anxious that he should take the scholarship, while his mother's influence was thrown, in the end decisively, against it. Why had she not wanted him to take the scholarship? Anderson wondered afterwards, and decided that the incident provided a clear indication of the extent and limits of her snobbery. The limit of her ambition had been reached with occupation of 'Tudor Vista', dainty teas and people in for auction bridge. She understood the social scale represented by attendance at the local grammar school, and membership of the tennis club; public school and university, however, meant nothing to her but an alien world whose inhabitants had queer aspirations beyond anything she could conceive. Mrs Anderson divided people into three social classes: 'stuck up', 'a nice class of person', and 'rather common'. It is probable that she disliked those who were stuck up even more than those who were rather common.

It was beside the imitation Tudor fireplace and within the leaded light windows that Anderson grew up, a curly-haired boy with an easy smile, exceptionally intelligent and reasonably good at games. His parents were, it may seem, exceptionally snobbish, exceptionally unimaginative in regard to any way of life except their own. But is such complacency really exceptional? Mr and Mrs Anderson had moved into the lower reaches of the middle class, and were able effectively to conceal their comparatively humble origin; such worldly success may be thought adequate for one lifetime. In the morally ambiguous but practically distinct division between satisfied sheep and unsatisfied goats, they belonged to the sheep. Sociologists have remarked that such satisfaction carries with it obvious emotional limitations. The sheep achieve an illusion of security within their class by observing approvingly certain institutions outside their reach (Mrs Anderson had an encyclopaedic knowledge of the genealogy of the English Royal family) and regarding with uncomprehending disapproval the behaviour of dissatisfied goatish figures (like those treasonable miners) well below them in the social scale.

When it had been decided that Anderson should not take up the scholarship, his parents planned their child's career in a simple and satisfactory way. Grammar school would be succeeded by bank or insurance office, at first in a junior and later in a managerial position: such a course appeared to them not only desirable, but almost inevitable. They were baffled, therefore, as well as distressed, by their son's deviations from their own way of life. The first of these deviations might, indeed, have upset any parents; for Anderson was expelled from his grammar school for theft. The affair was altogether discreditable and disturbing; he was found in the changing-room engaged in transferring five shillings from the pocket of another boy's trousers to his own. His parents were most injured, perhaps, by the social disgrace to themselves that attended his expulsion. As far as their son was concerned personally, they were pained equally by the fact that there was no possibility of belief in his innocence, and by their inability to induce in him knowledge of moral wrongdoing.

It would, clearly, have been rash to expose such a boy to the monetary temptations of a bank; Anderson became office boy in a firm of shipping merchants. Here his conduct was for a time exemplary. He was promoted after a year to the position of junior clerk, wore striped trousers and a black jacket and carried a carefully rolled umbrella to work every day. At the age of seventeen, however, when he was earning thirty shillings a week, Anderson showed an extraordinary inability to produce the pound which his mother deducted for his board and lodging. Mrs Anderson kept careful watch upon her son, and discovered that he was constantly in receipt of letters addressed in a backward sloping hand upon salmon-pink envelopes. It was a short step from realization that the backward hand was a woman's to execution of a parental duty in steaming open the letters; and another disturbing and discreditable affair was disclosed. Anderson had become mixed up (the phrase was his mother's) with a girl named Ethel Smith, a shop assistant whose father was a railway brakeman. The missing weekly pound had been spent upon Ethel, and the process of mixing up had gone so far that she was expecting a baby. What was most upsetting to Anderson's parents in the affair was the revelation of their son's taste for low society. 'How could you?' Mrs Anderson asked him. 'With a girl of that class?' But the time was one not only for reproaches, but also for swift and decisive action. Mrs Anderson saw Ethel, Mr Anderson saw the railway brakeman. Hard words were exchanged; but money was exchanged also. One more letter came in a salmon-pink envelope, to tell Anderson that Ethel had taken a job in Bradford; and that was the end of the affair. When Mr and Mrs Anderson talked it all over in later years they agreed that their son had narrowly escaped a shameful marriage through their promptness; but at the same time they were able to convince themselves, by a curious feat of mental legerdemain, that the whole of Ethel's mixing-up story was false. 'That girl certainly pulled the wool over our eyes,' Mr Anderson, who had now retired, would say to his wife; and this instance of duplicity in the lower orders of society afforded them a satisfaction which was at least some compensation for the money laid out on their son's behalf.

And what of Anderson himself? The central figure in this

small drama appeared hardly interested in the fate of his carefully cultivated and costly relationship. His only comment when
his parents tried to discover a reason for his actions seemed to
them ridiculous. 'Why don't you find some nice girl of our own
kind?' his mother asked. 'I can't think what you could see in a
common girl like that.' Anderson said then, as though the
remark had some relevance: 'She always had dirty fingernails.'
He added after a moment's reflection: 'She was rather dirty
altogether. Her feet were never clean.' His mother was triumphant. 'There you are,' she said. 'Disgusting. I don't suppose
she took a bath once a month.' Anderson said nothing more,
and since his father and mother never spoke of disagreeable
subjects if they could be avoided, the affair was dropped.

It is perhaps instructive that the fact that a letter addressed
to him had been opened never became a subject of argument
between Anderson and his parents, because such conduct
seemed to all three of them perfectly natural.

Soon after the end of the Ethel Smith affair, Anderson began
to write poetry and short stories. One or two of his poems
appeared in a local Ealing paper, and one was published in the
*Poetry Review*; his short stories, however, were all rejected. At
about the same time he gave up the striped trousers and black
jacket and began to wear a bright-coloured shirt and a sports
jacket when he went to work. He was sacked from the shipping
firm for slackness, and for nearly two years was out of work.
Most of his time was spent at the public library, or upstairs in
his bedroom reading. He made little effort to look for a job,
and it took all his parents' skill in mental conjuring to separate
the lower-class won't-works who were a menace to the country
from the unfortunate can't-get-works represented by their son.
He did not make life at home very pleasant for his parents, and
at times his attitude seemed to them quite incomprehensible.
When his father tried to have a heart-to-heart talk Anderson
said simply: 'You've taken responsibility for me. Very well,
keep me.' When his father asked what kind of work he would
like to do, Anderson said he was not interested in any office
job. When his mother asked again why he didn't find some nice

girlfriends, he said that he feared she would not approve of his choice of acquaintance.

It is impossible to know what might have happened to this unhappy household had not the pattern of their family life been suddenly altered. The habit of ignoring unpleasantness can extend from mental to physical matters; when Mrs Anderson paid a long-delayed visit to her doctor she learnt that the fears which had often kept her awake during the night had become reality. It was nine months before the cancer finally killed her, and during that time she was hardly ever out of pain. Her physical suffering was appalling; but the doubts she may have begun to feel about the way in which their son had been brought up were cancelled by the remarkable change in his behaviour. Anderson attended his mother in her illness with extraordinary devotion. He brought her breakfast every day, played endless games of cards with her, and behaved always in her presence like the charming curly-haired boy she remembered. During the last weeks, when she was too weak to leave her bed, he sat by her side for hours reading light romantic novels to her. In the three days before she died he was with her almost constantly, although at this time her appearance was ghastly, and the stench that surrounded her was so unpleasant that her husband could hardly bear to enter the room. It was Anderson's hand that his mother grasped when, pitifully yellow and gaunt, unrecognizable as the plump middle-aged woman who had visited the doctor nine months before, she completed the long journey to death.

Soon afterwards Anderson, now twentyone years old, obtained a job as a clerk in the accounts department of the Nation-Wide Advertising Company. At the same time he left home, and went to live in lodgings. His father sold 'Tudor Vista' and became a paying guest with some distant relations in Birmingham named Pottle. Communication between father and son was spasmodic, and soon became limited to two or three letters a year. When Anderson last met his father he greeted a little grey bent man who seemed bewildered by the lack of purpose in his life; his father saw a young man with a thin, hard, keen face, unusually serious for his age, who wore a neat blue suit, carefully brushed and pressed. Transferred to the Production Department of his firm, Anderson had attracted the attention of his superiors by making rough layouts embodying new advertising ideas for their clients, which he left lying about on his desk. He had been tried in the firm's Studio, where he showed insufficient artistic ability for a layout man, and then in the Copy Department, where at last he settled. 'Your mother would have been proud of you,' Anderson's father said to him shakily. 'She always said you'd make good.' The young man made no reply. Some three months later his father died suddenly of a heart attack.

Anderson was not a great copywriter, but he possessed a combination of practical common sense and verbal ingenuity which is unusual in advertising. After three years he left the Nation-Wide and from that time onward moved from firm to firm, each time improving his position a little, making a reputation as a figure of solid talent. In 1939 he came to Vincent Advertising, a firm which people either left in a month because they could not stand Vincent, or stayed with for years because they liked him. Anderson stayed. During the war Vincent Advertising, like other firms, handled their share of Government advertising. Anderson was first deferred, and finally exempted from war service, because he was employed on the work Vincents were handling for the Ministry of Knowledge and Communication.

In 1942 Anderson married a girl named Valerie Evans. They had no children.

# VI

There is a part of London near the Buckingham Palace Road, behind Eccleston Bridge, where the large stucco seediness of once-fashionable squares, Eccleston and Warwick and St George's, fades into a smaller shabbiness. There are streets here of small identical red-brick houses, fronted by ugly iron railings; these streets branch off the main stem of Warwick Way, that backbone of Pimlico where large houses converted into a dozen one-room flats offer typists and secretaries the chance of developing an individuality untrammelled by the presence of parents or the inhibiting eyes of childhood neighbours. Such self-contained lives typify the decay that is spreading slowly over the fabric of our great cities; to be part of this decay, to visit the ballet frequently and to fornicate freely, to attain a complete irresponsibility of action – that is, in a sense, the ideal life of our civilization. And if such a life can be lived comfortably enough in the four-storeyed houses of Warwick Way, it can be lived more easily still in the little red-brick houses of Joseph Street. You might find similar houses in any London suburb, where they would be the homes of clerks, schoolmasters and small businessmen; but the people who lived in Joseph Street were male and female prostitutes, unknown actors and film extras, artists and journalists who had given up worship of the bitch-goddess Success and were content to earn a few pounds here and there which they drank away at the Demon round the corner in Radigoyle Street while their teeth fell out and their tongues grew furry and their eyesight failed. Among these characteristic occupants of the small red-brick houses, however, were a few eccentrically successful figures, people whose presence in this raffish area could not have been easily explained, even by themselves. Joseph Street numbered among its inhabitants two company directors, a dress designer, an important gynaecologist and a retired trade union official. Anderson, who might also be regarded as eccentrically respectable, lived at Number 10 Joseph Street, in a house distinguished from its fellows only by the window boxes carefully cultivated by the Fletchleys, who lived in a self-contained flat on the first floor. Anderson had bought a ninety-year lease of the house at the time of his marriage.

He turned out of Radigoyle Street into Joseph Street this evening, passing the bright lights of the Demon without so much as a sideward glance. Flossie Williams, one of the Joseph Street tarts, smiled at him as he passed and Anderson, breathing deeply, caught a whiff of her cheap scent. He felt a mingled exhilaration and depression as he approached his home, an obscure sense of wrongdoing mingled with an equally obscure feeling of pleasure. His key was in the lock when something touched his shoulder. Pivoting quickly on his heel he faced the great bulk of Fletchley, shaking with laughter in the Pimlico dark. 'I crept up on you,' Fletchley said. 'I saw you pass the old Demon. You never heard me. Me in my rubber-soled shoes.'

'Are you drunk?'

'Old boy,' Fletchley was reproachful, 'I've had a pint to drown my sorrows, not a snoutful. A snoutful is out of the question, much as I should like it. Tonight I have to write immortal verse. A dozen orders to fill, old boy.' He declaimed:

> 'I don't know much of rhyme and metre,
> So I'll say "God Bless Mummy". Peter.

That's from a little kiddy, six months old, to his mother. A nice sentiment, eh?'

'Where's Elaine?'

Fletchley wavered on his feet and then said: 'Out. Won't be back till late. I'm turning an honest penny on my lonesome.'

Fletchley was a man of many curious occupations, all of them appropriate to an inhabitant of Joseph Street. He had made money by starting chain letters and pyramids, he had held at one time a valuable insurance book, he was an agent for the pushboards by which small cricket and football clubs raise funds. His latest way of earning money was by supplying rhymed Christmas and birthday greeting wishes. The customer would give details of the recipient's age and character and Fletchley would make notes reading: 'Uncle Bill, birthday, from niece Mary. Big nose, retriever dog Laddie, granddaughter Phyllis learning to talk. Humorous.' Uncle Bill would then receive on his birthday a card which contained two or three printed verses embodying the points Fletchley had jotted down. Fletchley set up these cards, which were of a sentimental, humorous or reverent nature, on a small hand press, and his charge for them varied between half a crown and five shillings according to the length of the message. The business was largely seasonal, but there was a steady birthday demand throughout the year.

The house had been clumsily converted into two flats, with a hall common to both. Anderson was just about to open the door of his flat when Fletchley said: 'By the way, old boy, that police chap called round to see you this evening. He doesn't seem to be a bad fellow. We had quite a chin-wag.'

'You'd better come in,' Anderson said. He turned on the light. 'What will you drink? Gin or whisky?'

'Won't say no to a little drop of something to keep the cold out. Whisky – and don't kill it. Can't think where you get the stuff.'

'Valerie got it – black market.' Anderson poured himself a drink. 'What did he want?'

'Who? Oh, the copper.' Fletchley shook again, a pinpoint head wobbling uncertainly on an enormous sagging body. There were food stains on his jacket, and above a mountainous belly the tapes of pants were visible, held by his braces. 'He's mustard,' he chuckled.

'What do you mean?'

'Mustard, old boy, mustard. His name's Cresse and he's hot as mustard, see? But what did he want? He wanted to see you. Something to do with Valerie. He's a nice sort of a chap.'

'What did he ask you?'

'I didn't give away any secrets, don't worry,' Fletchley said and winked portentously. It seemed to Anderson that there was something strange about Fletchley tonight. His whole body was trembling slightly, as though convulsed by some elaborate inner joke. Sharply, Anderson said:

'Secrets, what do you mean, secrets? And why should I worry?'

'Only my joke, old boy.' Fletchley was momentarily solemn, but Anderson had an uncomfortable feeling that this solemnity was maintained only with an effort, and that if the fat man let himself go he would burst out laughing. 'Do you know he's got two kids?'

'Who?'

'He's got two kids and he wants me to write birthday messages for 'em. Fancy sending birthday wishes from a CID Inspector. He is CID, isn't he?'

'But what did he want to ask you?'

'Pretty near everything from the time I get up in the morning to the width of my pyjama stripes. All sorts of questions,' Fletchley rambled. 'You wouldn't believe the sort of questions he asked.' And again it seemed to Anderson that there was something very odd, something almost menacing, about the tone of the fat man's voice. But this impression was no sooner in Anderson's mind than it was gone again, as Fletchley drained his glass and put on his mask of good-fellowship, if indeed it was a mask and not a true reflection of the sentimental birthday-greeting soul within his great bulk. 'I must be going. Night, old boy.'

'Good night.'

The door closed and he sat still for a moment in the armchair, staring straight ahead of him. Then, as his eyes slowly focused to take in the furnishings of the room, the modernist grey carpet with its jagged pattern of blue and orange picking up the same colours in the curtains, the chromium standard lamp, the Lalique glass on the mantelpiece, the chromium electric fire, the white ghastly light from the fluorescent strips on the ceiling, as he took in the whole brassy brightness of the place he thought: *I must get away from here; this is nothing to do with me.* For if the choice of neighbourhood was Anderson's, reluctantly agreed to by Valerie because it was almost impossible to find a place to live in, the flat itself was Valerie's, just as Elaine Fletchley was Valerie's friend. There was one incongruous thing, however, which stood out as an oddity in that room of chromium furniture and tubular lighting; a Georgian writing desk which stood between the electric fire and an angular wall light. This writing desk had belonged to Anderson's parents, and his father had given it to him when he moved from home. He walked over to the desk now and opened a drawer below the main body of the desk with a small key. He felt at the back of this drawer, pressed a small protrusion, and another small hidden drawer was revealed, just large enough to contain a book with a cover of black leather and stiff marbled corners. Anderson took this book in both hands, holding it carefully as if it were a fragile object. Then he sat down at the desk, staring at the black cover. Anderson had first written in this book a week ago, and had sat up four nights in succession, writing each night for several hours. Every night since then he had felt compelled to read the story put down between the black leather covers with marbled corners. He had written the story himself, and yet he felt so remote from it that a sensation of utter strangeness overcame him while he read, so that he seemed to be reading of somebody else's life and not his own. And now the craving to read what was written in the book had become so strong that it was the first thing he turned to when he came back from work.

Tonight he had gone to the cinema, but in front of the Hollywood faces he saw quite distinctly the shape and appearance of the book. Now he sat looking at the cover, holding the book in both hands. I can do whatever I wish, he thought. A movement of the hand and this book returns to the drawer, another movement and the drawer is closed. But if a person dissociated from the figure Anderson recognized as himself – the slick executive, in line for a directorship – if somebody else had put down what was in this book, could not a similarly dissociated figure put back the book in the drawer? Was it possible to experiment, he wondered, to make one's mind a conscious blank? And while he thought this, his grip upon the book must have relaxed, for it dropped to the floor, landing with a soft *plop* upon the carpet. Anderson picked up the book, opened it, and began to read.

Now it is all over. The funeral is over, the inquest is over, the verdict has been given. Two people who had very little in common have ceased to live together. One has fallen down a flight of stairs and broken her neck; the other continues an existence in which he regards his own ridiculous occupation with extraordinary gravity. Is there anything more to be said?

Yes, there is a great deal more to be said. Why should Valerie and I have lived together for years? What possible meaning can one attach to our life together, how can one understand it? And if such a ridiculous end to a shared life is possible, doesn't this illuminate the absolute absurdity of existence itself? Now that Valerie is dead, I see quite certainly that I didn't love her. I am absolutely unable to understand why I married her. I can't see why I didn't push her down the stairs long ago. Wyvern, at the office, has a phrase which he uses every now and again when things are going wrong: 'Why don't we all get in one great bed and – one another?'

Well, why don't we?

But of course that kind of thing won't do – that pure abandonment to the idea that life is nonsense. There must be somewhere an explanation of human activity which isn't purely biological, which interprets life in terms of some kind of meaning. It's to try to get some idea of what it all means that I'm putting down this individual case history of my life with Val.

I met Val first at party given by Elaine Fletchley. At least it was given by *Woman Beautiful*, the high-class fashion magazine she works for, and Elaine was a hostess. They asked somebody from all the bright advertising agencies, and I went from Vincent's. It was a very dull party. I had a bit of chat with other advertising figures and was just working my way over to say goodbye to Elaine when I bumped into a girl and upset her drink. 'Oh dear,' she said. 'Oh dear, my poor frock.' She stared at me with wide-apart eyes of a curious hazel colour. Then she said: 'But I want another drinky.' There was just the faintest suggestion of a lisp in the way she rolled her r's. So I got her a drink and we talked, and it turned out that she worked for *Woman Beautiful*, too, as an assistant fashion editress. I told her that I was a copywriter and she said: 'Oh, but you must be awfully clever.' She was so short that she had to look up at me, and she did so with a kind of starry gaze. I can remember wondering what I was doing talking to her. She was just the kind of girl, I can remember thinking, for whom I had no use at all. How is it possible, then, to account for my next action? I leaned over (I can see myself doing it quite clearly) and said: 'Let's get out of this din and go somewhere else?' And what did she say? She giggled and answered with quite a definite lisp: 'I say, you are a quick worker.' We left the party, had some drinks – she soaked up drink like a sponge – and she stayed at the flat I lived in then, in Kensington. When she left in the morning we arranged to meet that evening. We did. And the next and the next. In six months we were married.

So there it is, or there's the beginning of it. During the whole of that six months if I'd ever asked myself whether I liked Val, the answer would have been an unhesitating 'No.' I dislike girls who lisp, girls who are kittenish, girls who drink too much. Valerie did all of those things. Why did I marry her, then? Partly I'd got into the habit of seeing her – but what made me start the habit? Partly no doubt I was the victim of that feeling war and bombing gave you, that no relationship you formed mattered much or was likely to be permanent – and how damned mistaken that feeling was. Partly she was good in bed, and although I was over thirty when I met her I hadn't much experience of that sort of thing. Although Val was nearly ten years younger than I was, I gathered she'd had plenty. But although I enjoyed our times in bed, I wasn't all that interested. That certainly won't do for a main motive.

And why did Val marry me? If I can't explain my own motives, I certainly can't understand hers. I think she found me attractive – although few women have done so. I believe she liked men older than herself. And – although I may be quite wrong – I believe she regarded me as a very different person from the man I am. Subconsciously I assumed that we should stop drinking and going to parties after we got married. But Val assumed that we should go on drinking, and go to more parties than ever.

So we started off wrong. And then there was trouble about this house. Val was essentially what I think of as an Earls Court girl – nice gay parties with people in the rag trade as she called it, a few commercial artists, some bad actors. Well, you can get all that in our bit of Pimlico if you want it, but in rather too sordid a way for Val. She liked a bit of glamour spread over it – not too much, just a thin layer. She was horrified when she first saw the house and even more so when I told her I liked it. 'But how *can* you like it? It's so vulgar. That woman Flossie Williams – she's just a tart.' And what are your friends, do you think? I asked her. And what are you? Didn't you sleep with me the first time you met me? The only difference was that you got marriage instead of a spot cash settlement. At that she burst into tears, and it's true I was unfair, because Val was a one-man woman. I say I think she found me attractive, but I'm doing myself an injustice. The fact is that she never looked at anybody else at all. She told Elaine Fletchley so, and Elaine told me. And how can one explain that? That's as nonsensical as the rest of it.

So Val burst into tears. She was always bursting into tears; it was one of the most irritating things about her. Then she asked me again why I liked living here, but I couldn't answer that, because I didn't know. There was just something about the streets and the people and the atmosphere, that's all.

But if Valerie couldn't get her own way about the house, at least she made it look the way she wanted. It's all round me now, as it's been round me for years – the glaring colours, the fumed oak paradise in the bedroom. 'It's so bright and gay and new,' she'd say – but with the lisp, of course. 'I hate old stuff. I'd like life to start again every morning. New people, new job, new places, new everything. Wouldn't you like that?' And when I said truthfully that I'd like nothing less, she'd be upset. And she not only had her way about the look of the place; she got Elaine to live in it as well. First she said the house was too big for just the two of us. Maybe there'll be three one day, I said, but she didn't want children. Then she wanted Elaine to come and live here with us. I didn't want it; I wanted to be alone. But she had it her way. We turned the place into two self-contained flats and we had the ground floor and the Fletchleys had the first. We shared the cellar, where we both kept a small stock of drink. Elaine is a neat, tarty little piece, slick and smart and hard. What did she see in Fletchley to marry him? That's another problem, but I can't go into it now.

Val had kept her job on *Woman Beautiful*, so when Elaine came the girls could talk office gossip all evening long. Fletchley never seemed to mind, just as he never seemed to mind Elaine going out with other men. 'She always comes back,' he used to say to me. 'She always comes back to old Fletch.' But at that time, when they first came here, Elaine didn't go out much. She would talk office gossip with Val in the evening until I was nearly crazy. Occasionally I thought she was intending to make a pass at me, but Fletchley never seemed to notice, so perhaps I was wrong. I got so crazy with their talk that I suggested in desperation to Val that we should go out and drink. Six months ago she'd have leapt at the suggestion, but now she didn't much want to do anything but drink a glass or two of black-market whisky by her own comfortable electric fireside while she chattered to Elaine. And when we did go out it wasn't any good, because I didn't really care for drinking and I could hardly even be polite to Val. 'You're never nice to me, Andy, the way you used to be,' she'd say tearfully, and look at me with her head slightly on one side. Was it true? Had I ever been nice to her? I can't believe that I ever was. She'd invented my niceness in the past to contrast with my horridness in the present. We can't recreate the past, but we can always soothe sorrow and vanity by inventing it.

So drinking was no good, and after a couple of years there was another thing that was no good, too. I couldn't work up the least flicker of interest in Val while I was with her. When I was away from her – in the office writing copy, interviewing a client, sitting round a conference table – then very often I would positively shiver with desire for her. The most powerful and violent sexual images came to my mind, and they were not merely vague images – they had a positive association with Val. As soon as I saw her, though – as soon, even, as I knew I should see her within half an hour – they vanished altogether. It would all have been comic if it had not been deeply humiliating.

All this sounds like a good case for divorce, or at any rate separation. But strangely enough, Val never wanted a separation – throughout the whole of our life together she was absolutely devoted to me. And why did I stay with Val? I find the question absolutely unanswerable. It would have been difficult, I suppose, to arrange a separation. She would have wanted to go on living with Elaine. I should have had to get out of Joseph Street, and I didn't want to get out. Then again I should have been lonely. She had become a habit, and we live by our habits. But there was something outside all that, something that held me to her. It was, it seems to me, precisely *because* I disliked her, because she filled our home with hideous furniture and empty chatter, that I wanted to live with her. The things that I most detested were the things I most desired! Shall I put down the image that came to me most often when I saw Val, tearstained and reproachful, or limply acquiescent in my unkindness? It was of my mother, and the ghastly house we lived in so many years ago – and of holding my mother's hand as she lay, a pitiful and repulsive skeleton, upon her deathbed.

But now I come to the real reason for writing in this book – the effect Val's death has had on me. We lived together for several detestable years. For the whole of that time I had seen with irritation the grease on her face at night, and her intolerable cheerfulness in the morning. I'd listened all that time to her inanities about clothes and film stars. Unconsciously, I must dozens of times have wished her dead. But now that she *is* dead, and the bathroom is free when I want to use it and I no longer find hairpins in the bed, I am oppressed by an extraordinary sense of loss. Not loss of Val exactly – that seems not to enter into it. Rather, part of myself seems to have disappeared. I feel like one of those insects that goes on living even after being cut in half.

On Monday, February 4th, we went to work as usual. Val sang 'Berkeley Square', from her repertory of out-of-date songs, in her bath. I had a worrying day at the office.

There the writing ended. Anderson's perfect absorption in the black book had been such that he had forgotten to turn on the electric fire, and he now became conscious that he was cold. He was sitting also in an uncomfortable position, so that something in his pocket pressed sharply into his side. He put his hand in his pocket, drew out the pot of Preparation Number 1, and placed it upon a red-topped table with chromium legs. He flicked a switch, and the firebar glowed. But there was some other cause for disturbance – what was it? Sickly-sweet chimes sounded in the room. Of course! Val's musical doorbell. Anderson put the book back in the small secret drawer, and closed and locked the desk. Then he went to the front door, and opened it to reveal a burly figure. The street lamp cast the shadow of this patiently waiting figure into Anderson's hall. The face was left dark, but Anderson recognized Inspector Cresse by his bowler hat.

'Come in,' Anderson said with self-mocking gaiety. 'Come in, Inspector.' With a catlike, almost mincing step, he led the way into the room he had just left. The Inspector followed more deliberately. Under the tubular lighting his face showed large, blue-white, slightly dented, with two strongly marked lines running from nose to mouth. The whole face was flattish, the nose a large blunt wedge, the mouth broad and shapeless, but turned down slightly at the corners in an expression both clownish and severe. But the balance of these heavy features was changed altogether when the Inspector took off his bowler hat, revealing a great white head that was completely bald. What had been menacing now appeared ludicrous; and such sudden changes of appearance and gesture appeared to be part of the Inspector's stock-in-trade. He had presented, Anderson thought, a quite farcical figure at the inquest; and yet at odd moments there was something in the firm fit of his clothes and his blank forward-looking stare that gave an impression of intellectual strength, though not of subtlety. Behind the figure of farce lay the man of power, behind the man of power lurked the irrepressibly clownish comedian. The comedian was uppermost when the Inspector took off his hat, and placed it, with a wonderfully whimsical gesture, upon the red table by the pot of cream.

'A drink?' Anderson almost danced round the thick-set figure. 'A cigarette? Sit down. It's rather cold in here, I'm afraid.' He shivered in an exaggerated manner.

The Inspector sat in one of the chromium-armed chairs, his hard bulk filling it without overflowing. His voice was rich and thick, and at times he did not articulate with absolute distinctness. 'I'll take just a little whisky. Thank you, Mr Anderson. Nothing in it.' He held the amber liquid in one large blunt paw. 'I called earlier this evening.'

'Fletchley told me. You wanted to know the width of his pyjama stripes. You Gallup Poll policemen!' Soda-water sizzled in Anderson's glass. He almost giggled.

'We had a little chat,' the Inspector said vaguely. 'He's a man with a sense of humour, which is something I always enjoy.' On another chromium chair, bent deferentially a little forward, Anderson smiled agreement, rocked by an obscure secret merriment. 'A nice idea of his, to write those cards for birthdays and Christmas. Ingenious, too.'

'A nice sentiment.' Anderson rocked again.

'That's right. Or don't you think so?' A vacant orb, emptied of expression, the Inspector's eye rolled.

'I am not called upon to express an opinion.' Anderson spoke a little huffily.

'But I'm interested' – the Inspector's great head nodded in puzzlement – 'to know what you think. An intellectual man like yourself; you'd call yourself an intellectual now, wouldn't you?'

'An advertising man merely.'

'Those verses he writes – you couldn't call them great art now?' Anderson shook his head. 'But they help to increase friendliness between human beings, don't they? Isn't that a good thing?'

With complete self-possession Anderson smiled at the heavy

face opposite him. 'The verses Fletchley writes are in every way contemptible. They pander deliberately to the vulgarian who lives in all of us. They exploit the lowest depth of public taste. That's what is wrong with Fletchley's rhymes.'

With clownish pleasure the Inspector said: 'I do admire the way you talk, now. But tell me – as a plain man now – if there's a demand for something, can it be wrong to supply it?' The vacant eye rolled round the room. 'You don't have a woman in,' he added. Anderson was taken aback.

'What?'

'Dust.' The great bald head was slowly shaken. 'You're letting things go, Mr Anderson. This room looks altogether different from the way it did when I first saw it. That was three weeks ago. Your wife kept it very nice, if I may say so. Not my own taste, of course, – but – ' The great flat hand moved embracingly to include carpet, curtains, chairs, lamps, everything. 'Very nice. And now look.' One great finger moved on the red table, sketched a face in dust, skirted the bowler hat and picked up the pot. 'Preparation Number One,' he read as slowly as a peasant. 'Preparation for what, if it's not a rude question?'

Anderson leaned forward again, pleased that the conversation had moved away from his wife. 'That little pot, Inspector, contains a cream designed to eliminate shaving from our lives for ever. It is a small part of the twentieth-century revolution.'

'And what might that be, when it's at home?'

'Hygiene, asepsis, artificial insemination.'

The lines on the great blue-white face deepened as the Inspector laughed. 'You're in favour of modernity, though, Mr Anderson. How about the refrigerator in the kitchen? And' – his hand moved embracingly again – 'all this.'

Anderson said stiffly: 'My wife furnished this flat.'

'Ah, she was a modern,' the Inspector said sepulchrally. 'I'm old-fashioned. But hygiene and asepsis – I'm modern enough to believe in them.'

'But don't you see that they're unimportant?' Anderson cried. He was moved suddenly by the need for explanation.

'Unimportant?'

'When a doctor saves human lives he is committed to the belief that they are valuable. But he may be quite wrong. It's only during the past few hundred years that we've come to assume that there is something intrinsically important about the fact of life itself, and now soil conservers are telling us that the world's population is too large for the amount of food available, that we're slowly starving to death. Improved maternity statistics and better dental treatment have no importance in themselves. The important thing to find out about any man or woman is whether he's preserved his soul alive.'

The Inspector looked at Anderson. Anderson looked at the Inspector. 'Have you got a match?' the Inspector asked vacantly. Anderson gave him a box of Swan Vestas, and the Inspector lighted a cigarette. 'Matches,' he said absently. 'That's what I was going to say.'

'What?'

'Nothing.' The vacant eyes rested on Anderson. 'Have you got any enemies?'

'Enemies?'

'We have received a letter – in fact, we have received two letters.' Suddenly two pieces of paper were in the great hand. 'We don't pay much attention to such things in general, but just in this case we'd like to know who sent them.' Anderson read the letters. The first suggested that he hated his wife and made her life miserable for years. It asked why Anderson's statement at the inquest that his married life had been 'normally happy' had been left uncorroborated. The second said that Anderson had been persistently unfaithful to his wife. *And then he insured her life for £5,000. And then she fell downstairs. Cui bono?* Anderson read the letters and returned them without comment.

'Typed on a Remington 12 machine, posted in Central London, no fingerprints,' the Inspector said. The clownishness had dropped from him, the heavy face was alert, the eyes' vacancy might be interpreted as alertness. 'The first of them came a week ago, the second three days after it. Nothing since. You've no idea who wrote them, I suppose?'

'No.'

'Stuff like this now – in one way it's beneath contempt. And yet in another it's interesting. It's the sort of thing that sets us thinking.' With a return to clownishness, the Inspector ran a hand over his great bald head; the humorous action was somehow more menacing than a threat could have been. 'A clever chap like you now, you're thinking all the time. But a policeman only thinks when he needs to, and that's not very often. A bit of low cunning's enough for our purposes usually, when we're dealing with the uneducated classes. But with a gentleman like yourself – '

'I went to a grammar school,' Anderson said sharply, to check this ponderous humour.

The Inspector was unperturbed. 'That's just what I mean. You're a well-read man, an intellectual. A policeman's got to be clever to keep up with you. When we got these letters we thought back over the case, and do you know what we discovered? We hadn't been clever enough. But that won't be any surprise to somebody like yourself.' The Inspector slapped his knee with a meaty hand, and laughed.

'Not clever enough?'

'We had failed to read our Sherlock Holmes. The curious incident of the matches. Although, of course, in a way the reverse of *Silver Blaze*. You've read that, of course.'

'I'm afraid not, no.'

'Detective fiction,' the Inspector said with a sigh. 'But the box of matches worries me, I must confess. You don't understand me?' Anderson shook his head. In his thick voice the Inspector said: 'Your wife left the sitting-room – '

'The kitchen. She was cooking the supper.'

'Left the kitchen, passed through the sitting-room, went out into the passage, to the head of the cellar stairs, turned on the switch and found that the light had fused. Unhappy that the light should have fused, is it not, just at that particular moment? Tragic, even. She then struck a match, began to descend the stairs, slipped – ' The Inspector paused delicately, and then looked up. 'Where did the box of matches come from that was found by her body?' The question was asked in a gentle voice.

Anderson goggled at him. 'She would hardly have taken matches from the kitchen when she supposed that the cellar light would be on? Of course she wouldn't. She would not find matches in the passage. She didn't come back or call to you when she found that the cellar light was out of order. And yet – a box of matches was found by the side of her body.'

'Her frock,' Anderson said. His voice was hoarse.

'Woollen. No pockets. It's a problem. I don't see where the box of matches could have come from, do you?' The Inspector's voice rumbled softly; it was ridiculous to think that his eyes could ever have been vacant. 'What the anonymous letter said about the five thousand pounds insurance – that was right, wasn't it?'

Like a man emerging from water, Anderson shook himself. 'Inspector Cresse, are you insinuating that I killed my wife?'

The Inspector looked astonished. 'Why, what a question to ask! I came here about those anonymous letters.'

'Then why do you ask about the insurance? You know perfectly well that we each had an insurance on the other's life. I am not short of money, Inspector.'

'Now, now, Mr Anderson.' The meaty hand was raised, soothingly. 'Nobody said you were. You don't get the point. Nothing was mentioned about that insurance at the inquest. The person who sent that letter must know you pretty well. You might think it over and see if you can identify him – or her. But the whole affair, that unfortunate business about the light that fused, and so on, raises what you might call a moral problem.'

'Oh yes, a moral problem.' Shall I say it? Anderson wondered, and then gripped the arm of his chair and spoke earnestly. 'Tell me, Inspector, if I told you that I killed my wife, would you arrest me?'

'Ah ah.' Like gigantic scissors the Inspector's legs shifted and were crossed from right to left instead of from left to right. 'Precisely the moral problem.' Anderson poured out fresh drinks for both of them. When he passed the Inspector's glass, however, some of the whisky splashed on to the hard, fleshy thigh. Anderson exclaimed in dismay, drew out his handkerchief and

rubbed the offending spot. The Inspector, apparently unconscious of these ministrations, stared ahead of him at the pentag-
onal looking-glass fixed over the fireplace. 'Precisely the moral
problem. You killed your wife, Mr Anderson.' Anderson sat
perfectly still, holding his own glass, staring. 'You killed her, I
mean, in the sense that had you pursued some other course of
action she would not now be dead. You might have taken her
out to dinner. You might have gone down into the cellar in her
place, might you not? And then perhaps when you found it in
darkness, you might have mended the fuse – you are a handy
enough electrician for that? Or perhaps you might have
accompanied her to the head of the cellar stairs instead of
reading the paper in the sitting-room. Then you would have
cautioned her no doubt – you would have said: "Be careful of
that slippery step half-way down." And then, who knows –
perhaps she wouldn't have slipped.'

'You attach blame to me? You think me guilty?'

'Ah ah,' the Inspector said again. He drank three-quarters
of the whisky in his glass. 'That question is not for an ignorant
policeman, but for an intellectual. A man like yourself. It's a
problem of morals.' He spoke with a gravity to which Anderson,
his partner in this curious verbal knockabout, responded with
restrained jocosity.

'So you will not arrest me?'

'Arrest you?'

'Even though I said *Mea culpa*, I confess my guilt.' Anderson
beat his breast in mock despair. 'What do you propose to do
about it? Supposing I said that – just supposing!' With a revival
of his earlier gadfly spirit, Anderson walked mincingly across
the room to straighten a picture.

'What do *you* propose to do?' The Inspector's features had
lost altogether their joviality. The strong lines threw into pro-
minence the great blunt nose, the loose lips were joined in an
appearance of resolution. 'We can do nothing without you.' He

stood up and clapped the bowler hat on to his bald head. It was like the curtain coming down on a play.

'Nothing!' Anderson echoed triumphantly.

'Nothing.'

# THE TWENTYSIXTH OF FEBRUARY

## I

The sickly light of morning, filtering through pink curtains, illuminated Anderson asleep in a double bed. He slept in a position curiously contorted, one arm thrust over his head like a signal, the other holding a pillow tightly to his chest. His knees were drawn up like those of a man making a jack-knife dive. His yellow face looked younger in repose. The top of his pyjamas, open, revealed a body surprisingly white.

An alarm clock rang by the side of the bed. Anderson opened his eyes. They stared at his wife's photograph, which stood beside the alarm. While a hand silenced the alarm clock, Anderson continued to stare. His wife, head slightly to one side, eyes melting, lips bent upward in a smile, seemed joyfully to meet his gaze. Anderson's stare shifted from the photograph to the pink curtains, to the pink quilt on the bed, to the china knick-knacks on the mantelpiece, to the pink ribbons tied round the top of the dressing-table, back to the photograph. A slight film seemed to be spread over the glass. He touched it gingerly, and exclaimed: 'Dust,' remembering the Inspector. The flat had not been dusted or cleaned since his wife's death. Groaning slightly, Anderson got out of bed, ran a bath and put two slices of bread in the electric toaster. Plates and dishes with small pieces of food on them stood in the sink. He bathed quickly, and looked at his face in the shaving-glass. Magnification made the pits of removed blackheads look like craters of the moon, but he stared particularly at the blue growth on and underneath the chin. Each hard bristly hair was plainly distinguishable; the total effect was exceedingly unattractive.

Anderson put his watch in front of him and then, like a nervous bather, dipped a finger in the pot of *Preparation Number 1*. Gingerly he smeared the stuff on to his face. He felt at first nothing at all, then a prickling and burning that was not unpleasant, then again nothing. Obviously, the stuff had failed to work. He checked by his watch, waited another half-minute to give the preparation a chance, then damped a flannel and wiped his face. He looked to see the blue stubble. It had gone. His face was absolutely clean to the eye, and to the touch of fingertips felt babyishly soft. The preparation, in fact, did exactly what had been claimed for it; Anderson, an advertising man accustomed to publicizing goods that did perhaps a quarter of what was claimed for them, gasped with astonishment at such a consummation.

## II

The swing doors hissed behind Anderson. Miss Detranter was reading from notes, ticking off each item as she read. 'Flowers,' she said to Jean Lightley. 'Flowers for the directors' rooms. Flowers for Mr Anderson's room. Flowers for each department. Secretaries' typewriters neat and tidy. Tell the Studio they must get straightened up. All of them working, but everything bright and clean. Tell the production boys to get blocks stacked one side of them and proofs the other. Tell Miss O'Rourke – '

Anderson stared and listened. The black book with marbled corners, the Inspector's visit, belonged to another time and world; within these doors he was an advertising executive, a man with a purpose in life. 'Hey,' he said, 'that's my secretary.'

'VV's orders,' said Miss Detranter sweetly. 'He rang up in a flap and said get all the girls to work on it. I can't leave Reception. Jean won't be half an hour, will you, Jean?' Jean gasped like a fish.

'Flowers in February. What's it in aid of?'

'Mr Divenga's coming round.'

'And who's Mr Divenga?'

'I simply haven't a clue,' said Miss Detranter. Anderson made his way down the corridor. As he turned the corner, he heard: ' – tell Miss O'Rourke she must have some vital statistics on hand. Charts and graph on the wall – '

Anderson went into his room! Figures scurried past in the corridor. Reverton's secretary, Miss Flack, came in with a duster. 'Just dusting,' she said with a smile and flicked rapidly at cupboard, chairback, hatstand and desk. 'Mr Divenga's flown over,' she added with a bright smile, and went out. The telephone rang. 'Oh, Mr *Anderson*,' said Miss Vine, 'Mr Vincent said to tell you that Mr Divenga's coming in this morning.'

'I've grasped that.'

'If you have an outside appointment, will you please postpone it if possible. If it can't be postponed, please let me know. Otherwise will you please be available.'

'I'll please be available.' The operator giggled. 'Who's Mr Divenga?'

'I don't know him from Adam, I'm afraid, Mr Anderson.' The operator giggled again.

Anderson sat down in his chair. As he did so he noticed that Miss Flack, when she dusted the desk, had shifted a letter at the bottom of his pile of mail, so that it was out of place. His hand moved to replace it, and then he noticed the handwriting. It was a letter from Val.

Anderson sat quite still. His head seemed to be the centre of a whirlpool, going round and round and round and round. He closed his eyes, and in the whirlpool there were faces – the round bland face of Lessing, the square dependable face of Reverton, the triangle of VV's great forehead and small pointed chin, the long chalky nose of Molly O'Rourke. Anderson opened his eyes again, and gripped the sides of the chair to stop himself from falling. When he felt better he picked up the letter and read the hastily scribbled lines: *My darling. I love you so much, and it seems so long since I held you in my arms.* Somebody has stolen the letters she wrote to me, Anderson thought with a bitter anger that surprised him. And then, as he turned the page and read the unfamiliar words, he realized suddenly why this letter had been put on his desk. This was not a letter Val had written to him; it was a letter she had written to somebody else. 'I love you *dearly*' were the last words, and then came the scrawled signature *Val*. Val had loved Anderson – or so he had always thought; but she had never ended a letter *I love you dearly*. And yet this letter, written in the light blue ink she used, on dark blue paper, was unmistakably in her writing.

Anderson sat looking at the letter for a period that might have been seconds or minutes. Then he pushed it clumsily into his pocket and almost ran out of the room. As he slammed the door the telephone rang. With blundering emphasis Anderson moved along the corridor, head down. His swinging arm struck something soft, and a voice said 'Good morning'. Anderson looked up to find Mr Pile regarding him severely through his rimless pince-nez. 'Is anything the matter?' Anderson muttered. 'You don't look well, Anderson. Perhaps you had better go home.' Mr Pile's tone made it clear that he did not care for executives who were unwell and went home.

'Mr Divenga,' Anderson said.

A withered smile passed over Mr Pile's face. 'Ah yes, he is coming round this morning. But he won't expect to see our senior men rushing about head down. Are you quite sure you feel all right?' Anderson nodded. Mr Pile stood still, fumbling for the true and appropriate phrase. At last he found it. 'Well, more haste less speed.' He passed on.

Anderson went into the Copy Room. The neat brown-suited figure of Greatorex rose to receive him. 'I put that list of names on your desk – '

'Where's Lessing?'

'I haven't seen him this morning, Mr Anderson.' Greatorex was apologetic. 'Shall I ask him – '

'Doesn't matter.' Greatorex looked at him in surprise. Outside the door of the Copy Room, Anderson stood and wiped his hand over his forehead. Anger and urgency drained away, and his body felt simply weak. He walked along slowly and aimlessly, turning right and left, until he came to the door marked simply Research. Molly O'Rourke's head popped out. 'Oh, it's you,' she said. 'Come in.' He went in. 'You can lend a hand with this chart. Just pass it up to me, will you.' She stood on a chair, and he passed up to her an enormous chart made up of different blocks of colour. Above each colour block, on the left-hand side of the chart, was a percentage figure. The centre part of the chart was divided into geographical areas. The blocks on the right-hand side were split into months of the year and had cash figures over them. 'Take this,' she said. He held one end of the chart while she pinned it to the wall. They both stood looking at it. 'In case you wonder what it all means, it tells you the percentage of cakes of Happiday Soap sold in England in comparison with all competitors. It gives you an area breakdown. It relates advertising cost to sales returns in all districts. It tells you – '

'Wonderful,' Anderson said. 'And when you've got it what have you got?'

'You haven't got much and that's a fact. This is all two years out of date. Fortunately the date was at the bottom and we've cut it out. It looks good on the wall. Part of the red carpet for Mr Divenga.' She stared at Anderson. 'You look terrible. What's the matter? Here, never mind. Take a nip.' She drew out a bottle from the drawer of her desk. Anderson looked round for a glass. 'Ah come on, drink it like a man.' He took out the stopper, tilted back his head, and drank until tears came into his eyes. 'My my,' said Miss O'Rourke, 'that must have put several hairs on your chest. What's the matter? Tell mamma.' Her black curls shook, her chalky nose was near to his face.

'Look, Molly,' Anderson said, 'did you see anybody go in my office early this morning?'

'Since I can't see round several corners the answer, old cock, is No. Don't tell me somebody's been stealing your ideas.'

'Somebody's playing a funny kind of joke on me, and I'd like to find out his name.'

'Sure it's a him?'

Anderson fingered the letter in his pocket. 'Quite sure.'

'Girls can play some pretty funny jokes sometimes.'

'This one was played by a man.' The house telephone rang. Molly said: 'Yes, you've run him to earth. Yes, I'll tell him.'

She put the telephone down. 'Birdseed is on your tail. Something about some drawings – '

'Christ!'

'But more important, Mr Divenga is on his way round. Will everybody please be in their rooms. You'd better run along. Feeling better?'

'Yes.'

Molly was casual. 'Care to repeat the dose this evening if you've got nothing better to do?'

Anderson hesitated and then said: 'All right.'

She put her hand on her heart and grimaced. 'My, you just sweep a girl off her feet. Come here, your tie's crooked.' She straightened Anderson's tie and gave him a little push out of the door. On the way back to his room Anderson met Reverton, walking down the corridor pipe foremost, with a look of intense concentration. He raised a hand and would have gone on, but Anderson stopped him. 'I say, Rev, who's Mr Divenga?'

Reverton stared at him in surprise. 'I thought you knew, old boy. He's the managing director of Multi-African Products. Just flown over unexpectedly. Going to meet him now. Will you be available?'

'I'll be available.'

'All a lot of bull, of course, showing him round, but you know how it is.'

'I know how it is,' said Anderson.

## III

Falsely hearty voices roared along the corridor in waves. The door opened and they all came in, laughing. But where was Mr Divenga? 'And this is Mr Anderson,' VV said. 'Our copy chief. He will be in control of the creative side of your account – under me, of course – and if I may blow somebody else's trumpet without immodesty, you couldn't have a finer man on the job. Anderson, this is Mr Maximilian Divenga of Multi-African Products.' Anderson stood up and from behind the smiling Reverton there darted a little figure something less than five feet high. He was dressed in a tightly waisted lilac suit with a fawn waistcoat, he wore spats above crocodile leather shoes. But it was not these things that made Anderson gape at Mr Maximilian Divenga, nor his beaky Jewish nose, but the fact that the lower part of the little man's large head was almost completely covered by a great black spade beard.

'You are happy, yes?' Mr Divenga asked, gripping Anderson's hand with fingers like pincers. 'Are happy in creation?'

'Mr Divenga thinks it most important that the creative minds in charge of an account should feel thoroughly integrated with the work they are handling,' said Mr Pile plummily. He turned to the gaily dressed dwarf. 'That is a consideration we always bear in mind, my dear Mr Divenga. We pondered very seriously the problem of which of our creative minds should handle your account. Mr Anderson already has the whole question of shaving at his – ah – fingertips. He handled another shaving-cream account with great success when he was – ah – working with a rival agency some years ago. Isn't that so, Anderson?'

'Iss goot,' said Mr Divenga before Anderson could assent to this complete untruth. Then he turned menacingly on Mr Pile, and gave his chest several steely prods. 'But iss not *another* shaving-cream account. Preparation Number One iss not shaving cream. *Shaving iss finished*.'

'Finished,' said VV triumphantly, and the others took up the cry. There was a short silence. Were they all thinking as he was, Anderson wondered, of Mr Divenga's great black beard?

'I've been giving your preparation a test, Mr Divenga,' he said. 'My chin's pretty blue normally, but Number One leaves it smooth as silk.'

The little man stepped up close to Anderson, passed a hand over his chin and breathed. 'Ahh.' He turned to the three directors. 'You have felt?' Obligingly VV and Pile touched Anderson's chin and exclaimed in wonder, although as Pile retreated Anderson seemed to remark a slight frown behind the pince-nez. Mr Divenga turned to Reverton. 'You have felt?'

'Don't need to, Mr Divenga. Tried it myself yesterday morning. Absolutely miraculous.'

'Miraclus, miraclus,' said Mr Divenga. 'Always in South Africa are performing miraclus. Have marketed many miraclus – clasp-knife changes to tooth-drawer, paper flower breathe on and opens, card of pretty girl with clothes on – hold to the light and is pretty girl without clothes on.' The three directors and Anderson laughed heartily, but with a trace of puzzlement. VV became oratorical.

'Engaging toys, Mr Divenga, but this is something different. I assure you, my dear sir, that I believe – that we believe – your preparation to be the greatest boon ever brought to twentieth-century man. It is – '

'Iss miraclus,' said Mr Divenga, whose attention seemed to have wandered. 'Pleased to meet, Mr Anderson. Shall we go on now?' The directors about-turned.

'Is Number One the final form of your preparation?' Anderson asked. 'I ask partly because I think we should impart a slightly different odour to the one it has at present before putting it on the market, and partly because I felt a rather curious sensation when I used it this morning.' Then Anderson made the most awful error of his advertising career. 'I don't know whether you've ever tried it yourself, Mr Divenga – ' Three directorial faces looked back at him from the doorway, frozen in expressions of horror. Anderson stopped, speechless. But Mr Divenga seemed merely puzzled. 'Senashun, what is senashun?' he asked.

'A kind of burning feeling just for a moment or two.'

An expression almost of alarm appeared on the little man's face; but it vanished in a moment. 'Iss sample,' he said, pointing to the pot on Anderson's desk. 'Iss all the time more miraclus. Experiment lavatories,' he said with a smile at Anderson which showed a mouthful of splendid teeth, 'soon get rid of senashun.'

He was gone, and the directors followed him. Mr Pile cast one backward glance over the top of his pince-nez at Anderson, and the glance was not friendly.

# IV

Jean Lightley stood awkwardly in front of his desk, with her weight resting on one foot.

'So you brought in my mail at about twentyfive past nine.'

'Yes, Mr Anderson.'

'You're absolutely certain that this letter wasn't with it?' He held up Valerie's letter upside down, and some distance away from Jean.

'I'm sure, Mr Anderson.'

'And it wasn't lying on the desk when you brought in the mail?' She shook her head. 'How do you know? It might have been put under another paper. That's possible, isn't it?'

A tide of colour went up from Jean Lightley's neck into her face. 'Yes,' she whispered, 'but I don't think so.'

'Now look, Jean, this is important. Are you sure you didn't see anybody come into my room between half past nine and the time I came in this morning?'

'I didn't, Mr Anderson,' she said earnestly. 'Truly I didn't.'

'All right, Jean.' He remembered the calendar. 'Has that magic calendar of mine been behaving itself?'

'Yes,' she whispered. She almost bumped into Charlie Lessing at the door in her eagerness to get out. The copywriter looked after her.

'What's on your mind?' Anderson asked. 'And by the way, where were you at nine-fortyfive this morning?'

Lessing looked injured. 'I was at the BM historically researching into the history of shaving. The old English was "sceafan", perhaps derived from the Latin "scabere", which means scratch, or the Greek "skapto" which means dig. "We're not going to sceafan any more" – yes?'

'No.'

'A shaving tool was first known in the twelfth Egyptian dynasty,' Lessing said imperturbably, 'and became common in the eighteenth. "The Egyptians had a word for shaving – modern man uses Depilo." '

'Don't keep calling it Depilo, that's no good. Have you seen Mr Divenga?'

Lessing grimaced and spread out his hands Hebraically. 'Depilo? De pillow? Ain't that what you sleep on, no? So there's nothing to history, eh? Out, damned history.'

'Keep it up your sleeve. But I don't think we'll ever get past VV. Let's look at that list of names Greatorex has made.'

'Some of them aren't bad.'

They bent over the list. 'All these portmanteau names are no good,' Anderson said. 'Can't be patented. And things like Secshave are no good either. But we might put forward – ' The house telephone rang and he picked it up. VV's voice said: 'Hey presto.'

'What's that?'

Gleefully the voice repeated: 'Say hey presto.'

'Hey presto.'

'No no. "Say Hey Presto" – can you see that at the top of an eight-inch triple? "Say Hey Presto – and forget about shaving." "Say Hey Presto for a silk-smooth jawline." "Say Hey Presto and no more cottonwool." '

'Cottonwool?'

'After you've cut yourself shaving.' VV's voice was faintly dubious. 'Perhaps that one's a bit obscure. But you see the possibilities. I think we've really got something with Hey Presto, don't you?'

'I thought we were out for humanity, not humour.'

VV chuckled happily. 'This is human and magical at the same time. Think it over, boy. Then come in and see me.'

Anderson put down the telephone, and began methodically to tear up the sheet of paper containing Greatorex's names. Reverton's square head was poked round the door, for once pipeless. He said with mild interest: 'Copy Department having fun tearing up copy?'

'VV's had a brainwave. He's found a name for our antishave preparation. Hey Presto.' Decisively Anderson tore the sheet of paper across again, and dropped it in the wastepaper basket. 'There go about a hundred ideas for names.'

Reverton's square face and Lessing's round one both looked serious. 'It's got something,' Lessing said.

' "Say Hey Presto – and forget about shaving." ' Anderson was ironic.

'Yes, I can see that,' Reverton said. They were his highest words of praise. 'You don't like it, Andy?'

'It's not whether I like it – though I think it stinks. But it's just exactly the line he told us not to work on.' Reverton raised his eyebrows. 'Humanity, not humour, he said, and I think he was right. Is "Hey Presto" human? It sounds pretty comic to me.'

'Now look, Andy,' Reverton said earnestly, 'you're losing your sense of proportion. It's good this name, don't you agree, Charlie?'

'I think so, yes.'

'All right, then. You know me, Andy. I'm one of the boys myself; I think like you, I know what's in your mind. You like ideas to come from the copy boys and the Studio and then go up to the directors, not come down the other way. So do I. We all know that directors are pretty dumb – I ought to know, I'm one myself.' He laughed heartily. 'But it can happen that a director gets hold of a bright idea. This is it.'

Perversely, against the sense which told him he had better keep silent, Anderson said: 'I still think it stinks.'

The telephone rang. Anderson picked it up and made a face. It was Bagseed. Reverton and Lessing went out. With an effort, Anderson adjusted a tone of false joviality over his voice and said, with the forestalling technique familiar to advertising executives and others engaged in selling material which they have had no hand in producing, 'I know what you're after, Mr Bagseed, you're after those drawings.' The forestalling technique was justified upon this occasion by the fact that, at the moment these words were spoken, Jean Lightley came in with the drawings in her hand. Mr Bagseed whined, cajoled and threatened until Anderson said brightly: 'Those drawings are on the way up to you *now*, Mr Bagseed.' He looked at the drawings, which showed odiously fat little girls and unnaturally demure little boys wearing a variety of clothing, and told Jean Lightley to send them up immediately to Kiddy Modes. When she had left the room he tilted his revolving chair back against the wall, and sat staring at the green carpet. Looking up, he was surprised to see the neat brown suit of Greatorex in front of his desk.

'I knocked, but you didn't answer.' Greatorex coughed. 'I wondered if you'd had a chance to look at those names for the new preparation.'

Anderson pointed to the wastepaper basket. 'There they are.' He held up a warning finger. 'Don't get the idea they were no good. I thought two or three of them were pretty bright. But that doesn't matter.' He let the revolving chair drop to the ground with a bump. 'What matters is that VV has had an idea himself.'

'That's Mr Vincent?'

'That's Mr Vincent. He's decided to call the stuff Hey Presto. That's the decision and there's no argument about it, unless VV changes his mind. So – ' He indicated the torn-up pieces of paper.

'Hey Presto,' Greatorex said. 'Well, that's a pretty good name.'

'I think it's a terrible name. I'm the creative man on the account. But that doesn't matter either.' Anderson tapped the desk with his finger. 'Lesson number one in advertising. Be original, but don't be too original, because people won't like it. And remember that until you get near the top nine-tenths of what you do won't even be considered. You'll sweat your guts out for no purpose whatever. It's disheartening, but that's the way it is. Now, here's advertising lesson number two.' He laid another finger on the desk. 'Have you got another copy of that list? All right then, don't throw it away. VV may change his mind – or the client may not like VV's idea – then that list might be very useful. Understand?' Greatorex nodded, but looked at him oddly as he left the room. Anderson reflected again that he was a fool to be saying such things. A month ago he would not have said them. Why was he saying them now?

He pulled out of his pocket the letter from Val, spread it

before him on the desk, and read every word of the letter carefully as though in the hope that the wording of those hurried phrases or the shape of the handwriting or the texture of the blue paper would tell him something of the circumstances in which this letter had been written, and of the utterly unknown and unsuspected lover who now lay like a shadow across his past life. Who had been her lover? Somebody in his own office, somebody to whom Val had talked of him, laughing about him as a cuckold almost too easily deceived. Who could it have been? Reverton, Lessing, Wyvern, Vincent? She had known them all slightly, and thought little of them. It was impossible that she could have written to any of those men the words on the sheet of paper, that she should have said to any of them, 'I love you dearly.' And yet she had done so; in death she triumphed over him through these hasty words of love. What assignations did this letter represent, what clandestine meetings, what furtively delightful brushing of hands even in his presence, what pleasant deceits! Reverton, Lessing, Wyvern, Vincent: which of them had been her lover? The letter gave him no answer.

## V

The small window of Anderson's office looked on to the backs of three similar blocks of office buildings, separated from Vincent Advertising by a deep, narrow well. On three sides, looking out of Anderson's window both upwards and downwards, one could see through other windows girls typing, men surrounded by sheets of paper, girls looking in filing cabinets and sharpening pencils, men making notes in books or speaking to strange machines, tea being made and drunk. Wyvern was fond of standing at the window and saying that the contemporary world could be seen in microcosm; with, he added too aptly as he stared down the dark well, the bottomless pit which was the destination of all worshippers of Mammon, all those who sold their souls for a mess of pottage, all who had installed a piece of clockwork in their heads in place of a mind.

Anderson's room was never fully illuminated by sunlight, but on sunny afternoons a bright searchlight shaft would cut across his desk, liven the colour of a small, sharply defined area of carpet, and play upon the hatstand. This February afternoon was sunny; and, giving himself an occasional quarter-turn in the revolving chair, Anderson sat watching the parallelogram of sunlight become narrower and narrower until it was a thin finger-strip touching one edge of his penstand and gleaming on a worn segment of carpet. The telephone rang, people came in and out asking questions and bringing tea; he made no attempt to do any work, but sat staring in front of him. He thought – although the word is not truly applicable, for the images that passed through his mind seemed almost entirely casual and involuntary – of Val in relation to those four men, of her gestures and actions in their company. One day at the annual outing Lessing had helped her out of a charabanc. Anderson saw now with strange clarity the grip of Lessing's hand upon her arm just above the elbow, fingers pressing deeply the soft flesh of the upper arm. Lessing, Lessing, a randy married man? Once at a party, Val had been missing for half an hour and then had returned, dragging somebody by the hand, saying: 'Look what the cat's brought in.' There, smiling behind his pipe, letting himself be pulled into the room, with a great show of good-humoured reluctance, was Reverton. But Reverton, like Lessing, was a man happily married, with two children. Surely not Reverton. Wyvern? A disappointed artist, tediously cynical, always droning on about his obligation to his mother. But then Val had always liked them to go out drinking with Wyvern because she said he was such good company. There was a particular ridiculous phrase they used instead of saying 'Cheerio.' Anderson saw Wyvern raising his glass and saying 'Shorter days,' and a clink as Val's glass struck it and she responded: 'Longer nights.' And VV? But he could recall nothing about VV in connection with Val, except a vague impression of the elaborate courtesy with which he always treated women.

The afternoon passed away; the sunlight faded, and the daylight; Jean Lightley came in, touched the electric switch and exclaimed: 'Why, Mr Anderson, you're sitting in the dark. I thought you had gone home.'

Anderson, slouched in the revolving chair, moved a little. 'No, Jean, I had not gone home.' And I should like, he thought, as he caught among those other glimpses of the past a picture of the pink bedroom, the modernist sitting-room, the dishes in the sink, the thin layer of dust over all, I should like never to go home.

# VI

'Down hatches and mud in your eye,' said Molly O'Rourke. 'This is my fourth and I can't feel a thing. They've doctored the whisky. I say, I say,' she called. The barman came up. He was a large man with a sad, ugly prizefighter's face. Several strands of almost colourless hair were plastered down on his head. Molly thrust her nose and her glass forward at the same time. 'Is this stuff doctored?'

'I beg your pardon?' The barman's voice was surprisingly almost a tenor.

'Castrated, if you'll pardon my French. Do you a-dul-ter-ate,' Molly O'Rourke said with a twitch of her chalky nose, 'the po-ten-cy of this allegedly Highland dis-till-a-tion with an ad-mix-ture of – '

'What's that?'

'Skip it. Care to tickle your tonsils?'

'What's that?'

'Lift the elbow. I mean to say,' said Miss O'Rourke patiently, 'have a drink.'

'Oh ah. Just a little drop of It, then. I like a little drop of It.' The barman poured a drop of It. 'Good luck. You've certainly got a funny way of talking.'

'We're in advertising. That explains everything, doesn't it,

Andy?' She swung her body in its uncreased blue tailored suit round on the bar stool.

'If you say so. Look, Molly, there's something I want – '

The barman leant forward a little. 'All sorts we get in here, you wouldn't believe.' He made a gesture that embraced the empty bar. 'Had a raid last week and it's done for business. But they'll be back.'

'Who'll be back?'

'The boys'll be back. You don't scare 'em away for long.'

'What boys?' Molly asked, and the barman's sad look lightened. He put a hand on his thick waist.

'You know – the boys. The boys that wish they was something else.'

'Oh, *those* boys.'

'Antics they get up to sometimes. I could tell you – '

'Two more whiskies,' Anderson said. 'Look, I want to talk to you, Molly.' He pointed to the little empty tables in one corner of the bar. The barman was offended.

'All right, then, all right; you want to be alone, that's all right. I can take a hint. I know when I'm not wanted.' He poured two nips of whisky. 'But I've got my feelings like anybody else. Your young lady got into conversation with me, don't forget that. I was passing the time of day in conversating when asked, that's all.'

'No offence,' said Anderson. 'Have another drink, Jack.'

'No offence at all. I shouldn't like you to think I was pushing, that's all. I'll just have another drop of It. But my name's not Jack.'

'What's your name?'

'My name's Percy.'

They left him at the bar, and sat down at one of the empty tables. Molly O'Rourke's knee was warm against Anderson's leg. 'What's on your mind, Andy?'

'Molly, how well did you know Val?'

She leaned back and let out breath in a sigh. 'Still chasing lost causes. Why don't you give up and make a fresh start?'

'What did women think of Val? Did they like her?'

Molly placed one lean bony hand upon the breast that pushed out her jacket. 'If you're asking one woman the answer is no. I thought she was a snake in the grass. I never went for that dewy innocence. Whatever she got was what was coming to her.'

Anderson put down his glass quickly upon the table top. Some drops of whisky bounced out. 'What do you mean by that?'

'Mean? I'm not using up any spare handkerchiefs on her, that's all.'

'You said she got what was coming to her. What did you mean?'

'Oh, I don't know, Andy, I don't know.' She looked away from him and said: 'I suppose the thing is I never thought she was good enough for you. That's all I meant.'

'What about men friends? Did she know anybody well – anyone in the firm?'

'Here, here.' She moved her knee away from Anderson's leg. 'What's all this about? What does it matter now, anyway?'

'Oh, it doesn't matter.' Anderson was elaborately sarcastic. 'It's just that I'd like to know who she was running round with, that's all. Just that I'd like to know how long I'd been wearing horns.'

'Look here, Andy, I don't know anything about this. But I think you've got it all wrong somehow.'

'I've got nothing wrong,' he said violently.

'I mean I don't think there was anyone in the office.'

'There was someone in the office.'

'If there was I don't know about it. You believe me, don't you, Andy? But I tell you who would know all about it – if there was anything to know. That girl she worked with – Elaine Fletchley.'

They were both silent. Then Anderson said: 'Let's get out of here.'

'All right, let's go and eat.'

'I don't want to eat.'

'Right you are, then, let's go and drink. Where shall we drink?'

'I know where to go,' Anderson said.

As they went out Molly called: 'Good night, Percy. Don't mix any gin with that It.' The barman ducked his head and looked pleased. Outside, a thin rain blew into their faces. Anderson called a taxi. When they were inside Molly placed her bony hand on his. Charing Cross Road went by, the bookshops all in darkness. Irving's statue stared under the lights of fluorescent blue.

'Look, Andy, I know it's none of my business, but you're taking this too hard. People are talking. Little Jean had some tale about your giving her a calendar and saying it was magic. It's all over the office.'

'Somebody was altering my calendar.' Anderson leant back on the cushions. 'Every time I was out of the room it was changed to February the fourth. That's the day Val died.'

'Why – you poor darling.' Molly's hand gripped his convulsively. 'Who would have done that?'

'That's what I want to find out.'

'Sure you didn't imagine it?'

Anderson pulled his hand away. 'What do you take me for?' The taxi lurched as they turned into the park and he was thrown against her. As they kissed her hard fingers dug into him, moving furiously over his back, holding him tightly as if he were a plank that might save her from drowning. In the flickering darkness her head moved down to his neck, and her corkscrew curls bobbed over his face. He jerked his head back and pushed her away. 'I like you, Andy,' she said. 'I've always liked you. There goes Buckingham Palace. Goodbye, Buckingham, and goodbye, Palace. I'll tell you something, Andy – shall I tell you something?' Her body rested in the crook of his arm. 'Percy didn't doctor that drink.'

He grunted. How many times, he thought with a nostalgia that surprised himself, how many times have Val and I ridden in petrol-scented darkness past Buckingham Palace and down these streets. The bombs dropped a mile away, pieces of shrapnel clattered on the pavement like toys, reminders of the delightful impermanence of life. On such nights Anderson had come as near as it was possible for him to come to a confused love for everything around him, love for the people who might today or tomorrow be killed quite casually, love for the civilization being reduced to rubble under his eyes, love even, momentarily, for Buckingham Palace and his companion in the cab. Such possibility of sudden death imposed upon life a design. But tonight there were no bombs and life had no design and a different companion rested in the crook of his arm.

They stopped. 'Here we are,' Anderson said. 'My home ground.' He glanced upwards at the sign, faintly visible in the light streaming from the saloon bar, of a grinning figure with cloven hoofs, harlequin clothes and flames coming out of its hair. Underneath the sign, in mock-Gothic lettering, could be read *The Demon*.

Molly seemed disappointed when they got inside the pub, although she did not refuse a drink. 'I thought we were going home.'

'Home, home? I have no home.' Ironically, Anderson declaimed: 'Let Rome in Tiber melt and the wide arch of the ranged Empire fall. Here is my – home. Drink up.'

'Oh, be your age,' she said a little impatiently. 'Where can I go to spend a penny?' When she had gone he stood pressing his fingers upon the glass and looking at the imprint. He slipped one hand into his pocket, and fingered Val's letter, assuring himself that it was still there, a perfectly tangible proof of disaster. Why disaster? he thought. Why disaster when I never loved her? Because, he answered himself, because the letter had opened up one of those terrible gaps in personal relations which we all know to exist, but are generally able to ignore, the sudden revelation that, in the lives of the people we know best, there exist great unexplored areas of jungle, places where primitive loves and hatreds fight silently together like tigers. Anderson asked for another drink. 'Sorry, Mr Anderson, no more whisky.' He ordered gin. A boy came round selling the Greyhound Special, printed slips which showed the results of the evening's dog racing. A big dark man with a broken nose standing near Anderson bought the sheet. A man with a check cap and the pointed nose of a weasel looked over his shoulder. The third member of their party, a small faded blonde woman wearing a pink dress under a cheap fur coat, sipped a small port apathetically.

The big man exclaimed angrily, 'Your bleeding Melksham. The bleeder never even showed.'

'You musta got the wrong race, Jerry. Couldn't come unstuck, Melksham.' The weasel nose appeared over the big man's shoulder, little eyes looked hastily over the sheet, thin lips exclaimed, 'Would you Christmas Eve it! Never showed.'

'I thought it couldn't lose,' the big man said bitterly. 'I thought it could win on three legs. I thought the others weren't in the race.'

'It was a racing certainty, Jerry.'

'And what kind of a bleeding certainty do you call that? Never even showed.'

'It couldn't lose on the book, Jerry.'

'Couldn't lose. Couldn't lose. What about your info that cost me half a nicker?' The little woman moved convulsively, but did not speak. 'What about the others being ready to lie down?'

'Do you know what I reckon, Jerry?' the check cap asked solemnly. Molly came back. Anderson, absorbed, pointed to her drink upon the counter. 'I reckon it's next time out.'

'Next time out!'

'Look at it this way. It's a good thing tonight, see. It can't lose. So it's three to one, maybe five to one on. So nobody can really make a killing. Next time it's odds against, see, and you get right in with both feet.'

'Next time! It's cost me ten bleeding nicker *this* time.'

Like a clockwork toy suddenly moved to action, the small blonde woman gave a small scream, and spoke in a voice of the utmost refinement. 'Not ten pounds, Jerry. Oh really, not ten pounds.'

The big man did not look at her. 'He's smart. He knows it's a good thing. He has the inside dope it can't lose. He tells me to step in with both feet and help myself.'

'You got no call to say that, Jerry.'

'But ten pounds, Jerry. What about the rent?' The little woman stared with horror at her port.

'Now don't you stick your nose into this.'

'But the rent, Jerry. Are you sure the rent's all right?'

' – the rent.'

'Oh, Jerry, you've spent the rent money. I never thought you'd do it.'

The big man shook his head like a dog. 'That's enough now. Let's get out of here.' But the clockwork toy, wound up, was not now to be denied action. Without a word the little woman launched herself at the check-capped weasel. The table at which they sat went over. Beer flecked Anderson's trousers and Molly's stockings. Red marks appeared on the face of the check-capped man. He pushed at the woman, not hard, and she fell over. The big man roared angrily and advanced, not upon check cap, but upon the woman. With one hand he pulled her to her feet and with the other struck her in the eye. She would have fallen again, but for the hand that held her up. Molly cried out. The barman ducked under the counter, caught hold of the big man by neck and waistcoat and ran him out of the door. The big man made no attempt to resist, but maintained firm hold of the woman, who was crying and holding a hand to her eye. The man with the check cap picked himself up, dusted himself and went out after them. The barman came back, looking rather pleased. Molly said to Anderson: 'Aren't you going to do something?'

'Never interfere. That's my good-neighbour policy.'

'But he might kill her.'

'Not he. She'll have a black eye tomorrow, that's all.'

Her nose was twitching. 'It's horrible.'

'Haven't you seen a fight in a pub before?'

'That's not what I mean. It's the way you just let them out of your sight and then don't worry about them. Suppose he *did* do some injury to her – we should be responsible.' Anderson shrugged. She put down her glass and ran out of the pub door. Anderson followed her. Under the sign of *The Demon* the faded woman in her cheap fur coat sat, crying feebly and trying to staunch a flow of blood from her nose. There was no sign of the two men. Molly knelt by her side, Anderson stood above them. A confused flow of words came to him: 'Nose . . . rotten little devil . . . the rent . . . Rampole Street . . .'

'We've got to get her home,' Molly said. 'Forty Rampole Street. She says it's just round the corner. That swine!' she said encouragingly to the woman. 'I'll tell him something if I see him. Give her your handkerchief, Andy.' Reluctantly Anderson applied his handkerchief to the woman's bleeding nose, and helped to lift her to her feet. She was as shapeless as a feather pillow. 'I suppose there isn't a spare room at your place for her,' Molly said.

'There certainly isn't.'

'She shouldn't be left with that man.' Together they supported her, each with an arm around her. The woman took not the least notice of them. She lurched forward with Anderson's handkerchief against her nose, muttering. A policeman looked at them suspiciously. They turned the corner into Rampole Street and suddenly the woman came to life again, darting out of their arms to a figure half visible in a doorway. 'Jerry!' The big man with the broken nose emerged. 'Oh, Jerry, take me home.'

'Come on, then,' the big man said. With one malevolent glance at Molly and Anderson he strode away along the street. The woman followed a step or two behind him, still clutching Anderson's handkerchief to her nose.

Anderson burst out laughing at the expression on Molly's face. 'You've worked in advertising too long; it's softened you up. Come to my place and have another drink.' They walked back. Anderson felt suddenly and unreasonably gay, but as they passed the *Demon* he was oppressed for a moment by a sense of foreboding. Something had happened when he came out of the pub; he had seen something strange, something out of place. What was it? The thought escaped him, and he put it away.

The tubular lights flickered, and then illuminated their two figures. 'Drink,' Anderson said, and poured it. Molly looked round the room curiously.

'Not your taste.' With his back almost turned to her, Anderson shook his head. 'Val's, eh? Just what she'd like. My my, you need a spring clean, don't you. What's here?' She opened the door to the bedroom and stood, hands on hips, surveying it. 'Blimey, a symphony in pink.' When Anderson came in she had Val's photograph in her hand. Something about her tall bony figure drinking in the room and the photograph, sniffing it all up with her big nose, shamed and excited him. 'Put that down,' he said, and then as she turned in surprise he gripped her by the shoulders and pulled her over to the bed. The glass of the photograph frame broke as it dropped to the floor. Like a man burning with fever dropping into a cool stream, he coupled with her.


# VII


He was conscious at first only of a sound rhythmically repeated, the pattern of a train's wheels perhaps, the sound of a sewing-machine, but more nearly – more nearly – the scream of a train's whistle as it passed through a tunnel. One tunnel and another and another, and then the noise was transformed into a long thin whistle pulled, one might almost say, through the hole of a needle that was stubbornly resistant of it. And then, as he opened his eyes and stared upwards, he realized that the sound was a snore. Awake, on an instant awake and aware of what was happening, he turned to see the white shoulder turned away from him, mounting high among the bedclothes. For a moment he hesitated and then touched that shoulder with his forefinger, half expecting to find a marble statue by his side. But the shoulder was warm, it shuddered to the finger's touch, the arm moved slightly and was then flung out along the pink quilt. The whistling ceased, the body turned to him, he saw the face. It was the face of Val. In the half-darkness of early morning he could see the features distinctly, the wide space between brows, the short nose and upper lip, the tiny mole by the side of the chin. As he traced those familiar features he saw, with a shock of terror, the eyes open slowly and heavily like a doll's eyes and stare at him. His hands moved to push away that face, to close those eyes. . . .

A shrill cry awakened him, and a thrashing and beating like that of a trapped bird. Claws tore at his arms. Molly O'Rourke sat upright and naked in the bed, clutching her neck. 'Christ,' she said, 'Christ, you nearly strangled me.'

He stared at her without understanding. 'But you're not Val.'

'And thank God I'm not if that's what she was let in for every night.' The marks of his fingers were on her neck.

'I had a dream – a nightmare,' he said humbly.

'Well, don't have another. Go to sleep.' She turned away from him, and in a few minutes the whistling sounds began again. Anderson lay on his back, staring up into the half-darkness which became slowly half-light. He thought about the letter, and then he remembered what had disturbed him when he came out of the pub.

# THE TWENTYSEVENTH OF FEBRUARY

## I

Upon Anderson's desk there lay an envelope, white, with no name written upon it, placed centrally on his blotting-pad. He stood above it, staring down, passing a hand over a chin treated with Hey Presto, which felt remarkably like polished glass. A jumble of thoughts moved in his mind, thoughts of fingerprints and of Val's face as he had seen it in the night and of the red marks round Molly O'Rourke's throat. The telephone rang and he picked it up, staring at the still untouched envelope which contained, perhaps, nothing at all, that was related to Val. Listening with less than half his mind, he heard Bagseed's voice, nasally imperative: 'Action.'

'What's that?'

'I say they won't do, Mr Anderson. Mr Arthur has never seen anything like them in his life.'

For ten minutes Anderson argued about the merits of the drawings at which he had merely glanced. The neck of a frock had been too much rounded, a sleeve was too short and a lapel too wide. The effect was to depreciate the class of goods sold by Kiddy Modes. Mr Arthur had been much upset. Anderson made notes on a pad and said that he would send up for the drawings and get alterations made.

Bagseed's voice took on a note at once conspiratorial and gleeful. 'One more point, Mr Anderson. Have you looked at drawing number eleven?'

'Number eleven?'

'I don't think you can have looked at it closely. Mr Arthur said, and I was bound to agree, that it really is disgusting.'

'Really?'

'Disgusting. It's the one with the gym tunic.'

'The gym tunic, yes.'

'A gym tunic must always be treated carefully, Mr Anderson. It's a risky garment.'

'And you feel the artist hasn't treated it carefully enough.'

were advertising men, and remember only that you were human
beings in dealing with this thing. I admit it, I was wrong. Don't
hold it against me.' Anderson watched with reluctant admiration
as VV joined both hands together in prayer. There it is, he
thought; that's the way to do it. He knows he's been contradict-
ing himself right and left and he's persuading us that black's
white, like a conjurer. 'Let me tell you the result of much
cogitation and burning of the midnight oil. I see a need here
for drama. There must always be drama in advertising – advertising is the drama of the masses; but here we have a product
which is in its essentials dramatic. But there is also, as Rev
here has seen with his particularly practical mind, a need for
education. How can we combine the two?' Behind the pipe
Reverton's face was serene, but he did not look at Anderson.
So he's been doing a little idea-stealing again, Anderson
thought. Was it possible to imagine that square jaw, that placid
face, belonging to Val's lover? Was it Reverton's hand that had
placed the envelope, neat and square and empty of writing,
upon his neat square empty blotter? He would never have the
imagination, Anderson thought, and felt momentarily amused.

'Run the two schemes side by side.' VV's hands moved outwards in a flourishing gesture. 'For big spaces the dramatic
scheme. This face reflected in the glass, the face of a supremely
contented man. The face of a man who has done with shaving
for ever. And to drive it home simply the slogan. The basic
slogan will be "Say Hey Presto – and forget about shaving." I
have indicated some others very roughly, and the genius of
our copy boys will find some more. For the smaller spaces an
educational campaign. What is this wonderful new cream that
has revolutionized men's lives? What are its properties and its
make-up? What precious oils enter its manufacture?'

'What do?' croaked Wyvern. He spoke so rarely in conferences that they looked at him in surprise. VV regarded the
question rhetorically.

'What do? That's the question to which we give an answer,
sober yet interesting, lively without being sensational. Jack, my
boy, here's your chance as a typographer. Something chaste,

something discreet, something elegant. Andy, here's an opportunity for good straightforward educational copy. Don't be afraid of packing it. Be factual. Be informative. Let yourself go. Set out what you've got to say under headings. One. Two. Three.' VV punched one hand into the palm of the other.

Reverton scratched his nose with his pipe. 'Doesn't sound too lively.'

'It *can* be lively,' VV insisted. His eyes were gleaming with love and inspiration. 'Make it question and answer. *What is Hey Presto?* It is a cream that etcetera. *What are its constituents?* The rare oils of the tgojumba tree are blended with etcetera. *How is it prepared?* Analytical chemists working in conditions of aseptic etcetera. Christ, do I have to write them all for you?'

While VV talked Anderson had been staring at his mobile face, alight with enthusiasm. He was moved suddenly by a desire to turn that constant enthusiasm and good humour to anger. He coughed. 'Did you say this was factual advertising or a patent medicine campaign?'

There was a moment's silence. Then VV spread out his hands again, imperturbably good-humoured. 'Ah now, Andy, you expect too much. Advertising is persuasion, not medical science. But do you see what I'm after? We've got to persuade, yes, but we can do it decently not vulgarly; we can set our persuasion in Times Roman instead of . . .' He let the sentence die away and sank back in his chair. His doglike eyes, half closed, moved from face to face.

Reverton scratched his nose again. 'Silence reigned,' he said humorously. 'And we all know what happened after that. Shall I tell you what I think, VV, speaking as one who's seen a bit of life on both sides of the fence – Board Room, Copy Room and Studio?' Body flung back, too tired completely to open his eyes, VV slightly nodded. 'I think I'm speaking for the boys when I say that they'd like to feel they're not bound by this scheme of yours, that they – '

Anderson ceased to listen. How many solemn conferences of this kind had he attended over the years? Conferences on the best way of selling boots and toothpaste and machine tools,

vacuum cleaners and antiseptics and motor-cars? They peeled
off in layers from his mind, the ridiculous failures and even
more ridiculous successes, the occasions when by a mixture of
wheedling and bluster he had jockeyed a superior or a client
into accepting his own presentation of an idea. To win it was
necessary above all to know when to fight, when to laugh, when
to argue earnestly. To an equal the rueful smile: 'I'm sorry, but
I just can't see it that way, old man.' To a superior propounding
ideas the youthfully enthusiastic tone: 'I say, sir, this really is
grand stuff; this'll knock 'em sideways.' He had been
accomplished in playing those parts and many others, but now
something had gone from him, and he could think only that one
of these three men might have been his wife's lover.

'Isn't that so, Andy?' Reverton looked at him with a slightly
quizzical gaze. 'The guinea-pig's come to no harm, has he? Hey
Presto really works?'

With a conscious effort Anderson brought himself back.
'Girls, just feel my chin.'

'No five o'clock shadow?'

'No five o'clock shadow.' He ran a hand over the slightly
chilly smoothness of his face. 'If I were a boxer I'd say I had a
glass jaw.'

They laughed. That's it, Anderson thought; you can still do
it when you try, you can't teach an old dog new tricks but he
doesn't lose the ones he's learnt. Providing, he noted mentally,
he can summon up the energy and interest to go through them.
Consciously summoning up the necessary energy, Anderson
spoke for ten minutes in a manner both passionate and serious.
He said that it was absolutely essential that they should obtain
more information from Mr Divenga. He said that informative
copy, even if dedicated to the art of persuasion, must have a
firm basis of fact. He was judiciously doubtful about the proposal
to split the campaign into halves. He suggested that they worked
on this idea of VV's, but kept their minds open to other possibilities. He suggested also that a memorandum should be prepared covering the whole subject. Reverton listened with every
appearance of interest. VV still lay back in his chair, but his

eyes stared at Anderson keenly. Wyvern looked out of the window.

Ten minutes later the meeting broke up. Anderson was the last to leave the room. He was at the door when VV said softly: 'Andy.' Anderson pivoted on his heel. VV hesitated and then said: 'What are you doing for lunch?'


# III


'Nutmeat steak, jacket potatoes and salad with grated new carrot,' VV said. 'Is that all right?'

The waitress, a brick-red girl with a fanatical eye, bent over him. 'Perhaps you'd sooner have the mock-chicken with sea-kale? Or spaghetti and tapioca savoury?'

'Nutmeat steak,' Anderson said hurriedly, and when she had gone away, 'I didn't know you were a vegetarian.'

'My boy, I haven't touched meat for six weeks,' VV said with the enthusiasm of the reformed drinker. 'My stomach was in a terrible state. Insomnia, indigestion, sharp pain after food. I knew there was only one thing for it – a clean break. I've made a clean break with meat.'

'Do you feel better for it?'

'Of course I feel better. If it weren't so difficult I'd eat nothing cooked, nothing but raw food. Do you know the protein content of grated raw cabbage? Do you know what percentage of protein value is destroyed by cooking?' He stared at Anderson indignantly, and then suddenly burst out laughing. 'Andy boy, I'm getting to be a bore in my old age.'

Anderson joined in the laughter politely. 'Last year it was steam baths.'

'And before that it was brown paper next to the skin.' VV's hearty laugh rolled round the restaurant, startling pale long-nosed men crouched over their date and nut salads and their large-footed bare-legged wives munching raw vegetables. 'Do you know the trouble with me, Andy? I'm an advertising man.

It's an incurable disease. There's nobody more easily sold on a simple nostrum for all human ills than a good advertising man. And do you know why that is?' He flung himself back and stared at Anderson.

'Why?'

'Because we make such a mess of our own lives. We know how to sell other people on happiness, but we've never been able to sell it to ourselves.' VV's brown eyes melted with self-pity. The waitress brought the nutmeat steaks. She carefully wiped the edge of each plate and stared at its contents lovingly before she moved away. 'I'm a failure,' VV said as he stuffed nutmeat steak into his mouth. 'I've made a mess of my life.'

VV had several moods well known to his immediate subordinates. They fell into the chief divisions of self-congratulation, self-condemnation and self-pity. These were all capable of refinement into subdivisions by characteristic modifications. There was, for instance, self-congratulation with mock self-mockery: 'You struggle to get to the top of the tree, and when you've clambered up it what do you see? A desert.' Thus also VV's moods of self-condemnation were based upon recognition of his own wasted genius, and his self-pity was compensated by recognition of his courage in surviving the hard knocks of fate. Anderson ate some food which tasted like sawdust covered with breadcrumbs, and waited for self-condemnation to be replaced by self-esteem.

'And why have I failed?' VV pointed a finger and turned it into a fist. 'Because I possessed too many talents. You think that's a good thing? Andy, my boy, it's as fatal as having no talent at all. Composer, singer, painter – did I ever tell you that I had a picture in the RA when I was sixteen?' Anderson, who had been told this story many times, made a surprised noise. 'I composed an opera when I was twelve. But one's restless, one turns from this to that, and at last one becomes – what? An advertising man.' VV attacked his jacket potato furiously. 'It's a sad end for an artist. I always say thank God for the wife and kiddy, Andy, thank the Lord for the personal life. Though even that – ' He sighed heavily and left the sentence unfinished.

'How is Mrs Vincent?' Anderson scraped pieces of under-done potato out of a burnt jacket. It was Vincent, he thought; he is an attractive man – Vincent was Val's lover. This kind of histrionic nonsense is the kind of thing all women enjoy. Vincent and Val rolled together on the pink bed in the pink room. Anderson had once gone swimming with VV and noted the remarkable furry hairiness of his body. It was this furry animal that he now saw holding Val in a firm grasp, her gaze adoring while out of the animal's mouth poured a sickening stream of self-pity and self-praise. Suddenly Anderson thought of Molly O'Rourke, and of the mask that had turned to him in the night. Nausea overcame him as he stared down at his plate. 'I can't – ' he said, half rose from his chair and sat down again. One or two long-nosed men looked round.

VV said in alarm: 'Andy boy, are you all right?'

'Quite, thank you.'

'This stuff takes a bit of getting used to. You have to stick at it.' VV pushed his own plate away and played with a tooth-pick. His stare at Anderson, for all its self-absorption, was remarkably shrewd. 'I'd like you to know, Andy, that I feel for you about Val.'

'My wife? Yes.' Was this, Anderson wondered, the prelude to a confession?

'She had gaiety. That's a great quality in a woman. My wife, now – she lacks it. Never well, you know. A nervous condition. The doctor can't find a cure for it.' VV spoke with a touch of pride. He leaned forward and said gently, almost lovingly: 'Why don't you take a holiday, Andy?'

'You haven't eaten your nutmeat? Didn't you like it?' the waitress asked accusingly. Anderson shook his head. 'It's very good for you. What sweet, please? Prune mould is rec-ommended.' They ordered prune mould.

'A holiday,' Anderson said vaguely, and then: 'You called her Val.'

'That was only a manner of speaking. I hardly knew her, of course. You need a holiday, Andy; you're not looking the thing. Let the office do without you for a couple of weeks.'

'Did she ever write to you? You'd know her handwriting if you saw it, wouldn't you?'

VV's spoon dipped into a confection of a purplish colour and blancmangish texture with a strip of arsenical green running along its spine, and then was carefully put down. 'I don't understand you. What are you trying to say? I'm telling you that you need a holiday, Andy. Don't make it too hard for me.'

As though he were outside his own body, Anderson could hear his voice, shrill: 'What do you mean?'

'It's being talked about. You're losing your grip – only temporarily, of course, but people get to notice. There was something Rev told me about a desk calendar – '

'Rev? That snake?' Anderson cried. He heard himself and was appalled. 'You want to get me out of the way, is that it? And what about the letters?'

'The letters?'

'You'd send them on, I suppose, Post Restante. But I'm not going. You can put them on my desk as usual. There's nothing wrong with my work. This is Rev's plot to get rid of me.'

VV was trying to be jocular, not very successfully. 'Hold on now, Andy. I'm a democrat, but remember Rev's on the board. If there's anything you want to talk over, let's talk about it sensibly.'

'A plot,' Anderson shrieked. His outswept arm jerked the glass dish containing his own prune mould to the floor. The purplish mould mingled with the red carpet. There could be no doubt that they had attracted attention. One or two of the women were talking urgently to their companions. There was a flurry at the end of the room. The brick-red waitress was hurrying up to them. At the next table a young man writhed round in his chair and asked politely: 'Were you asking for a clergyman?' Anderson stood up. Below him and, it seemed, small, as if seen through the wrong end of a telescope, VV's face stared in astonishment and distress. The waitress confronted him, a solid wall of flesh, her face redder than before with annoyance. 'You haven't eaten – ' she began. Anderson stepped aside to avoid her and his heel crunched on the glass dish. Pushing aside her

statuesque body so that she staggered across a table, he ran out
of the restaurant.

## IV

*Few interesting or reliable statistics are as yet available regarding
the course of mental breakdown. We can chart with certainty
the thought-patterns only of those unfortunate people who are
incarcerated, more or less permanently, in mental homes; but
these are extreme cases, and they must surely be unsafe guides to
the psychopathological conduct in which every human being now
and then indulges. Anderson's conduct in the restaurant was,
beyond doubt, irrational; but it was the result of extreme
emotional pressure, and it would not be safe to make assumptions
from it about his future behaviour, or about his competence to
fulfil his functions in everyday life.*

These reflections passed through Anderson's mind as he
walked aimlessly about the streets of central London, wandering
from Tottenham Court Road through Soho, thence down to
Piccadilly and into Mayfair. He thought of himself in the third
person, so that responsibility for the actions of this hypothetical
Anderson did not concern him. Nevertheless he *was* concerned,
concerned in the sense that he felt a need to trace the illogicality
of Anderson's actions. Such concern led him to ignore the cor-
poreal universe in which he moved; and with his mind set on
problems which he knew to be insoluble, Anderson's body cannoned into other bodies, crossed the street against traffic lights,
bought a paper and looked at it without noting its contents, and
behaved generally like a rudderless boat. Some people when
drunk lose all surface knowledge of their intentions, and yet are
able to fulfil them. In much the same way Anderson, after
an amnesiac interval, found himself standing outside a small
hairdresser's shop in Melian Street, near Shepherd Market.

There was nothing remarkable in the shop's appearance. A
sign over the door said in letters of faded gold, *Antoine's*, and

in smaller letters, *Ladies' and Gentlemen's Hairdressing*. Two flyblown windows offered toothpaste, powder and lipstick. The door was closed, and the pane of glass in it opaque; but Anderson had been here before, and knew what he would find inside. Like an echo, as he stood on the pavement, words came into his mind that he had read long ago: *In dreams begin responsibility*. He pushed open the door and was in a narrow passage between plywood walls. A door to the left said *Gentlemen*, a door to the right said *Ladies*, and from behind these doors came the clip of scissors and the murmur of voices. At the end of the passage a young Jew sat behind a counter on which was displayed shaving cream, toothpaste, face powder and razor blades. The counter, like the front window, was dirty. The young Jew, on the other hand, was very clean. His dark glossy hair was waved, his nails were manicured, and there were two rings on his fingers. He was playing a game resembling Diabolo, in which he threw up a marble-sized ball and caught it in a small ornamental cup. A spring in the cup released the ball to varying heights, but the young man invariably caught it. Anderson waited. When the young man had thrown up the ball three times and caught it with unfailing dexterity he gestured towards the counter and said: 'Was there something?'

'Lily.' This was the first word Anderson had spoken since leaving the restaurant, and it came out harshly.

'If you're wanting flowers you'll do better round the corner.'

Anderson cleared his throat. 'My number is MM51. Is Lily free?'

The boy paused with his fingers on the spring. 'Just now she's busy. Was there anybody else?' Anderson shook his head. 'All right, MM51, you said.' He picked up a telephone by his side, spoke into it inaudibly and said: 'You know where to wait?' He gestured at a red curtain behind him.

With his hand on the curtain Anderson paused. 'That's a clever trick. You must have put in a lot of practice.'

'And where does it get me?' The boy flipped up the ball again. Anderson passed to the other side of the curtain, let it drop behind him and walked upstairs. Miss Stepley met him at the top. She was a neat woman of fortyfive with greying hair. She wore a white coat, and looked like a doctor. She said pleasantly: 'Lily's engaged. Will you come into my room? I'm afraid we're rather busy today.' She opened a door and stood holding the handle. Anderson was about to move past her into the room when he stood still, immobilized by something extraordinary that he saw. It was, at least, Anderson's impression that he saw this thing: at that moment he believed fully the evidence of his eyes, but perhaps, he thought afterwards, he had been mistaken. He was standing on the landing, and Miss Stepley was in front of him, holding open the door to her room. A long passage lined with red plush stretched ahead, and the passage was dim, because there were no windows and the only light came from small fittings set into the ceiling. The door of a room just down the passage opened and a girl came out. Anderson had seen her before; her name was Marjorie. She nodded to him as she handed a small card to Miss Stepley and then pushed open a door neatly labelled *Rest Room*. That was not the extraordinary sight: but when Marjorie left the room she did not close the door completely, and through the gap a man's figure was visible. The man sat on the edge of a bed with his hair disarranged. He was engaged in pulling on some fulllength underwear, and he looked up, with an expression of annoyance on his slightly flushed face, at the open door. As the man looked up Anderson saw, for a moment, his face; only for a moment, because Miss Stepley quickly moved across and closed the door. There was nothing extraordinary, either, about seeing a man in that room; the extraordinary thing was the man's identity. For the man Anderson thought he saw in the room, pulling on winter underwear, was Mr Pile.

'This way,' Miss Stepley said brightly. Her room contained a large desk, filing cabinets, a table, four spindly chairs. On the wall were a number of machines that looked like time clocks. Miss Stepley looked at the card given her by Marjorie, and pressed a lever on one of the clocks.

'That looks like a time clock.'

'It is a time clock. We have one for each of our girls.'

'Really? That's a new idea, isn't it?'

'Absolutely. After every engagement a girl fills in a card like the one which Marjorie handed to me. It tells us the length of time for which she was engaged. By clocking in on this machine we can tell her working hours each week. By comparing that with fees paid we can also assess her hourly rate of pay. Of course, the recorders reveal a number of other things, too, like peak periods and slack times. We can tell which girls aren't pulling their weight in the organization.'

'What happens then?'

'We warn them. This is a free enterprise organization, and there is no room in it for inefficiency. The customer is always right, and if a girl's earnings drop it is because she has ignored that elementary fact of economics. If she shows no sign of improvement – '

'You turn her out to look after herself.'

'Good gracious, no.' Miss Stepley looked shocked. 'What do you take us for? This is a business like any other, and we recognize our responsibilities towards our staff. Besides, it is not in our interest that girls should be on the streets in competition with us. No, the organization finds them jobs elsewhere. Girls who have no particular talent in our profession may make excellent assistants behind a shop counter.'

'Don't you find that girls ever try to cheat you out of money?'

'Unhappily, yes,' said Miss Stepley with real distress. 'It's very difficult to obtain a thoroughly satisfactory staff-management relationship. But we obviate that difficulty as far as possible by arranging payment in advance. If, after that, clients still offer gifts to our staff, we can't stop them doing so. But it is an anti-social practice like tipping, and we hope before long to have educated our clients so that they realize our fee covers a full service from the staff. And by the way' – she ruffled through a card index – 'you're MM51, aren't you? I see you've paid us three guineas on previous occasions. Would you care to – '

Anderson placed three pound notes and three shillings upon her desk. 'Does MM mean anything?'

Miss Stepley looked up from her cash box and smiled briskly. 'Speciality masochism, quality mild.'

'And everyone's known by a number?' She nodded. 'Then it's no use asking you who it was I saw through that open door – he's just a number, too? I thought I knew him for a moment, but I don't think it can have been the same person.'

'He is simply a number to us. But in any case it would be a breach of professional ethics to discuss one client with another.'

'Yes, I suppose so. You seem to have everything excellently organized.'

'Love is a business like any other,' Miss Stepley said solemnly. 'It was high time somebody understood that.'

'It's rather unromantic.'

'But hygienic. Frequent staff inspections are carried out. We deal with reality here. Romance can be left to the women's magazines.' There was a buzz from the switchboard by Miss Stepley's side. She put on a pair of headphones. 'Yes, Lily. I have another appointment for you. Category MM. Can you receive him?' She smiled brightly at Anderson. 'Lily is ready for you now. Room 5.'

Anderson went along the corridor to his appointment.

Afterwards Lily said: 'Ten minutes to spare. Got a fag?' She lay on the bed naked, smoking, a big blonde Cockney girl.

Anderson passed his hand over his face, which felt slightly numb. He felt empty in mind and body, curiously light-headed. 'Do you like it here?'

'It's all right. Only, of course, you're not free like the way you used to be. It's like living at home.'

'Really? I should hardly have thought so.'

'You don't see what I mean. They're always going on at you, wanting to do things for your own good. Makes you sick, sometimes. We get three evenings off a week, see, and we have to be back by eleven or our pay packet's docked. Then there's the pension scheme – they dock so much for that. Very good it is, but I'd sooner have the money. Then if you ever pick up a man outside there's trouble if Step gets to know about it. So I generally just go to the pictures with one of the other girls. I love the pictures, don't you?'

'Sometimes.'

'I saw ever such a nice film last week, an old one; it was on at our local fleapit. *Mrs Miniver*, it was called. Walter Pidgeon and Greer Garson. Have you seen it?'

'I haven't, as a matter of fact.'

'Oh, you ought to. They're ever such nice people, Mr and Mrs Miniver, and it's the war you see, and – ' Lily's voice went on. Anderson closed his eyes and wondered why he had come here. What was the relation between his urgent bodily need and that awful scene in the restaurant? His mind shied away from thought of the exhibition he had made of himself. ' – and the planes are flying in formation and they stand watching them from the ruins of the church. That's the end.' Anderson opened his eyes and saw that Lily was crying. 'It's so sad,' she said. 'Have you got a handkerchief?' She lay on the bed naked with Anderson's handkerchief to her eyes. As Anderson put on his shirt and trousers and stared down at her, he felt desire for her again. 'Lily.'

She looked at him and then sat up on the bed. 'If you want another appointment you'll have to speak to Step. Time's up for this one.'

'No.' Anderson was not sure that he wanted another appointment, and anyway he was not prepared to spend another three guineas. He finished dressing, walked along the corridor and down the stairs. Outside the red curtain the Jewish boy was still playing cup and ball. He did not look up as Anderson passed him. In the street Anderson saw a broad-backed bowler-hatted man in front of him. Something about his figure was reminiscent of Inspector Cresse, but the man turned down a side street and when Anderson reached the corner there was no sign of him.

# V

The time was four o'clock. It was difficult to return to the office, but more difficult not to do so. Anderson looked up at the sign which said VINCENT ADVERTISING VINCENT ADVERTISING VINCENT and settled his black Homburg hat firmly on his head. Then he walked in and the swing doors hissed behind him.

Upon his table lay the drawings returned from Kiddy Modes and an envelope addressed to him by VV. He tore open the envelope and read in VV's sprawling hand:

Andy,
    What was all that about? Come and tell me when you feel like it. Not today – I'm at a conference all afternoon, New World Coolers.

VV.

There was a postscript in small writing: *Dare I repeat that you need a holiday?* Anderson laughed. VV was a good chap. He put the note in his pocket, and looked at the drawings. Bagseed had made notes upon every one of them in a gentlemanly copper-plate hand. 'Collar on this jacket won't do. Refer to model. J.B.' 'This dress hangs wrongly. Refer to model. J.B.' 'Neck of frock incorrect as per our discussion. J.B.' The drawing with the gym tunic was marked with a large cross and the word 'No' simply. This 'No' was also initialled 'J.B.'

As he looked at Bagseed's comments Anderson found himself becoming angry, and by the time he had read the curt letter that accompanied them he felt the kind of fury known only to advertising men who think they are being treated unfairly. He called in Jean Lightley and pointed to the drawings. 'Do you see anything wrong with these?'

She saw Bagseed's comments and gasped: 'Oh, isn't he fussy?'

'He is.'

'Mr Crashaw won't like making alterations, will he?'

'He will not. Write to Bagseed and tell him that we have

looked at the drawings and cannot agree that they are of a nature to depreciate the class of goods sold by Kiddy Modes. We are, however, having alterations made upon the lines laid down in his instructions. Yours, etcetera. Then write to Crashaw: "Dear Crashaw, Kiddy Modes have shot these drawings back at us with comments made and bureaucratically initialled. Out of our many pestilential clients Kiddy Modes are perhaps the most pestilential of all. As far as I can see their criticisms on this occasion, as on others, are incompetent, irrelevant and immaterial, and I can hardly blame you if you decide to throw in the sponge on this job. I hope, however, that you'll feel able to play along with us and make the necessary alterations. We have to take the rough with the smooth as you know, and Kiddy Modes are just about the roughest there is. They demand just about six times as much attention as any other client of their size. If you can help us out on this occasion it will be much appreciated by me. Sincerely." '

Miss Lightley gasped. 'That's very strong.'

'So are my feelings. Get those typed as quickly as you can and send them up by hand.' When she had gone Anderson took Val's letter out of his pocket, read it again and put it back. The telephone rang and the switchboard operator said: 'Oh, Mr Anderson, Mrs Fletchley, Mrs Elaine Fletchley, rang twice while you were out. She said it was important.'

'Try and get her for me, will you? At *Woman Beautiful.*' The house telephone rang as he picked up the other receiver. He put it to his ear and said: 'Anderson.'

'O'Rourke.'

There was a pause. 'What do you want?'

'Haven't we got a date for tonight?'

'We haven't. I'm busy.'

'What about a drink?'

'I'm sorry. I told you I'm busy.'

There was another pause. 'I want to see you, Andy.'

Somebody opened the door. 'All right,' Anderson said. 'I'll come in in five minutes.'

'Am I interrupting something?' Wyvern asked. 'I can come back.'

Anderson waved him to a chair. 'Not a bit. What's on your mind?'

'I dunno. Bloody old Hey Presto, I suppose. What do you think of that scheme? Tell me honestly, if there's any honesty among account executives. I've got the boys working on half a dozen different ways of presenting that face in the shaving-mirror idea, but they all look pretty corny to me.'

'Ours not to reason why,' Anderson said absently. Was he mistaken in finding something strange about Wyvern, a suppressed excitement in his manner, a hint of uncomfortable revelations about to be made? Wyvern's long legs in corduroy trousers were stretched out against the carpet, his lopsided smile seemed to have a special meaningfulness. Anderson slipped his right hand into his jacket pocket. The telephone rang. He pulled out the letter and placed it on the desk, looking all the time at Wyvern.

'Switchboard, Mr Anderson. Mrs Fletchley's in conference. They'll tell her you're in the office as soon as she comes out.'

'There's another thing,' Wyvern said as Anderson put down the receiver. 'Do you know where VV got his bright idea from that he's thought up all of a sudden? I've found the identical layout presentation – face in mirror, product name up above and slogan below – in an old *Saturday Evening Post*, used by Topmost Shaving Creams. What do you know, eh? Doesn't it stink?'

'We all know there's nothing new.' Anderson began to play with the sheet of blue writing-paper on which Val's letter was written, curling it up in his fingers and uncurling it, looking steadily at Wyvern.

'Nothing new – it's bloody well dishonest, and you know it.'

'Dishonest – come now.' Anderson opened out the letter carefully and began curling it the other way.

'Perhaps it's not in a way – I know what you mean, old cock. You mean VV probably doesn't realize his own dishonesty; it's just something that's stayed in his mind. And you're quite right, of course; if there's one thing advertising men do better than taking in the public it's taking in themselves. This whole bloody hullaballoo shows that.'

'How do you mean?'

'Why, nobody but an advertising agent would believe this story about a magic cream extracted from the juice of whatever it is. That stinks, too. Don't tell me there isn't something phoney about Mr Divenga. With that beard!'

'But – ' Anderson raised the letter coiled round one finger and tapped his smooth chin with it. The house telephone rang. Molly's voice said: 'Five minutes, remember?'

'When I'm free.' He put it down.

'I know, I know,' Wyvern said amiably. 'Don't tell me. It works. It's the most revolutionary etcetera that *Homo sapiens* has ever invented to ease his spirit in the era of the atom bomb. I see it. But I still don't believe it.' During all this time Wyvern had not appeared to notice the letter in Anderson's hand. Now he suddenly said, almost with embarrassment: 'What the devil are you doing with that bit of paper, Andy?'

Anderson hesitated for only a second. 'That bit of paper, as you call it, is a letter from Val.'

'A letter from Val!' Wyvern stared and then said: 'Poor old Val. It was a damned shame; the sort of thing that makes you wonder what life's all about. You know what – I was remembering only the other day that silly toast we used to drink.'

'Shorter days – longer nights.'

'That's right.' The suppressed excitement had gone from Wyvern's manner, if it had ever been there. He now looked simply uneasy. 'Forgive me for saying so, Andy, but it's no use harking back. We all do it, I know. I often wonder what would have happened to me if I'd left home when I was twentyone. My mother wasn't bedridden then, and I could have done it. If I had done – but you see it's no use harking back. Get rid of memories, destroy letters, otherwise they haunt you.'

'Haunt you?'

'When I was out in the desert I used to look up at the stars and think about my mother, make decisions about what I'd do when I got back. I was going to leave home and make her an allowance. I was going to get out of advertising for good. And there you are – look at me now.'

Anderson was not listening. 'This letter arrived yesterday morning,' he said.

'Yesterday morning! But, Andy, Val died more than three weeks ago.'

'That's exactly what I'm getting at. I found this letter on my desk yesterday morning.'

At last he had spoken out, and for the first time had told another human being the incredible truth. The moment remained in Anderson's memory through a pattern of colours. The green carpet, the brown panelling on the walls, Wyvern's stone-coloured corduroy trousers, the white hands resting on them that tightly pressed his knees. He felt, with a kind of triumph, the tension in the room. Something significant had happened, something more significant still would happen in a moment, a gesture would be made or a word spoken that had the quality of a revelation.

The house telephone rang. Molly. He snatched at it and shouted: 'I said when I'm free.'

'This is Rev here, Andy. You sound het up.'

'I'm sorry, Rev. I thought – '

'That's all right. I know you're up to the eyes. Can you come in just for a minute? It's only a little job to be done.'

'Right away.'

He replaced the receiver, and the moment had gone. Wyvern was standing up, a long thin figure looking down with the oddest expression on his face. 'I wanted to know if you had any other Hey Presto ideas we could work on, but we can talk about it some other time.' He stopped at the door and said: 'If I were you I'd forget all about that letter. I wouldn't tell anyone else about it.'

When Anderson left his room to go in to see Rev he heard the sharp rings of the house telephone, but he did not go back. The little job that Reverton wanted done was, as he had said, only a little job: what he had omitted to say was that it was a job he was supposed to do himself. The job was connected with the Crunchy-Munch account. Vincent's had obtained the Crunchy-Munch advertising on the strength of a slogan invented by VV: 'First you Crrrunch it Then you Munch it – that's CRUNCHY-MUNCH.' This slogan, with a few variations, had been the basis of Crunchy-Munch advertising for several years. Now they had suddenly become dissatisfied with it; and although every bar of Crunchy-Munch was sold on the chocolate ration, they had begun to worry about the effect of the advertising on their sales when sweets were unrationed. 'Shall we be ready to go full steam ahead,' the Crunchy-Munch advertising manager had asked, in one of those metaphors favoured by all advertising men, 'when we get the green light?' He was paid a handsome salary for worrying about such things, and it was customary to send him a yearly memorandum, which had become a sophistical exercise in evolving theories about the effect of various advertising approaches on the technique of sweet-selling, if it ever became necessary to sell sweets. The purpose of this memorandum was to give the Crunchy-Munch advertising manager something to occupy his time, and also to present a picture of the situation which implied both that a continual jockeying was taking place for future leadership in the confectionery field, and that in this race Crunchy-Munch, thanks to the mental agility of their advertising agents, were always leading by a quarter of a length. This year, however, the memorandum would be a little different; it would have to justify the new scheme which was to be discussed the following morning. Reverton suggested that, since Anderson was in charge of the new scheme, he should write the memorandum, too. 'It's not the kind of job I like to delegate,' Reverton said with a shake of his square sensible head, 'but I've got so much on my plate I think I'll just have to. Anyway, you're right on top of the new scheme, Andy; you're the man to write the memo.' Reverton paused and added casually: 'By the way, what is the new scheme?'

'We're putting up two ideas.' Reverton raised his eyebrows. 'One's Lessing's and one's mine. The studio are working on them now. They'll be on the table tomorrow, for you and VV.'

'Two schemes, eh? Differences of viewpoint?' Reverton said mildly.

'Just two ways of presenting it. When will you want the memorandum finished?'

'If we pass the scheme through tomorrow, Andy, early next week for the memo. Can do?'

'I suppose so. I don't know when I'm supposed to work on Hey Presto.'

'Better hand it back, then, if you haven't got time for it. Mustn't let anything stand in the way of Hey Presto. I was going to give you the dope, but it can stay here.' Something in the way in which Reverton tapped the papers on his desk, the readiness with which his own mild grumble had been accepted, seemed curious to Anderson. He felt, with no obvious reason, that he had fallen into a trap.

'That's all right,' he said; 'I'll manage.'

'Grand. Weight off my mind.' Reverton handed over the papers with a smile and tamped the tobacco in his pipe thoughtfully. Anderson felt, as he had done a few minutes ago with Wyvern, that there had been a sudden drop in the emotional temperature. There had been a moment of crisis, and now it was over; but the nature of the crisis baffled him. He expected, nevertheless, that Reverton would pursue the subject of the memorandum, so that the next remark took him completely by surprise.

'What do you think of Charlie Lessing?'

Anderson quite frankly stared. 'Charlie Lessing? As a copywriter, you mean?'

'All round. There's more to being a copywriter than writing copy; you know that.' He waited expectantly.

Anderson said: 'I don't know just what you want me to say. He's good at classy copy, stuff with plenty of snob appeal, not so hot when something down to earth is wanted.' He ended almost with a question. Reverton puffed away at his pipe.

'A nice chap, is he? Easy to get on with?'

'I get on with him. Some don't – think he's a bit superior. Why?'

'One just likes to keep a finger on the pulse,' Reverton said with quite uncustomary vagueness. 'Harmonious running and all that. So you'll tackle that memorandum after our meeting tomorrow.'

Anderson said he would tackle the memorandum. Back in his own room he found Jean Lightley and Molly O'Rourke. Jean was standing guard over the two letters he had asked her to type; Molly was at the window, staring out at the figures on the other side of the well, moving about in their little lighted boxes. She looked round as Anderson came into the room, and then turned her back on him and stared again out of the window.

'Your letters,' Jean said.

Anderson looked at his watch. 'You could have signed them yourself. It's late.'

'I thought perhaps – that one to Mr Crashaw – you'd like to look at it.'

'You're quite right.' He signed the letter to Bagseed, and then read the one to Crashaw. It was strong, but not too strong. He signed it. 'By hand.'

'Oh yes, Mr Anderson.' In gasps she brought out: 'Mrs Fletchley rang through and spoke to me. She's had to go out and you can't reach her. She'll be at a party later on this evening – at the Pollexfens', she said. She said it was something important.'

Anderson looked at Molly's hostile back. 'The Pollexfens', yes; thank you, Jean.' She went out. Without turning round Molly said: 'Five minutes.'

Anderson put down the Crunchy-Munch papers and said with elaborate patience: 'I told you I was busy.'

'Too busy to come in and see me.'

'That's right.'

'Too busy to see me tonight.'

'That's right.'

'But not . . .' Since Molly was still standing with her back to him, addressing the window, Anderson could not hear her.

'If you'd turn round,' he said, and at that she turned round and showed tears running down either side of her great nose. Her voice was choked.

'Not too busy to see Elaine Fletchley.'

'I haven't seen Elaine.'

'You've been trying to see her. Ringing her up.'

The tears blotched Molly's powder. Anderson contemplated her with distaste. 'You know why I want to see her. I asked you last night if Val had an especial boyfriend. Now I'm going to ask Elaine.'

'Why?'

Suddenly Anderson's control left him. He smacked the desk lightly with the palm of his hand. 'Because Valerie was somebody's mistress.'

'So what?'

'And it was somebody in this firm.' Now, Anderson thought, I've done it; the cat's really out of the bag. But to his surprise Molly seemed not to find the news exciting.

'What does it matter? She's dead. It won't bring her back. And anyway, you never loved her.' Molly dabbed at her eyes. 'I must look awful. I'm making a fool of myself. I've never met a man who didn't give me a runaround. And do you know another thing – I've never failed to come back for more. I'm a fool, that's all, I'm a fool.' She began to cry again, weakly and without conviction. Anderson picked up the Crunchy-Munch papers again, and pretended to study them. 'You don't want to make love to me.'

'Not at this moment, thank you.'

'You don't even want to kiss me?'

'No.'

She tottered towards him on her high heels. 'Give me a kiss to show you don't hate me.'

'For God's sake, Molly, we're in the office.'

'It's time to go home. Everybody's going home. Nobody will come in. Just one kiss.'

'Very well.' Anderson got up and advanced towards her round the desk. Her nose at this distance, and under harsh electric light, was revealed as one of ghastly shape and size, almost like a false nose put on for a charade. Was it possible, if one kissed her, to avoid a jarring contact with that forward and hunting proboscis? It appeared not; and yet it had been possible, no later than last night. Very gingerly Anderson's lips approached the tear-ravaged face. Reluctantly he felt the warmth of her body against his own. He closed his eyes, like a child about to drink medicine, and thus he did not see Molly's withdrawal from him, but simply felt it in terms of decreased warmth. He opened his eyes again. Molly was staring past him. He turned round and saw VV standing in the doorway, hatted, overcoated, staring at them.

# VI

At one moment VV was standing there before Anderson's astonished eyes. In the next moment, without speaking, he was gone. Had he really been there at all? With a vigorous gesture Anderson pushed Molly away from him and opened the door. He ran down the corridor in time to see the door of VV's room close and present to him so blank an oak face that he was moved by the kind of fear he had known in childhood when he had been found out in wrongdoing and had been locked in his room, not, as his mother impressed on him, as a punishment, but so that he could 'think it out'. He felt at those times a weight of guilt that could be dispersed only by contact with the judge, his mother, even though when he saw her he had nothing to say. So now, with the sense of betrayal strong upon him, he felt it essential to see VV. He crossed the landing, tapped on VV's door gently, and entered.

The bright, inquisitive, intelligent face that was turned towards him seemed wholly friendly; it showed no consciousness of having witnessed that scene in Anderson's office a moment ago, no recollection of that appalling luncheon. Anderson felt again, as he had felt several times in the past fortyeight hours, that the events in his life somehow failed to be interconnected, as events should be in a life properly organized and rational; the happenings of yesterday, the errors of luncheon, the visit to

Miss Stepley's establishment, seemed to bear no relation to what was happening here and now. Had those things really happened? If they have, Anderson thought, they must be on the tip of VV's tongue; they will surely be mentioned. But VV, instead, presented him with two thumbs triumphantly raised. 'New World Cooler,' he said. 'Everything went like a dream. Approved this, approved that, approved the other – only two small copy revisions. Lessing's scheme, wasn't it? Well, it's very good work. Congratulations all round are in order. Copy, Studio – even the man who took it up and sold it to them takes a bow.' Gracefully VV bowed, and added solemnly: 'It's times like these – intelligent scheme, intelligent client, no quibbling – that make one feel advertising is worth while.' He looked at his watch and showed a rare trace of nervousness. 'What are you doing for dinner tonight? Can you come back with me? Belsize Park, you know. Only *en famille* – but it's rather an occasion in a way. And we should have time for a talk.' With an upward look, humorous and shy, he said: 'We ought to have a talk, you know.'

Anderson had dined once before with VV and his wife, but that had been in a restaurant. Was it a mark of favour to be asked to dine with him at home? While he was pondering this point, VV said with a small intimate smile: 'Better get your hat and coat. And get rid of your – visitor.'

'I'd like you to understand, it's – '

'Not another word. I do understand, my boy. I understand perhaps better than you think.'

Molly was still in Anderson's room. She looked at him as if he were a stranger. 'Where are you going?'

Anderson put on his overcoat. 'I'm invited out to dinner with the boss.'

She continued to stare at him. 'There's been a telephone call. It was a policeman named Cresse. He wanted to know if you'd be at home tonight. I told him I didn't think you would. He said he'd call anyway.'

'That was absolutely right.' Anderson adjusted his black hat at a jaunty angle. 'Did he say anything else?'

'He said that the air was unhealthy in Melian Street. He said you'd understand.'

VV's high spirits were gradually dissipated on the way out to Belsize Park. In the underground train they were packed as close as tinfoil, and he talked about travelling conditions. 'I admire,' he said loudly to Anderson as they swayed on the same strap, 'the enormous capacity of modern man for endurance. But it's unhealthy. The real, healthy thing is the capacity for rebellion. I don't see any sign of that around us.' His waving hand, with a large parcel in it, described a small part of a semicircle and then was stopped by contact with a bulky figure in dungarees. The figure glared. VV glared back, but he stopped talking. After they got out at Belsize Park he was monosyllabic, and they trudged up Haverstock Hill in silence. Then VV said: 'Marriage is a terrible thing.'

'What's that?'

'I say marriage is a terrible thing. Have you met my wife? She's a terrible woman.' Anderson found nothing to say. 'Sometimes I wonder why one does it all. Advertising, I mean. Working, working, working – abandoning an artistic career – and for what? To support a woman who just doesn't care.' VV's rich voice was low and emotional, as though he were about to cry. 'I sometimes think you've got the best of it. A girl like Molly – '

'Look here,' Anderson said, 'I shouldn't like you to think that was anything serious. It's not.'

This time VV was able to make the semicircular arc without obstruction. 'I'm a man of the world, Andy. I understand these things. I don't want to enquire into your private life. Probably none of our private lives will bear inspection.'

'But – '

'Though there are compensations. Did you know I had a stepdaughter? Her name's Angela. She's a nice girl. It's her birthday today. Fourteen.'

'Shan't I be in the way?'

'Oh, not at all,' VV said gloomily. 'Quite the contrary. And we must have our talk, don't forget that.' His voice was now almost threatening.

VV lived in a large block of flats. They went up three floors in a lift and down to the end of a corridor. As he turned the key in a highly varnished maplewood door VV gave a low-pitched whistle. There was a sound of running feet. The door opened and a large girl flung her arms round VV's neck. 'Daddy!' she cried. With a look almost of idiocy VV put his arms behind his back. 'Daddy, what have you got? Oh, who's this?' Anderson found himself shaking hands with the girl. She was large-boned, red-haired, slightly freckled, and attractive in a peasant-girl manner. She looked at least sixteen years old. 'It's my birthday,' she said. 'Have you brought me a present?'

'I'm afraid I haven't,' Anderson said. 'But many happy returns, all the same.'

'Thank you. Oh, Daddy, what are you hiding?'

With ghastly agility VV skipped behind Anderson, holding the brown paper parcel still concealed. Angela shrieked and pursued him. Using Anderson as a fixed central pole, they danced round the little hall, giving cries and shouts of pleasure. At last Angela caught her stepfather and they struggled together as she tried to get the parcel. 'Catch,' VV said. The package came flying through the air to strike Anderson chest high. He hugged it in both arms as a door opened and a voice said: 'What is this brawl?'

Anderson remembered Mrs Vincent as large and bony. She now appeared smaller, but bonier, than he remembered. Her face was long and thin with a knifelike nose between high cheekbones from which the flesh fell away. Her breastless body was clothed in a long dark sack tied at the waist. Her hands, dropped at her sides, were long and colourless. She stood framed in a dark doorway, looking at her husband and daughter. 'Victor,' she said, 'don't be disgusting.'

VV removed his arm from Angela's waist and took off his overcoat. 'My dear, I'm glad to see you up.' His tone was one that Anderson had never heard him use before, the gentle placatory tone that an actor uses to a stage invalid. 'This is Mr Anderson from the office. Perhaps you will remember him.'

'Go and wash your face and hands, Angela. You look grubby.' With awful gentility Mrs Vincent said to Anderson: 'How do you do? We have met at the firm's dances, have we not? But this is an unexpected pleasure.' Anderson tucked the parcel under one arm and took her limp hand.

'VV was good enough to invite me at very short notice. I hope I haven't put you out.'

'Nothing puts me out,' Mrs Vincent said, not reassuringly. She was staring at the parcel under Anderson's arm.

VV made a gesture towards the parcel. 'And what do you think? He's brought a present for little Angela's birthday.'

'That was kind,' Mrs Vincent said. 'And particularly clever, at such short notice. But unnecessary. What is the gift, may I ask?'

'A pair of ice skates,' VV said hurriedly. Anderson patted the parcel and idiotically repeated the words. Angela ran out to the hall again and cried: 'A pair of ice skates.'

'Happy birthday,' Anderson said, and dumped the parcel in her arms. She looked at him uncertainly. Mrs Vincent's thin voice said: 'Thank Mr Anderson for his gift.'

Angela opened the parcel. A card dropped out, which she glanced at hurriedly and put into her pocket. 'They're lovely,' she said. 'Thank you awfully.'

In words as clear as drops of water Mrs Vincent said: 'A card, too. How very thoughtful Mr Anderson is. What does it say?'

'It just says happy birthday.'

'I am sure it must say something more interesting than that. Give it me, Angela.'

'Would anybody mind,' Anderson said, 'if I took off my overcoat?'

'My dear boy.' VV rushed forward. There was a little flurry. Anderson was freed of his overcoat. He turned round to see that Angela had torn the card to shreds. She faced her mother defiantly and said: 'You shan't see what's on it.' Mrs Vincent's limp hand came up and struck the girl upon the cheek. To Anderson she said with perfect politeness: 'You'll excuse me, I am sure, Mr Anderson. I have a sick headache.' She was swallowed up in the darkness behind her.

Angela stood facing her mother's closed door, cried two words at the top of her voice, and ran into another room, holding the ice skates in her hand. The first word Angela cried was 'You'. The second pulled Anderson's mind away from his surroundings to the establishment in Melian Street. Would there be any place for such words in Miss Stepley's sexual paradise? Probably not. Or perhaps they might be uttered only by special dispensation as erotic stimulants.

VV sighed. 'I expect you'd like a drink.' He led the way into a pleasant but untidy sitting-room. 'You see how it is. Of course, she's not well. Any excitement upsets her and she has to go to bed. Nervous trouble – but I told you that didn't I? What can you do?' VV fiddled with the glasses. He was so unlike the benevolent dictator of the office that Anderson felt he was talking to a stranger.

He said with a shade of understatement: 'She doesn't get on with Angela?'

'That's the trouble. The fact is that I love Angela like my own daughter. You'd think Mary would be pleased. But is she pleased? Instead she does everything she can to make life miserable for all of us. Do you know the cause of all this trouble just now? The theatre.'

'The theatre?'

'We were going to the theatre tonight for Angela's birthday. But – Mary has a sick headache.' VV laughed without amusement, and yet with a faintly histrionic air. 'I know what you're going to say – why don't we go without her? Impossible, my boy, impossible. She goes to our neighbours' flats and becomes hysterical. She sleepwalks if she knows she's alone. Once she fell out of a window. That was not here,' VV said in a regretful voice. 'It was a first-floor window. Little damage was done. But she can't be left alone.'

'I don't quite see where I come in.'

'We've got to have our talk.' But VV said it with little energy or interest. 'And the fact is, she's been more than usually difficult lately. I thought a visitor might – ease the strain. Perhaps I was wrong. Ah, here comes Angela. Now we can – ah – have supper.'

Supper had a certain surrealist quality. VV ate only lettuce, seedless raisins, grated carrot and nuts, but he was anxious for Anderson's welfare. 'Eat up,' he said. 'Take plenty of everything.' Anderson found it difficult to follow this advice. The food had come from the delicatessen counter of a very high-class store, and it was all covered with jelly. Anderson ate sparingly of cold consommé followed by prawns in aspic and by chicken in a huge square jelly casing. The jelly stuck like glue to his teeth; the Russian salad that accompanied the chicken, on the other hand, tasted like small cubes of ice. Angela told him that Mrs Vincent had put it into the cold storage department of the refrigerator by mistake. The white wine afforded a contrast to the Russian salad, for it had inadvertently been placed by an electric fire, and was lukewarm.

'Mother ordered everything from the food department of Jockney and Hanson,' Angela said demurely. 'Did you think she had done it all herself?' She had changed both her dress and her appearance. She was now wearing a green evening frock and had swept up her red hair to reveal neat ears remarkably like her father's. Only, of course, Anderson reflected, he was not her father, but her stepfather. The effect of the new hair style was to make her look eighteen instead of sixteen.

Anderson sloshed some warm wine about in his mouth. It removed pieces of jelly from his teeth and unfroze some small cubes of Russian salad. 'Are you really only fourteen today, Angela? You look much older.'

'Do I?' She glowed. 'You hear that, Victor?' VV nodded gloomily. She turned again to Anderson. 'You didn't buy me the ice skates, did you? The card said: "For Angela, with love." You wouldn't have said that, would you?'

'I might have said it,' Anderson replied gallantly, 'but I didn't buy the ice skates.'

'But still it was sweet of you to try to get us out of trouble.' She looked archly at VV, who was scooping the last mouthful of carrots and raisins from his plate. 'We're always in trouble with Mummy, Victor and I. Do you like ice skating?'

'I've never tried.'

'It's so graceful – you just fly along. Victor sometimes comes with me, don't you? I say, this wine is nice, isn't it?'

'Delicious.'

'Mummy doesn't let me drink wine. Isn't it lucky she's ill?' She gazed from one to the other of them.

Anderson coughed. 'Perhaps she would like a little – a little consommé.'

'Oh no, Mummy enjoys being ill. I say, shall we have some more wine? I know where there's another bottle.'

VV said weakly: 'You've had enough to drink.'

'It's my birthday,' she pouted. She was certainly remarkably pretty. 'And I want it. I'm going to get it.' She jumped up and ran out into the kitchen. While she was out of the room VV rolled his brown eyes ceilingwards in mock appeal. Angela came back with another bottle. VV pushed away his plate with an air of hunger. 'I think I might have a little sweet. What is it?'

'Fruit and ice cream.' Anderson brightened, but the fruit arrived embedded in jelly. His spoon slid off the stiff surface of the ice cream. He thrust furiously at the jelly and succeeded in extracting small, tasteless pieces of cherry, pear and banana. VV pushed his sweet aside and sat picking his teeth with a silver toothpick. Angela ate the whole of her sweet with much apparent enjoyment. Anderson tried a mouthful of wine and found that the second bottle was, if anything, warmer than the first.

'It's good wine, isn't it?' Angela said. 'I mean, I don't know anything about wine, but I like this, don't you? Oh, but I asked you that before. You are a couple of deaf mutes, you two, aren't you? I mean to say, can't we do something? Oh well, if you're not going to talk, I shall go out and make coffee.' She disappeared again.

Conspiratorially, VV leaned over the table. 'I suppose you

wouldn't like to take Angela to the Palladium? I've still got the tickets, you know, and – '

'I'm afraid not,' Anderson said firmly. 'I mean, I should like to, but I have to go to a party.'

'You could take her with you.'

'And what about our talk?'

'Oh, that can wait. Will you take her to the party?'

'Well really, I'm afraid – '

'No? No, I suppose not. You don't mind my asking, do you?'

Angela came in a little unsteadily with coffee and biscuits on a tray. 'I say, let's dance. You do dance, don't you?' Anderson admitted that he did. 'And so does Victor, only he never will. But tonight you *must*, because it's my birthday.' She darted over to VV, took his hands and pulled him from the chair.

'But what about the noise? Your mother – '

'Oh, she won't hear if we have it low. After all, it's my *birth*day. Next to ice skating, I love dancing more than anything in the world. Don't you, Mr Anderson? I say, what's your Christian name?'

'That's something I never reveal.'

'Then I shall call you Andy. I'll turn on the radio. Oh, but I suppose you want some coffee.' Anderson half expected the coffee to be warm jelly, and was pleased to discover that it was quite drinkable. Encouraged, he bit into a biscuit, but his teeth refused to close on it. The biscuit bounded from his mouth on to the table. Angela was convulsed with laughter, as she explained that these rubber bouncing biscuits were kept specially for guests. Even VV came out of his abstraction to venture a sad smile. Anderson did not find himself much amused. The incident made him aware that he was painfully hungry.

In the sitting-room the radio was playing dance music very softly. Only one light was switched on, faintly illuminating walls and chairs and bookcases. 'Come *on*,' Angela said. 'Let's dance.' She seized her stepfather by the waist and they began to shuffle over the carpet together. Anderson dropped into an armchair and twiddled with the half-full wineglass which he still held in his hand. Like somnambulists the two figures swayed in their erotic clinch as the radio played

> 'It was all over my jealousy;
> My crime was my blind jealousy. . . .'

The *Radio Times* was by his chair. Anderson picked it up and saw that the programme was 'Hit Tunes of 1942'. Nineteen-fortytwo, he thought, nineteen-fortytwo. What did the date mean? That was the year when he was thirtythree years old. That was the year when he married Val. That was the year when he might have been called up – when, in fact, he would have been called up, but for Reverton. In that year Vincent Advertising had been told that they must cut down their staff. They cut, and cut again; and at last there came a day when either Anderson or a man named Goble had to be relinquished. Goble was a studio artist who made layouts for the Ministry of Knowledge and Communications schemes, on which Anderson was then writing the copy; he was thirtyfive, two years older than Anderson; he had two children. Anderson would have had to go, there was no doubt of it, but for good old Rev. Good old Rev had been a tower of strength; good old Rev had not much liked Goble, who was inclined to be independent and sometimes came in late and had a habit of taking things to VV direct over Rev's head; good old Rev saw a chance of placing Anderson permanently in his debt. All that had been understood when good old Rev said: 'It's a toss-up, I don't mind telling you that, Andy, but I'm going into that Board Meeting to fight like hell to have you retained. We've always got on together, haven't we? But it's not a question of that; it's just a matter of which man is the most valuable to the organization.' And then good old Rev had paused, had taken the pipe out of his mouth and had looked shrewdly and sharply at Anderson. 'Unless, of course, you feel that you must go, Andy.' That was the decisive question, the decisive answer, that put you in Rev's power. For after you had equivocated, after you had said that if you had to go you'd do your bit as well as the next man, that if you really thought you'd be more useful in the army than here doing essential propaganda work you'd go like a shot, but it was obvious that you weren't – After you'd said all that you'd delivered yourself over to good shrewd old Rev, and you could never really argue with him on even terms again. And that was all recognized when good old Rev put his pipe back again and said: 'I want you to know, Andy, that I'm going to do my damndest to swing it for you.' And good old Rev had swung it (or perhaps there had been no question of swinging it, perhaps that was just Rev's fun, perhaps the votes of all the directors had gone to him without question), and Goble had been released from deferment and conscripted, and had died on the Normandy beaches, earning himself a posthumous MC. And the curious thing, Anderson thought as he sipped his lukewarm wine, is that I shouldn't have minded the army at all, that I shouldn't have minded dying, that I should have been very capable of the act of enforced heroism, the courage to which there existed no alternative. And why did I accept good old Rev's offer? Because it was the smart thing to do, because it was always foolish to stick one's neck out. There, but for the grace of good old Rev . . .

'Andy, Andy,' Angela was calling him. 'Come on, Andy. I've kept this dance for you on my card.'

VV's face was very red. He dropped into a chair which was completely in shadow.

'VV,' Anderson said, 'will you tell me something. Do you remember Goble?'

'Poor old Goble.' VV nodded.

Good old Rev and poor old Goble. 'You remember we had to release him. Either he or I had to go; that's right, isn't it?' VV coughed. Anderson waved his hand impatiently. 'I know that's how it was. What I wanted to ask was this. How did the discussion go at that Board Meeting?'

'It's a long time ago, Andy.'

'Don't tell me you can't remember,' Anderson said rudely.

With a trace of his vanished Olympian office manner VV said: 'I was going to say it's a long time ago, and I don't see it can do any harm to tell you. There wasn't any discussion. We knew you were the man we had to keep.' He sighed. 'And so poor old Goble went.'

'Oh, come *on*,' Angela said. 'Don't stand jabbering.' She pushed herself into Anderson's arms and he smelt her hair. Good old Rev, Anderson thought; he fought for me right to the last ditch, only there wasn't any fighting to do. He became aware that Angela was speaking. 'I beg your pardon.'

'I said don't you think this is a miserable way to spend a birthday?'

'I'm sorry. I'm afraid I'm not exactly gay company.'

'Oh, I don't mind. I don't suppose you like me at all, though, do you?'

'Certainly I do.' As much, he said to himself, as I like any girl or woman.

'I've always liked older men. I mean, you're fairly old, aren't you?'

'Nearly forty.'

'That's what I mean.' They shuffled round and round. A crooner sang

> 'I never said thanks
> For that lovely weekend,
> Those few days of heaven
> You helped me to spend . . .'

'I never did hear such a soppy old song,' sang Angela. 'Did you?'

'Perhaps not. It was popular when I married my wife.'

'Oh, you're married. Where's your wife?'

'She died this month.'

'Oh yes, I've heard about you.'

'What have you heard?'

'Only that you were upset, behaving oddly, couldn't forget her. I bet I could make you forget her.' She moved closer to him.

'Behaving oddly?'

'Excuse me cutting in on you.' Anderson felt himself pushed away. Angela giggled and slipped into her stepfather's arms.

They swayed together, making the beast with two backs, the single and intolerable beast, in the deeply-shadowed room. In the very darkest recesses of the room, in the deepest double-beds of shadow, Anderson thought, what secrets might be drawn forth by this sickly music and this sweet warm wine? He stood with one arm on the mantelpiece and, with a slight alcoholic drowsiness, watched the beast swaying.

The lights went on. The recesses were exposed to light. The whole room was rich with it, yet strangely the effect was that of a torch shone directly at a face in sleep. The sleeper turns and twists, but he has been speared firmly by the hook of light; and behind the torch he knows there is a judge's hanging face. So, wrenched from their private dreams and lusts, Anderson and VV and Angela blinked and rubbed their eyes and stretched like figures dropped from a congenial extra-terrestrial existence into the real unpleasant world. The cause of their translation, Mrs Vincent, stood in the doorway. She still wore the dark sack, but her hair was disordered, and Anderson saw with pity that she had been crying. She strutted slowly, like a breastless pigeon, into the room, infecting them all with her overpowering sense of guilt and shame. Anderson, certainly, waited expectantly for some final pronouncement to drop from her tongue, some word that would make plain the nature of the lotus-land into which they had inadvertently strayed. He found it incongruous that the word she finally ejected like a stone from her lips had a positively banal appropriateness. 'Disgusting,' Mrs Vincent said, and without warning dropped with firmly closed eyes on to a convenient sofa.

Her faint, however transparently simulated, had the effect of jerking into action the three figures who had seemed set in their surroundings like flies in amber. Angela darted off once again to the kitchen. VV, crying 'Her salts, her salts . . .' ran out of the door that led to the hall. Anderson, left alone with the recumbent figure, rather feebly patted its cold, long hands which showed no awareness of his touch. The application of smelling salts to the narrow nostrils, and the pouring of brandy between the colourless lips, however, proved more effectual.

As suddenly as she had dropped down Mrs Vincent, with rather the effect of a Jack-in-a-box, sat up and stared at the three faces bending over her. She spoke, but only to Anderson, as though the scene she had interrupted proved a theorem long argued between them. 'You see.'

But as she straightened Anderson straightened also, so that the effect of her confidence was lost. 'I must be leaving, I fear. An appointment.' VV also straightened and nodded to Anderson, as though in relief.

'An appointment,' Angela said mockingly. 'It's not an appointment; it's a lovely party. I heard you say so when I was in the kitchen. And you won't take me. Why won't you take me?'

Mrs Vincent, whose comments at this time had the merit of brevity, ejected another stone, this time directed straight at Angela. 'Strumpet.' At once a screaming match began between mother and daughter. Their styles were interestingly contrasted, for Angela screamed with the full force of youthful lungs, and Mrs Vincent faintly and with an awareness of her own irony, as though each faint scream might be her last earthly pronouncement.

'Dirty old sow.'

'Strumpet.'

'It's your filthy mind, you dirty old woman.'

'My daughter!'

'And if I were it would be your fault. You hate sex.'

'Sex!' Mrs Vincent looked as if she might faint again, but managed to stay upright on the sofa.

'Repressed, repressed, you're repressed. You look through keyholes. You ought to be in a home.'

'Ha ha ha!' Mrs Vincent's falsetto laughter was positively frightening. She dropped her voice, most effectively, to a conversational level, as she said: 'A period in a reformatory school would do you a great deal of good. I shall make enquiries – '

'They'll put you in the loony bin,' screamed Angela. She began to dance round her mother, rolling her head idiotically, flapping her hands, and chanting: 'The loony bin, the loony bin, they put her away in the loony bin.' Anderson and VV left the room unnoticed. Anderson put on his coat in silence, while VV ran his hands through his hair over and over again, saying: 'Sorry, sorry, I'm really awfully sorry.'

'Say goodbye to your wife and stepdaughter for me.'

'I'll see you downstairs.' When they stood in the vast gilt hall that was the entrance to the flats, VV sighed. 'A problem child.'

'There are no problem children,' Anderson quoted sententiously. 'Only problem parents.'

'And stepparents?'

'And stepparents.'

'I must go back there. We don't seem to have had a chance to have our talk, do we?' VV took Anderson's hand and gripped it. 'I'm sorry about the way everything's turned out.'

'That's all right.'

'I hope it's a good party.' VV stood on the steps, waving goodbye. He looked extremely forlorn.


# VII


Adrian and Jennifer Pollexfen had a tiny mews house at the back of Portland Place. They were the constituent elements of a firm named Pollexfen and Pollexfen, and in that capacity called themselves 'Design Consultants'. They were prepared, for a suitable fee, to design in a modern manner anything from a teapot to a motor-car, an electric toaster to a radiogram, a hockey stick to a new range of cosmetics. The occupation is one recently discovered, but once discovered quickly seen to be indispensable to industry. It will be readily appreciated that the design consultant has an honoured place in the advertising profession, and also that each design consultant will be likely to have his particular variation of style. All design consultants, of course, adhere, in their fashion, to modern conventions: but some are still old-fashioned enough to be stuck in a Le Corbusier doctrine of fitness for purpose, while others have passed beyond that to the belief that some form of ornamentation, or even of free idea association in design, is permissible. The particularly distinctive feature of Adrian Pollexfen's style was that he managed to make the most disparate objects look like pieces of sculpture by Henry Moore. 'UPD,' Adrian would say, which being interpreted meant *Utility plus Beauty equals Design*; and he would point to the teapot with its hollowed centre and its lid strongly resembling one of the pinheads to be found on Moore's gigantic figures; to the surprising radio cabinet which had dials for breasts and was divided at the crutch; to the abstract shapes he had designed for Mary Magdalen cosmetics. Jennifer added the weight of an enormous mass of statistical information to Adrian's artistry on the drawing board; she was very ready to show the design development of a particular article since its invention, and to analyse the reasons for the various modifications of existing shapes in historical, economic and artistic terms. Jennifer, it was said by the unkind, first blinded prospective clients with science and Adrian then slew them with charm. The Pollexfens were great party-givers. They were anxious to be intimate friends with as many people as possible; and it is well known that there is no better way of being intimate friends with people than by introducing them to other people at parties.

Anderson wondered, as his footsteps rang on the cobblestones, what he was doing here. Why did Elaine want to speak to him? What could she possibly have to say that was important? In the dark mews the Pollexfens' house was a block of light. A kind of subdued hum came from it, a medley of sounds such as one might expect to hear at the recording of a meeting at the Tower of Babel. Anderson went up the narrow staircase, giving a glance at the alcoves on either side where Pollexfen designs were displayed under perspex; the electric iron like a recumbent woman, the double-headed refillable shaving tube which squirted brushless cream from one head and talcum powder from the other, the toys resembling elemental human figures. At the top of the stairs Jennifer Pollexfen met him, her round face grave as usual, her hair hanging down her back in two long pigtails. They had met once or twice before, but he was surprised by the warmth with which she greeted him. Anderson looked at the thick wedge of humanity behind her, and was reminded of the pictures he had seen of American football.

'There's someone you'll like to meet,' Jennifer Pollexfen said. 'But a drink first. We'll have to fight, I'm afraid.'

'I don't mind about a drink. I'd hoped to see Elaine.'

'She's about somewhere,' Jennifer Pollexfen said vaguely. 'But let's – ' He could not hear the next words for, beckoning him to follow, she threw herself, pigtails waving behind her, into what seemed the most crowded part of the scrum. Surprisingly, it parted for her; arms were withdrawn, legs seemed to bend away as though made of plasticine, and miraculously they came out into a backwater occupied by a square-headed man with cropped hair and a grey beard who stood munching a sandwich from a paper bag. Jennifer Pollexfen beamed with the consciousness of achievement; her round face was rosy. She spoke, but the words were inaudible, until Anderson suddenly heard 'Professor Protopopoff.' He extended a hand and the Professor, stuffing his sandwich into the bag and the bag into his pocket, squeezed the hand in a powerful grip and grinned as widely as a cat. When Anderson looked round Jennifer Pollexfen had vanished, swallowed up in the scrum. The Professor was talking, but the noise around them was so great that Anderson could not hear a word he said. This failure in audibility by the Professor was like a break in the sound track of a film – except that the break involved the Professor alone, for all around them the sound track was only too plainly audible. A beefy young man at Anderson's side had obviously just made a joke. He roared with laughter. 'Ha ha ha,' he yelled, and dug into Anderson with his elbow at each roar. 'Ha ha ha,' cried a girl in poison green and a man in an egg-yellow pullover. The three of them rocked gently before Anderson's eyes. And then suddenly the Professor's sound track was working. In perfect English, but with a slight accent, he said: '. . . of the syntagma.'

'I beg your pardon.'

The Professor was perfectly audible. 'I said that, for me, a syntagma is a grammatically free group of signs correlating a determining with a determined term in a binary structure. Now, from the mnemonic point of view – ' his eyes rolled alarmingly – 'from the mnemonic point of view, a partial syntagma of discourse is a complete mnemonic syntagma if by a mental association it can be reduced to a sentence of which the determined term is the subject.'

'Oh.'

'Take advertisement.'

'What?'

'I say take advertisement. That is a virtual syntagma, is it not? And yet it is reducible to – '

'You'll have to excuse me,' Anderson said. 'I'm looking for somebody.'

'But, Professor – '

'I'm not a professor. My name is Anderson.'

'You are not Professor Protopopoff? The grammarian? No?' The grey-bearded man looked extremely offended. 'You have been trying to make a fool of me.' He turned his back on Anderson and took out his paper bag again. Anderson lowered his head and charged into the crowd. But the bodies that had parted before him when he had followed Jennifer Pollexfen's pigtails now seemed to have taken on an obstinate quality of resistance. At one point his way was blocked by two men with enormous stomachs which swelled out of their bodies like balloons. A long way above these touching balloons their mouths were opening and shutting; below, the balloons were supported on spindly trousered stalks. For a moment Anderson was seized with a desire to drop down and crawl beneath that bridge of stomachs. Instead he stared angrily at the men and said: 'Excuse me.' The two heads, as he spoke, seemed to diminish, the stomachs to expand threateningly; then normality returned, the men were men and their stomachs merely sizeable, and he pushed a way between them. At another time, and quite unexpectedly, he found himself transformed from the outside to the inside of a conversational group. He had been beating on them unavailingly with apologies, with 'Would you let me pass' and 'Excuse me please', with unnoticed shoulder taps and unsuccessful sidelong shuffles. They seemed not to notice his existence. And then suddenly he was in the middle of them, a drink was pushed into his hand, he drained it with a confused impression that it was something unusual, and received another, he was clapped on the back and the chatter, instead of moving away from his ears, was all aimed directly at him.

'So this bastard said to old Jock, he said, every well-read man reads *The Economist*.'

'And then Jock says, well, I'm as red a man as most, and e con o mist comes over my eyes when I see that paper.'

'And this bastard says I tell you frankly, Jock, I don't think you're pulling your weight.'

'Weight, Jock says, weight, you could do with losing some weight, and I tell you what, says Jock, you've lost me. You know what you can do with your job, says old Jock.'

'Trust old Jock.'

'He's a lad is old Jock.'

'Stay out the month, the bastard says, and old Jock said I'll not stay a single day.'

'Swept up the things from his desk, packed them in his briefcase.'

'Raised two fingers to Smallbeer, the managing director.'

'Turned Smallbeer's secretary over on her desk and whacked at her with a slipper.'

'Kissed the telephone operator goodbye.'

'Said a soldier's farewell to the Art Department.'

'Blew a raspberry at Production.'

'Cocked his leg up as he walked through Space.'

'Wished Research joy of it.'

'Walked down the street to Rafferty, Hay and Pilkington and got a job at another five hundred a year.'

'Taking the lung tonic account with him.'

Anderson drained the second glass, said 'Hurrah for old Jock,' and flung himself at a gap in the circle of figures surrounding him. The figures parted and he was through, but not with a clear passage, for now he bumped against another enormous mass of flesh. A voice said: 'Hey there, Andy, watcher doin' to y'r ol' pal Amos.' The mass of flesh, great hands and thighs, large feet, blubber face with small twinkling eyes, was resolved into Fletchley.

'Fletchley!'

'My ol' pal Andy's lookin' a little the worse for wear.' With his hands round Anderson's waist, clasping him with the insistence of an anaconda, Fletchley sniffed the glass which Anderson still firmly held. 'Dat ol' debbil Pernod's bad ol' debbil,' he said, and shook his head.

'Where's Elaine? She said she'd be here.'

The comedy was wiped away from Fletchley's face. The corners of his mouth turned down in an expression of stage misery. 'Gone.'

'What do you mean? Gone home?'

'Oh no, she's not gone home. She'll never go home again, Andy boy, she'll never go home again.'

'She's left you, then?' Anderson asked brutally. He now had Fletchley not only in focus but in colour, the bluish bags under the eyes, the pasty white cheeks, a hint of carbuncle on the nose.

'She says she's left me, but she'll never leave me. That's one thing Elaine could never do to her old Fletch. She always comes back. She's been here tonight. Now she's gone again, but she'll come back.'

'Then where is she?'

'At this moment, old boy, she's probably careering round Regent's Park in a taxi, making love to a young man. Film star – not a star, that is, but film actor. Good-looking. Young. Got everything. She deserves everything; she deserves the best, and what's she got? Me?' Tears were in Fletchley's eyes. 'But I want you to know, Andy, that I'm not jealous. Whatever I may have said or done, it wasn't done in jealousy.' The great drops of liquid overspilled the lids, surmounted the bags beneath them, and coursed down Fletchley's cheeks. He put out his tongue and licked at them.

The realization of Fletchley's condition made Anderson feel fully sober, although he was not in any case suffering from drunkenness in any easily recognizable form. His speech was clear, his mind normally, perhaps even abnormally, active; the room and the people in it had now settled into what was almost a state of slow motion. He could observe in detail every movement of a hand, every flicker of expression. His perceptions seemed to be sharpened so that, for instance, the colours of Fletchley's suit, a close-woven herringbone, stood out with extraordinary distinctness. He put out a hand and touched the cloth, and a remarkable improvement in his tactile sense was also apparent; his fingers rubbed against material not to be classified simply as rough or smooth but identifiable, rather, in terms of emotion. This, Anderson seemed to realize, was the way in which life itself should ideally be apprehended. What stirs in my stomach at the touch of this cloth? What subliminal urges move me when I feel fur? What words can tastebuds find for richness of cream? *Softness*, indeed, and *richness* – how inadequate they are.

'Words,' he said to Fletchley, 'not feelings.'

'What's that, old boy? I didn't quite catch.'

'Richness, softness, what do they express? What do any words? Not feelings. Words were deceivers ever. The true feelings lie here.' Anderson placed his hand on the top button of his waistcoat.

'Deceivers ever.' Fletchley's great head swung pendulously from side to side and two more tears rolled smoothly over the blubber of his cheeks. 'Who could 'a thought that a girl like Elaine would go off – go off night after night. A well-set-up girl like Elaine. Who could 'a thought it.'

'Take advertisement. A virtual syntagma.'

'But I want you to know, Andy, that nothing said or done was in jealousy. You believe me, old boy, don't you?'

Fletchley was obviously much moved. Anderson said: 'I believe you.'

'A well-set-up girl. Say what you like, at *Woman Beautiful* they're all well-set-up girls. Like Val. Your little woman was a well-set-up girl and where did it get her?' Fletchley began to sob, loudly and miserably. 'She died. Your little woman died a miserable, a sudden death.'

The words dropped, dropped, how did they drop – like bombs, like vitriol? – into the pool of Anderson's peace. He felt anger and yet peace, the sense of the profound unimportance of what Fletchley was saying, underlay the anger which (like perhaps, a thick coating of oil?) rested on the surface and made his own voice say sharply: 'A sudden death – what do you mean, a sudden death?'

'Sudden and sad. I wrote today, old boy, one of my little pieces. *She will not feel the spring, nor hear the bluetit sing, nor see the lambkins gambol in the meadow*. I thought of Val.'

'*Sudden* death. You mean – ' As Anderson spoke the words the peace below anger was aware of their ludicrousness, their relation to football matches and music hall jokes – 'you mean *foul play*.'

'My dear old boy.' Fletchley's tears stopped.

'That's what you mean, is it? *Foul play*.'

'Don't get me wrong, Andy.'

'If not *foul play*, why *sudden death*? Out with it, Fletchley.' The peace still existed deep down, very deep down, but the surface anger was fairly boiling away, there could be no doubt of that.

Half turning away, rubbing fat tear-stained cheeks, his whole sagging body shivering with disdain, Fletchley muttered words well in the tradition of *foul play*: 'If the cap fits – '

From the depth of his inner peace, remote in a fastness impenetrable by anger and insusceptible to words, Anderson saw and felt what happened next: the endlessly deliberate action with which his right arm moved, forward and upward (would it never reach?) until it collided violently with an obstacle. Violently, violently; and yet in that happy seclusion where his spirit rested imperturbable, Anderson was almost unaware of the impact of fist on flesh, experienced it only as one feels the disturbance of a hair that has strayed across the face. He saw, however, the colour of a fist, strong, brownish, hairy, against unhealthy white; he saw the badly articulated body move slowly backwards and sink to ground; he saw the pin of blood, that gathered to a large ruby, and was then comically a river of red tears. But the whole thing became at last a fag, too much trouble to follow: quite deliberately he withdrew his eyes from the body wriggling on the floor, his ears from the orchestra about to spray over him prompted by his fistic overture; deliberately he withdrew from it all and settled in that landscape of the heart which he had always known to exist, but had never before been lucky enough to find.

## VIII

He was walking down a long narrow road which seemed to have no ending. Tall houses upon either side turned upon him their unfriendly night faces. Nobody but he seemed to be moving, so that it must be late, perhaps very late. Where had he been and what had he been doing? He found himself wishing for a door to open and show behind it a rich panel of light from within, for the scream of a radio set, for some footsteps other than his own to tap the pavement. There was something disturbing in this apparently purposeful but actually aimless movement of leg after leg. He could not be quite sure that he was awake.

A hand placed, quite casually, upon his forehead, came away wet. Was it with blood? But beneath a street lamp's yellow light he saw that a fine straight rain was falling. His forehead, of course, was wet with it. But he was conscious that for some reason or another his forehead should not be wet. Why not? And then the same hand passed over his hair revealed that he was not wearing a hat. He must have left it at the party.

At the end of the endless road he turned left into a road apparently identical with it. The circles of faint light round the street lamps; the high, blind houses; the absence of people or noise. But there was something else wrong, some strange stiffness affected him. His movements, he discovered, were like those of one struggling against an impediment. Could he, in

some way, have been injured? He began gingerly to prod ribs,
side and shoulders. Then he realized the cause of the trouble
and began to laugh. He was wearing the wrong coat.

Anderson could not have said why the discovery that he was
wearing an overcoat much too small for him should have amused
him so much. Crowing and hooting with laughter, he capered
down the road, and in a moment heard the distant hooting of
a motor horn. The sound gave him much pleasure. He passed
a shuttered and silent public house. It was, then, after eleven
o'clock – but, of course, he knew that, for he could not have
reached the Pollexfen party before ten. And as he remembered
the Pollexfen party his mind moved back to the strange triangle
at VV's flat and he laughed again, laughed until he felt that he
must burst the buttons of his borrowed overcoat, and at further
thought of the overcoat stood, quite helpless with laughter,
propped against a sign outside the pub. He turned his face
upward to the sky to catch the rain and as he did so distinguished
in the faint light the outline of a figure with cloven hoofs and
harlequin's clothes. Above the figure was the word *Demon*. It
was strange, he thought, that there should be two *Demons* in
London with exactly the same sign. Then his laughter was
stopped as tape is cut by scissors. There were not two *Demons*.
This was the *Demon* he knew, the pub at the corner of Joseph
Street.

It is again impossible to explain rationally why the discovery
that his legs had guided him home should have cancelled Anderson's uproarious mirth, but it is a fact that he was remarkably
reluctant to turn the corner into Joseph Street and enter his flat.
He felt that some disastrous news awaited him there; and it was
only by a great effort of will that he pushed away from the
signpost that had supported his uncontrollable laughter and
turned into Joseph Street. Then he stood still. Joseph Street,
like the other streets through which he had walked, was dark
and silent. But not altogether dark. Through the windows of his
own flat, inadequately contained by the gappy curtains, two
fingers of light stuck out into the road.

Anderson's next actions, the thirty steps taken to his own front door, the key inserted in lock, entrance hall crossed, and the last decisive action of turning the Yale key to open the door of his own flat, were as difficult as any he had performed in his life. When they were done he felt relief, although he had no idea of what lay behind the closed door of the sitting-room. He smelt cigar smoke, which somehow reassured him; and, opening the door, he saw Inspector Cresse filling one of the chromium-armed chairs, hands folded on stomach, staring placidly ahead of him like a musical comedy Buddha. Cigar smoke was thick in the room, a cigar was in the Inspector's mouth, and the stubs of two more lay in an ashtray. Slowly, and it seemed in several movements, the Inspector rose from the chair. The two men stood looking at each other and then the Inspector, a courteous host, waved a hand. 'Come in, come in, and make yourself at home. There's been a little trouble.'

'Trouble?' And now Anderson, looking round the room, saw that a great wind might have blown through it. The carpet had been pulled up and then thrown aside, a pouffe had been slit open, seats of some chairs had been removed. The pictures, stacked against the wall, had their backs cut away. The Inspector followed Anderson's roving gaze with heavy interest. 'And the tubular lamps,' he said, 'and the fire elements. Unscrewed them to see what they could find. Thorough.' He nodded amiably towards the bedroom door. 'In there, too. Chaos, I'm afraid. Mattress and pillows, all that kind of thing. Even took the back out of that portrait of your wife. I don't call that playing the game.'

'And the writing-desk? Anderson had carefully refrained from looking at it; but that, he realized, might be in itself suspicious. He looked, and the Inspector's eyes, at the moment singularly mild, followed. The writing-desk was open. Bills, letters, papers, lay confused within it. The drawer beneath had been opened also. Had the searcher discovered the hidden panel, and the limp black book?

'Quite a neat job,' the Inspector said. 'Didn't force the lock there. Used a skeleton key.' Anderson stared and stared, in bewilderment. Presumably the person responsible for this raid was Val's lover? But what could have been his purpose? To get some more letters, perhaps, which he knew Val had left here? But that seemed ridiculous.

'You're looking a bit under the weather,' the Inspector said. 'Let me pour you a drink, and perhaps you won't take it as a liberty if I pour myself one, too. I haven't done so, because I never take drink or bite in another man's home without invitation.' He stopped in the act of pouring whisky. 'Is this your coat? It seems to be a very bad fit.'

Anderson struggled out of the overcoat, and threw it on a chair. 'I picked it up by mistake at a party.'

'Gadding about.' A large finger wagged at Anderson. Behind it the white face with its two deep furrows was placid. 'Do you know it's one o'clock? I've been up here two hours. But you guessed that, I daresay, by the stubs. They're Upmann cigars – take nearly an hour to smoke – two and a half gone. I ought to charge them up to you.'

'Why are you waiting for me? What are you doing here?'

'The ingratitude of mankind.' Now, for the moment an absolutely farcical figure, the Inspector ran a hand over his shining bald head. 'Usually we policemen are slated for inefficiency. Try to be efficient, try to help people a little, and are they pleased? They certainly aren't. But let me tell you about it.' He produced a notebook from an inner pocket and referred to it. 'At 8.48 this evening PC Johnson observed that the front door of Number 10 Joseph Street stood wide open. He rang the bell and, receiving no reply from upper or lower floor, entered the hall. The door to the upper flat was closed, but he found the door to the lower flat standing open. He entered and found – ' the Inspector stopped reading – 'this.'

'That tells me nothing.' Anderson stared now unashamedly at the open lower drawer of the writing-desk. 'It doesn't tell me why *you're* here.'

'I take an interest in you.' The Inspector's hands were clasped again on his stomach.

'You pursue me.'

'Oh now – really.' The furrows deepened, the mouth curved in deprecation.

'What about this afternoon? A message left for me in the office given to a girl who might make anything of it. *The air is unhealthy in Melian Street.* That sort of thing is disgraceful, I say, disgraceful. It is persecution.' Anderson had not meant to shout, but the sight of this large man sitting in his wrecked room, drinking whisky, somehow induced anger with this policeman and all his kind.

'Now now, Mr Anderson, I'm really surprised at you. Persecution, indeed. I was trying to be helpful.'

'Helpful!'

'A word to the wise, you know. I happened to notice you coming out of that – establishment, shall we call it? I was surprised – not shocked, you understand, but surprised – and I was worried. Within a few days that establishment may be raided. It would be a pity if you were there, wouldn't it? Wouldn't look well. I was trying to be thoughtful, but do you appreciate it? No, you think I was persecuting you. Really, Mr Anderson, sometimes I agree with Gilbert and Sullivan.'

'Gilbert and Sullivan?'

'A policeman's lot is not a happy one. That's a very true saying, though not intellectual enough for you I expect.' In the same comfortable voice, almost apologetically, the Inspector said: 'But I shall have to ask a few questions.'

'Me? Ask me?'

'Why yes, Mr Anderson. I must tell you that we are not satisfied.'

'Not satisfied?' Anderson repeated stupidly. He sat looking round at the disorder of the room.

Without ceasing to look at Anderson, the Inspector pulled a nail file from his pocket and began to file his large well-kept nails. As he did this, he went on talking in the same conversational half-tone; and beneath his quiet, coarse voice there lay the faint rasp of the file. 'I'll tell you something now, Mr Anderson. This morning we had another of those anonymous letters. Very nasty, too; beastly things they are altogether. Don't ask me what it said, because I can't tell you, but you can take my word for it it was nasty. Take no notice, you may say, and that's all very fine, but then what about this business tonight? A few days ago you told me you hadn't an enemy, but it looks a bit as if you have. Eh, Mr Anderson?'

'I didn't speak.'

'I thought you mentioned a name.'

'A name?'

'Your enemy's name. You told me a little while ago that you had no enemy. That's not true, is it? You have got one, and you know who it is.'

'You want to know the name of my enemy?'

'That would be interesting.' The Inspector stopped filing his nails.

'The name of my enemy,' Anderson leaned forward and spoke with an intensity the remark hardly warranted, 'is Anderson.'

Obligingly, the Inspector leaned forward, too. Poised on their chair edges, they confronted each other like eager dogs. 'Your brother, is that? I didn't know you had one.'

'Myself!'

The Inspector's interest notably diminished. He dropped back into the lap of his chair and as he did so dropped the emotional level of the conversation. 'A man's worst enemy is himself! Well, I suppose you're right, but it hardly answers what I want to know, does it?'

The Inspector's obtuseness made Anderson anxious to disentangle his own fine shade of meaning. 'You don't understand me. These things that you describe – the anonymous letters, the wrecking of this flat – they are things that I might have done myself. They awaken a response in me. The anonymous letters – spying through the keyhole and telling the world the secrets we've seen inside the room – that's a thing I might have done. And then the flat – look at it now. Do you remember what this room looked like the last time you saw it, how every ghastly object was in the right place, every filthy little cushion and lampshade just as my wife had them. Now I see it all utterly disordered, everything completely boss-eyed, and do you know what I wonder, Inspector? I wonder why I didn't do it all myself years ago.' Anderson had meant to speak perfectly quietly, but in spite of himself his voice had risen a little. The Inspector, nevertheless, continued almost perfectly obtuse.

'You say the oddest things sometimes, Mr Anderson. I don't hold much with all this modern psychology stuff myself.'

It was injudicious to shout, Anderson knew, but now he fairly shouted. 'Psychology, nonsense. Don't be a fool, man. I'm saying that the actions of this man, whoever he is, are actions I can understand. The desire to destroy, that's what I'm talking about, is that plain enough for you? Because he wasn't searching here for anything, there was nothing to search for. Hatred was moving, hatred of me, the wish to wreck my life, to destroy anything that belongs to me. And I feel that impulse, too. Do I make myself clear? To make disorder out of order, to wreck, tear, kill – ' Abruptly Anderson stopped. The word hung in the air between them, a word for which, in the Inspector's terms, there was no possible explanation or excuse. But, so far from asking him to explain it, the Inspector merely sat filing his nails. When at last he spoke it was to take up Anderson's remarks at one remove and with a rambling clumsiness, a missing of the essential point that seemed, on this evening at least, characteristic of him.

'It's funny, now, that you should be talking about order and disorder, because my wife's great on them, too. Did I tell you I was married? Well, anyway, I am, and two kids as well. Here we are in the front garden.' With the pathetic pride of an amateur conjurer the Inspector whipped from his wallet a photograph. Anderson looked at a small pretty woman in an overall, flanked by two young boys. Their slightly bovine faces, staring earnestly into the camera, were recognizably of the kind that would later attain their father's flat weightiness. A rather younger Inspector, less bulky and with a thick fringe of hair round the side of his head, looked at them with the affection of an overgrown bulldog.

'Very nice,' Anderson said. He handed back the photograph

and thought: *Wreck, tear, kill* – what could have possessed him to use such words. He had been drunk, it was true, at one time in the evening, and now it was very late, and he was so tired that he hardly knew what he was saying. He looked at his wristwatch. Two o'clock. Would the man never go?

'The apple of their mother's eye – and their father's too,' the Inspector said earnestly. 'But I was telling you about my wife. *Order*, she says, you must have order or how can life go on? And she tells that to the kids, and makes them understand it. There's a time and a place, she says, for skylarking, and the time's not lunchtime and the place isn't the dining-room. And she makes the punishment fit the crime – to use another Gilbertian phrase. If the kids throw food about at the dining-table they have to do the washing up, if they come into the house with muddy boots the wife puts mud on their clothes and makes them clean it off. She's got a sense of humour, and that's a wonderful thing.'

Good God, Anderson thought, no wonder the poor little creatures look bovine. But the Inspector was droning on. 'I say to the wife that it's only a little bit of fun they're having, but she will have it I'm wrong. Disorder, she says, is wicked. I must tell you, though,' the Inspector said with one of his devastating lapses into bathos, 'that she was brought up a Nonconformist. I say to her sometimes that the state of disorder is a state of nature. Do you know what she says to that? The state of order is the state of grace. It's from the impulse to disorder, she says, that these Mussolinis and Hitlers gain power. And if she were here tonight she'd say to you that it was quite right to say that the impulse to make disorder out of order was the same as the impulse to kill. Killing is disorder, that's what she'd say. And what would *you* say to that?'

Anderson felt suddenly a quite overwhelming anxiety simply to get rid of the Inspector at any cost. 'I should say she was a damned fool' he answered harshly, 'and was going the right way to make Fascists out of her children.'

Surprisingly the Inspector laughed. 'You'd be perfectly right. I made it all up.'

'What?'

'All that stuff I was saying just then. The wife's thoughts don't rise above the kitchen sink. I was curious to see what you'd say. It's getting late.' At last, at last, Anderson thought. The Inspector stretched like a hippopotamus and yawned. 'But somehow I don't feel tired. Insomnia, that's my trouble; one of my troubles, I should say. Do you mind if I have another little drop of Scotch?' He poured a drink and wandered about the room, stopping to peer out into the street. 'Not what you'd call a very salubrious neighbourhood. But I suppose there's no accounting for tastes. One man's meat is another man's poison, as they say. How are you getting on at the office?'

'The office?' Anderson lay back exhausted. As he did so his eyelids, like a doll's thick lids that shutter the staring eye when it is laid flat, closed.

'Everything all right, not feeling the strain or anything like that? You look as if you're feeling the strain, you know. But it's interesting, all that stuff about order and disorder, isn't it? Philosophical, too. I feel in a way it's my business, and sometimes it worries me.'

Behind the closed lids Anderson could see the Georgian writing-desk. Put your hand inside, open the secret drawer and there, in the mind's eye, was the black book with its marbled edges. In the mind's eye, ah yes, in the mind's eye.

'Order's got to be preserved; we're all agreed on that, I hope,' the Inspector said, rather as if he were addressing a public meeting. 'But how far are we justified in using disorder to preserve it? That's the kind of question that worries me when I can't sleep. Supposing a man's arrested on suspicion, now; you know as well as I do that the boys give him a little going over on the way to the station. Very useful it is, too, often enough, in taking the starch out of them. But is it right? That's the thing I've started worrying about in my old age.'

The doll's lids flickered. 'Ethically no. Practically yes.'

'I'm very glad to hear you say so – because practice makes ethics, doesn't it? Though I'm out of my depth even when I'm thinking about this kind of thing, let alone talking about it. Still, methods like those wouldn't be any use in dealing with a superior man such as yourself, say. Would they?'

'They might extract a confession. Isn't that always what you're after?'

The Inspector's voice was plaintive. 'It certainly is *not*, Mr Anderson. Only incidentally. A policeman is like God. He wants to know the truth. And he's bound to believe that any means are justifiable – any means, do you understand me – if he can find the truth through them. The truth, the clean and perfect truth – that is what we shall reach tomorrow if not today, next year if not tomorrow. The truth!'

The voice was suddenly loud, and like a bell. Anderson opened his eyes and saw the Inspector standing, overcoated, in front of his chair. Seen from this angle and at this moment, he was no longer a comic figure. The deep vertical lines that ran down the cheeks were cruel, the pudgy features had assumed a coherent severity, power and the will to use it lay in the great bald skull. For a moment Anderson lay defenceless, sprawled in his chair, ready for raping by this ogre of order. From behind his back the Inspector then brought forth – not a whip, but his bowler hat. Clapping upon his head this symbol of order the Inspector turned upon a respectable black heel. 'Good night.' The words rang through the disorderly room. The front door closed. For perhaps five minutes Anderson lay in the armchair, deprived of movement, looking at the writing-desk. It does not matter, he told himself, whether the notebook is there or not. What does the notebook say, after all? It says our marriage was not ideally happy – but what marriage is happy? No, no, he told himself, the notebook does not matter in itself. But which of them could have wanted something in this flat so badly that they committed burglary to get it? Lessing? Reverton? Vincent? Wyvern? But Vincent was ruled out, was he not, by the fact that he had been in Anderson's company? Lessing, Reverton, Wyvern? Or – remember the open door, the figure pulling up the long pants – Pile? Ridiculous, ridiculous.

Like a sleepwalker, Anderson moved over to the writing-desk, fumbled, found the protrusion, pushed. The secret drawer opened. It was empty.


# IX

Awake, it seemed that he was still asleep. His feet touching the floor had the lightness of a dream; but entirely real was the pain that beat in his head, and the tightness of his face, which felt as if it had been coated with varnish. He applied Hey Presto and wiped it off. He felt absolutely nothing, for the varnish was apparently impermeable, but the blue growth on his chin disappeared magically. The toast he cooked and ate, the coffee he boiled and drank, had similarly no taste or smell. An automaton pushed food and drink into its mouth.

This numbing of the senses continued on his way to the office. The omnibus came noiselessly along the street, he saw but did not hear the click of the conductor's punch. He stood between a fat woman who breathed in and out, deeply but apparently noiselessly, and a figure holding a newspaper. This figure was interesting. Two delicate hands were visible at either side of the paper, which faced Anderson, and occasionally an edge of the paper flicked his face. It became important to Anderson that he should see this newspaper-holder. The hands seemed to be those of a woman, and yet the trousers, as he saw on looking down, were a man's. A woman in slacks? Anderson swayed forward against the newspaper, but it remained obstinately raised. When somebody by his side got out he said, although to him the words remained inaudible, that there was a seat vacant. The figure accepted the seat, without for an instant lowering the paper. Infuriatingly, when the man-woman sat down, somebody else pushed against Anderson and he was still unable to see over the newspaper barrier.

The figure rose, still holding the paper before its face – and then in a flash the paper was folded and the figure, presenting its back to Anderson, was on its way out of the bus. Excuse me, Anderson said, excuse me, but by the time he had reached the end of the bus the figure had dropped off and was running across the road concealed in a duffle coat which effectively concealed sex as well as identity. Anderson jumped off the bus. For a moment a taxi was in front of him, then it swerved aside and he saw the driver's shaken fist.

Running, running across the wide road he saw the figure, ahead of him, enter an office block. He ran in after it and found with astonishment that he was in the reception hall of Vincent Advertising. The figure sat at the reception desk with its back to him, but turned as he approached the desk. The newspaper still held in front of the face was slowly lowered, and behind it he saw the laughing features of Molly O'Rourke. He stood still in astonishment. She bowed her head in mock acknowledgement, showing all her fine teeth in laughter, and then pointed down the corridor towards his room. He ran down the corridor and at the first bend turned to look at Molly. He could see nothing but the newspaper held at the edges by two delicate hands.

When he reached the door of his room Anderson paused with one hand on the door handle, and then dramatically swung the door open with such violence that it struck the inside wall (but noiselessly, noiselessly–). He saw then how he had been deceived, for a figure stood by the desk, back to him, and this figure also was wearing a duffle coat. Slowly, very slowly, the figure turned to face him, and Anderson saw, with a shock that was yet no surprise, the round face of Charlie Lessing. Lessing, too, was smiling, and he held in one hand, waving it with gentle mockery back and forth, a letter from Val. Even across the room Anderson could recognize the blue paper and the careless handwriting.

'You!' Anderson cried, and for the first time heard his own voice. 'You, you, you!' Lessing stood there by the desk, waving the letter, smiling. His smile did not waver even when Anderson in a great spring across the room had him by the throat, forcing the hated face further and further away from him over the desk, gripping tighter and tighter the flexible round neck above which the gums still showed in a ghastly smile, while from the pink gullet came wild and agonized screams, while the eyeballs started outwards and the throat screamed, while the face reddened and the throat screamed and screamed and screamed . . .

The screams echoed in his head long after he woke and lay staring at the ceiling in the half-light of early morning. A nightmare, he thought; it was nothing but a nightmare; there was no reason to think badly of Molly or of Lessing because in a dream he had invested them with diabolical smiles. He straightened up in bed and saw that the hands of the alarm clock said half past five. On the floor lay Val's photograph, out of its frame. He picked it up, put it by the bedside lamp, switched on the light and stared at it. The eyes looked lovingly back at him, the full mouth was smiling.

# THE TWENTYEIGHTH OF FEBRUARY

I

When one wakens after a nightmare, actuality may seem unreal.
Anderson opened his eyes to see a patch of sunlight on the bed.
His head ached violently and the skin of his face felt tight. The
time by his alarm clock was twentyfive minutes to ten. This is
another dream, he thought, and turned over in bed. But his
head went on aching, the skin of his face still felt drawn. He
stretched, yawned, closed his eyes, and then rolled over again
to look at the clock. Twentyfive minutes to ten. He picked up the
clock, and shook it, but it continued to tick. Had he forgotten to
wind the alarm, or had it failed to wake him? The question was
academic, beside the fact that he was extremely late.

He jumped out of bed, washed hurriedly, applied Hey Presto
to his face. *In the dream* he thought, *I felt nothing; it was as
though my face were covered with varnish*. And when he
removed the Hey Presto he felt none of the pricking or burning
sensation that had accompanied previous applications – nothing
except, perhaps, a slightly increased facial tension. It was not
pleasant to have the dream pattern so nearly approached; fortunately his senses of touch and hearing appeared to be unim-
paired. He had no time to discover whether his sense of taste
was still functioning, because he left without eating breakfast.
He put on a raincoat and his second-best black hat, and threw
over his arm the overcoat collected at the party. When he had
closed his own front door he remembered the Fletchleys. Elaine
would be at *Woman Beautiful* by now, but he ought to apologize
to Fletchley for the blow on the jaw. His wristwatch, however,
said a quarter to ten. He decided to telephone later.

The sense of unreality stayed with him as he ran to the corner
and jostled on to a bus. He stood; and there, sure enough, as
in the dream, the person standing next to him held a newspaper
in front of his face. The bus stopped abruptly and threw them

against each other; Anderson, with a movement apparently involuntary, pushed at the newspaper and it was lowered immediately to reveal a petulant small indeterminately male face quite unknown to him. The journey continued without incident. Anderson jumped off the bus and ran across the road to the office. At the desk sat not duffled Molly O'Rourke but pneumatic Miss Detranter. She called to him, but Anderson, one hand raised in greeting, hurried down the corridor. At the door of his own room he paused with one hand on the handle, as he had paused in the dream. He flung open the door, and was surprised when it struck the inside wall with a crash. That was a surprise; but he received a shock that took him back to the dream when he saw Lessing standing by the desk. Lessing had his arm round a girl who was crying on his shoulder. He looked extremely uncomfortable, and on Anderson's appearance said with relief: 'Here he is.' He saw that the girl was Jean Lightley.

'Oh, Mr Anderson,' she said. 'Oh, Mr Anderson.' Her speech failed in a series of gasps.

Anderson took off his hat and raincoat and put the overcoat over a chair. The telephone rang. He moved over to pick it up and Jean Lightley called: 'Don't answer it.' She put her head back on Lessing's shoulder.

'Listen,' Lessing said. 'Here's what happened. It's pretty rough. Yesterday you wrote a stalling note to Bagseed about the drawings he'd sent back for correction. And you also wrote a fair stinker to old Crashaw. Well, somehow the letters got mixed up.' At these words Jean Lightley, who had shown signs of recovery, burst into great hiccoughing sobs. 'Raper of Kiddy Modes has been on raising hell. That's probably him on the line now.'

Anderson listened carefully to what Lessing was saying; and yet he could not forget that the villain of the dream was this same Lessing, spectacled incurious amiable Lessing, who now looked at him with such friendly concern. The telephone rang again.

'You don't seem very worried,' Lessing said. 'I wonder if I've made it clear. Shall I take the call?'

With a supreme effort Anderson brought himself back to reality, this kind of reality, the reality of advertising and of holding down a good job. He put on even (but with what an effort, what an effort) the mask of language and of manner that had served him so well in the past. 'I'll handle it,' he said. 'Get that weeping Jenny out of here. No, wait a minute; I want a copy of the letter I wrote to Crashaw.'

Jean Lightley removed the handkerchief from her face long enough to say: 'It's on your desk.' Then she ran wailing from the room. Lessing sat at one corner of the desk and swung his leg.

Bagseed's voice was quaveringly severe. 'Mr Arthur would like to speak to you. Please hold the line.' Anderson stared at Lessing's foot. A voice like ice water dripped into the telephone. 'Mr Anderson, this is Arthur Raper speaking.'

'How are you, Mr Raper,' Anderson said heartily. 'A long time since I've had the pleasure of seeing you.'

The voice said politely: 'That can be remedied. Perhaps you will make it convenient to come up and see me now.'

'Right, Mr Raper. I'm just making some enquiries about – '

The voice said: 'Now, please, Mr Anderson.'

'I should like ten – ' The line was dead. Lessing got up. He was plaintive. 'I wanted to talk to you about Hey Presto. How's the personal test doing? You look a bit funny.'

'What do you mean, funny?' He could feel the tightness of the skin round his cheekbones.

'Strained or something, I dunno. Are you going up now? Is there anything I can do to help out?'

'No, I don't think so. Yes, there is.' Anderson remembered the Crunchy-Munch conference fixed for ten-thirty. 'Will you present those two Crunchy-Munch schemes instead of me?' Lessing nodded. 'Strictly anonymous, you know. They don't know anything about them yet.'

'Strictly anonymous,' Lessing said and winked. 'But I shall do my best on my own behalf. I say, the Crunchy-Munch meeting can't take long. There's something on this morning at eleven-fifteen, Board Meeting or something. Rev's saying nothing, but looking full of it. Maybe they're going to give us all a rise.'

'Maybe.' Anderson put on his raincoat.

'I say,' Lessing was amiably but unusually curious this morning. 'That your coat on the chair?'

'Why?'

'It looks uncommonly like one Greatorex wears, that's all. Got a paint mark on the sleeve like his. Good luck. Don't let Raper rape you.'

'Thanks.' Anderson went along to the secretaries' office where Jean Lightley sat red-eyed, staring at her typewriter. Anderson said kindly: 'Jean, I'm sorry I blew off. I'm going up to see Kiddy Modes now.' She looked up at him. Her underlip was quivering. 'While I'm up there I want you to find out exactly what happened about those two letters, just how they got sent to the wrong people. Try and trace them right from the moment I handed them to you yesterday afternoon. It's not a question of responsibility; I just want to find out what happened. Understand?' She nodded. As he closed the door he heard a fresh storm of sobbing.

# II

Arthur Raper was a small grey man wearing a neat bow tie, who would have been identifiable as a very respectable elderly clerk if one had met him in the street. But he was not now in the street, but behind a large desk in a large room. To one side of the desk, springing up from an uncomfortable chair at Raper's command, was Bagseed, a stringy indigestible, nervous, old-middle-aged kind of man, obviously worried about the security of his job. At the other end of the room, separated from Mr Raper and his henchman by some yards of mulberry carpet, sat Anderson, bolt upright on the edge of an over-stuffed armchair. In a thin, polite, exhausted voice Mr Raper said:

'I am going to read you a letter, and I want you to tell me

what you think of it.' With a little cough he picked up a sheet of paper from the desk. It was, Anderson saw, the letter to Crashaw. 'Dear Crashaw,' Mr Raper said. He read the letter very slowly, pronouncing each syllable with care. At the word 'pest-i-len-tial' Bagseed shook his head gravely, at 'in-com-pe-tent, irr-el-ev-ant and im-mat-er-i-al', he plucked with dry fingers at his skinny neck. Mr Raper did not speak loudly, and at the other end of the room Anderson did not hear him very well, but he tried to give the impression of a keen and interested executive. It was necessary to crawl, he had decided in the taxi, but it would be fatal to crawl too fast or too far. We're all human, that was the line, we all blow our top sometimes and write things we regret five minutes afterwards. So when Mr Raper asked him to give an opinion of this document Anderson said firmly: 'I take full responsibility for writing that letter, Mr Raper.'

'Are you proud of your handiwork?'

'Far from it. I don't want to excuse writing such a letter. But I'd like to explain it.' Anderson launched the speech he had prepared in the taxi. 'That letter, sir, was the product of a week at the office in which we haven't known whether we are on our heads or our heels. It's the kind of letter all of us sit down and write a few times in our lives. Five minutes after we've written it we regret it. If we're sensible enough to delay posting it for half an hour we look at it again – and tear it up. I'll be frank, and say I wish I'd done that. I'll be franker still, and say that when Mr Bagseed received the letter and saw the kind of thing it was, and that it had come to him by mistake, I should have expected him to read it, laugh at it, tear it up, and perhaps write me a line saying that we were the most pestilential advertising agents he'd ever dealt with.' Mr Bagseed's hands clutched at his high, old-fashioned collar as though he were being strangled.

'Do I understand you to say that Bagseed should have concealed this letter from me? That he should have . . .' The rest of the sentence was inaudible to Anderson.

'I didn't quite hear you, I'm afraid.'

The ice tinkled more sharply. 'That he should have betrayed

his duty to me? You suggest that?' Bagseed shook his worn old head in anguished denial of such a possibility.

'Why, of course not. But one's got to make a distinction between a piece of spontaneous emotion like a man swearing when he kicks his foot against a stone – '

'I regard bad language as bad manners at any time,' said Raper. Bagseed sucked in his false teeth sharply.

'Ah, you're too good for the rest of us erring mortals, Mr Raper.' Anderson managed a laugh.

'Leaving aside your curious view of Mr Bagseed's responsibilities, I must confess surprise that I have heard no expression of regret from you regarding the contents of the letter. But perhaps you think no regret is called for. If that is your view it would be honest to say so. I respect honesty, Mr Anderson, above all things.'

It was the crawl then. 'Of course, I regret extremely the expressions I used in a heated moment.'

'But some of them, perhaps, you still feel inclined to justify.' Mr Raper's lips moved, but no words were audible. Had his voice, perhaps, been deliberately lowered?

At the other end of the mulberry carpet Anderson said: 'I beg your pardon?'

'I said "Out of our many pestilential clients, Kiddy Modes are perhaps the most pestilential of all." Does that phrase have the ring of truth to you, Mr Anderson?'

Not only a crawl, but a belly crawl. 'Certainly not. I should like to apologize for the use of that phrase.'

' "Their criticisms on this occasion, as on others, are incompetent, irrelevant and immaterial." Does that seem to you a fair observation?'

'It was thrown off in the heat of the moment.'

'That is not an answer to what I asked. Do you wish to justify that remark?'

'No no, certainly not. I should like to apologize for it – to you and to Mr Bagseed.'

Bagseed looked startled. Mr Raper made the very faintest inclination of his head.

' "Kiddy Modes demand just about six times as much attention as any other client of their size." Was that a proper remark?'

'I apologize for that, and for the whole of the letter unre-
servedly.' Is it possible for the head to get lower than the belly
when you crawl? It is at least possible to try. 'I don't wish to
make excuses, but a few weeks ago my wife died. I have not
been myself since then.'

'Please accept my sympathy in your bereavement,' Mr Raper
said primly. 'But I am sure you would not wish that factor to
influence my judgement of this deplorable letter in any way.'

'Naturally not. I only – '

'I am very glad to know that you agree with me about the
nature of this letter. Had you seriously thought us at fault I
should have felt bound to make a thorough investigation of the
circumstances. Nevertheless, I had to make up my mind whether
a firm which expressed such views would be quite happy with
our account.' The thin voice was now penetratingly clear. 'I
consulted with Mr Bagseed, and he agreed with me that once
the perfect confidence that should obtain between client and
agent has been broken it can never be mended.' Bagseed was
picking at the knees of his trousers and staring at the floor. 'Do
I make myself clear, Mr Anderson?' Anderson was speechless.
'Do I make myself clear?'

'You're taking away the account?'

'Precisely. Here is a letter terminating the contract. Formally,
it has still two months to run, but I imagine that in view of this,'
Mr Raper tapped Anderson's letter, 'Mr Vincent will not wish
to argue that point. Mr Bagseed will make all the necessary
arrangements for our change-over to another agency.'

So the belly crawl was useless, had been useless even before
he contemplated it. He had been a perfect mouse for this neat
sadistic cat, a mouse who gave the greater pleasure because he
clung to the illusion of freewill. And what could he say now? It
would be a mild pleasure, perhaps, to call Raper names, but by
doing so he would give the little man one more satisfaction. But
even while his thoughts moved thus rationally, Anderson was
inarticulate with rage. He stood up, walked stiffly over the

mulberry carpet to the big desk, and picked up the letter terminating the contract. The temptation to put his fist into the small face upturned towards him was almost, but not quite, irresistible. Anderson folded the letter carefully, put it in his pocket, and left the room.

## III

We all of us retain, for the greater part of our conscious lives, the impression that we are in control of events; not exactly in any world-shaking, Hitlerian or Napoleonic way, but in the sense that the performance of certain actions has predictable results. The exact nature of the links that make up the chain of cause and effect is concealed from us, and to most people, indeed, the links are of no interest; but it is essential for our mental well-being that the chain itself shall not be broken. When a switch is pressed the electric light must shine; the formal conversational gambit admits of only one formal reply; a letter, stamped and posted, must reach its addressee. No common logic is, in fact, applicable to the postal service, the return of conversation and the supply of electricity; few of us are concerned, however, to trace such things to their origins, but merely to receive a traditional result from a traditional action. It is upon this illusion of freewill (an illusion in the cases mentioned because the effect of our actions is really based upon the inventive genius, the courtesy or the labour of others) that our civilization has its slender basis; damage to this illusion in the case of any individual may render him incapable of dealing with the simplest problems, so that he is afraid to push the bell of a street door or to pull a lavatory chain because he has come to believe that life is in its essence illogical and irrational.

Something like this loss of belief had been suffered by Anderson. His mind had served him well in his work as a business executive, his judgement of people and situations had been almost invariably correct. The realization that he had been hopelessly astray in dealing with Raper affected him profoundly. It had never occurred to him that Raper's action might be the decisive one of severing relations altogether; the whole of his own conduct had been based upon a set of wrong assumptions. It was true that even a correct analysis of the situation could not have saved the account, but that point was irrelevant to Anderson's shocked consideration of his own condition. Such a gross error was out of the natural order of events; so far out of it that Anderson, when he left the room with the mulberry carpet, was a changed man. The change affected his thought and by extension, naturally, his conduct. There are two great classes in European civilization, those who do things, and those to whom things are done. Anderson entered the room with the mulberry carpet as (in his own view, at least) a member of the first class; he came out of it a member of the second. His energies had hitherto been divided between the attempt to preserve his position as an advertising executive, and the desire to discover the identity of his wife's lover. The first of these objectives he now abandoned. Not quite consciously, he felt that his power to apprehend the external world was failing; he had always believed that whatever happened constituted a norm of rationality, so that inability to understand the happenings around him naturally appeared as a defect in rational apprehension. He gathered together, therefore, as it might be said, his remaining forces, and launched an attack on the mystery of his private life, the vital part of the enemy position. His business flank was necessarily left exposed.

It was symptomatic of this changed attitude in Anderson that on return to the office his first move was to telephone Elaine Fletchley, and not to see VV. She was out at a fashion show. He telephoned Fletchley at Joseph Street, and got no reply. He asked for VV, who was still in the Board Meeting. Jean Lightley, who told him this, also gave him the result of the investigations he had asked her to make about the changeover of the letters. It seemed that a boy from the Dispatch Department, in an excess of zeal, had taken the letters from Jean Lightley's desk. In the Dispatch Department, where the drawings were being packed up, he had dropped the letters and when he picked them up had put them into the wrong envelopes. It was as simple as that; and to Anderson, now, it seemed so unimportant that he did not even ask the boy's name. When Jean said that she hoped Kiddy Modes had not been too angry he smiled, but made no reply.

To some natures there is something consoling in the perfect knowledge of the worst that can happen; it is, for a little while at least, satisfactory to be saved from the belief in the possibility of beneficial action. Such false tranquillity blessed Anderson now. He felt as the prisoner condemned to death may feel after his appeal has failed and the Home Secretary has refused to intervene. To know one's fate inevitable – is that not also to know peace? Anderson, a plastic and suffering figure, waited now for what might happen with the resignation he had shown in air raids during the war; feeling now, as then, certainty of disaster. But, in fact, he had come through the war unchipped, and no doubt there remained in some part of his mind the thought of escape which added an edge of contradictory pleasure to his perfect despair.

Anderson remained in this mood for about half an hour, staring into space unseeingly; and then his eye, coming, it seemed, into focus and roving over the neat room, was caught by something out of place. It was the blue overcoat he had brought away from the Pollexfens' party. What was it Lessing had said? That it looked like a coat belonging to young Greatorex? Anderson got up slowly (his movements, since his return from Kiddy Modes, were slightly hesitant like those of an old man), picked up the overcoat and went to Lessing's room. The copywriter was not there, but Greatorex sat at a desk in a corner of the room with a guard book open in front of him, and the telephone in his hand. He replaced the receiver as Anderson came in.

Anderson held out the coat. 'I picked this coat up in mistake last night. Lessing said he thought it might be yours.'

Was he mistaken in thinking that the blond young man hesitated before answering? He must surely know if he had lost an overcoat. 'Yes, it does look rather like mine.'

'And you lost yours? At the Pollexfens' party?'

'That's right.' Greatorex nodded, and smiled ingenuously and charmingly. 'To tell you the truth I had rather a lot to drink and don't know whether I was coming or going. I wasn't sure where I'd left it. But that's mine. I recognize that mark on the sleeve.'

Anderson held out the coat. 'You know the Pollexfens?'

'Not really. My uncle, Sir Malcolm, gave me introductions to a few people, and they were among them.'

'I didn't see you there.'

Greatorex smiled discreetly. 'You'd gone, breathing fire and brimstone, before I could make my way across the room to say hallo. You created quite a stir.'

Of course – Fletchley! Anderson had forgotten about him. 'Was Fletchley all right?'

'Was that his name? I don't think he sustained any vital injuries. He seemed to spend most of the evening crying about his wife. I believe he stayed the night. At least, he was still there when I left. Yes, this is my coat all right.' Greatorex looked at the label, put his hands in the pockets. 'I suppose you didn't leave anything – ' His hand came out with an envelope in it. He looked at it and said: 'This is yours.' Upon the envelope, in typewriting that somehow seemed familiar, was printed *Mr Anderson*.

Anderson put the envelope in his pocket and walked out of the room without saying anything. Back in his own room he extracted a cream-laid card of medium thickness. On it was typed:

> Yet Ile not shed her blood,
> Nor scarre that whiter skin of hers, than Snow,
> And smooth as Monumentall Alabaster:
> Yet she must dye, else shee'l betray more men:

Corny, Anderson thought, corny. Somebody's done five minutes' work with Stevenson or Bartlett. He remembered now why the typing seemed familiar. It was, he felt sure, the same as that on the anonymous letters shown him by the Inspector. And yet the quotation, corny as it was, stirred something in him, probed gently and painfully into a very tender and deep recess. But how had the card got into the pocket of that over-coat? It could not have been put in while he was at the party, for nobody could have known in advance that he would leave wearing Greatorex's coat. In pure theory it could have been slipped into the coat after he had put it on, and was about to leave, but somehow that seemed very unlikely. Somebody, it was much more likely, had put the card into the coat pocket this morning while it lay in his office. Somebody, anybody, X. But Val's letter and the blank sheet had been put on his desk. Why should X have chosen to put this card into a coat pocket, rather than on the desk? To that question Anderson could find no answer, until with a flash (there seemed, quite literally, to *be* a flash and a kind of crack inside his head, so that he put up both hands to his temples, covering his eyes) an answer came to him. Postulate Greatorex as X, say that the card had been in Greatorex's overcoat last night ready for delivery at some convenient time. By bad luck Anderson had taken away the coat with the card in it; and when Greatorex discovered that fact he must have been on tenterhooks in case Anderson had put his hand in the pocket immediately on leaving and dis-covered the card. In fact, Anderson had not done so; and when Greatorex found that out this morning he had, with the utmost coolness, delivered the envelope as he had meant to do last night. Neat.

By this process of reasoning which, Anderson conceded to himself judicially, seemed remarkably plausible, Greatorex was X; but Greatorex, as far as Anderson knew, had been altogether unknown to Val. Greatorex was in the office only because he happened to be the nephew of Sir Malcolm Buntz. Greatorex as X was, in fact, at once plausible and ridiculous.

When Anderson had progressed this far in his reasoning he became aware that something in front of him was shining. The shining came from his desk and was something more than the reflection of electric light upon its polished surface. Something actually upon his desk was shining, and, peeping through the fingers that still covered his eyes, he could not be sure what it was. He must, then, remove his fingers to see the object; but that proved to be, for some reason, remarkably difficult. It seemed to Anderson minutes, although it was doubtless not more than one or two seconds, before he drew away fingers from eyes; and when he did so he was conscious of a positive screech of separation, as though they had been attached by sticky tape. His eyes, naked and defenceless, were confronted by the shining object. Anderson was looking at a brand new chromium desk calendar. The date showing on it was the thirty-first of February.

The sight of this calendar filled Anderson with an unreasoning terror which nullified altogether the logical process of reasoning by which he had been seeking to identify Greatorex as his wife's lover. He put out a finger and touched the calendar, very timidly, as though afraid that it might contain some poisonous spike that sprang out at a touch. He ran a fingertip over its shining surface, placing it upon the figures 3 and 1 as if to convince himself of their existence. He was still staring at the calendar when the door opened and Lessing said, 'How did it go?' and then, 'Why, what's the matter?'

Anderson swallowed and spoke. 'The calendar.'

'What about it? New, isn't it?'

'Where did it come from?'

'How should I know? Probably a gift from your faithful secretary.'

Anderson swallowed again and said: 'Look at the date.'

Lessing looked and sighed. 'What little things do amuse little girls. The thirtyfirst of February. Doesn't it show that the oldest chestnuts are still the ones that rock 'em in their seats?'

'You think it's a joke?'

'If you call it a joke for a young girl to be coy.'

'Coy?'

'What's the thirtyfirst of February but a sort of super Leap

Year, quadruple Leap Year or something? But how did it go with ropy Raper and birdseye Bagseed?'

Still looking at the calendar, Anderson said: 'We lost the account.'

Lessing's small mouth rounded into an O of surprise. 'Do the big boys know?'

'Not yet.'

'They won't be pleased.'

With an effort Anderson stopped looking at the calendar and looked instead at Lessing. 'Rev's always said it was a pain in the neck.'

'Saying's saying and losing's losing. A twentyfive-thousand-pound pain in the neck is worth having. But it's your baby, not mine. Only I've got some bad news, too. Rev's done you in the eye over Crunchy-Munch. He produced a scheme of his own at the meeting and pushed it through against our two ideas. Ghastly stuff. "The kind of sweet that mother used to make." Two curly-headed children and a good brawny housewife wiping her hands on her apron. VV fell for it like a ton of bricks. Did you know Rev was working out a scheme of his own?' Anderson shook his head. 'It's a dirty trick,' Lessing said indignantly. 'How's Hey Presto?'

'It's made my face stiff,' Anderson said and then broke off. 'There's Jean.' He was out of his chair and at the door. Jean Lightley came in, panting slightly. Anderson pointed to the chromium desk calendar. 'Did you put that on my desk, Jean?'

'Oh *no*.'

'Do you know who did put it there?'

She stared at him nervously, and blushed. 'I thought you did, Mr Anderson. Because you didn't like the other one, did you? So I thought you might have bought a chromium one because you liked it better. It was on the desk when you came in this morning.'

'And you didn't put it to that date.'

'Oh *no*, Mr Anderson.' She crimsoned and fled. Anderson turned to Lessing. 'You see.'

'So you've got an unknown admirer. Should you worry? You've got other things to worry about, believe me.'

'What do you mean?'

Lessing's gaze seemed innocent of duplicity. 'I'd be worrying about Kiddy Modes and Crunchy-Munch and Rev if I were you.'

The door opened, and Wyvern's narrow head appeared. 'Comintern's still in session. It's a general salary cut, never a doubt of it. Those who stay put will be getting a rise. Coming for a drink?'

The telephone rang. Anderson picked it up. The switchboard girl said: 'I've been calling and calling, but you were out. Mrs Fletchley will be in Riley's Long Bar at a quarter to one if you can manage that. She said be sure and let you know.'

Anderson put down the receiver and said: 'I've got a date.' He arranged with VV's secretary to see VV at half past two, and went out. As he passed through the swing doors he heard feet in the corridor, and the sound of the directors' voices, loud with self-congratulation. Then the doors sighed behind him. In the street outside he cannoned into a little man who was bouncing along in a shuffling two-step, head down, wagging one finger in the air. As they hit each other Anderson distinctly heard the little man say: 'Three four *five* six, three four *five* six.' After they had collided the little man staggered away, said 'Sorry,' and resumed counting. He ran past Anderson into the building.

Within two minutes Anderson had forgotten the little man. He was convinced that he would learn something important, something that would destroy the whole nonsensical web in which he was trapped like a fly in treacle, when he met Elaine Fletchley.

## IV

Riley's Long Bar was crowded, but Elaine Fletchley was not in
the crowd. Anderson bought a beer and settled in to wait. After
a quarter of an hour and two beers he asked the barmaid
whether she had any message for him. The barmaid clicked her
fingers. It had gone completely out of her head that Mrs Fletchley had telephoned to say that she had to take a couple of clients
to El Vino's. Could Mr Anderson join her there? Anderson
went to El Vino's, where a bland blond barman told him that
Mrs Fletchley had left a few minutes ago, leaving a message
that she would be lunching at the Chinese restaurant in Frith
Street, and that Mr Anderson should join her there. There is
no Chinese restaurant in Frith Street, so that obviously somebody had made a mistake. Anderson tried the Shanghai restaurant in Greek Street, Ley-On's and Maxims in Wardour
Street, the Hong-Kong in Shaftesbury Avenue, Shaffi's in Ger-
rard Street. He looked in the French pub, the Swiss pub, the
Scotch House and the Irish House. He did not find Elaine
Fletchley. The skin of his face felt as tight as a lampshade.

## V

Molly O'Rourke, wearing a bottle-green coat and skirt with a
grey blouse and a red tie, stood outside the door of her room.
She caught hold of Anderson by the sleeve and said 'Hey.' He
looked at his watch. 'Ten minutes,' he said. 'I've got to see VV.'
They went in the room. She shut the door and stood against it,
staring at him. 'Men,' she said, 'aren't they all the bloody same!
You give them all you've got; they take it without saying thank
you, and leave without saying goodbye.'

'What?'

'I'm not a floozie, Andy, you know that. They all think I'm
hard-boiled, but I'm not a floozie, though God knows I've been

unlucky in my men. You've no right to treat me this way, Andy.'
A tear dropped off her cheek and splashed to the coloured chart
on her desk. A little yellow ran where the tear had dropped. 'I
gave myself to you.'

'Don't be ridiculous, Molly.'

'All right.' She sniffed and stopped crying. A tear hung like
an icicle on the end of her long white nose and then dropped,
emasculating a little block of red on the chart. 'This kind of
thing's no good, is it? not what men go for at all – I know that.
Aren't you going to see me again, Andy?'

'What am I doing now?'

'Oh, you know what I mean. What about tonight? Busy, I
suppose? And tomorrow night, and the night after tomorrow?
I'm a fool to ask, I know that. Don't bother to lie to me. And
a fool to buy you a present. You haven't even noticed it.'

'What present?'

'A bloody little desk calendar.'

'Desk calendar.' He began to laugh, but the laughter came
out in choking hiccoughs.

'Stinking little chromium thing. Saw you'd got rid of your
other one. I put it on your desk this morning. What's funny
about it?'

'You put it on the desk.' Anderson went on laughing until
he remembered. 'What about the date? What date did you put
on it?'

'Why the right bloody date of course, today's date, the
twentyeighth of February.'

'You're sure of that? You're sure you didn't have a little
joke?' He took hold of her arm. 'Didn't you have a little joke
with me and put the date of the calendar at the thirtyfirst of
February?'

'The thirtyfirst of February?' She glared at him in astonishment. 'Why, there's no such date.'

VV sat tapping his desk with a paper knife. His look was friendly
but reserved, and a little sad. His magnetism was flowing at only
about a quarter strength. 'You wanted to see me, Andy.'

Anderson explained about Kiddy Modes. As he explained and showed VV the letter terminating the contract he felt the absurdity of his own words. A year ago, a month ago, what he was saying would have made sense; today it was merely ridiculous. And what was ridiculous, he vaguely realized, was not simply agitation about losing Kiddy Modes' account, but the whole social structure propped by advertising campaigns and board meetings. This, he wanted to say to the sad gnome who sat opposite him tapping rhythmically at the desk, this is not reality as I know it, obscene and raw. Reality, Anderson wanted to say, is what I have experienced in the last few days and am enduring now; reality is the cellar stairs, the hidden diary, the changing expressions on a policeman's face, the life torn in ribbons. Reality is the fourteen-year-old red-haired seducer slipping into her stepfather's arms, the disastrous disgust with the world and herself in Mrs Vincent's thin face. And if that vivid recollection of VV, his face red with suppressed desire, was true, the figure opposite him now who held the power of rebuke or praise was a preposterous mask; if the disordered flat, the open drawer, the stolen diary, were real, this solemn recitation of the insignificant must be a dream. Now, indeed, he saw with all the minuteness of a dream the yellow pattern on the green curtains that hung before the window, the hairs sprouting richly from VV's nose and ears. He stopped talking; and, like an actor taking up his cue, VV began. What was he saying? Anderson knew that the words must be important. He tried hard to listen, and even to make apposite replies; but he was all the time aware that what was said and done here could have no effect upon a fate already decided, though still imperfectly known. Snatches of speech came through to him. *Last night*, he heard, *last night* – what did that mean? – and *unfortunate incident* – could that refer to the burglary of his flat? But of course – the realization was delayed, but emerged finally – VV was saying that he had meant to discuss Anderson's position last night, but hadn't done so because of the trouble at dinner. *Holiday* – well, that was plain enough.

'I don't feel inclined to take a holiday,' Anderson said firmly.

He added, with a feeling of rich absurdity: 'I have a job of work to do here.' He pointed to his face. 'Hey Presto!' A joke! But his face felt as though it might crack if he bent it in a smile, and VV's resigned sorrow did not change. His expression became, if possible, more serious as he picked up the telephone and spoke inaudible words. They sat staring at each other. Supposing, Anderson thought, that I said: 'Let us talk about something important. Tell me, did you sleep with your stepdaughter last night?' Would that open for both of us the floodgates of confession, should we be able at last to speak honestly with each other, meet face to naked face? But he knew that the alien words would never be permitted to come through in true simplicity by the censor operating in VV's mind, that they would emerge as something quite different from what was intended, as an insult or an attempt at blackmail. And would they not, after all, be that in a sense?

Two figures had crept into the room. How had they done so without Anderson's knowledge? Creeping up behind my back, he thought indignantly; and it was literally true that anybody who entered the room must have done so behind his back, because the chair in which he sat had its back to the door. But it was still a dirty trick that these two grotesques, made in the shapes of Reverton and Pile, should have sneaked in on tiptoe as they must have done. Now they sat, solemn as statesmen pondering the fate of Empire in an old *Punch* cartoon, sadder even than VV, mutes at a funeral. But at least their lips were not sealed. The mouths of these Charlie McCarthy characters opened and shut. *Holiday, holiday*, Anderson heard. Surely he had made his position clear? He leaned forward and said again, very slowly: 'I don't want to take a holiday.'

The dummies shrugged, inimitably lifelike. VV made a long speech. VV was an intelligent man, a man who could tell a Dover sole from a packet of crisps. Perhaps he would tell the dummies about his stepdaughter? But he talked instead about Kiddy Modes. Anderson shut off, as it were, the power current necessary to make connection with the words, and stared at the complicated whorls of smoke rising from Reverton's pipe. While

VV talked the faces of the marionettes grew sadder and sadder. *Makes no difference*, VV said. Anderson could not forbear a smile for they were echoing, a good while afterwards, his own thought. It made no difference, absolutely none, whether they lost this account or all their accounts. Was that not what was meant? Perhaps not, for a moment later, without intending to eavesdrop, he heard another connected phrase: 'Extended leave on half-pay.' And then – it brought, almost, tears to his eyes – 'Sympathy.' Ah, sympathy! What errors, casual injustices, deliberate villainies, are covered by thy name!

Now VV had finished speaking, and one of the marionettes would no doubt begin. But instead they waited for him, they deferred to him almost, they seemed to seek his opinion on the nonsense VV had been talking. He felt inclined to let them have it, to pepper these three stuffed or mechanical figures from the unworld of dream with a few rounds from the popgun of his private knowledge. *Pile, old boy, what's your sex classification in Melian Street? VV, whose room did you sleep in last night? Who have you laid the finger on now for a judicious spot of emotional blackmail, Rev, do tell.* Or something simpler, something friendly, a piece of personal exhibitionism which might provoke the desired Buchmanite reaction. *Gentlemen – half magnetizing, half-baked geniuses of the half-world – here it is, what you've been waiting for, the unadmitted revelations of my whole inner life. Listen, and you shall hear.*

There were the words, shiningly visible. Had they, in fact, been uttered? Looking round foxily at the three faces set in their stiff masks of regret, Anderson decided that they had not. It was better perhaps that they should stay unuttered in the presence of these dummies. Sinking back into the comfortable chair provided for him the prisoner at the bar smiled, waved a hand, refused to plead. His judges pronounced sentence. Anderson, now physically and emotionally limp, lounging in his chair with almost insulting ease, felt the immediate slackening of tension as he abandoned momentarily the world of reality. The sound track came back; and like a corpse miraculously granted the power of hearing, he listened to the elegies read at his graveside.

It was not, said good old Rev, removing his pipe from his mouth as a token of respect to the dead, it was not, Lord knew, that any of them wanted to lose old Andy. The copy lads who worked with him had always liked Andy, the production boys liked Andy, the Studio liked Andy, and – last and no doubt least important – the Board liked Andy. He had been a grand team man, constructive, keen, tireless, a man who was on the job twentyfour hours a day. And Rev spoke with very special feeling, he said, about the question of team spirit, because he had been one of the boys himself not so long ago. He knew the difference between working with an awkward and with a decent copy chief. He would like to say about Andy that Andy had always played the game with everybody. But for the last few months, Rev was bound to say, Andy's work hadn't been what it was. It had been efficient all right – Andy was never less than efficient – but it had somehow lacked the spark. He wouldn't enumerate all the little points he'd checked up on and worried about, Rev said, but Andy would remember them. He'd tried to take some of the work off Andy's shoulders, but there it was – the dear chap was just a glutton for work, and was just the least bit huffy if you suggested he might be overdoing it. And then less than a month ago old Andy had taken just about the hardest knock a man could take. Since then his work – Rev pursed his lips, looked down at his pipe, shook a sad head – it was better to draw a veil. He'd just like to say, though, how pleased he was that Andy was being given this period of six months off duty. Beyond that time, of course, they couldn't say anything, on either side. If he felt like coming back afterwards, Rev would be the first to welcome a good fellow, and a great team man, back into the organization.

And now Pile, that hard-eyed dry little old man, L. E. G. Pile, cast his handful of earth upon the grave, addressing himself as he did so to the virtues of that conspicuously English institution, family life. Who would have supposed that the old man had so much sentiment in him? For his voice quavered, or at least Anderson thought with too much flippancy, semi-quavered, as he told what his own family had meant to him, bustling Mrs Pile and the four little Piles, four little kiddies to have their napkins changed, their mouths filled, their clothes put on (more and more clothes put on, larger and larger meals eaten), their school fees paid – the two others fidgeted, but Anderson listened with the closest attention as old dry Mr Pile told how the institution of the family had helped to preserve him from fornication, drunkenness and extravagance. Anderson, said Mr Pile, had not been granted, alas, the blessing of a family. Might he be forgiven for discovering in the absence of the infant's cry the lack of that inspiring energizing influence that alone could bring a man unharmed through the valley of the shadow of death. (Who would have thought the old man had so much poetry in him?) They had seen and known this friend of theirs for years, they had valued Anderson's advice and respected – nay, in his own case, been dazzled by – his intellect. His departure from them, unavoidable as it was by the keen standards of business ethics and efficiency to which Anderson would be the first to adhere, was nevertheless a tragedy. Might he be forgiven for saying, as he wished Anderson Godspeed and good luck, that it was a family tragedy?

A family tragedy? Anderson saw the long pants, the thin ruffled hair, the goatish expression changing to one of annoyance. Aren't all tragedies family tragedies? he heard himself asking. But these words, like the others, remained unspoken.

With the corpse now firmly underground, VV judged it safe to attempt a little act of resurrection – nothing spectacular, nothing serious, a mere gesture to placate whatever gods may be, gods who might think that full justice had not been done to Anderson. This was not to be looked on, VV then cried with a ghastly joviality not meant to convince, this was not to be looked on as a parting. Pull not those long faces. Say au revoir but not goodbye. Andy did not want a holiday – very well, then, he need not take a holiday. Let him take a rest cure, go to some little place where he would be well looked after. Let him return in six months' time a new man, a well man, not disturbed any more by these terrible calendars that changed their dates (oh yes, VV injected parenthetically, *that* story is all round the firm and we can't ignore such things, my boy). Let him come back to us then and – VV added with a self-conscious drop from grand to commonplace – we shall be pleased to have a chat.

There was silence. The judge-executioners had done their work, and now they stared at him. Anderson returned their looks with a suitably dead gaze. Quietly, conscious of irreverence, Reverton coughed, and VV was startled into action. The question then arose, he said, of Andy's – we are bound to use the word – successor. We thought at one time of promoting young Lessing –

Good old Rev took his pipe out of his mouth to say: But you told me yourself yesterday that people didn't get on with him.

And we felt, pronounced Pile, that while excellent at his present work, he might be weighed down by a position of too much responsibility. But we have been fortunate enough to find a really excellent executive type –

A man with a distinct personality, said VV.

A friendly type, Rev remarked, and with good connections.

A man with a keen administrative sense, added Pile, whose name is Blythe-Pountney.

VV rang a bell. A man came in. Andy my boy, said VV, meet Mr Percival Blythe-Pountney. Mr Blythe-Pountney, Mr Anderson.

Anderson had seen Percival Blythe-Pountney before. He had then been walking along, wagging a finger in the air and saying: Three four *five* six. Now the little man stuck out a hand, looking both guilty and sly. Anderson took it, and burst out laughing. The laughter, uncontrollable as last night's laughter, rocked him so that he had to lean against the wall. Mr Blythe-Pountney looked modestly, but still slyly, at the floor, but three pairs of eyes stared at Anderson with frozen disapproval. There is, after all, no return from the dead.

# VI

There is no return. But was it not possible, Anderson thought again, that the whole thing was a dream? At times during the afternoon he thought so, said to himself: It is quite impossible that I should be showing this man Blythe-Pountney the progress of my accounts, introducing him to the Production Department, the Space Department, to Studio, Research, Vouchers, Accounts, Dispatch. Blythe-Pountney, at first accompanied by Rev, but later left entirely in Anderson's hands, did no more number counting or finger wagging. He developed during the afternoon, however, a nervous tic which caused him to wink prodigiously at awkward moments, and his limb movements were poorly articulated. An arm, moving in a wild unnecessary semicircle, would now and again thud against Anderson's body, or a flying elbow be dug suddenly into his side. Blythe-Pountney seemed able to control these unexpected thrusts in the presence of women, but he gave Wyvern a great dig in the stomach and flicked the manager of the Space Department lightly across the face with his hand. His two-step overcame him at the oddest times and places. He might run a step or two down the corridor, or break into a brisk foot tapping while details of space bookings and insertions were being explained to him. It was difficult, certainly, to believe in Blythe-Pountney as a representative of reality.

The news, nevertheless, had to be broken. Anderson broke it, gently and carefully, like eggs into a basin. 'I'm taking a long holiday,' he said, and added with what he hoped was an obvious note of irony, 'At the directors' request.' When he told Lessing the copywriter shook his head, eyes grave behind his hornrims. 'Bad luck,' he said. 'Kiddy Modes?'

'No,' Anderson answered. 'Life. The missing wail in the nursery.' Lessing looked puzzled. 'This is Blythe-Pountney, who is taking over from me.' Blythe-Pountney twitched, winked and shuffled. Greatorex was brought from his corner desk and introduced. 'Are you leaving us for good, Mr Anderson?' he asked.

'For good or ill. Never be surprised by sudden departures in the world of advertising, Greatorex.'

Blythe-Pountney said to Lessing: 'You'll be working for me on that – um, ah – new account, won't you? Hey Presto. Big stuff. I like it. Scope for ideas. Let me see what you've done on Monday.'

'With you.'

'What's that? What's that?' Blythe-Pountney winked.

'Andy and I work with each other.'

Blythe-Pountney twitched. 'That's what I said.'

'The word is *with*, not *for*.'

'Oh.' Twitch and two-step. 'Oh yes. Jolly good. Yes, I see.' A gargantuan wink. 'With, not for. Yes, I see your point.'

In the studio Wyvern carefully wiped off paint and took the hand offered by Blythe-Pountney with an accompanying two-step. Wyvern said nothing at all, but Blythe-Pountney seemed hardly to notice silence. He stuck his nose into the rough layouts Wyvern was making for Hey Presto, was enthusiastic about some designs for labels that had already been rejected by a client, pinched the arm of a girl working as apprentice in the studio, and criticized a photographic montage of buildings which was being pieced together for a construction company. 'Modernistic stuff, eh, modernistic. Very interesting. Like it, do you? Can't say I do myself. Simple, strong, vital, that's what I find clients generally like. Just like the girls,' he said with a wink and a sudden dig of his elbow at Wyvern. 'Most interesting place in an advertising agency is the studio, I always say. Like to spend all my time in it. Got some layout ideas myself, you know, full of ideas. Be bringing them down to you; you'll be seeing a lot of me. 'Bye till Monday.' Blythe-Pountney two-stepped forward, grasped Wyvern's hand, winked and two-stepped away. Anderson said: 'I'll be in tomorrow, Jack, to clear up and say goodbye.' Wyvern stook, hands on hips, looking after them.

When Blythe-Pountney had gone Anderson sat in his office, staring at the diminishing finger of sunlight on the carpet. His mind had gone back, for no obvious reason, to the day in his boyhood when, coming downstairs to breakfast, he had seen by his mother's plate the salmon-pink writing-paper and recognized Ethel's hand. His mother had wept, shouted, screamed at him; but when she knew that Ethel was going to have a baby shouts and screams were replaced by gentle wheedling. 'You don't really want to marry her, do you, dear? A girl of that class. You've made a mistake, but we must see if you can't patch it up, so that you can wait until Miss Right comes along.' Patching-up meant the last letter in the salmon-pink envelope to say that Ethel had gone to Bradford, but what else did it mean? His father and mother had spoken of the affair thereafter only as a narrow escape from danger, a trap which through their clever-ness had never, quite, been sprung. But what had happened to Ethel? He could recall nothing of her but a nervous giggle, employed upon the most inappropriate occasions. On the common under the bushes Ethel had giggled and giggled, quite unable to control herself. She remained as a giggle and a salmon-pink envelope, but what had happened to the seed within her? Had it been allowed to live? Was a child of his loins, a young man or woman, now talking with Bradford accent, training as an engineer or student of ballet? How astonishing that in all these years he had never thought of Ethel Smith and of their child. One brings down the curtain, Anderson thought, and never looks behind it. And why was he looking behind it now? Suppose the seed exterminated, might one say that murder had been done when Ethel was sent to Bradford?

The thin beam of sunlight had vanished when, looking up, he saw Reverton standing, pipe in mouth, smiling a little ruefully. Vincent, Reverton, Wyvern, Lessing, which of them gave my wife his – blessing? 'I've come to say goodbye,' Reverton said, with such finality in his voice that Anderson was startled.

'Goodbye?'

'I shan't be in tomorrow. Going down to see Crunchy-Munch. I was sorry to have to butt in with my own ideas there, but you know how it is sometimes. Anyway, it's over now. Andy, it's all for the best, believe me. It may be only temporary.' A far-away look came into Reverton's eyes. 'We've had some good times together. I'll miss you, Andy. We've been a great team, but I've got the firm to think of. We must all think of the firm. Frankly, I've had a feeling lately that you haven't really been – believing in your work.' Tribute had been paid to sentiment. Reverton took the pipe from his mouth, looked at it, tapped it on his heel. 'You won't forget the Hey Presto when you come in tomorrow, will you? Divenga rang up about it today. As a matter of fact, there's some snag.'

'Snag?'

Reverton was looking hard at his pipe. 'This particular sample may not be absolutely suitable for every type of skin. He doesn't want us to go on using it. Seems it contains some substance which may irritate some delicate white skins, though it's quite all right for others. They're sending over other samples which have gone through some new refining process. They're experimenting all the time, you know that.' Reverton paused, apparently expectant of a reply. When he did not get one he said again: 'You won't forget to bring it back tomorrow. I shouldn't go on using it.'

'I won't forget.'

'No hard feelings, Andy.'

There should be hard feelings, Anderson thought, but in fact there are no feelings at all, nothing but numbness and a memory of Ethel Smith. 'No hard feelings.'

'Sure you're all right?'

'Perfectly.'

'Well.' Reverton tucked away the pipe, shot out his muscular, reliable hand. 'Goodbye Andy, and good luck.'

'Goodbye.'

The afternoon grew darker. Anderson sat at the desk while spots of light appeared in the offices visible through the window. At last he got up, put on his hat and raincoat and reached the door. There he switched on the light and stood looking at the desk still littered with papers, the green carpet, the hatstand; aspects of a dead life. He said aloud, not knowing what he meant: 'It won't do.' As he walked away from the office the telephone was ringing. It seemed somehow to be a comment on his career.

# VII

The sense of impending event, awful in its significance, disastrous in its effect, that hung over Anderson was accompanied by a strange numbness and emptiness. He was frightened at the thought of return to his flat; the disordered room, the empty drawer, the dirty sink, the Inspector's presence hanging about the place like his cigar smoke, were things that moved through his numbness to cause irrational apprehension. It was with a sense that he had absolutely nothing to do but wait, combined with a contradictory feeling that some kind of action was demanded of him, that Anderson turned into the *Stag* after leaving the office. There, sitting in one of the partitioned alcoves, hat on the back of head, sat Wyvern. He pointed a finger at Anderson.

'Bang bang bang, so they got you. The gipsy's warning was right. Let me set them up. Cheers. Let me guess what my old pal Rev said to you. He said: Goodbye Andy, it's been lovely knowing you; if I were a crocodile I'd weep; I'm sorry, but you've stopped believing in your work. Right?'

'Not far wrong.'

'I know I'm not far wrong. Don't say I didn't warn you. But why did they fall for St Vitus? Because of his old school tie? He's no advertising man; he just stocks a nice line of bull. Anybody with half an eye can see that. Well, he'd better not come playing round in my department or he'll be out on his ear.'

'Another drink.'

'Thanks, mine's a Bass. It's a damned shame the way they've treated you. It is the boot, isn't it? Rev said you were taking a long rest, and might not come back.'

'I shan't come back.'

Wyvern held his long nose with two fingers. 'When you smell stinking fish, there you smell advertising. That's my view of the profession.'

'There's nothing like that to it,' Anderson said wearily. 'They've got as much right to get rid of me as I've got to leave them. I don't complain.'

'Then you bloody well should complain. When I think of those complacent bastards sitting there and then think of my old mother – ' Wyvern tilted his glass and took a long drink. 'Though from what they tell me you've been a bit off the beam lately. I mean, old boy, magic calendars and letters flying about to the wrong people – they just won't do.'

'Who told you?'

'My ear is to the ground.' Wyvern cupped one ear. 'What are you going to do for that little girl?'

'Jean Lightley, do you mean?'

'Jean Lightley.' Wyvern made a noise. 'I mean Molly.'

'I had forgotten about Molly.'

'Ah, there you are. But she hasn't forgotten about you. She wants you, Andy.'

Anderson thought of the long chalky nose, the ride in the taxicab and the tears staining the little squares of colour. He said flatly: 'But I don't want her.'

'Why did you make her think you did, then? Why did you sleep with her?' Anderson stared in astonishment at the face stuck forward indignantly into his own. 'Hell, man, everybody knows it. You've only got to look at her to see the difference.'

'You can't see a difference,' Anderson said mechanically. He was looking at a hat which lay on a table by one of the alcoves opposite. The hat was a bowler, rather old but quite respectable. A coat, beside it, was dark blue. The occupants of the alcove were invisible, but it seemed to Anderson that he knew both hat and coat.

'Shall I tell you the trouble with you? I feel all the sympathy in the world with you, the dirty way you've been treated, but shall I tell you the trouble with you? Self-centred, you're too damned self-centred, Andy. Suppose we were all like that? Take me and my mother now, what do you think happened the other night? I was just going out – '

A hand, holding a glass of beer, was visible outside the partition. The beer was placed upon the table by the hat. Before the hand was withdrawn Anderson saw the thick, hairy wrist. At the same time he heard a laugh, light and boyish. The laugh, like the overcoat, belonged to Greatorex. Anderson stood up suddenly and knocked over the table. Beer flowed over the floor and on to Wyvern's lap. 'Sorry,' Anderson said. 'Sorry.' He got out of the alcove and ran from the pub without looking into the alcove opposite.

# VIII

Trafalgar Square, Leicester Square, Piccadilly, Shaftesbury Avenue, Charing Cross Road. Neon signs flashed at him in coloured lights messages which had a desperate depth of meaning. BOVRIL – BOVRIL – BOVRIL, said the lights in Trafalgar Square, where the fountains played excitingly their song of sexual aspiration. In Leicester Square the houses of pleasure invited him, Gable and Grable, Garbo and Harpo, Tracy and Lamarr. In Piccadilly Circus a sign said excitingly *Drain it to the last drop*. Ah, to belong again to the world of Bovril and Moussec, to know and love the realities of Gable and Grable, to be unconfused by the agonies of choice. *Reality*, said Dr Johnson, leaning forward and pinching one elegant thigh with his rude fingers, *Here is reality, sir. Thus I confute you*. Oh, Anderson cried, wandering among the civilization of the Corner House and the Milk Bar, jostling gum-chewing girls, passing the contraceptive doorways of chemists – oh to believe that such a visible world exists in its ideal simplicity; a world away from the disordered flat, the anonymous letter, the unseen figures in the alcove. He stopped outside a cinema which said MORE BRUTAL BENNY – MORE LUSCIOUS LUCY – FIERCER AND FRANKER THAN EVER. Lucy Lalange presented an expanse of thigh ten feet high, Brutal Benny Baily stood snarling by her side. Anderson passed over his pieces of silver and went inside.

Within the air was warm, delicious; he shivered with ecstacy in his thin raincoat; his shoes sunk in rubbery pile. From the walls, as an epauletted attendant conducted him towards Mecca, looked down benevolently the gods whose names were music, whose words were law, whose look was love – Astair, Iturbi, Goodman, Dorsey, Bogart, Cagney, Scott and Ladd, Turner, Stanwyck, Lockwood, Bergmann. Under different names from those given them at birth, serenely fixed in one attitude, displaying for ever a smile or a fist, the gods watched the progress of this neophyte in the service of reality.

Upon the screen, when Anderson first saw it, enormous faces met, blonde and dark hair mingled, Benny Baily's voice, rich, warm, American, said to Lucy Lalange *Everything is going to be all right.* But everything was not all right. The music, emphatically discordant, recorded the progress of Benny Baily, sitting grimly at the steering-wheel of a long lean car. Rain drove at the windscreen, scenery slipped by, Benny stared ahead, moving the steering-wheel rapidly from time to time as the car shaved others by the width of a coat of paint. Round and round, ceaselessly, Benny's jaw moved, masticating the juice of the healing gum. Now a barrier had been placed across the road to stop him – poof, he was through it without so much as a batted eyelid, his jaws moving a little faster to indicate strain. And now a rapid patter of shots came from behind bushes, the windscreen glass splintered, Benny drew a revolver from under his armpit. Crack, crack, crack through the car window and the villain, his face distorted ludicrously, staggered and fell. Round a hairpin bend – and far, far below another car was visible racing along the ribbon of road. For a moment Benny stopped chewing.

But back in the city two men had come for Lucy Lalange. Flashing badges beneath their coat lapels, they pushed her into a car and drove away. Pug-nosed, cauliflower-eared, hard-lipped, squint-eyed, they were not the cops Lucy in her sophisticated innocence had taken them for, but gangsters. Out of the car and through a back door they hustled her (a quick cut revealed the front of the building as an exclusive niterie), and into a room containing a safe, a settee, and a carpet. In this room a thinly moustached man sat picking his teeth.

Now Benny's jaws were at work again. His long greyhound of a car nosed its way round bends, skidded with two wheels the edge of precipices, ate up the shiny road. Slowly, and then quickly, it gained on the other car whose occupant, weak and shifty-eyed, looked nervously back at overtaking Nemesis. Shifty turns the car into a side road and scrambles down a hillside, clinging to bushes with one hand, holding in the other a bag. But Benny is after him, now he is on him, he grasps Shifty round the neck. Shifty struggles, however, writhes and writhes, brings up his knees to a vital part. Benny staggers, falls to his knees, drops to the ground, and Shifty draws back his foot for a kick that will send Benny half a mile down the hillside to the rocks below. We see the look of pleasure on Shifty's face, cut to the foot in its heavy steel-tipped boot drawn back to kick, cut back to see dismay replace Shifty's gloating expression. Benny has his teeth sunk deep into Shifty's calf, Benny has him down, Benny gives Shifty's neck one quick backhand cut with the heel of his hand. Shifty's neck is broken, head hangs sideways, tongue drops out. He is no good any more. Benny pitches him down on to the rocks, looks in the bag, nods to show that the bonds or jewels are still there and says reflectively: 'Where's my gum?' The audience laughs, Benny finds his gum and starts chewing again.

(Anderson became aware of a pressure against his left leg. Without looking away from the screen he pressed back.)

Back in the gangster's office Lucy Lalange has been tied up. She is required to tell something or do something; it is not clear which. It is abundantly clear, however, that she refuses. Her head shakes from side to side, her great eyes roll about in terror. Pug-nose One, thin-lipped, hits her across the face, quickly back and forth. The chief goes on picking his teeth. Pug-nose Two, slobber-mouthed, looks on disgustedly, saying: *Aw, chief, gimme a chance – why don't you gimme a chance?*

(A hand found Anderson's hand. Pointed nails dug into his palm).

In police headquarters the superintendent puts down the telephone. A car is out, two cars, three cars, a whole fleet of cars screaming along the road. The gangster chief nods to Pug-nose Two, who lights a gas-ring, chuckling. Benny, looking at the loot, has somehow discovered the gang chief's complicity. Jaws moving faster than ever, he is on his way back. Quick cuts show Lucy's rolling eyes, the police cars racing, Pug-nose Two heating curious instruments over the gas flame, Benny racing and chewing, the gangster chief picking his teeth.

(The hand moved up Anderson's arm, nails tearing at the skin. A foot found his foot.)

The gang chief stops picking his teeth, walks over to Lucy, looks at the nails on her hand, sighs and motions to Pug-nose Two. Lucy rolls about like a sick cow, Benny arrives at the back door. The police draw up in the front. Pug-nose Two advances on Lucy, drooling a little.

(A heel dug at the side of Anderson's leg, stripping away it seemed the flesh.)

Benny breaks down the back door, rushes up the stairs and into the room. He kicks Pug-nose One in the stomach and jumps on his hand as it reaches for a gun, catches Pug-nose Two around the neck and throws him towards the gang chief, who has drawn his own gun. The gang chief's shots go through Pug-nose Two who is still holding his instruments of torture. Enraged, Pug-nose Two lurches forward against the gang chief pressing him against the wall, pushing the hot irons into his eyes. The gang chief screams.

(Hand and leg were withdrawn. Anderson felt his wrist tenderly.)

And then the formalities: the police, congratulations, bag handed over, Pug-nose One confessing, Pug-nose Two dead, the gang chief blinded. Another close-up of the dark head and the fair. Benny pushes his gum to the side of his cheek and winks. Lucy, her eyes cast down in a maidenly manner, looks up suddenly and winks, too. Curtain.

The lights went up. Anderson turned to his left. There he saw, with a shock of surprise almost equal to that given him by the sight of a bowler hat and an overcoat in the *Stag*, a small suburban woman in her late forties. She wore horn-rimmed glasses and had on no lipstick and very little powder. Her dark brown coat was dowdy. As Anderson stared at her unbelievingly she turned to him full face for a moment and bestowed upon him a mild, dull gaze. This failure of correspondence between the visible and the imagined struck Anderson most unpleasantly. He got up hurriedly and went out.

As he was crossing the rubber floor of the foyer he heard his name called: 'Andy.' An obscure connection with the incident in the cinema made him walk on faster. 'Andy, Andy." He recognized the voice, and turned.

Elaine Fletchley advanced towards him, swinging a little umbrella in one hand, the other resting lightly on the arm of a young and fierce-looking Guards officer. 'At last, Andy. Wherever did you get to at lunch?'

'I had an international lunch in several Chinese restaurants. They told me to look for you there in El Vino's.'

'Not Chinese, darling – *Turkish*. Bonzo was with me, and we waited and waited. He didn't like it.' She patted the stiff Guards arm. 'This is Bonzo. He's a good dog.' Bonzo growled unintelligibly. 'Andy, I've got to talk to you. Bonzo darling, you must go.' The guardsman growled again. 'Now, don't be silly. Andy and I have got some business to do, that's all. Oh, I haven't introduced you. Bonzo, meet Andy. Andy, meet Bonzo. Now you're friends.'

Anderson's hand felt as though it had passed under a steam roller. Elaine Fletchley pinched her lip. 'Bonzo, go home and collect the baggage. I'll meet you at the station in half an hour. If you've been a good dog I'll give you a biscuit.' The guardsman growled again, but the growl was hesitant. Under the great peaked cap his face was round, pink and immature. She swung the umbrella lightly against his buttocks. 'Go on, go on, don't be a foolish Bonzo.' The guardsman growled again. 'I shall be all right. I've known Andy for years.' The guardsman raised a hand to the peaked cap in a half-salute, about-turned and strode away, moving with the precision of a mechanical toy. Elaine watched admiringly until he had turned a corner. 'What do you think?' she said. 'Not very intelligent, but he has such beautiful shoulders.'

'We were going to talk.'

'My God yes, we must talk. I've wanted to find you all week, Andy. Where have you been hiding yourself? And where shall we go? Let's go to the Corner House; it's handy and I've got to be quick. Did you like the film?'

'Not much.'

'It gets you where you live, I think. At least, it got Bonzo. He was mad about it. We're going to get married.'

'Married!' Anderson said incredulously.

'I'm not married to Fletch, you know. We never got that far. That's why he's so madly jealous, jealous of everybody you know, jealous of you even. That's half of the trouble, I think.'

'Jealous of me. But he hadn't any cause.'

'Since when do you need a cause to be jealous?'

'What do you mean half of the trouble?'

'I'll tell you when we sit down.' Elaine trotted along with neat, accurate steps. She was a small woman of thirtyfive who looked as if she were made of brass. Bright yellow hair was curled in great coils about her ears, her coat was richly yellow, and brass buckles gleamed on her shoes. These were outward manifestations; but her voice and manner also were hard, bright and shining. They attained a gloss that might be mistaken for wit, as her face achieved through cosmetics a freshness that might be taken for youth.

They sat with coffees at a check-clothed table. She stirred with a spoon and said: 'I hate that policeman. He frightens me.' Quite irrelevantly she added: 'Bonzo comes of good family, you know. He's the Honourable Roderick Manly. And he suspects because of Fletch. He's a swine, that man. He knows about Bonzo and he couldn't get back at him, so he got back at you. It's not my fault, Andy, honest to God I had nothing to do with it.'

'To do with what?'

Elaine rarely listened to what other people were saying. 'So now that policeman suspects.'

'Suspects what?' Anderson asked with extraordinary patience. 'What does he suspect, Elaine?'

'He suspects you.' Anderson moved. 'Don't tell me, Andy, I don't want to know anything about it. I don't want to be mixed up. I've done the best I can.' She added absently: 'He came to see me.'

'Who?'

'The policeman, of course. He came to the office and told me about it.'

'He came to the office,' Anderson repeated dully. 'And told you. Told you what?'

'About the letters, the anonymous letters. Fletch sent them to the police.'

'Fletch sent them.' He gasped. Why had he not realized it before? Why had he not understood Fletchley's own hints and the Inspector's questions about an enemy? 'But why?'

'Don't ask me why. He's not sane, that man. I tell you, he's crazy with jealousy. He admitted sending them as soon as they asked him. But that's not all. He told them about the switch.'

'What about the switch?'

Elaine Fletchley was busy stirring her coffee. This is the revelation, Anderson thought; when she has told me what she knows all my questions will be answered. 'You told them,' she said slowly, 'about the switch being fused. So that Val fell downstairs.'

'Yes.'

'That was at a quarter to eight.'

'Yes.'

'Fletch told them he went into the cellar at half past seven and the light was working all right then. Fletch said he hadn't offered the evidence at the inquest because he hadn't realized it was important. So then they came and asked me.'

'Asked you?' Anderson found himself simply unable to grasp the meaning of all this. 'Asked you what?'

'If we were having an affair, you and me. I told them no.'
Flatly she said: 'I don't think they believed me.'

Suddenly she said: 'What's the matter with your face? It
looks funny.'

His face was certainly taut with strain and tension. But his
questions were not yet answered. 'Elaine, you were Val's best
friend, weren't you?'

'Well?'

'You'll know then – you must know.'

She looked at her gold wristwatch. 'I must be going.'

'No no, you can't go yet. There's something I must know.'

But it was difficult to ask the question, the decisive question.
He moved uneasily on his seat. 'That you should have told me.'

The voice was now altogether brass. 'Told you what?'

'Elaine, look here; you were her best friend, she trusted
you.' Somewhere in Anderson's mind was a terror of what he
was going to hear. Among the check tablecloths, the suburban
families and the respectable clerks, some final word was to be
pronounced. 'You can tell me the name,' he said with difficulty.

'What name?'

'The name of her lover.'

At the next table the waitress dropped knives and forks with
a clatter. Elaine leaned a little towards him. 'What did you say?'

Anderson put his hand to his throat. He felt as if he were
choking. 'Her lover.'

The smoothness of her ageing forehead stayed uncreased,
but her bright eyes stared at him with an unfathomable gaze.
'Her lover?'

The waitress was apologizing to the young couple at the next
table. 'I'm ever so sorry,' she said. 'It's my nerves. It's a dream
I had last night. I've got a little boy and I dreamt I saw him in
a coffin. Been upset ever since, I have.' The young couple
looked at her doubtfully.

'You know who it was,' Anderson said. The check tablecloth,
Elaine's wasp-yellow coat, and her intense stare – he sought for
some kind of meaning in these things, and did not find it.

'But – ' she said, and then looked again at her wristwatch. 'I've got to go. I simply must fly.'

'No.' He pushed away the coffee-cup, leaned over and caught hold of her wrist. 'Not until you've told me.'

'For heaven's sake.' She wrenched her wrist away. 'You're barking up the wrong tree, Andy.' The young couple picked at their food, watching.

'What do you mean, the wrong tree? You know the name, I can see you know it. Tell me.'

'Andy, I don't know what you're talking about.' She was not convincing; she was trying to shield somebody, she did not know of the irrefutable evidence in his pocket. He tried to tell her of it, to speak calmly, logically, but the phrases tumbled out in the wrong order or in no order at all. He heard his own voice, pitched too high. Somebody in his office, it was saying, the letter on his desk, in Val's writing, how could she explain the letter? But of course she couldn't explain – nonsense to pretend, to shield people – who was it? The young couple put down the forks with which they had been picking at their food and looked at it distrustfully.

Elaine had been opening and shutting the clasp of her black bag. Now she stood up, small, neat and determined. 'I've got to go.'

But the letter, the letter, Anderson heard his voice say whiningly – how can you explain? Look, here it is, here, here.

'Now, Andy,' Elaine said loudly and clearly and slowly, 'you're not well, Andy. Listen to me. You should go home and straight to bed and have somebody see to your face.'

The fingers dragged out the blue paper, and held it up. She glanced and snorted angrily. 'That's a bill. Now look, Andy, go home and see a doctor.'

He stared at the piece of paper unbelievingly. It was a tailor's bill. Then the letter – the fingers fumbled again, but she was still talking. 'I knew Val better than anyone, and I tell you you're all wrong.' Anderson stretched out his hands imploringly. The young couple at the next table looked at one another, pushed away their food and got up.

Now the voice was saying it could find the letter, and was crying out over and over again. *Tell me the name, please tell me the name.* And the blow fell, the blow he had expected and feared. She turned on him, the bag snapped tightly, finally, as tight and final as the look on her face. 'You're crazy, Andy. I didn't want to say it, but you've made me.' She paused – the young couple and the waitress waited eagerly, expectantly – and spoke the irrevocable words: 'Val was sold on you from the day she met you. She never had a lover. You've invented him.' She walked with hard, firm steps on her high heels, past the cash desk and out of the restaurant.

# IX

He stepped out of the small safe box of the taxi, into a world full of enemies. It would be unwise, no doubt, to let the driver know where he lived. He got out at the Demon, tipping the man a half-crown, watching carefully to see if he betrayed any extravagant reaction. But the driver merely tested the coin with his teeth, said 'Thanks, guv,' and put in his clutch. Anderson leaned forward confidentially and made a gesture with his thumb at the Demon behind him. 'I don't live there.'

'You don't, eh?' The driver laughed, showing projecting teeth. 'I wish I did. 'Night, guv.' And he was away, leaving Anderson standing shivering in his raincoat, on the pavement. The rain, thin and slanting, damped his face and his uncovered head. His uncovered head; he remembered now that he had taken off his Homburg – his second-best Homburg – in the taxicab and put it by his side. Would the man bring it back? How extraordinary it was that he should forget his hat after, last night, forgetting his hat and taking the wrong coat. The wrong coat, the lost hats – they had a meaning, he knew, but what was it? He recognized a meaning, also, in the words Elaine Fletchley had spoken; although its precise significance still eluded him, although for that matter he could not remember exactly what she had said, he knew that he had ground for being deeply upset. But that was all too tangled, too difficult: and besides, it distracted his attention from the immediate problem. Was his home being watched? He walked to the entrance of the Demon, paused as though about to go in, and then moved quickly into the shadow by the side of the pub. In this shadow, not impenetrable but deep, he tiptoed to the corner, and stared into the darkness of Joseph Street. The house *was* being watched. In the front portico a figure lounged, unidentifiable, just out of the range of the street light. Anderson drew back. His whole body was trembling.

The clumsy fools had stationed somebody outside the front door. He could have laughed aloud. But this was not a matter, after all, for laughter. It meant that the instinct which had warned him not to return here – the distasteful and even terrifying images that had risen in his mind at thought of the disordered rooms, the empty drawer of the desk, the broken picture, and, yes, the cellar, the uninvestigated cellar – that instinct had been right. It would be falling into the trap, the trap for which that motionless and weary figure was acting as bait, if he turned the corner and walked across the road.

Is that what I believe, then? Anderson asked himself. Must I turn round and go back? Let me be logical. And now a whole set of completely different arguments came into his mind. Was it really likely that they would be as clumsy as that? Was there not an obvious motive for stationing a man just where he would be seen? Wouldn't Anderson, in fact, be playing into their hands by running away like a scared child, failing to remark that a double trap had been laid for him? Anderson began to laugh. He said aloud: 'Come on now, give them credit for a bit of subtlety. They're not fools – we all know that.' But beneath these uttered words, or above or behind them or anyhow existing in some relation to them, were the things Elaine had said, the things he had forgotten and could not now try to remember. He spoke again, without knowing the meaning of his words. 'The letter,' he said, and turned the corner. With rain blowing directly into his face he stepped firmly into the roadway. The figure in the door straightened up, moved slowly to the gate, tucked a newspaper under one arm and then ran to meet him. They met in the middle of the road. It was Molly O'Rourke. 'Andy,' she cried, 'Andy, are you all right?' He said nothing, but stood looking at her consideringly. 'What's happened to you, Andy? Why are you looking at me like that?'

In a voice so consciously soft and low that he could not recognize it as his own, Anderson said: 'Who sent you?'

'What do you mean? I heard about it this afternoon.'

Distracted for a moment, he said: 'About what?'

'All those filthy internal politics to get you out. When you're not well, too.'

What was she talking about? But the last phrase caught in his mind and was linked with other things that had been said recently. 'What do you mean not well? Who told you I was not well?'

'Andy, we can't stand here in the rain. Let's go and talk.' Quite passively he allowed himself to be led to the kerb, and then broke free of the hand she had placed on his arm. He said, again with that conscious gentleness: 'Who told you I was not well?'

'Anybody can see it for themselves. You're shivering. And – what's the matter with your face?'

'You don't care to give me the name of your informant?' he said politely.

'Oh, don't be silly.' Now they were at the front door. 'Give me the key.' He handed the key to her obediently, but as she turned it in the lock he moved swiftly. He was inside the front door, and had snatched the key from the lock. He held the door open a little, facing her and laughing. 'My dear girl, you must be very simple to think I should fall for *that*.'

'For what, Andy? I don't know what you mean.'

He laughed again. How easy it had been to outwit her. 'I'm afraid you'll have to go back to them and report failure. Suggest that they should try something subtler next time.'

'Let me in.' She took a step forward.

'Ah, ha,' he said, and laughed again. 'No nearer.' But now

she darted forward, with a suddenness that took him by surprise
and they were struggling together in the doorway. He had been
over-confident, he had relaxed his guard, and the result was a
fight to expel this creature who was all hair and claws, who
sobbed even as she tried to push past him. She had come out
now, however, thank goodness, in her true colours; there was
no subtlety about it, she was simply trying to come in where
she was not wanted, and as they swayed together he felt the
exhilaration of one whose dubieties had been lost in the satisfaction of righteous action. He heard a voice crying out something
of this, but he was unable to listen closely, because his energy
was given to the struggle with the enemy. Her approach might
have been clumsy, but she fought cleverly, eel-like, eluding his
grip, trying to get past him. But he was filled with the strength
of ten, he caught her by the throat and when she tore his hands
away brought up his knee as Shifty had done to Benny Baily.
She cried out, and sprawled on the ground with her skirt up,
showing a patch of thigh. Somehow the evening paper that had
been in her hand was inside the door, as though it had been
delivered by a newsboy. He picked it up, slammed the door
shut, and burst out laughing.

But that, after all, was not the end of her. She got up, kept
her finger at the doorbell, which chimed most musically, and
cried to be let in. What stupidity! And what effrontery! Did she
take him for a fool? He was suddenly very angry and, standing
on the other side of the door, shouted at her a mixture of insults
and obscenities – rather shameful words, perhaps, and he waited
for Fletchley to come down. But Fletchley did not come down;
Fletchley was out somewhere. *Go away*, Anderson heard a voice
screaming. *Go away*. And at last she went away, walking slowly
and dejectedly, dabbing at her face with a handkerchief. He
opened the door of his own flat, tiptoed into the sitting-room
and looked out through a window (the curtain edge lifted the
merest fraction) until she had turned the corner. He had won
the first round. Now to sit back and take stock of the situation.

But the kind of stocktaking he had promised himself – the rational working out of his own position, the plans for his own defence – proved impossible, after all. For when, hesitantly, he had pressed the switch and the fluorescent light, cold, even and blue, shone out into the room, it illuminated also the fact that only yesterday the enemy had been here, poking and snuffling, opening doors and sniffing out secrets. How ridiculous to have made that prodigious struggle to keep the woman out tonight when yesterday she or her friends had invaded his privacy and discovered the mysterious things they wanted to know. Looking round at the room, catching sight of the dirty whisky glasses, he felt utter hopelessness. And beneath the hopelessness, fear.

He sat in a chromium-armed chair and put his hand in his pocket. And now the first thing he pulled out was the letter from Val, creased and crumpled but unmistakably in her hand. Another dip – and here was the anonymous letter that had strayed mysteriously into Greatorex's overcoat. Why had he been unable to find these things when he talked to Elaine? He stared at them, spread out upon his knees. But the words were blurred in front of his eyes, and he quickly lost interest in the letters and let them drop to the floor.

Groping on the carpet for these dropped letters, he found the evening paper that had been dropped so neatly and, it now appeared, cunningly inside the door. They had had a purpose in leaving the paper, for they had a purpose in everything. Was it to try to scare him with a paper dated February the fourth? He looked at the type, but it danced away from him. It danced away – and yet after a moment the date was clear, although everything else wavered up and down. The date upon the newspaper sneered at him in letters and numerals that grew larger until they exploded in his brain. The date was the thirtyfirst of February. And at that moment, when clear warning was given him – but warning of what? – he noticed the smell.

Head raised, nostrils sniffingly apart, he was able to separate from the faint odour of dust another smell equally familiar: the smell of a particular scent, *Lovely Evening*, that Val used. And the smell, pungent now in his nostrils (how could he have failed to notice it before?) came from the bedroom. Now he knew that the struggle and victory outside had been an illusion. On the thirtyfirst of February the last fight must be fought and won before he could rest.

How many seconds, how many minutes, how many hours, were used up while he switched off the light at the door, moved silently to the door of the bedroom, and then with one decisive gesture flung it back? The darkness within was almost complete, but still his eyes recognized, deceptively motionless upon the bed, the faithless woman he had married. This, then, was the struggle for which the events of these last days had prepared him; and shouting again and again like a battle cry, *The Thirty-first of February*, he flung himself upon the bed.

But this woman was a hundred times more cunning and skilful than the one in the street. She slipped into his clutches and out again; it was impossible to get a grip on her; she fought silently and at times invisibly. His throat was constricted and, gasping, he pulled at the invisible hands, breaking their grip, tearing at collar and tie as he rolled to the floor. *The Thirtyfirst of February*, he cried again and, struggling wildly with her, felt his face cut by pieces of glass, the blood running down it warmly. He kicked out, but something heavy came down and suddenly struck him in the stomach. He moved his head, and something else was shattered just where his head had been. He brushed a hand across his eyes and pursued her again, unable to see clearly where she was, blundering round the room, catching and losing her.

The light came on, and he stood still. If she had brought in reinforcements there was little hope. Panting, he turned slowly to face the door. There, solid as a bowler-hatted bulldog, with legs apart and face graven into sad lines, stood her chief ally, and behind him faces that he had known in a past life, the woman at the door, a young fresh face that was unrecognizable, men in blue. Would they be too much for him? It was with the consciousness of defeat that he cried for the third time *The Thirtyfirst of February*, and was among them, fighting with the strength of virtue, knocking off the bulldog's hat and getting the snarling beast down to the floor, squeezing the corded throat. Then he felt a dull pain in his head, spreading all over it, his hands became strengthless, he slipped down, down, down into defeat, into permanent and shameful defeat.

# THE FOURTEENTH OF APRIL

The two men walked up the gravel drive towards the large grey building. They walked in step, without speaking. Neither of them noticed the brightness of the blue sky, or the geometrically neat gardens on either side. At the door of the building the younger of the two, a fair-haired inconspicuous figure in a brown suit, paused and said: 'What are you trying to prove?'

His companion was taller and bulkier, and he looked even larger than he was, because on this April day he wore a thick, dark overcoat. He lifted his bowler hat, wiped his forehead, replaced the hat and said: 'What?'

The man in the brown suit turned his back on the building and stared out over the empty grounds. 'I sent in my resignation this morning.'

'*Resignation*,' said the bowler-hatted man incredulously. In a heavily jocular tone he added: 'And why should you want to resign?'

'You're an old hand,' the man in the brown suit said with deceptive mildness. 'But, you see, this is the first time I've ever driven an innocent man mad. I didn't like it.'

'*Innocent*,' the other said with the same bursting, incredulous impatience. 'You don't mean to tell me he pulled the wool over your eyes, too. Listen.' He ticked off points on his fingers. 'One, the money. Five thousand pounds is not to be sneezed at when you're slipping in your job. Two, he hated his wife. You remember that journal? "I can't see why I didn't push her down the stairs long ago." How do you explain that?'

'There's no need to explain it. It doesn't prove anything. The kind of thing any man might write who didn't get on with his wife.'

'Didn't get on with his wife.' The big man snorted. 'And he'd been playing round with Elaine Fletchley.'

'She denied it.'

'What would you expect her to do – give it to us on a plate?

He blew the fuse on that cellar staircase deliberately. Or how was it that Fletchley a few minutes earlier found the light still working? Then he hit his wife on the head and fractured her skull, she fell down the stairs and broke her neck.'

'You don't know that Fletchley told the truth.'

'Why should he lie? And what about the matches? What can you say about the matches?' The man in the brown suit said nothing about the matches. 'Where did those matches come from that lay by her body? She left the kitchen to go to the cellar – Anderson said she had no matches in her hand. She had no pockets in her dress. She walked along a passage where there was no ledge on which matches could have rested. She switched on the cellar light and found it didn't work. She started down the stairs – where could she have got hold of the matches? There's only one explanation for them being by her body. Anderson put them there after he'd killed her. What other explanation can you offer, can anyone offer?'

'I don't know,' the other man said. 'I don't know. Perhaps she was holding a box of matches in her hand and he didn't notice them. Perhaps someone had left a box at the head of the cellar stairs.' He said weakly: 'Funny things happen.'

The big man seemed not to have heard him. 'But now,' he said softly, 'what were we going to do about it with proof to satisfy ourselves, but no case to take to court? Would the cause of justice be served by letting this wife murderer get away with his foolproof crime? Do you suggest that?'

'You hated him, didn't you?' Greatorex said suddenly. 'You hated the kind of man he was.'

The Inspector looked up at the sky. 'I don't hate anybody.'

'You sat in judgement and found him guilty. You played God. A policeman shouldn't play God.'

'A policeman,' Inspector Cresse said, 'is God – or he is God's earthly substitute.' The strong shape of his body was firmly outlined against the grey building. 'Justice should be intelligent, not blind. If we are obstructed by the forms of legality in reaching the end of justice, the forms of legality must be ignored. And what did we do that would distress an innocent man? A few hints were dropped here and there, a telephone call to Sir Malcolm Buntz and you were installed in the firm as his nephew, his calendar was changed, his flat was searched. What was there in any of that to upset an innocent man?'

'The letter,' Greatorex said. He seemed during this recital to have shrunk inside his suit, and in spite of the warmth of the day he was almost shivering.

'The letter,' said the Inspector blandly. 'A tribute to your skill as an amateur forger, although, of course, it would never have deceived a handwriting expert. And after all, what was the effect of the letter?'

Still shrinking inside his brown suit Greatorex said: 'It helped to send him off his head.'

'Not at all. At the most it tipped the scale for a man who was obviously guilty. But take it for a moment that you're right. What was there in the letter to frighten an innocent man? Why didn't he tell me he was being persecuted? Why didn't he say his journal had been stolen? Because he was afraid of the truth. If he hadn't gone off his head,' the Inspector added meditatively, 'he would have broken down and confessed within fortyeight hours.'

'And events helped us – if you call it helping,' the younger man went on as if the Inspector had not spoken. 'All the trouble at the office – the mess he got into over Kiddy Modes, Reverton playing internal politics, the Hey Presto business.' He shuddered. 'I shall never forget his face that night all puffed and red with that poisonous stuff, and bloody where he'd cut himself fighting with a ghost.'

'And by the way,' the Inspector said with undisturbed good humour, 'I understand they're not putting that stuff on the market. It's back in the experimental stage. One person in ten has a skin allergic to it.' There was a silence. 'No use hanging about any longer,' the Inspector said. He turned to go in. Greatorex caught his arm.

'I can't go in.'

The Inspector turned to look at him. The vertical lines in his face were hard. 'Don't be a fool.'

'Look here,' said Greatorex. 'What do you expect to prove? What do you think he'll tell you?'

'If he's able to recognize me I hope he'll confess.'

Greatorex spoke with the utmost earnestness. 'I'll make a bargain. If he confesses I'll withdraw my resignation. If he doesn't confess – '

'If he doesn't confess?'

'I want you to resign, too. It ought to be a matter of conscience.'

The Inspector stared at him. Then he began to laugh. The laughter grew until it filled his whole hard body, until he took off his hard hat and revealed the great shining bald head. Between gusts of laughter he said: 'You know, Greatorex, I'm not sure you shouldn't be in this place.' He was still laughing when he entered the grey building.

Inside the asylum he was received deferentially, but perhaps a little ambiguously. 'You must be prepared for a change in him,' the doctor said. 'He has grown a beard. He has a horror of shaving.'

'I've seen worse things than a man with a beard,' the Inspector said. 'Can he talk sensibly?'

'That depends,' said the doctor. He had a fresh face and a shock of white hair. 'What do you want to talk about?'

'I want to ask a few questions about the murder of his wife. Can it do any harm to discuss it?'

'I don't think,' the doctor said, 'that anything can do him harm.'

'You mean he's incurably mad.'

'That is hardly a clinical way of putting it,' the doctor murmured. 'But he will certainly never stand trial, if you have that in mind. Shall we go?' The Inspector nodded and the doctor pressed a bell. To the burly white-coated man who came in he said: 'How is Anderson?'

'Quiet. He's writing.'

'Writing,' the Inspector said, 'That may be important.'

'We shall see,' the doctor said.

Inspector Cresse was not an impressionable man, but he felt

a little strange when the door of the room was opened and he saw what appeared to be a complete stranger bent at a table, writing. 'Is this – '

'This is Anderson,' the doctor said. 'Here is a visitor for you, Anderson.'

The man at the table hurriedly closed the book in which he had been writing and pushed it into a drawer of the table. Then he looked at his visitors. The lower part of his face was hidden by a straggling beard of a dull brown colour, but the features themselves had changed curiously in shape and texture. The whole face was fatter and somehow blunted, and had lost its look of intelligence. The eyes, which had in the Inspector's memory looked watchful and hunted, were now like dull buttons.

'Well, Mr Anderson,' the Inspector said, 'so we meet again. You remember me, don't you?' He held out his hand, but Anderson did not take it.

'Certainly I remember you. Your name is Rex.'

'Cresse.'

'Rex Imperator, son of the Almighty.' Anderson stood up and made a mocking bow. 'Where is your companion?'

'My companion?'

'The greater Rex, your drinking friend, advertising manager to God. An amiable youngster, but deceitful. He told me God fathered him on Sir Malcolm Buntz.'

The Inspector said to the doctor: 'Are you sure this isn't all put on? I believe he knows quite well who I am.'

'We shall see,' the doctor said. 'What have you been writing, Anderson?'

The blunt features twisted into an unpleasant expression of cunning. Anderson shook his head.

'About *her*?'

Anderson nodded.

'May we see it?'

With a look of alarm Anderson shook his head again.

'Let us see it, Anderson,' the doctor said pleasantly. 'I will keep her away.' He said to the Inspector: 'He thinks his wife comes to torment him, and that writing in the book is the only thing that stops her.'

'You can't keep her away,' Anderson said. He took the book out of the drawer, and held it close to him.

'I shall put a spell on her.'

'She knows all your spells,' Anderson said. 'She came last night, tearing and scratching. She knew the date.'

'What date?' The doctor glanced at the Inspector.

'The thirtyfirst of February,' Anderson said. He began to cry out in a high voice, over and over again: 'The thirtyfirst of February, the thirtyfirst of February.' He stood up in the middle of the room and flapped his arms like wings. 'Here she is,' he screamed. The book dropped to the ground. The doctor picked it up.

The room was square, with no furniture in it except the table and a bed, both bolted to the ground. Anderson ran from side to side of the room, holding his hands to his head, uttering shrill unintelligible noises, like an animal in pain. He blundered into the three men standing there as if they were statues. Then, still with those inhuman cries coming from his slack mouth, he began to knock his head against the wall. The man in the white coat locked Anderson's arms behind his back and threw him on the bed. There he lay quietly, with his face turned from them.

The doctor opened the book. Each page was covered with thousands of fine lines of incoherent scribbling written across, up, and down the page. A few disconnected words could be made out on various pages: *London, God, wife, scheme*. The doctor looked at the Inspector. The Inspector shrugged his shoulders.

Outside in the April sunlight Greatorex was waiting. The Inspector said nothing, but clapped his bowler hat on his head.

'What happened?'

'Nothing happened. He's mad.'

'He made no confession.'

'No.'

'Then we shall never know,' Greatorex said. 'We shall never know whether he was guilty.'

'He was guilty,' the Inspector said. 'But he is mad. There will be no confession.' He took out a pipe, looked at it, filled it, and felt in his pockets. 'I thought I had a box of matches, but I must have left it – '

Greatorex said in an odd voice: 'There's a box by your feet.'

For a moment the Inspector looked almost disturbed. Then his face cleared. 'A hole in my pocket. They must have dropped through it.'

'A hole in your pocket.'

Very slowly the Inspector bent and picked up the matches, struck one and lighted his pipe. 'A hole in my pocket,' he said. 'And what of it?'

Smoke rose from the Inspector's pipe. The two men stood looking at each other.

All Pan Books are available at your local bookshop or newsagent, or can be ordered direct from the publisher. Indicate the number of copies required and fill in the form below.

Send to:     Pan C. S. Dept
              Macmillan Distribution Ltd
              Houndmills Basingstoke RG21 2XS
or phone:    0256 29242, quoting title, author and Credit Card number.

Please enclose a remittance* to the value of the cover price plus £1.00 for the first book plus 50p per copy for each additional book ordered.

*Payment may be made in sterling by UK personal cheque, postal order, sterling draft or international money order, made payable to Pan Books Ltd.

Alternatively by Barclaycard/Access/Amex/Diners

Card No.

Expiry Date

_____

Signature

Applicable only in the UK and BFPO addresses.

*While every effort is made to keep prices low, it is sometimes necessary to increase prices at short notice. Pan Books reserve the right to show on covers and charge new retail prices which may differ from those advertised in the text or elsewhere.*

NAME AND ADDRESS IN BLOCK LETTERS PLEASE

................................................................................................................

Name _____

Address_____

_____

_____

_____

3/87